Also by Abigail Hing Wen

Loveboat, Taipei

ABIGAIL HING WEN

SIMON & SCHUSTER

London   New York   Sydney   Toronto   New Delhi

First published in Great Britain in 2022 by Simon & Schuster UK Ltd

First published in the USA in 2022 by HarperTeen,
an imprint of HarperCollins Publishers

1 3 5 7 9 10 8 6 4 2

Simon & Schuster UK Ltd
1st Floor, 222 Gray's Inn Road
London WC1X 8HB

www.simonandschuster.co.uk
www.simonandschuster.com.au
www.simonandschuster.co.in

Simon & Schuster Australia, Sydney
Simon & Schuster India, New Delhi

A CIP catalogue record for this book
is available from the British Library.

PB ISBN 978-1-4711-9296-8
eBook ISBN 978-1-4711-9295-1
eAudio 978-1-4711-9994-3

This book is a work of fiction. Names, characters, places and
incidents are either the product of the author's imagination
or are used fictitiously. Any resemblance to actual people
living or dead, events or locales is entirely coincidental.

Printed and bound by CPI Group (UK) Ltd, Croydon, CR0 4YY

MIX
Paper from
responsible sources
FSC® C171272

For my children

XAVIER

LOVEBOAT TALENT SHOW AND AUCTION

NATIONAL THEATER, TAIPEI

AUGUST 8

When your life has been a series of fuckups, it's hard to believe any one thing will actually go your way. But now I'm backstage behind the velvet curtains, watching Sophie try to auction off my mural to two thousand people—and a weird hope beats in my chest.

"Now for tonight's final item . . ."

Sophie gestures a hand at my painted dragon, hung high on the backdrop from my stage wing to hers. An electric fan makes him ripple and fly like he's sprung to life. He's all shades of green: like wet grass, peacock feathers, the ocean, and mint. Like the mountains of Taiwan and the coolness under a leafy tree.

At least, that's what was in me when I painted him into existence.

"This dragon is the work of an anonymous Chien Tan student." The microphone lifts Sophie's voice over a blur of faces in the audience. She smooths a stray lock from her mass of black hair, which is swept off her neck and pinned with a silver clasp. "Notice the impossible number of hues in its scales. The power of its wings . . ."

Somehow, she's making it sound real. When my whole life, Ba told me not to waste my time with art. Once he melted my pastels into a puddle and left them to harden on my desk. But this summer, I got brave and started to draw again. This dragon is the biggest thing I've ever done. I've never felt so exposed; way worse than if I ran naked across the stage.

"Do I hear three thousand NT?" Sophie asks.

To my surprise, several white paddles rise in the night.

A hundred bucks for a smear of green, blue, and gold pastels.

"Six thousand?" Sophie asks. "Twelve thousand? Picture this impressive dragon guarding the halls of your office!"

Sophie was born to command an audience. The numbers climb, making me dizzy with their speed. I couldn't believe someone was willing to fork over a hundred US bucks. Now there are several someones willing to pay seven.

Eight.

Nine.

At a thousand US dollars, Sophie is down to three bidders. I crane my neck to see them. The darkness obscures a woman standing in the balcony, a man in the back, another to the side. Unbelievably still raising their paddles.

At five thousand US dollars, the man to the side drops out.

"And sold at two hundred thousand NT!" Sophie cries. "To the man in the white jacket. Thank you, sir, and congratulations! Please meet me at stage right after the show to claim your mural."

The applause vibrates the floorboards beneath my feet. I nearly spill onto the stage trying to follow the spotlight as it searches the faces for the guy who shelled out over seven thousand US for my anonymous dragon—almost as much as the rest of the auction made tonight. A supporter of the arts? Or just someone who liked what he saw?

The spotlight stops on a man in a snow-white jacket and pants. Head and shoulders erect, with a familiar military bearing. He takes his seat again, raising one modest hand to acknowledge the applause.

Wait, I know him.

It's Ba.

CAST OF CHARACTERS

LOVEBOATERS

Chien Tan Campus

Xavier Yeh (Xiang-Ping)

Sophie Ha (Bao-Feng)

Ever Wong (Ai-Mei)

Rick Woo (Kuang-Ming)

Marc Bell-Leong

Spencer Hsu

Debra Lee

Ocean Campus

Emma Shin

Bert Lanier

Priscilla Chi

Joella Chew

Jasmine Chew

YEH FAMILY

Chao-Xiang Yeh (Ye-Ye): Xavier's grandfather

Ako Yeh: Great-Aunty One

Yumiko Yeh: Great-Aunty Two

Jasper Yeh (Ja-Ben) (Ba): Xavier's father

Lynn Noel Yeh (Chun-Hwa) (Ma): Xavier's mother

Edward Yeh: Jasper's younger brother, Uncle

Rose Chan: Aunty Three

Lily Yeh-Abebe: Aunty Four

Lulu Chan: Cousin

Lin-Bian Yeh: Cousin

Gloria Yeh-Abebe: Cousin

Xiang-Ping "Xavier" Yeh

WOO/HA FAMILY

Sophie Ha

Rick Woo

Camilla: Sophie's mom

Sophie's brothers: Kevin, Steve, Dave, Kai

Aunty Claire

Uncle Ted

Their children: Fannie, Felix, Finn

1

SOPHIE

TAIWAN TAOYUAN INTERNATIONAL AIRPORT

AUGUST 9

You're smarter than 99 percent of the planet. Last I checked, that includes most guys in existence. So why don't you go make your own millions of dollars?

Ever's voice plays in my head as I watch her and my cousin Rick lock into the farewell kiss of the century. They're dressed in complementary blues, backdropped by a billboard advertising furry baby pandas arriving at the Taipei Zoo next week—it's too bad we'll miss them.

Debra, Laura, and a bunch of the guys are dressed in comfy chic, exchanging contact information, vowing to video chat every week. Swearing that our summer cultural immersion trip means we'll be friends forever. Everyone scrambling to plant last seeds they hope will blossom into romance.

Not me. I'm swearing off guys for the next four years of Dartmouth. Maybe forever.

And for good reason.

Loveboat, for me, was A. DISASTER.

I threw myself at Xavier Yeh, son of Dragon Leaf CEO Jasper Yeh, because I was supposed to marry a rich husband and support my mom and four brothers. Instead, I got my heart shredded, my reputation pulverized, my eye blackened by an asshole—and I did some terrible things I will never forgive myself for. I hit rock bottom, to say the least.

Then Ever caused a cataclysmic shift to the axis of my world.

Why don't you go make your own *millions?*

Now I'm going to Dartmouth. I can make my own future! Maybe every other girl already knows she can do this, but I actually, truly didn't. But I have a second chance to blast off into the stratosphere.

I just pray I don't get in my own way.

Like I did with Xavier.

"Boarding first class for Los Angeles," says a woman's voice over the PA.

I take a seat in the waiting area and open my phone to check school emails for the first time all summer. My home screen is my favorite picture, bought years ago here in Taipei—white moon lanterns floating into the night. I dig into a mess of emails—from friends, high school wrap-up . . . then one from Dartmouth jumps out at me, from a month ago.

My heart misses a beat.

"Hey, Xavier. You slumming it with the rest of us?" Marc Bell-Leong asks.

I glance up. Of course. Xavier Yeh himself is walking toward us, slouchy in his finely woven black shirt with the silver threads. Tastefully understated without even trying or caring: that's Xavier. His wavy black hair's falling into his eyes. He hitches up his orange Osprey backpack and tucks his sketch pad deeper under his arm.

"What happened to the private jet?" Marc asks. I hadn't even known Xavier had one, and I'm glad I didn't. *Ooo, Xavier, let's fly to Paris!* I'd have acted like an even bigger fool.

Fortunately, Xavier isn't judgy. We're good. And I'm over him.

Xavier's smile is grim. "My dad's been pushing me to go to some school in Massachusetts. So I'm on the next flight to LA. Someone offered me a gig working on the set of a play."

He drops into the seat beside me. "Hey, Sophie."

"Hey, Xavier." His knuckles are white against his sketch pad in his lap, and smudged with blue pastel. I frown. "You okay?"

"Yeah. Just . . . can't believe summer's over." He pulls paper-wrapped white rabbit candies from his pocket and offers one, then nods at my phone. "Don't let me interrupt."

I chew on the mild milk candy as I scan the Dartmouth email.

> Dear Student,
>
> The deadline for registration for Introduction to Artificial
> Intelligence has passed and we have not yet received
> your course fee. . . .

My stomach dips with dread and I swallow hard. "Shit."

"What's wrong?" Xavier asks.

"I missed a deadline. I didn't know there was a fee, and now I'm on the waitlist for my most important class." I should have been laser focused on Dartmouth ins and outs, but instead, I was laser focused on trying to impress Xavier.

"That sucks. But it's just one class, right?"

"I don't know! I'm on a special scholarship for girls in tech with a lot of requirements. If I can't keep my scholarship, my mom can't afford to send me to Dartmouth." I'd have to leave . . . and then what? I need to stay on top of this. I can't afford any more mistakes and to permanently flush my future down the drain.

My fingers shake as I sign up for the waitlist. "I'm number two hundred thirty-one! I need to find out how to get in."

"Wish I could help," Xavier says.

Ever's scanning her ticket at the gate. Rick is gone.

"My flight's boarding." I rise, grabbing my bag. "Be careful in LA. And good luck!"

"Wait, Sophie." Xavier's hand closes on my wrist.

He's looking at me with those dark brown eyes that see

everything and everyone, in a way that makes my insides shrink back a bit. It's a terrifying thing to have someone see you to your core, and not know what it is they are seeing. In Xavier's case, he's seen the very worst, of everything in me.

"Will I . . . ever see you again?"

He releases me, but his question stumps me. So much went wrong between us. Why would we see each other?

I've never been to LA. My Aunty Claire paid for my plane ticket to Taiwan. "I don't think I'll be in LA anytime soon. . . ."

"Well, once I finally get my trust fund, maybe I can visit. Everyone. New England in the fall is awesome. All the leaves changing colors. Maybe I can come by Dartmouth one weekend?"

So he wants to visit?

A stupid little hope flails in me, a wanting I can't afford. Not when I need to pour every ounce of emotional energy into college.

And poor little rich boy has to wait for his *trust fund* so he can jet off to see his friends? Ugh. Dom Perignon problems.

Putting him in that box, at least, builds a necessary wall around my heart.

"Boarding all rows Los Angeles," says the woman over the PA system.

"You gotta go." Xavier gives me a one-armed hug that makes that traitorous little hope hiccup. I slip free and turn to go.

But pause at the sight of a familiar man bearing down on us, flanked by two men in navy uniforms. Steel-gray hair and a snazzy navy sports coat.

The guy who bought Xavier's mural last night.

"Oh, shit, Xavier. Your dad's here."

2

XAVIER

Ba comes at me like a torpedo, flanked by two hulking body-guards. His hair is cut so sharp he could grate cheese on its serrated edges. Which matches his temper when it's directed at me.

Friends from Loveboat turn to look at him. I know he's a big deal. He's been on the cover of *Forbes Asia* three times since he took over Dragon Leaf, the company my great-grand-father started more than a hundred years ago. The logo's even embroidered on the guards' breast pockets: the bristly tree-like character that means "leaf," my last name 葉, surrounded by a wreath formed by a long-bodied dragon. I hear it's the proudest day in a guard's or driver's or whoever else's life to put on that badge of Yehdom.

But not for me.

I rise warily, holding my sketchbook to my chest like a shield. I spent the morning with it sitting on the Chien Tan lawn, one last try with my worn-down pastels to hang on to the feelings I had there. My sketches are changing. The face that's haunted my pages most of the summer has changed. For the first time, I'm not drawing Ever Wong. She chose Rick, not me, and I've let her go. And I'm seeing things differently now, but all these feelings are hard-won and fragile as silk threads.

Not something I want Ba to touch.

"Where do you think you're going?" Ba grabs my arm in a pincer grip. "You were supposed to fly to Boston for classes."

Everyone falls silent, and I wince.

"Told you already," I say. "I'm going to LA."

Ba yanks my sketch pad from my hands, moving so fast he blurs. Before I know what's happening, the sketch pad whales me across the face.

"Stop!" Sophie yells. "What the hell are you doing?"

White lights swim in my vision. My head rings. Everyone else is pulling back from me, eyes cast away, hurrying onto their flight. In case the fucked-up-ness of my life might be contagious.

Ba's shoulders surge as he tears my sketch pad in half. He hands it to his bodyguard, who tosses it in the trash bin. A book full of everything I saw all summer, transferred from my soul to my fingers to a page.

Gone.

Ba's dark-eyed gaze is grim. Short, angry breaths heave at my chest. I want to hurt him back. I have imagined—*fantasized*—what would hurt him most. If he lost all his money. If the family's reputation went down the toilet. If I had him tied up in a metal chair, helpless and powerless, while I punched him in the gut over and over.

Except I'd never even get a first punch past his guards.

Tangerine-orange silk flashes in my periphery. Sophie's fingertips graze my elbow, a steadying gesture of support—so she's still here. I'm surprised, actually. She was the ex from hell after we broke up, although she went through her own share of unexpected hardships. I'm not entirely sure I trust her—or at least her and me and the shitstorm we were together—but we're on better footing. Still, I'm not sure I want her here, not right now.

"What do you want from me?" I ask Ba.

"I put you in a summer program with students going to Yale, Harvard, Berkeley, Oxford. All summer, you were supposed to be learning Mandarin with them. This is what you do instead." He gestures to the trash bin. "Now you want to go to LA so badly? Very well. You're getting on the jet with Bernard, and Ken-Tek and Ken-Wei here will take you straight to a high school there that I've convinced to take you. Harvard-Westlake. I've set you up with an apartment to finish your senior year."

What the fuck? He wants me to repeat high school?

"Your cousin Lulu is also a senior there. She is very studious. You will follow her lead. No more girls, no more parties. And you *will* graduate."

High school *again*? "I'd rather pimp myself out," I snarl.

"You *need* to *learn* to *read*." He doesn't react to what I actually say. Never does. "When I was your age, I booked my own meetings on three continents. I ran a business unit for Dragon Leaf. Your cousin has been apprenticed to your Uncle Edward since he was thirteen."

He snaps his fingers and his bodyguards come at me. I know what's coming. I back up. My fist strikes one in the nose. My foot pulls a grunt from the other. But it's over in a heartbeat. I'm a black belt in tae kwon do, but Ba has three-time world champions as his bodyguards. They grab my arms in fists like iron cuffs, one on each side.

I glower at Ba. "You bring two guards to take on one son?"

"Xavier, do you want me to call someone?" Sophie's face is full of fear. Her phone is in her hand.

"Thank you for your concern, but there's no need," Ba says curtly.

"Xavier?" She looks to me. The waiting area is deserted except for the gate attendant, who is looking away. Which means she's been briefed. Yet Sophie stayed.

The rest plays out in my head: we call the airport guards, Ba flicks his wrist and sends them away. Yeh-crested or not, the entire fucking island is in his pocket.

"It's okay, Sophie." I force my voice steady. She's pretty brave, actually. No one stands up to Ba. They kiss his shoes. Lick them clean. But I don't want her witnessing things that shouldn't be witnessed by anyone. "You need to catch your flight."

Her eyes are dark with worry. "I—I'll call you when we land."

The bodyguards move me before she's done talking. Their fists are cutting off circulation in my arms. They march me down the corridor. To anyone looking, it doesn't look bad. Like I sprained my ankle and they're helping. But I'll be bruised in the morning. A reminder of who's in charge.

For now.

Because in two more days, my trust fund vests. I'll be in charge of my own destiny, and then I'll hire my own bodyguards to fight off his.

Two more days, and Ba can't ever touch me again.

He turns a corner, and the Kens steer me after him. I glance back at the LA gate. Sophie's still watching me, cell phone raised. I wish she could unsee everything she just saw. I must look so weak and stupid to her.

Then a coffee shop comes between us, and she vanishes from sight.

Ba's shoes make sharp clicks on the floor. "What can you do without a high school diploma, Xiang-Ping?"

"I'm doing art."

He scoffs. "Art doesn't make money. Even Shakespeare had the queen to pay for his scones and jam."

He fucking knows everything. If I could put everything I know into a circle, he could draw ten concentric ones around it.

But here's where he's wrong. Seven fucking thousand dollars' worth of wrong.

"Art *can* make money." I match his calm voice, although

everything in me wants to crow the whole ironic truth over the PA system. "That dragon mural you paid all that money for? Turns out *I* painted that."

I whistle the sound effect of a missle falling, complete with splat on the ground. Who gets the last laugh now, Pops? I lift my jaw and lock eyes with him—waiting for the truth to hit him harder than my fists ever could.

"Xiang-Ping, you are so naive. If I had not intervened, your feeble little scratches would have sold like a peddler's ware. I knew it was yours. It's the dragon at the head of your grandfather's dragon boat—the photo has been in our living room since before you were born. I bought it to spare us the shame."

The truth *has* landed. In my gut.

"And until you graduate, I've locked up your trust fund."

"What the fuck?"

"Yes, Xiang-Ping." He smiles.

"You're—you're lying! It's official." It's *mine*. "You can't!"

"I did."

"Ma left that trust to me before she *died*." I lunge at him, wanting to claw that smugness from his face. But the irons on my arms tighten to death grips. My fists clench helplessly at air. I'm sweating suddenly; cold air from a vent blows at me, a reminder that I don't even have the power to stop it from messing with my hair. "It was the last thing she asked for! *You're* the one always talking about showing respect for her memory. She had the lawyers draw up the papers while she was in the *hospital*."

"And if she were still with us, she would be as disappointed as I am. So my lawyers just undrew them."

Ba is a billionaire for many reasons, but one of them, I'm sure, is that each preciously guarded cell of his body is oriented toward one goal:

Checkmate.

"Graduate, Xiang-Ping," Ba says calmly, as if he doesn't know he just detonated a grenade in my life. "Graduate from high school like the rest of the world. *Attempt* to become useful. Then—and only then—you'll get your money."

3

SOPHIE

I worry about Xavier the whole plane ride back to the States. The red blotch rising on his cheekbone. His dad basically kidnapping him! Most of all, that helpless rage on his face—how could I have judged him for his Dom Perignon problems? I wouldn't want his dad for all the champagne in the world.

As soon as my plane lands in LA and I have cell reception, I call Xavier. The phone rings, then goes to voice mail.

I press the phone tight to my ear as my plane slows. "Hey, it's me. Just making sure everything's okay. Hope you're safe. Let me know if I can help or if you want to talk."

I hang up slowly. Would his dad hurt him? Cut him off from friends? If Xavier's coming here, should I report what happened?

I text him:

Checking if you're okay. LMK if you want to talk

A minute later, my phone chimes. It slips from my fingers and I have to fish for it under the seat in front of me before I can read Xavier's answer.

All good thanks

It's like someone grabbed my reins and yanked me back. *Whoa, horsie!*

A memory flashes: a night at a club. Me clinging to his back with my hands locked around his neck, my knees gripping his waist, trying so desperately to keep him. Until Rick had to yank me down and Xavier ran off . . . and I ran after him . . .

All good thanks

This dynamic feels way too familiar. Me chasing him; him pushing me away.

My cheeks heat. I feel a little foolish as I tuck my phone away. In the Taipei airport, I just wanted to be there for him. But not picking up, not calling back, *all good thanks*—translation: it's none of your business. Yet as usual, there I was in his space.

I grab my bag from the overhead compartment and head off to catch my connecting flight home to New Jersey. I can't keep thinking about him and I sure as hell don't want him visiting, even if that offer still stands. I have big plans: get into the AI class at Dartmouth, major in AI, work two years in a kickass job, go to business school, make my own millions—and prove to

15

my family (and myself) that I'm not the pathetic MARRYME-SOPHIE we all once thought I was.

Dartmouth.

Crisp air. Green foliage. Historic brick buildings, hot cider, and opportunities I never even dreamed off. I plunge headfirst into a weeklong firehose of information on activities, school clubs, classes, and majors. I meet all the kids in Lord Hall. I send out thirty applications for a job around campus, and most importantly, I hit up the registrar's office, where a woman tells me to attend the first day of Introduction to Artificial Intelligence to figure out the waitlist. I'm a Sophie-make-it-right machine, putting everything back on track.

On my way to a library tour, I spot the dean of Dartmouth, glowing in a snow-white power suit: a waterfall blazer over leggy trousers that flare from her knees. She passes the white-brick Dartmouth Hall, and the effect is stately Dartmouth—inspiring and intimidating.

I snap a photo and open my Instagram account to post it. I only have a few dozen followers, but my account has been more for me to sort my favorite photos from the summer: Taipei 101, the Night Market—and about five hundred more amazing outfits like hers.

To my surprise, I have a new follower: @XavierYeh.

My heart gives a little lurch. His icon is an inky purple dragon, curled in an S shape, powerful wings spread to either

16

side. His Chinese name, Yeh Xiang-Ping, overlaps it in artsy brushstrokes. It's awesome—the imprint of the chop he carved into soapstone on Loveboat and used to stamp his drawings.

And he's following me?

I pore over his account: he only joined Instagram a few days ago. He's following three people, with eight following him. His one photo is of water dripping off the underside of a bridge, magically made all gray shades, from water to concrete to sky. It aches loneliness. Is that how he's feeling? He can capture so much emotion in a single square, whether a painting or photo. That's his genius.

I zoom in on his photo. The sky was that same gray in Taipei the morning I woke up beside him after Club Kiss, savoring the warmth of his body curled against my back, his hand draped over my waist, the memory of his soft lips on my skin. . . .

Stop!

I follow him back on Instagram and send a nice but not too familiar note. "Welcome to IG. Hope you're well."

On Saturday, I charge into a dozen part-time job interviews: with the proprietor of a chocolate shop, a librarian, a girl in the bookstore. Two cancel before I arrive. Three send a fast rejection afterward: "Sorry, we've filled the role with another candidate." And the last—a clerical job for a balding guy in mismatched burnt orange—wrings his hands and says, "You're a beautiful girl. I just don't know if there's a fit here."

"I'm so confused. What did he mean?" I ask Ever on the phone that night. "I'm beautiful, therefore I'm not a fit? I'm not a fit, but should take consolation in being beautiful?"

"He regrets not being able to hire you because you're beautiful?"

"Hope not." I shudder, but I'm suddenly afraid she's right. "If that's the case, thank God it was no. I would have spent the entire term fending him off. I thought we had a very nice, professional conversation, too," I mourn. "It's actually kind of humiliating."

"It's *insulting. That's* what it is."

Thank God for Ever Wong. If she were any other girl, I'd have ended the summer as her wicked stepsister. But she's the most gracious person I know. Beats Cinderella hands down.

"Hey, so I need your help," she says. "I'm trying to learn how to put on eye makeup."

"For a virtual date with Rick?" I tease. I love that my best friend is dating my best cousin.

"I wish! I'm auditioning for an international dance scholarship tomorrow. It's for a full ride to a school of my choice, so a big deal."

"That's amazing!" At the end of Loveboat, Ever made the brave decision to withdraw from her seven-year med school program to pursue dance and choreography instead. We're all rooting for her. "I'll make you a video to help with your eye makeup after we get off, okay?"

"Thanks so much! And don't worry about that man. You have much bigger fish to fry!"

But I *do* worry. My only parent is a single mom with my four brothers at home. She barely pays the bills. Without this scholarship, I'd never even be here—and I really need a job to stay.

If Xavier's problems are vintage champagne, mine are Diet Coke.

As I head to my first class, I'm still obsessing over what went wrong with my interviews. Was I too energetic? Did I cross some invisible line?

The thing is, I can be a bit of a tornado in general.

In third grade, my teacher complained to my mom that I had impulse control problems. Once she told me to wait in my seat until she gave me permission to get up. She took the class to lunch, snapped off the lights, and left me alone in the dark. I still remember hanging on to my chair, trying to control my need to make a mad dash from the room toward people. When she returned twenty minutes later, I was so relieved and ashamed I burst into tears and promised I'd never get out of my chair without permission again. I kept that promise all year.

But I worry the tornado is still lurking. Like the horrible way I humiliated Ever over the summer because I was jealous that Xavier wanted her, the single worst thing I've ever done on impulse. And it's still there inside me. Ready to bust out and destroy whatever I'm trying to build. Friendships, relationships, jobs, a new goal. A plan.

Someone knocks into me, rushing for the auditorium doors just ahead. He's followed by a stampede of students, some clad in flannel pajamas, others in jeans, some in *Star Wars* T-shirts. Not a blush of color, which makes me look down at my azure long-line top. Did I overdress?

I follow them to find Introduction to Artificial Intelligence packed with more people than the New York City subway during rush hour. The sheer number of students is terrifying— they fill the rows across four sections, with dozens racing the aisles, searching for seats. Mostly guys. How many are trying to get off the waitlist, too?

"Gödel's incompleteness theorem is nothing more than a formalization of 'This statement is false,'" says a redheaded guy squeezing past me, talking to another guy.

"It's more complicated than a liar's paradox," his pal argues. "If you look at—"

Um, help! What language are they speaking? Part of me wants to about-face and make a run for it before someone demands to know why I'm here. But this class is my ticket to my new future.

Taking a deep breath, I plunge down the aisle.

At the blackboard, Professor Michael Horvath is chalking his name in bold script. He's young, in his early thirties. Handsome in a classical Greek statue way, with a strong nose and thick Beethoven-like brown hair. Great clothes—under his checkered blue sports coat, his vest is an exciting, violently orange print. My favorite color.

With relief, I spot a few open seats up front. I'm not usually a front-row student myself, but it's a new me!

"Excuse me. Excuse me." I squeeze past students all the way to the front and drop into a blue velour seat opposite the podium. I snap a photo of the professor's killer outfit, feeling more optimistic already.

"Hey, how's it going?" A guy takes the seat beside me, making me jump. "Whoa, sorry. Didn't mean to scare you."

"Um, no. Hi."

The sleeves of his blue button-down are rolled back to his elbows, the hem untucked over skinny black jeans. His black hair is closely cropped. Slightly more Asian than Asian American in style. He sets a sleek black-leather backpack at his feet. Canali— whoa, costs a thousand bucks, at least.

"I'm Victor." He flashes a nice smile, and I recognize the, uh, *interest* behind it. After so many years of chasing boys, you develop a radar.

My instinct is to bolt. But there's nowhere to go. Every seat in front is filled.

"I'm Sophie."

"Nice to meet you. Do you go by Sophie? Or a nickname?"

"Just Sophie."

He cocks his head. "You need a nickname."

"Never had one." I smile, going along with it. "Unless you count my dad calling me Cha Siu-Bao Face when I was a kid."

He laughs. "Pork Bun Face. I like it."

I've never shared that, but something about him invites realness. I used to love the idea that I was a warm delicious thing to my dad. But then he left. I guess I haven't really thought of it since.

"Hey, Victor, can we catch you after class?" Two guys in sports jerseys stop before us, blocking Professor Horvath. "We want your take on our Kaggle competition entry."

"Sure, no problem." They flash a thumbs-up and head off, and he turns back to me. "You must be a frosh."

My smile turns rueful. "It's that obvious?"

"No. But we've never met."

"And you've met all three thousand upperclassmen?"

"I would've remembered *you*."

Boy radar! *Ding ding ding!* But it's a new me. Which means it's time to deflect.

"Are you a sophomore? Junior?" I ask.

"Senior. I'm one of the TAs for this class. If you need help, that's why I'm here."

"Oh!" A teaching assistant! No wonder those guys wanted to talk to him.

"How was your summer?" he asks. "Did you study? Travel?"

"Both. Sort of. I was in Taipei for a language program—"

"Get out of here. Loveboat?"

"Yeah. You've been?"

"My family's from Taipei. My cousins have gone, but I missed out. That's why I'm still single." He winks theatrically. "So you

22

came back with a boyfriend, I assume?"

"Even better." It's the perfect opportunity to let him know where things stand. "I got all guys out of my system. *Forever.*"

He cocks his head. "How's that?"

"I dated Mr. Mistake and learned my lesson. Now I'm fully focused and ready to crush it with my career. This class is my first step."

There—flag planted. Although I feel a twinge of guilt—it's not really fair to reduce Xavier to Mr. Mistake, when I was a major part of the mistake. But Victor's brows rise. It's possible I've impressed him.

"Please take your seats," Horvath says into his microphone. Voices begin to die down.

"Well, you're right about this class," Victor whispers. "Horvath is a rising star. He's the youngest to make tenure at Dartmouth. He knows the heads of AI at Facebook, Apple, Netflix—you name it. Everyone who comes out of his lab gets their pick of AI internships in Silicon Valley. Our head TA's interning for Google AI. He's set for life."

A Google internship? I sit up straighter. The professor is plugging a cord from the podium into his laptop.

"Is that why you're here?" I ask.

"No. I work for my family," he says. "But that's why this class is jammed with upperclassmen. It's his last year teaching at Dartmouth."

I frown. "What do you mean?"

"Yale lured him away. Big new lab and all. This is the last

23

chance to have him. You're lucky you got in. Most freshmen don't."

"Oh, no. I'm actually on the waitlist—"

"Excuse me, this row is TAs only." A guy holding a briefcase, sandy hair prematurely graying in streaks, scowls down at me. He carries himself with authority.

I glance at Victor, who gives me a *yeah, sorry* shrug. "Guess we're out of seats up here."

The whole front row of guys—professor-like themselves— turns toward me as I rise. Someone in the row behind snickers, and my face warms. *TAs only*—how did I not know? But then again, I've never competed in a place like this before. I can't afford to do anything to screw up my chances of getting into this class. *Especially* since this is the professor's last.

Music begins to play. Two wall-length screens fill with the revolving image of a gray brain and *Introduction to Artificial Intelligence.*

"Down in front," someone yells, annoyed.

I hug my backpack and duck out of the line of sight. The aisle steps are packed with seated students, so I have to pick my way through bags and fingers, earning glares from a few guys craning to see. By the time I join the crowd standing in the back, my face is hot and damp.

I hug my bag tighter. I have to keep the tornado under control. My phone chimes, and I yank it out to silence it. Fortunately, the professor is occupied speaking to his TAs. Class hasn't started yet, so why is everyone so worked up?

A notification bubble has popped up on my phone. It's a post from Ever in the Loveboat alum chat group I put together to keep us all in touch.

> Ever: Hey guys, I'm a finalist for a dance scholarship! I'm going back to Taipei next weekend for the last round of auditions!
> Sophie: congrats! That's amazing!
> Ever: @Sophie i looked super profesh thanks to your eye makeup video
> Sophie: Yes, ALL ME. I practically did the dancing for you
> Rick: wish I could go too
> Debra: can I see the makeup video? I need it
> Laura: me too?
> Sophie: sure, I'll post on my TikTok
> Marc: I'd come to Taipei if I could afford tix
> Sophie: we all would! Go get that scholarship, E!

As Professor Horvath returns to his podium, I upload the eye makeup video for Debra and Laura and tuck my phone away. I'm so proud of Ever I could sing it from the back of this auditorium. She's going after her dreams.

And now I'm here to go after mine.

A video of Harrison Ford plays on the screens. Han Solo! His gray hair hangs neatly over his lined face. He raises a blue Yeti mug at us.

"Welcome to Introduction to Artificial Intelligence," he says. "You're in for the ride of a lifetime with my good friend Professor Horvath. I want to personally wish you well as you start the year. Also, I'm not actually Harrison Ford. I'm a deep fake. But I wish you well nonetheless."

I laugh with the class as Professor Horvath takes center stage, hooking a thumb in his pants pocket. "Welcome, as my good friend Harrison Ford said. First, a word to those on the waitlist, as I know we have several hundred anxiously waiting. I'm sorry to say we are simply limited by auditorium capacity. I encourage you to find alternative classes, but if you are still hoping for the Horvath touch, please audit the class for now and submit your project proposals for the first assignment, which I will tell you about shortly. If spots open in the next two weeks, I will admit waitlisted students based on the quality of your proposals."

A few groans go up. A guy in the seat in front of me heads for the doors.

The guy beside me motions to the empty seat. I almost refuse on principle, but I focus better when I can take notes, so I drop into it. This arrangement is actually good news for me. If I can jump the waitlist line with a kickass proposal, then I actually have a real shot at getting in.

"Now, onward. AI is revolutionizing everything from robotics to energy to healthcare, and everything in between. You will learn the fundamentals of artificial intelligence and how to build algorithms that are changing our world. Chatbots that talk to people. Tools to help doctors."

He launches into a world I've only ever associated with gamers. I type furiously, taking notes like I never have. I google (google!) every other word he says and scan Wikipedia for context—deep learning, deep fakes, chatbots. I'm going to learn the secrets to unlocking the universe. I'm going to learn magic.

Horvath introduces his ten teaching assistants. Turns out Victor is the only TA who isn't a grad student—impressive. The guy whose seat I took is the head TA, ugh! Hopefully, he won't remember me. I hang on to every word as Horvath lays out course expectations. It seems pretty different than high school. Our grade is all based on one major project: build a functioning AI program, to be turned in for grading in three chunks.

Another flutter of nervousness shifts my insides. This class is harder than anything I've taken before. A guy in front of me is already programming, his black screen flooded with white lines of code. I don't know anything about what's-his-name's theorem. Godiva? Godel? My cousin Rick is always chatting with friends on super-secure text messaging apps and playing AI-powered role-playing games. And me . . .

You're smarter than 99 percent of the planet, Ever's voice chides me.

"These projects are an opportunity for all of us to learn, myself included," Horvath concludes. "So no duplications—I'll authorize on a first-come, first-serve basis. Submit all proposals by Friday for my TAs to review. Any questions?"

The auditorium is silent as a tomb. I can sense the intimidation. This professor is SO HUGE.

"Very well, then—"

I raise my hand.

"Yes?"

Three hundred pairs of eyes swivel toward me. I shrink a bit, but it's too late to retract.

"Do you want projects focused on deep learning, or can we explore reinforcement learning?"

"Excellent question." He shades his eyes to peer up the rows at me. "Your name?"

"Um, Sophie. Sophie Ha."

"Well, Sophie. I'll cover that in the next lectures. But briefly, deep learning learns from a training set of data, while reinforcement learning learns dynamically through trial and error. Both are fair game, although my personal view is that many of the exciting developments lie at the intersection of both, as with DeepMind's AlphaGo." He gives me a smile like maybe I've impressed him. "Other questions?"

A hand goes up in front. "Is it true this is your last class at Dartmouth?"

"I'm afraid so." Professor Horvath rubs the back of his hair, rueful. "This is indeed the last chance to join the Horvath conspiracy before I move it to Yale."

More groans. A guy in a dirty white hat a few rows down to the left inserts a prong from his computer into a receptor. "Male and female. Get it?" he snickers to his seatmate. I ball a fist to keep from tossing my cell phone at his head.

"Something funny?" asks Horvath.

Dang. He has eagle ears. The guy sits up straight.

"No, sir."

"What is your name?"

"Jake Boneh."

"Please leave."

His eyes bulge. "Leave?"

"My class." A stunned silence follows. "Your seat will be given to someone who respects this subject and is eager to do the work."

"Damn," whispers the blond guy beside me.

"Is he allowed to do that?" I whisper back.

"Guess so."

"But . . . but I got in through the lottery," Jake stammers. "I want to learn about AI."

"Victor, please update the roster. Good news for those of you still on the waitlist—we have our first open slot."

In the front row, Victor's black head of hair bobs in a nod.

So there's a chance, but damn is right. One toe out of line— and BAM! Not a system that sets up a tornado for success. Another little shudder spasms through me and I sit up straighter.

"As for the rest of you, get to know one another," Horvath continues. "You'll be leaning on one another not just for this class, but the rest of your careers. You are the future of this field." He smiles. "Cheers."

The students begin to gather their bags. My phone buzzes with a text.

Victor here. Nice job, Sophie.

Huh. He must have access to my number as a TA. Nice job doing what?

"Wow. Day one and Horvath knows your name," says the guy beside me. He's wearing a Yoda T-shirt. "How did you even know about that stuff—reinforcement?"

"Reinforcement learning. I read about it while he was lecturing."

"You absorbed all that on the spot? *During* the lecture?"

"I was trying to catch up," I explain. "I've never done anything like this, but I'm so excited for the project. I really want to get in."

"I may drop off the waitlist. He's a hardass."

"Yeah, I can see that." And can I hack it? It won't be easy, but I want to. If I can conquer this class, I can conquer anything. "Look at what he's teaching us," I say. "It's like magic!"

"I understood a quarter of what he said."

I frown. Is he exaggerating?

"Also, it's a waste to do a proposal for a class you might not even get into. Not to mention risky to pin your whole grade on one project."

"Oh, but I have so many ideas."

"Like what?"

"Like a stylist bot that tells you the best outfits for your body type. Trends change so fast. And not everyone has the patience or eye for clothes—like my brothers." The reminder of my four little guys back home makes my throat ache. "Wouldn't that be useful?"

He shoves his laptop into his bag, preparing to leave. "Definitely sounds more magic than science. I need to keep my GPA up. This class is too cutthroat. Good luck, Sophie Ha."

I frown at his back as he heads off. Am I being unrealistic?

"Excuse me. Are you Sophie?"

I turn. An Asian American girl with startlingly blue eyes is standing in the aisle. Contacts? Her chin-length black hair frames an oval face. Her green Dartmouth sweatshirt has an untouched newness to it, and a tastefully small logo.

"Yes, have we met?" I join her in the aisle.

She holds out a slim hand, from which dangles an exquisite bracelet of twisted strands of cherry blossoms, each made from tiny pearls centered on a rose-gold blossom.

"No, but I'm Emma Shin."

"Love your bracelet." I shake her hand. "And your eyes." It's a weird thing to say, but I can't help but be curious.

"The bracelet's a present, with these." She touches a matching blossom on her ear. "And the eyes . . ." She shifts her fingers to her temple. "Someone in the family tree was indiscreet."

I laugh with her—I like her already.

"I'm a freshman, too," she says. "Victor sent me your way. He thought we could be study buddies." She gestures toward the

31

TAs, now gathered with the professor.

"How thoughtful of him. But I'm actually on the waitlist."

"You should have a good shot—they need more girls. Just have a solid proposal."

"I hope so!" I just don't want my gender to be a *dis*advantage. "What are you doing your project on?"

"Something with satellite imagery. Environmental. I program a bit, but no formal classes. My dad was a CS major here. He and Professor Horvath had the same mentor."

"Oh, wow, really? So you know him already?"

"I feel like I do." She smiles. "Victor mentioned you were on Loveboat this summer? I was at the Ocean campus."

"Oh, Ocean!" Loveboat had two campuses that didn't mix. With a thousand kids attending, it makes sense I'd run into another Dartmouth freshman. "I'm sorry you missed out." I smile. Ocean campus was isolated on the northern shore, far from the sizzling Night Markets and culture of Taipei.

"Seriously, all we could do was drink in the dorms and sing bad karaoke."

"Hope you got into *some* trouble," I tease.

"Our claim to fame is that ten guys broke into an antique shop."

"How rock star!"

She laughs. "That was Ocean. *So* glamorous. But we heard about your amazing talent show."

"Really? That was a good time." I flash my phone at her. "I started a Loveboat alum group—I'll add you. What's your

32

handle? We're at forty-four people now, lots of fun threads and it's getting chaotic. Feel free to invite friends. The more the merrier."

I add @Emma as a few guys barrel by toward the professor. A zipper scratches my shoulder and another body knocks me into Emma. She catches me, surprisingly sturdy.

"I shouldn't have worn heels." I rub the sting ruefully. "Didn't realize it was the wild west in here." I think of Professor Horvath's words. I'll need friends to make it through this class, and Dartmouth, and we already have a good energy together. I lift my bag onto my shoulder. "I brought mooncakes from home, if you want to come by later?"

She smiles. "Yes! I love mooncakes. I'm going to introduce myself to Professor Horvath now. My dad emailed him about me." She nods toward the crowd surrounding the professor so thickly that only his yellow hair is visible. "Want to come along?" Emma shoulders her bag. "Good to make a personal connection if you're trying to get in off the list."

"Oh, um . . ." Talking to Horvath feels like a big step. But apparently everyone is doing it. She's right. With this much competition, I need to show Horvath how serious I am about his class. Reinforce the positive first impression. "Sure." I start down the aisle as a new video loads onto the double screens. "Maybe I can run my project idea by him—"

". . . and don't forget to reapply your lipstick right before. It will make everything pop."

My recorded voice booms through the auditorium. Voices

die down as, to my horror, my face fills the screens. I'm magnified a hundred times, revealing my every pore and the zit over my eyebrow. Onscreen, my hand raises a tube of lipstick to my lips.

"Oh my God!" My makeup video. For Ever. Not for anyone else's eyes, and definitely *not* these three hundred people and Professor Horvath.

But below the screen, Professor Horvath tips back to look, along with the rest of the auditorium. "What's this?"

A few people laugh. Someone wolf-whistles and heads turn my way.

Emma's eyes widen with shock. "That's you."

"Turn it off!" I cry. It's obvious what's happened: in this room full of hackers, someone looked up Sophie Ha online.

But there's no turning it off. And I know exactly what's coming next.

On the screen, heartbeat-red lipstick smears over my lips, which blot together with excruciating slowness.

"They won't be able to ree-zeist you." I roll my Rs with a fake accent.

Then the Sophie onscreen blows a kiss at Professor Horvath and the entire future of the field.

4

XAVIER

LOS ANGELES

Sophie stayed at the Taipei airport when everyone else took off. She called to make sure I was okay. That's her instinct—she does what she says she'll do. Underneath all the layers, she's a good person. Turns out breaking up was one of the few good decisions she and I made on Loveboat. Now everything is less complicated.

I voice-dictate a text back and let her know I'm fine. But I'm not.

I'm trapped in Yehdom.

Ba set me up with a studio apartment on the third floor of a building with a crystal-blue pool, owned by the Yehs. The doorman wears the golden Yeh crest on his purple cap. Ken-Tek and Ken-Wei, still crest labeled, take turns guarding my door. Maid service drops off a steel-cut oatmeal bar for breakfast and gourmet beef noodle soup for dinner.

It's hell.

Then again, Sophie's worried about losing her scholarship. Having to drop out of Dartmouth. She'd have every right to say to me, "There are worse things than being forced to stay in a fancy pad and go to a fancy private school. So stop feeling sorry for yourself."

And she'd be dead right.

I run a coin over the backs of my knuckles and glance at the Kens. Is it worth trying to make a break for it? My arms are still bruised from their grip. The door opens and the Kens admit the caterer, carrying a cupcake lit by a single candle. It may as well be Yeh-branded, too.

Because all the teakwood lounge chairs in LA can't make up for the fact that I'm a prisoner on my eighteenth birthday.

On the first day of school, early September, the Kens escort me down the street to the Harvard-Westlake campus. It's all orange clay roofs and white stucco walls, Spanish architecture and about a thousand kids—movie star kids, film producer kids, kids who can *read* as easily as comb their fingers through sand.

The breeze is warm. It smells like eucalyptus, which I like. But I shiver as I climb the steps after Ken-Tek. I don't know anyone here, except my cousin Lulu, the studious senior. I remember when she got in, and how impossibly hard that was. Ba made sure to tell me. Now I'm supposed to find her and follow her good behavior. But when has that plan ever worked?

In the office, a receptionist moves aside her pot of minty herbs. She gives me a toothy smile.

"You must be Xavier."

"Yeah. That's me." I brace for what always comes next, when you talk to authorities. Behind me, Ken-Tek and Ken-Wei pretend to blend into the fleur-de-lys wallpaper.

"We may have had a scheduling mixup yesterday. You and your dad missed your meeting with your education specialist. We had a video call arranged?"

Right. Ba didn't bother to show either? Nice. Then again, Ed meetings have never been his thing.

"I don't need anyone else breathing down my neck."

Her smile dims. "We're here as resources for you."

I'm silent. The deal was school, not extra meetings.

Last night I got myself a new sketch pad. I drew a series of horizontal boxes one inside the other, getting smaller and smaller, until there was just a dot in the middle, but I know it keeps on going. Emptiness inside emptiness. That's what it means to come back to high school. If repeating senior year is what I need to do to break Ba's choke hold, I will—but my last shreds of pride won't let him overrun me completely.

She stands. "Well, come along. The dean is looking forward to meeting you."

I follow her past a few seated kids who watch me curiously. They've noticed the bodyguards. I shrink a bit, wishing I were invisible.

The dean's office is basically a western version of Ba's home office, with dark paneled walls and a bus-sized desk. Leafy potted plants brighten the room, but Dean Ramchandran himself is as dull as a foggy window: gray from hair to button-down shirt to the square rims of his glasses, which he puts on when he sees me.

"Xavier, so glad to have you. Please. Take a seat."

I slide into the chair opposite him.

"We're here to make sure you have a terrific year." Ramchandran's leather seat squeaks as he sits back. "I know you were put through the wringer at your old school." The *wringer*. There's the Dragon Leaf spin doctors hard at work. I fucking flat-out failed. But victims are more sympathetic than slackers, and so that's me: the misunderstood kid, poorly served by his previous institution.

"But I promised your father we would get you to the finish line."

"Let me guess." I lean back in my seat, mirroring him. "You don't get your fat wire transfer unless I graduate."

Ramchandran shifts uncomfortably. "Your father is very generous—"

"*My father* never gets taken for a ride," I say. "If you don't deliver, neither will he."

The dean tugs at his collar, then continues as if I haven't spoken. "We have specialists eager to meet you. They'll run assessments this afternoon. We'll go over your learning plan—based on the materials your father sent over, we're providing full accommodations. A reduced load. Eliminate the foreign language requirement since you don't need that additional complexity. Audiobooks. Double time for essays. Your locker, in the science wing beside the yellow fire extinguisher, has been specially arranged for you. We'll all work together to get you through this year." He pushes a small paper box and an envelope toward me. "This is a reader pen, and—"

"I get it." I have no idea what a reader pen is, and I don't understand half of what he's saying, but I don't need to. I jam the box and envelope into my backpack. "I'm stuck repeating senior year like it's fucking *Groundhog Day*. I'll have a million supervisors breathing down my neck. And I'm going to like it." I stand and sling my bag onto my shoulder. Every new person thinks they can fix me, until they can't. "I'm not coming back for those tests."

Dean Ramchandran rises, eyes alarmed. One hour into school, and I've put his grand plans into jeopardy already.

He holds out a lean brown hand. I ignore it, and he lets it fall.

"I hope you'll see we care about you, Xavier. Why don't you take some time to adjust and we can connect later?"

"You can't pay people to care about you," I say, and head out.

The fuck am I going through this again?

I head down the hallway in search of my locker.

As a kid in Taipei, I studied with private tutors instead of in school. After three years of my first tutor shoving character

39

sheets under my nose, he finally told Ba I couldn't learn. I got a massive beating and a new tutor, who told Ba the same thing. Uncle Edward said I should get lobotomized, Ma defended me, and Ba just turned on her, too.

I was twelve when Ma passed away. Ba dropped me off in Manhattan and enrolled me in a private Chinese-English bilingual school. I lived in an apartment with our housekeeper. I had an education consultant from Hong Kong. My teachers assumed I couldn't read English because it was new, and Chinese because I refused. By the time I hit high school, I'd figured out how to hire kids to write my essays, read for me, and prep me for class. I'm a good talker. And I didn't need to shine. I just needed to survive.

But that's not going to be enough for Ba. Not this time.

The hallway is emptying out, with kids disappearing into sunlit classrooms. I catch sight of a black sign with an atom—a nucleus orbited by dots. The science wing. *By the yellow fire extinguisher*—I wouldn't have admitted it to the dean, but describing its location, instead of giving me a number, means I might actually find it in this endless row of beige lockers.

But there's another problem: every locker bears the smug-nosed dial of a combination lock. My chest grows tight as I move down the rows. Clockwise and counterclockwise. I've never been able to tell them apart. My cousin the Douche Lord once locked me in a shed with a combination lock, along with the code. I was nine and could reach the lock, but no matter how many times I spun it, I couldn't open it. I pissed myself before our pilot, hours later, chopped down the door.

I still don't fully understand dyslexia. Just that my head's this way.

The locks grow more smug as I search for the extinguisher like a sucker for torture. There is no point visiting this locker that will remain locked all year, and yet my feet keep carrying me toward it.

Then the fire extinguisher leaps off the wall at me. It's not just yellow. It's banana, mango, sunshine alarming. Not even I could miss it. Is that the point? The locker beside it—mine—has a blue sheet of paper, printed with black marker, taped to it.

And instead of a smug combination lock, a steel padlock hangs from its clasp.

It's a friendly wave in a row of faceless enemies.

And the key?

I fish out the dean's envelope and spill a silver key onto my palm. It opens my lock as easily as sliding a knife into softened butter. Way too easy. I've been banging my head against closed doors all my life, and now—an opening.

My locker is empty except for the spare combination lock, its code still on a sticker on its back. I give its dial a spin. Now I won't have to use this, but my need for torture makes me drop the combination lock into my pocket. I shut the locker and snap the padlock into place. What else had the dean said? Double time on essays? Seriously?

Maybe this year won't be as bad as I fear.

The sign on the front—a note for me? A flyer? I reach for it, but a small hand darts in and snatches it off.

I turn to a face I haven't seen in a while. Lulu Chan, my cousin. We've never been close, but after the shitstorm with Ba, I feel a rush of relief to see a familiar face.

"Hey. Lulu."

She's still tiny—barely to my shoulders—but her baby cheeks are gone. Instead of a Disney princess T-shirt, she's wearing a cashmere sweater. Pearls in her ears. Two black pigtails run down her shoulders. I used to pull on them to piss her off.

But she's scowling at me so fiercely I wouldn't dare now.

She crumples the paper into a fat wad.

"You were supposed to be here an hour ago. You're late for class." Her scowl deepens. No warm fuzzies from her. Just the bristles of a porcupine. Then again, my dad probably owes her mom money or vice versa.

"Thanks for showing me around."

"You're family."

The word drops like a shard of ice. No surprise there. Family means something different to the Yehs than most people.

"What's that say?" I tap the wad in her hand. "I didn't have a chance to read it," I lie. Lulu doesn't know about my dyslexia. No one in the family does but Ba. I have a second cousin on the spectrum who was institutionalized when his dad ran for office fifteen years ago—to get him out of the way. That's the Yehs. If the truth about me had ever gotten out, Uncle Edward would have lobotomized me himself.

As for Ba, I know he'd still prefer me to will it away. A teacher my junior year told him I should get tested and as far as my school knew, he ignored her. But he *did* get me tested, and then doubled down on tutors. I'm guessing he only told Harvard-Westlake— and swore them to secrecy—because he had no choice. Which works for me. I don't want anyone knowing either.

"We should get moving." Lulu starts down the hallway at a brisk Yeh-like pace. The flyer crumples tighter in her hand. I hurry to keep up. No one would take us for family from a distance. A few heads turn, curious, and maybe Lulu notices, because she slows a fraction and says, "You're going home for the Mid-Autumn Festival next weekend, right?"

"Ha. No." Every year, Ba tries to force me to return for the mooncake pavilion my family sponsors as part of an international festival in Taipei. Every year I resist. The flight isn't bad—just an overnight sleep in the jet. The festival itself is great—the pumpkin glow of lights shining off the roof of each vendor's stand, music blaring over the lawn, and more types of mooncakes and teas than anyone can sample in a week.

But the *speeches*. Sitting on stage with Ba and Uncle Edward and Ye-Ye. Pretending I'm listening. Kill. Me. Now.

"There's a special reception for our grandpa's eighty-eighth birthday. It's at your place. Friday lunch."

"How nice." Even more reason not to go. Yes, eighty-eight is huge, double lucky number, but I'm not close to Ye-Ye. My cousin the Douche Lord spent his childhood kissing up to the patriarch, and maybe that was what sent me running in the opposite direction.

Lulu digs through her purse. "Damn."

"What?"

"I forgot a pencil. Have a math test today."

I open my pouch and hand her a newly sharpened one. She purses her lips, wanting to refuse. She doesn't want to owe me anything. I get it. Even small favors sometimes come with a price tag, though I'm not that way. She takes it. She's still walking fast enough to break the speed limit, but as she stops abruptly before a closed door, I crash into her back.

"Sorry—"

"Your English class," she cuts me off. "Teacher hates smart mouths and earrings. Just saying."

Was she this edgy before? Old habits die hard, and I tuck my hair behind my ear, showing off the stud there.

Lulu slams a fist into my stomach, sending the taste of my breakfast porridge back into my throat.

"What the hell!" I rub the ache in my middle. She's a black belt, too. Third dan. Should have remembered.

"I have a good reputation here. Don't you ruin it for me."

And there it is. The Yeh obsession with reputation. It's why they have a PR machine to bury bad press under six feet of dirt. Even when they have to bury a whole person. By now, it shouldn't bother me, not even from Lulu.

But it does.

"Sorry you have to slum it with me," I say.

She holds the crumpled flyer to my nose. "You wanted to know what this said? Because it doesn't take long to read." She

44

shoves it into my hand. "'Are these words too hard, dummy?'"

Oh, God. I can't do this again. There has to be an easier path to freedom than exposing my backside to kicks from all sides.

"No one was supposed to know," I say. Dumbly.

"That your dad bought your lazy ass into another school?" She heads off. Her voice cuts contemptuously back at me. "Not even Dragon Leaf's PR can keep *that* under wraps."

5

SOPHIE

They won't be able to resist you. They won't be able to resist you!

That vid was for Ever! To give *Ever* the confidence to blow away her *judges* and win a *scholarship*. And now Professor Horvath thinks I'm a boy-obsessed airhead.

I slump back against my dorm-room chair. I've been parked here since I bolted from the auditorium without a word, not even to Emma, who will probably never speak to me again. Three hours bent over my laptop, writing my fashion bot proposal because now *I* need to blow away *my* judge.

As it turns out, my scholarship *isn't* in jeopardy. That was a relief, although the fact I was so worried shows how scarily little I know. But now the problem is that this is Horvath's last class at Dartmouth. My only chance to show him what I

46

can do, join "the Horvath conspiracy," and maybe even land a Silicon Valley internship. It would be a game changer for me. I need it. So I need to wipe out any doubts that video planted in his head.

A text chimes on my phone. To my surprise, it's Xavier.

> Hey Sophie how's Dartmouth
> Did you get off your waitlist

I pick up my phone and move to my bed, setting my pillow at my back and my back to the wall. My heart lifts a bit. I know it's not good that I need this bit of connection so badly, but right now, I do. I write back.

> Not yet. The professor's brilliant and if he likes my project, I have a shot at getting in. I want to make a fashion app.
> That sounds cool
> How's LA? How are you feeling now?
> I'm drowning in assignments

Three raps sound on my wooden door. It creaks open, and Emma's bright blue eyes appear. Her cherry-blossom earrings dangle against her black hair. She's changed into a sky-blue blouse and printed skirt. So she came after all. A warm feeling, like wrapping my hands around a hot tea mug, floods through me.

"Sorry, I'm early." She sneezes.

47

"Gesundheit. No, come in. Great outfit. Just a sec." I text Xavier.

Hey, I've got to go. If you need help . . . pointers, I'm happy to help if I can.

A pause. Then . . .

Yeah later

Emma sets her mini roller bag by my dresser as I cross to my desk.

"I promised you mooncakes!" I flick the switch on my Zojirushi water boiler and shed the plastic wrapper on a golden lotus seed mooncake. I'm so glad she's here. I need friends. In the flesh. Girlfriends I can count on and a study buddy for CS. Especially now.

"That's a pretty one." Emma joins me. The mooncake is round, its flaky top imprinted with a rose.

"It's yum, too." I set it on a plate and pull out two mugs. "Green tea okay?"

"Yes, love it. I'm so sorry about that video stunt today." She sneezes again. "Sorry, pollen allergies." She pops a tablet into her mouth. "It was probably someone on the waitlist trying to get in. Sabotage."

"I should have shouted, 'It's a deep fake!'"

She laughs. "That would have been the perfect comeback."

"I never think of the perfect comeback until it's too late."

With a small, sharp knife, I slice into the mooncake's outer crust, revealing the sweet lotus-paste filling, the yellow orb of a salted duck egg yolk. I would normally be doing this for my brothers, who would eat it faster than I cut. A wave of homesickness washes over me as I slice quarters, then eighths, then hold the plate out.

"I end up eating the whole thing anyways," I admit. "I'm obsessed."

She takes a slice as I dispense the hot water. "There are worse obsessions."

"I have those, too," I say ruefully, and pop a sweet-and-salty bite into my mouth. "Mmm, *so yum*." I close my eyes and finish swallowing. "Well, now I *really* need to nail that proposal."

"Yes, just keep going. Turn in a fabulous proposal and Horvath won't even remember that video."

My phone chimes with another text.

"Go ahead," Emma says, and I pick it up.

Victor: I'll find out who did it and get the asshole kicked out of class

A smile touches my lips. Justice would be nice. But then I'll just have a hater at Dartmouth and, according to Horvath, for the rest of my career.

Sophie: Doesn't matter. Just let it drop.

Victor: Sorry, not up to you. It's harassment. And hacking the school system. Horvath wants us to look into it.

I frown. So it's out of my hands. But does that mean Horvath isn't holding it against me?

Sophie: I just need to focus on my proposal

Victor: Sure. Let me know if you want to talk, okay?

It's sweet of him, but I don't want to be encouraging. I've had to reject guys before, and things went south. It's better just to never get into the position of having to backtrack.

Sophie: thanks! ttyl

I set my phone down. Emma has crossed to the photo collection I pinned to the corkboard over my bed.

"Your brothers?"

"Yes." I snag another wedge of mooncake and join her. "I got them those shirts in Taiwan. They just sent me another photo of them wearing them."

"So cute." She touches the photos beside them. "Oh, fun! These are from Loveboat."

"That's my roommate, Ever Wong. She's dating my cousin Rick." Ever in red and Rick in black, crossing bo staves on the

50

stage of the National Theater.

"Lucky them. We had couples come together, too. Did you date anyone?"

I grimace. Xavier's photo is beside theirs, a group shot from a clubbing night. Everyone's dressed to impress: Ever, Rick, Marc, Spencer, me. Xavier in black is slightly off to the side, not smiling. "No one serious."

She touches Xavier's chest with a finger. "He's cute."

"Yeah." I let out a small laugh. "All the girls were after him. That's Xavier."

"Xavier?" She leans toward him, narrowing her eyes. "Xavier Yeh? Born in Taipei? Dragon Leaf Corporation?"

"Um, yeah."

"It *is* him!" Emma pulls the thumbtack free and takes the photo into her hand. "He's so grown-up!"

"You know him?"

"I grew up with him!"

"Oh, wow." There is about one degree of separation among Taiwanese who come to the States—but she *grew up* with Xavier. That puts her in another league.

"He was my little boyfriend. We used to pretend we were betrothed."

"*Betrothed?*" I choke on salted egg. Another *stratosphere*. "I can't picture him pretending to be betrothed. He's so . . . grumpy."

"Really? We were just silly kids." Her smile deepens. "Our

moms would have *swooned* if we actually got married. But I completely lost touch with him after I moved to the States." Emma is lit up like a paper lantern. "I have a picture somewhere." She scrolls through her phone. "Here, see?"

She shows me two six-year-olds with matching messy haircuts. Their heads are bent together over a black-and-blue butterfly on Xavier's outstretched finger. Emma's eyes are as blue as the butterfly. Her lemony dress flutters in a breeze, and Xavier is an inch shorter.

I study Xavier's young face. There's an innocence there. Enchanted soft eyes—nothing like the sarcastic charmer I swooned over on Loveboat. Or the pissed-off guy whose dad kidnapped him at the airport.

"How funny you know him, too!" Emma says.

"Um, so . . ." I open my mouth to tell her we *dated* on Loveboat. But it was so short and so heart-shreddingly disastrous that it almost doesn't count. "There were so many great people on Loveboat, you know?"

"What's he like now?" She pockets her phone, and I resist the urge to dig it out to examine Xavier more closely. "I haven't seen him since we were seven."

"He's an artist. He painted this." I touch the painting of Ever and me sitting on the shore of Sun Moon Lake. My sunset-orange dress pops against the blue waters and dark green trees. I hate to admit how much I've studied his rendering of me: my skirt fluttering over my tucked legs, my clipboard on my thighs. My black hair waterfalls down the side of my face.

My hand holds my pen, my elbow is awkwardly out, as it is when I'm writing fast. He saw me so clearly, and the hardest part was accepting it meant nothing to him. He made it for Ever, not me, and she gave it to me. And on the last day, he sketched portraits for Loveboaters who lined up in the courtyard to receive theirs. That's him.

"An artist! And wow, he's so *good*—who would have guessed? He was such a goofball. Is he in art school?"

"No, he's at Harvard-Westlake, finishing senior year."

She frowns. "I thought he was our year?"

"A year below."

"No, I'm sure he's our grade."

"I think he took an extra year when he moved to the States," I lie, and flip it back to her. "What was he like as a kid?"

"Oh, *so* sweet." She sinks onto my bed. "All his cousins had crushes on him, too, but since that was ick, I got him." She smiles. "He and his mom were always holding hands and laughing. That was the *real* love story, honestly."

More Xavier I can't picture . . . but then again, I can. There is a reason he's so closed off. "She passed away when he was twelve," I say. "He's been through more than most people our age." Still going through it, it seems.

"Oh, that's so sad. I remember hearing that. Poor guy." She pins the photo back on my board. "I can hang out and work for a while, if you don't mind."

"I'd love the company." Especially after today's disaster. "I was working on my CS proposal and haven't even finished unpacking.

My roommate's never here and it's a little lonely, you know?"

"Yeah. I'm in a single, actually."

She hauls her laptop onto my bed while I organize my clothes into five sections: dresses, tops, pants, skirts, jackets. I line up my sneakers, pumps, and sandals in a row. It's how I do it at home. That way I can grab whatever combination I want when I need it. Like the daring auburn leopard-print sweater that can go with my blue velvet pants, or the golden slip dress with the matching print, or crepe skirt with my don't-mess-with-me black boots. I love being able to stand before my closet and mix and match my day's look, depending on my mood: whether I'm feeling bright, somber, daring, fun.

On my bed, Emma tapes a colored flag to a page of her heavy textbook. Colored flags are moving up and down its entire inside edge.

"What are you doing?" I ask.

"I'm looking at the key sections so I know what the course is working toward," she says. "It helps me to see the big picture. I'm also checking the calendar so I don't have midterms and papers piled up the same week."

I'm impressed. "I'm pretty organized, but I don't think that far ahead."

"My dad told me time management is key. We always have too much to do, so we have to use our time well."

More of her legacy kid life. Like being brave enough to talk to Professor Horvath after class. If I was more like her, polished as a pearl, well spoken, not trying too hard or making goofy videos . . . this would all be so much easier.

"I'm the first person in my family to go to college in the States," I say. "So any advice—I'd be grateful."

"Sure, ask me anything. Anytime." She sits back, spinning her box of Post-it flags. "I, uh, kind of have something for you already."

The slant to her brow makes my stomach quiver.

"Yes?"

"You just spent over an hour organizing your closet."

"Oh, did I? Um, that's a crazy amount of time." I shut my closet door with a firm clank.

"It's not a bad thing, but your CS project . . . and I thought, time management . . ." She frowns. "Sorry, this is annoying, isn't it? My dad's always giving people advice. How to run their businesses. Super annoying. You don't need to hear it from me."

"Oh, but I do!" A Dartmouth alum dad running his own businesses. And obviously one of Taiwan's most prominent families, considering her childhood betrothal. I will take all the tips I can get. "I'm totally embarrassed I spent this much time on it. Stopping now."

A sheet falls from my corkboard and I hurry over to pick it up. It's Xavier's Sun Moon Lake. Like he's agreeing with her: "Get on with it already, Sophie." As I pin it back up, she says, "You can tell a lot about him just from his art. He's tough but sensitive. Smart."

"He's incredible," I say quietly. "He looked out for me when this asshole came after me." The guy who gave me the black

55

eye, who didn't mean anything to me because he wasn't Xavier. "Over the summer, he painted a picture of three old men in Taipei, just sitting in the sun. Not people anyone else would notice."

She gives me a probing look. "If he's so amazing, why didn't you go after him? I can't imagine him resisting *you*."

If only. Neither one of us is shy in the making-out department, or virgins. But even though I kept expecting more, wanting it, we never progressed that far. He always stopped us—the memories of him grabbing my hand back, rejecting me, even now make my skin heat with embarrassment.

"Honestly, he wasn't into me and I wasn't into him," I lie. "Not that way." I slip off the bed. "Also, I've sworn off guys."

"You have?" Her brow wrinkles, surprisingly concerned. "Why?"

"I'm a train wreck. I end up in bad relationships. Or I get . . . possessive?" I'm not even sure that's the right word. "Mostly, I can't afford to get distracted here. My secret weapon has always been my ability to charge into whatever I'm doing and just . . . drive it to the finish line. I missed the sign-up date for Horvath *because* I was distracted on Loveboat." By Xavier. "So I need to focus."

"I get it. I swore off guys last year, too."

"Same reason?"

She looks down at her thumbs, one rubbing along the base of the other. "More or less."

A disaster like mine? I can't imagine any real ripples in her ocean. I want to ask more, but she says, "But maybe you can reintroduce me and Xavier." She smiles. "If I mention him to my parents, they'll tell me he's on their list."

Their *list*. Of acceptable suitors. From the small circle of wealthy Taiwanese daughters and sons of the same age, like movie stars, who all know each other.

"Sure. If you're ever in LA," I say. "Or Taipei at the same time."

"We've probably both changed so much."

"He'd adore you," I say honestly. Beautiful and smart on top of fitting like a platinum puzzle piece into his world. And she's so steady. Xavier's a mess, like me. I've always thought Xavier needed a girl strong enough to take him on. Maybe what he actually needs is a girl solid enough to ground him. Like Emma.

"Want to go to Collis for dinner?" she asks.

"Sure," I say, and Emma packs her bag and heads for the door.

My phone buzzes with a text from Xavier.

Hey do you have a minute to talk

I snatch it up. Hell, yes. "You were betrothed?!" I want to say. I want to tell him I've been studying his painting and remembering how much I appreciated him looking out for me this summer. I want to hear how life in LA is going and if his dad has backed off.

Wait, what am I doing?

I've spent most of the conversation with Emma talking about him without even realizing it. Like organizing my closet for over an hour. This obsession is EXACTLY why I've sworn off guys, and Xavier in particular. I've. Sworn. Off. Boys. That's the anchor I need to cling to when my tornado wants to blow me off course.

Because my new friend is waiting and, as the video stunt showed me, I'm swimming with sharks.

Dropping my phone on my bed, I follow her out the door.

6

XAVIER

English, world history, geometry, physics—all my teachers pile on enough homework to sink the *Titanic* all over again. One assignment from *Hamlet*, even listening to audio files, takes me all night. I can't understand most of the words and keep track of everything asked for. I know I should feel grateful. Some kids with dyslexia probably never get a second chance.

But I'm too panicked to fall asleep for hours. I end up spinning the dial on the combination lock, trying to match the numbers on the dial with the code sticker, by moonlight. Until I jolt awake out of a nightmare into gray dawn. Ma was in it. Not the Ma who sang to me, or pretended to shower with me in a downpour, but Ma without hair in the hospital bed, who stroked my head as I lay on her chest and cried.

She would be as disappointed in you as I am.

My chest is tight. Have I even been breathing? On the coffee table across from me, *Hamlet* lies untouched. For some reason, I remember SparkNotes. I used it in my old school. I get out of bed and pull up *Hamlet* on the website, then use reading software on my laptop to read a modern translation.

It helps a bit. I've had to do hacks like this my entire life, but finding answers to the questions is still slow work. I have to repeat the audio again and again. I shove aside a congealing taro-pork clay pot. The dean told me I can work with my teachers to come up with alternative assignments . . . but I don't talk to teachers if I can help it.

But if I don't get on top of this mountain of work, I'll never get out from under Ba.

Sophie offered help, and I don't know where else to turn. Definitely not Lulu. But Sophie doesn't answer my text, so I place a desperate call the next day. Her photo blooms on my screen: ink-black hair twisted into a rope flowing down the shoulder of her tangerine dress. Oversized sunglasses over her heart-shaped face. I like how it's pure Sophie Ha: colors so deep and bright they won't let you ignore them. More attitude than smile to her mouth.

But my call goes to voice mail. After a second night playing SparkNotes, I try her again.

To my relief, she picks up.

"Hi. Xavier."

"Hey, Sophie." I push my earbuds deeper into my ear. It's

good to see her and hear her voice, when there hasn't been a friendly voice in this apartment yet. Although her expression is more closed off than I remember. "Everything okay?"

"Yeah. Fine. Sorry I missed your call yesterday."

She sounds distant. Then again, she's a busy college student who probably doesn't have time to talk to a guy who can't even get his ass out of high school.

"You have a few minutes?"

A short pause, then, "Yes, what's up?"

A million things crowd my mind. How the whole school knows I'm a fuckup. How I'm trying to fight my way out from under Ba's heel. How I got the bodyguards sent back today, finally, because Ba has me in a vise, and he knows it.

And of course, I want to ask how Dartmouth is going for her. But I shouldn't waste her time. "Have you read *Hamlet*?"

"'I am too much in the sun,'" she quotes.

"I'll take that as a yes. Do you mind if I take you up on help?"

"Sure, of course."

"Okay. Um, I can't believe I'm saying this, but I'm supposed to identify ten symbols. I have six. You remember any off the top of your head?"

"Easy—his clothes." Her voice warms. "He wears a dark blue cloak and black for mourning, even though his mom keeps telling him to stop."

"Right, makes sense. And seven's a passing grade. Thanks, Sophie." I flop down on my bed, where my sketchbook lies open. I've been drawing every moment I'm not studying. I should let her go, but I can't quite hang up yet. "I don't know how I'm going to do this for every single class."

"I'm surprised you're doing it at all."

"My dad took my trust back until I graduate."

"What? He can do that?"

I find myself filling her in—how Ba knew the dragon mural was mine. The deal with the dean to get me through high school.

"Your mural was amazing," she says hotly. "Two others were bidding until the end."

"Yeah, but he drove up the competition. He's good at that."

She scoffs. "He didn't force them to raise their paddles." She's right, but why can't I believe her? "It must be hard for you to be coming in senior year. Do you know anyone?"

"My cousin Lulu."

"There's the Loveboat alum group if you want to plug in more. I added you to it . . . I'm looking at it now, and it's almost eighty people now. Oh, ugh!"

"What?" I'm never in online group chats. They're not my thing.

"This guy Bert just posted a shirtless photo on it."

"Not pretty?" I smirk. "That's why I avoid group chats. It's never the people you want posing topless."

She laughs. "I guess I'd bail, but I need interaction."

We're such polar opposites. Guess we've always been. "I don't want to need anyone."

"Which is different from not actually needing them."

She's right. And that's Sophie. You think she's off in her own world, then she skewers you with penetrating insight. It's why

62

I can't actually imagine a conversation with her, because she's always saying things I'd never think of.

"My mom used to say we can't go it alone," I say. "But I'm making it so far."

My eyes fall on the white box on my coffee table, the one the dean gave me on my first day. I open it and spill out a fat plastic pen shaped like a torpedo.

Not what I was expecting. "Huh." I'm a sucker for pencils and pastels, and this pen feels surprisingly good in my hand. I hold it up for Sophie to see.

"What is it?"

"The dean gave me a reader pen. I just opened it. Never seen one before."

"What does it do?"

I drop onto my couch, pull the combination lock from under me, and open *Hamlet* to a random page. I glide the pen's flat tip over a sentence. Word by word, a robotic voice reads: "You come most carefully upon your hour."

It gives me a lot more freedom than my other hacks. I can flag and reread key passages . . . but this pen is an even bigger hack. It feels . . . wrong.

"Isn't this cheating?"

"The dean gave it to you. And I mean, isn't it like wearing glasses when you're nearsighted?"

"Yeah but . . . I thought I was supposed to *read* it." All of this—someone else reading for me, audio textbooks, double time on essays—I finagled these in my old school and kept them secret. Only this is way better. Teachers *expecting* my essays late. This fat-ass pen.

So it's legit? Is this how it should have been all along?

"Do you need help with anything else?" Sophie asks.

She's gone distant again. I set the pen down. I want to know how Dartmouth is going. I hope she's not having to fend off jerks like she had to on Loveboat. Sophie turned out to have surprisingly bad judgment when it came to guys. I just hope her next boyfriend is good for her.

And I hope she doesn't feel like I just needed her for homework help. Yeah, she nailed the *Hamlet* assignment for me. But that's not the only reason I wanted to talk to her.

But I don't know how to say any of this.

"No, that's all." I spin the dial on the combination lock. "Thanks, Sophie. Really appreciate it."

I missed my visual arts class on Tuesday by accident. On Thursday, I walk into the studio and feel my first spasm of hope. Bright sunlight and colors everywhere. Framed photographs of wild stonescapes. Blue cans with fat paintbrushes on easels flecked with paint. Along the top of the yellow walls is a scrawly border of green vines and words.

Maybe this is a class I can actually pass.

"'A picture is worth a thousand words, and a video a million.'" A woman steps up beside me, reading the words. She's wiping paint from her hands with a cloth that smells of turpentine. "It's a reminder to me how important our work is, so I decided to stencil it up there." She smiles, all warm browns: nest-colored hair, eyes, cross pendant, blouse, and printed pants. "You must be Xavier. I'm Ms. Popov."

"I could read that," I lie. "I'm not that bad."

She smiles good-naturedly and hands me a digital camera. The heft of it, like a solid rock, is oddly comforting. My thumb and forefinger close around the base of the lens. It feels like it belongs in my hand, and I lift it and frame a shot of the words.

"We're beginning a visual communications unit in preparation for the final project."

School's just begun and we're talking finals?

"What is it?" I ask warily.

"A six-minute short film. Any topic you'd like. The others are already outside. Why don't you join them? We'll share our photos and discuss during the second half of class."

Whoa. This is *school*?

For the first time all week, I feel more like myself as I cross the lawn, with the only goal to capture candy for the eyes. I head to the street into air that's actually breathable. I frame a photo of two black squirrels by a tree. A cluster of fungi at the base of a tree that could have come from another planet. A man sleeping on a bench. Images fill up my camera and I feel a sense of power, capturing each slice of life, one square after another.

"Xavier?" Ms. Popov waves, crossing the lawn toward me. Everyone else has disappeared, and I get the sense she's been calling me for a while. "Xavier, it's time to come back to class."

The other kids are working at the square tables, attaching cameras to laptops. I take a three-legged stool, comfortingly stained with oil paints and graffitied with arrow-pierced hearts and the names of those who've come before us.

"Folks, this is Xavier. Please make him feel welcome," Ms. Popov says to the students at my table. "Xavier, meet Rob, Jared, and Maddy."

"Hey," I say as Ms. Popov heads off.

"Hey." Maddy smiles, friendly. She's cute. Sleek blond hair in a blue headband, white faux fur lining the collar of her light jacket. "You're the new guy, right?"

Jared says hi, but Rob barely glances my way. "Maddy, Damien's got his old man's car Friday. He's meeting us after dinner."

"Sure, what time?" Maddy gives me an apologetic smile. The three of them pick up a conversation about tomorrow night. They're friends from the cradle. I'm the odd man out.

"Please choose six of your favorites to share." Ms. Popov's drawing a grid on the blackboard. "Upload them to Google Classroom."

Damn. I'd managed to forget the show-and-tell part. Art helps me put the oblong shapes and shadows inside me on the outside, so I can look at them. But I don't want all these people looking, too. Yeah, I got brave over the summer and showed my scratches to Ever, and at the talent show, but then . . .

I bought it to spare us the shame.

But did he?

I'm still on the fence as I download my camera's photos to my laptop. Maddy is posting a selfie to Instagram, and so I open my own Instagram account and find that Sophie's following me back, along with some family members. The Dragon Leaf PR machine must have gotten an alert when I created the account.

I peek at Sophie's feed. It's full of colors in motion: a guy in a crocheted blue octopus hat waving its legs, a lemony-layered skirt swinging like a bell on a model. She needs to crop her photos more closely to frame them better, but the images dance on her page. Until I joined Instagram a few days ago, I hadn't known she saw the world like this.

I heart the latest photo of her sitting on the steps of a red-brick building, leaning back on her hands with her head flung back and her night-black hair whipping across her face. Then, on a whim, I post the squirrels on my Instagram for her. They're energetic and fun. I think she'll like them.

"Xavier, your files haven't come through," Ms. Popov says. "Can you try again?"

Damn. She's holding me to it.

A classmate's photos—Harvard-Westlake buildings, the football field, and the same squirrels—glow on her big screen. I load my images into the classroom drive, but my insides have knotted with a cold dread. Maybe we'll run out of time and not get to mine. I hope so.

"Three of us caught those squirrels," Ms. Popov says. "What was it about them?"

"They're unusual," says a guy at the next table. "I mean, they're around campus, but we don't see them up close. Especially two together."

"We're drawn to relationships," says Maddy. "We relate to them."

"The way they sat in that shaft of sunlight," says another girl. "It was a photo asking to be taken."

I've never been in an environment like this, all brains bent on putting words to what's obvious to my eyes. I didn't know there *were* words. If my photos weren't in line to go under the microscope, I might actually enjoy this. I put my hand in my pocket and, with the edge of my thumb, spin the dial on the lock I'm carrying around for some reason.

"Let's talk about Xavier's now." Ms. Popov sends a bolt of panic through me. My photos appear on the screen.

The squirrel couple.

A woman pushing a blue pram.

A child hand in hand between Mom and Dad.

A golden stack of mooncakes, for sale by a grandmother and granddaughter.

A father with his son riding his shoulders.

Shit.

Ba used to carry me like that. Hanging on to my legs so I could see the world from up high with him. I rode hands-free like the kid in my photo, trusting he wouldn't let me go.

And now with my photos splayed up there with everyone looking, I see the pattern.

"Beautiful work, Xavier," Ms. Popov says.

"They're all . . . so lonely," says Maddy.

"Even though the subjects are together," says the guy in the front.

I squirm in my seat. I hate all their eyes seeing into me.

"Does family mean a lot to you?" Ms. Popov asks.

Fuck no.

Truth is, since I got shipped to the States, I've been alone. That's most of my life. Maybe it's messed me up? Somehow I've captured that on camera. And exposed myself like it was worth exposing.

I bought it to spare us the shame.

I fold my arms. "They're pictures. That's all."

Ms. Popov says, "Xavier—"

"Look, don't bother." I shove back my stool with a scrape on linoleum. The one class that could have been good . . . well, I'm out of here. I swing my backpack onto my shoulder. "I did the assignment. That's all. I didn't ask to be psychoanalyzed."

"Wait, Xavier!"

I head out the door, ignoring her.

7

SOPHIE

I feel a jolt in my chest when Xavier's purple dragon icon appears in my Instagram notifications. He liked my latest post. He saw it. The Westminster Quarters chime over the campus—shit, gotta run. I shove my phone into my pocket and pick up the pace toward the computer science building, chomping at my Gala apple breakfast.

Yes, I slept through my alarm. I'm seriously pathetic.

Ever since Xavier called about *Hamlet*, I haven't been able to get his voice out of my head. Especially the way he says my name. *Sophie*—like I'm the most important person on the planet to him. Which is bull crap. It's why I needed to cut our call short. To slice through those emotional cords thickening and tightening and threatening to reorient me toward Los Angeles, toward the stuff he's working through ... all the way across the country.

But one week into my official classes and the rest of my life, and I'm already losing. I want him to call and ask me about everything—*Macbeth*, *Midsummer Night's Dream*, his reader pen, his classmates, his asshole dad.

If he calls again, I'll take it, because I can't NOT take his call.

But I'll be sure the wall around my heart is built up thick.

My phone chimes. I fish it out with some fear and trembling, but to my relief, it's Mom.

"Hi, Mom! How are you? How are the boys?"

"Hi, sweetie. We're well." I cling to her voice as she catches me up: free skating lessons for Jerry at school, programming for James and Kai, who are following in my footsteps—ha! "And Kevin's really stepped it up as big brother. He's washing dishes."

"Amazing." I speak around the apple in my mouth. "It only took him till he was thirteen. I've spoiled them all."

"True." Her voice turns teasing. "And how are the boys at Dartmouth?"

No. I swallow hard, but the apple goes down like a cold stone. Even now, I can still feel those old expectations—*Have you met him yet? Don't give boys a hard time or no good ones will want you*—clawing for my soul. Yes, I've met a ton of boys here. Some in Lord Hall. Some in my classes. Cute guys, smart guys, hot guys. There were lots of vibes, and not just from Victor. If this were me three months ago and I was with Ever, all I would be talking about was whether to go for this one or that. But—

"I'm not here for boys. I'm here for my *CS degree*." My voice

71

comes out sharper than I intend. But I need her to believe it. I've limited interaction with Xavier. I stayed up late this week writing my proposal for Horvath until my eyes dried out and the sky turned pink over the trees outside my window. I've even tamed my outfit today to Understated Serious Student—beige slacks, cotton blouse, hair in a modest ponytail. "I'm a new me, Mom."

"It doesn't hurt to keep your eyes open."

She doesn't believe me. That's how it's always been. That's how it will always be until I prove otherwise.

I pass a group of guys heading into the auditorium. Someone makes a kissy noise. Ugh. The video. My face heats but I don't turn around.

"Mom, I'm almost to class." I toss the rest of my apple into a trash bin, my appetite gone. "I gotta go."

D. Please see me after class.

What?

My heart stops. I'm in my seat in the auditorium, staring at my grade at the top of my personal stylist bot proposal. I've never gotten a grade below a B in my life.

And a D is *definitely* not the way off the waitlist.

I reread my proposal.

> *I would like to build an app to help people find great clothes from all over the world. People can upload selfies of*

themselves, and the app will give recommendations. They can like or dislike items so the app can learn their taste over time.

I even designed the app prototype, with a non-girly, stylized sketch of a woman in a blue wrap dress. I named it Mirror, Mirror.

"What do I do now?" I ask Emma and Oliver Brooks, the guy who sat beside me on the first day, who decided to stick around a bit longer.

Oliver shifts his bag of kettle popcorn aside. He tilts his laptop to show me his proposal to train an algorithm to distinguish pictures of cats from pictures of dogs. Rejected, too, with a note:

Please do the assigned readings. As noted there, this problem has been solved many times.

"Ouch," I say.

"I called my dad." Oliver coughs up a kernel. "Sorry. He told me to take classes I'm good at. That's a big part of succeeding—being smart about what classes you take. Maybe computer science isn't your thing?" He ties off the top of his popcorn bag. "I'm done. I'm withdrawing from the waitlist. I'm considering law school and need to protect my GPA."

I frown. "If we can't take classes we like, what's the point of having so many cool ones to choose from?"

He makes a rueful face. "Guess it depends on your goals."

"Do what Horvath says," Emma says, then sneezes. Her

proposal to work on satellite imagery for climate disaster monitoring has been approved, with an offer to connect her with a leading researcher in the field. She points to the "see me" at the top of my screen. "Go talk to him."

I join a long line of students to speak to Horvath at his podium. His small-checkered black blazer over a creamy shirt and striped pants are a pretty risky choice, but he has a great sense of style. Surprising for a CS professor. Even more reason for me to hope I can get this project through.

The guy in front of me catches my eye.

"Hey, baby," he smirks. "How about a kiss?"

Oh, God. These duds really need some new material. A million comebacks present themselves. None of them can be overheard by Horvath.

I pivot out of line only to smack into Victor, smashing the cinnamon roll in his hand between his chest and my blouse.

"Oh, sorry!" I say as he steadies me by my elbow.

"Cha Siu-Bao Face, how goes?" He holds his smushed roll delicately between thumb and forefinger. The short sleeves of his Ralph Lauren polo shirt show off tightly muscled arms. He raises his brow at the guy, who quickly turns back around.

I brush cinnamon from my front, flooded with gratitude despite the buttery stain. "My mistake, telling you my nickname," I say ruefully.

"We caught the perp who leaked your video," he says. "A waitlister. He's outta here."

I'm surprisingly relieved that the guy's not in this auditorium anymore. I'm glad the school was braver than me. Although . . . could there be retaliation when I'm least expecting it?

Swimming with sharks. *Don't let your guard down,* I remind myself.

"Everything okay?" Victor asks.

"No." I show him my big D, and he winces.

"Talk to Horvath. You'll work it out."

"Thanks." The guys ahead of me step onto the stage.

"If you need help, that's what I'm here for. Bubble tea happy hour?"

"Oh, um . . . sure. So generous of you. Maybe this weekend?"

"I'm out of town for a family event. But Monday? Boba Babe?"

"Babe?" My face flushes hot.

"Boba Babe." He speaks around a big bite of the smushed roll. "It's the name of the bubble tea place."

He waves over my shoulder and I turn, stumbling on my own feet, as Professor Horvath says, "Next student, please?"

"Professor Horvath, you remember Sophie Ha," Victor says. "She's got great ideas. I'm happy to help—let me know."

His kindness buoys me onto the stage—he didn't have to do that for me. I'm sure he needs Horvath's good opinion as much as I do.

Up close, Horvath is even taller than viewed from the

audience. I can imagine his socks ironed and folded into squares, organized by size and color. His hazel eyes are intelligent and warm and he probably advises queens and noblemen. I have so much to learn from him.

"Sophie, how can I help?"

SO GLAD we're not talking about the video. I turn my laptop around to face him. "Um, hi. I'm Sophie." Right. Like he said. Ugh. Help! "Um, you asked me to see you."

He scans my proposal in about a second and a half.

"Ah, yes. I was surprised by this one. Tell me the thinking behind it."

"Well, I love clothes. I've dressed my brothers for years and my friends are always asking for advice. It's hard to stay on top of trends, and even harder to find clothes that are . . . you. So I thought, what about a bot that makes recommendations? Like Netflix does for movies."

"You have good ideas, as Victor said. But what you have here is a lot of description of clothing and barely any deep learning. You need more data to be analyzed so your algorithm can 'learn' why an item of clothing is fashionable. Or why it would flatter one user or another. What you have so far is . . . lightweight."

Ouch.

"I can add more data. Ratios of body parts. Cut, color, fit, and styles for different bodies. Scoop necks versus V-necks . . . I've already collected a huge database of dresses I love."

"You'll need ten thousand images to train the app, at

minimum. Label them with characteristics, the intelligence needed to make a useful suggestion. Making that data usable for training is a major effort. But if we step back, fundamentally, is there any substitute for trying on clothes?" He runs his thumb down the inside of his lapel. "Amazon has tried online clothing. People want to see the fit for themselves and touch the material. They want to *discover*. The entire retail industry is set up so you can browse stores—see the clothes, colors, and find them yourself."

I'm stumped—everything he's saying is true. But I can see a way around all of these hurdles. He lifts a finger at the line of guys behind me. *Wait a sec.*

"You'll be better served pursuing a project where you can research how others are doing it successfully."

I frown. "You mean, not a fashion app?"

"Yes, approved projects involve satellite imagery, or data from drug companies to predict candidates for new treatments. If you'd like to explore something softer, maybe consider something like converting graphic video game images into something photo-real." He swivels my laptop back toward me. "I expect one or two slots to open up after the withdrawal deadline next week, but I want to have a diversity of students. If you show me a viable project before the twenty-eighth, a slot is yours."

I put out my tongue and try to moisten my dry lips. "I hope my project will be good because it's good," I say. "I'll get it to you by—"

"Good luck. Next student, please?"

The stink of mildewed laundry floods my nose as a guy shoves in beside me.

"I'm a senior on the waitlist," he pants at Horvath. "Are you giving preference to us? Because you *should*."

8

XAVIER

Friday night, I step from the shower in a waft of steam when Ba texts me for like the billionth time. I know what he wants and it's more of the "yada yada have you graduated already, why not? dumbass" crap.

I grab my phone and fling it across the room. The small crash echoes in the apartment, but it doesn't make me feel any better. I'm boxed inside these four walls. No one gives a shit that I exist, unless they're trying to blot out my stains on the family altar.

"I've gotta get out of here," I say aloud. To my damp face in the mirror. To no one.

I don't know what good it will do. But as Ba continues to chime my phone by the wall, I towel off my hair, throw on a pair of shorts and a button-down shirt, and head out the door.

I don't really have a mission. I stop by the 7-Eleven a few miles from campus. In Taipei, 7-Eleven is my favorite store; I used to get a steamed baozi there every afternoon with Ma. Of course, 7-Elevens in the States don't sell baozi, but something about the layout of the store still feels like home.

I browse the cold drinks in the fridge and hover over greasy hot dogs rolling on their grill, then decide against everything and head back out.

To my surprise, Lulu is walking into the parking lot, hunched with her hands in the pockets of a black Harvard-Westlake hoodie.

"What are you doing here?" I ask.

She frowns at the sight of me. "Just clearing my head."

"Here for a baozi?"

Her brow quirks. Then she gives a rueful almost-smile. "Wish they had them here. Our moms used to take us for them."

"I was thinking the same."

The gutteral rev of an engine erupts down the block. We both turn. A Cadillac Escalade blinds me with headlights as it zooms up the street. The lamppost on the corner illuminates kids stuffed inside, catching the sparkle of necklaces, face glitter, sequins—everyone decked out for the night.

Lulu swears under her breath as it slows toward us.

"Who are they?" I ask.

"The guy driving is the one who put the sign on your locker."

Fuck. "Well, he can write."

"He can do more than write. That's Damien Martin. His dad's made blockbuster movies with, like, Bruce Willis."

"Got it. A big shot."

She falls silent as the black SUV stops an arm's length away. The passenger window rolls down. A girl with giant fake pearls swaying from her ears waves. The driver leans over. He's a thin guy in a black J.Crew shirt with a shock of piss-colored hair.

"Hey, Lulu, this your dum-dum cousin?" Damien asks.

Lulu frowns. "He's my cousin, yeah."

He appraises me. "Not as vacant eyed as I thought he'd be."

"I'm in disguise tonight." I shrug.

His brow knits with confusion. Then he grins. "Dum-Dum has a sense of humor."

Lulu grimaces. "It's been lovely. See ya." She starts toward the 7-Eleven.

I should get the hell out of here, too. But this asshole put that note on my locker. And I want him to take it back. Want them all to find out for themselves I'm not a waste of space.

I look Damien in the eye. "Where you all headed?"

"Xavier!" Lulu hisses. I ignore her.

"Club Pub. That's spelled P-U-B."

"Drinks on me if you give me a lift." I flash my black card. It's time to be *that guy.* I know exactly how this scene works, and it's the easiest path to making the rest of the year bearable. "My cousin needs a lift, too."

Lulu kicks the back of my calf. Damien and his girlfriend hold a quick conversation with the people in back.

"I'm busy," Lulu hisses at me.

"It's Friday night," I say. "It's your senior year." It's also piss-on-Ba night, and the nice thing about leaving my phone at home is that he has no idea where I am.

"Didn't peg you for a party guy." Damien's back.

"Yeah, well." I shrug. "There's a lot about me people don't get."

The back door opens. Rob from visual arts class sticks out a hand.

"Hop on up," he says.

Maddy from visual arts class smiles. "Hey, big guy."

So this was the party they were talking about. And now I'm crashing.

"Lulu, you're invited, too," says Damien's girlfriend.

I grab Rob's hand and he hauls me up onto a pile of laps. The AC is cranked full blast. Lulu scrambles in after me—so I got her. Nice. There are twice as many people in here than seat belts, but who's counting? This is feeling familiar. More like the summer sneaking out on Loveboat. More like me.

"He's cute," says a girl behind me.

Mmm-hmm. Definitely more like the summer.

"What's your actual name, Dum-Dum?" Damien asks cheerfully. He catches my gaze in the rearview mirror. I hear Lulu telling someone, "No thanks." Then a cold tin bottle is pressed into my hand.

"Xavier."

"Cool. X-Man."

I take a swig of not-bad whiskey. I don't mind *this* nickname, so already we're making progress.

"I'm Damien." He lifts an eagle-tattooed fist and I bump it with mine. Then his yell echoes off the windshield and we lurch forward. "Let's party, bitches!"

9

SOPHIE

Here I was flying along full tilt with my fashion bot, arms out like a Marvel hero—and I was flying in the wrong lane. All those late nights reading about machine learning and collecting photos of Prabal Gurung models. I even started to code the algorithm. Then *SPLAT*! Smack into the side of a skyscraper.

That video already made me look like I have cotton candy between my ears. Now Horvath is calling my project too *soft*.

It's late Friday night. I scarf down a cheeseburger and spend my evening in the library on an essay for Writing 5. Then I drag myself back to my dorm room and flop down on my bed. I have another campus job interview tonight—for a closing shift. Then I need to start on the next idea for Horvath. But I can't rally. Most of the good ideas have been claimed by now. How can I possibly start from scratch?

My phone buzzes with a text. I roll onto my back to read it.

Victor: How did it go with Horvath?

Sophie: I need to come up with a new project

Sophie: He said I'm at the top of the waitlist if I can show him a real project

Victor: That's great!

Victor: You'll nail it. Let me know if you want to brain-storm.

Victor: Lots of great work in deep learning and finance, robotics, Red Cross.

All topics my classmates are already covering. None that call to me.

Sophie: Thanks! I'll look into them!

My Instagram app is lit with new notifications. I scroll through some recent posts from Loveboat friends: Ever teaching a dance class of seven girls, including her little sister, Pearl; Rick with his arms around football teammates at Yale; a nostalgic Gang of Five photo from the summer at Taipei 101 by Marc Bell-Leong. "Miss the crew," he's written.

"Me, too," I write back. I scroll deeper and run into a pair of black squirrels on emerald grass, posted by Xavier. No caption, but none is needed. He's caught them in action: fur coats gleaming as they dance on hind legs, pawing at each other. One holds a seed in its paws, like it's playing a game of keep-away.

I smile. Only Xavier could make squirrels this fun. He seems okay. I'm glad he's not letting his dad stop him from capturing the world he sees.

I heart it and comment, "I needed this. Glad you're well."

My alarm sounds—time to get ready for my interview. It's at a mail and printing shop. I head for my closet. I need an outfit that *screams* I'm perfect for the role . . . practical, but tasteful. No more "beautiful" comments. I sort through my tops. Through my new Emma lens, I can see how some are pretty wild: a yellow peacoat covered in squares; a body-hugging purple-striped sweater. The problem is all my dressy clothes are from the MARRYMESOPHIE era, not the ÜBERSTUDENT one.

I glance at my roommate's closet. She said I could borrow whatever I wanted, then dashed off to run the Dartmouth Libertarians.

Minutes later, I'm dressed in her white camisole under my most conservative blazer, solid blue suede, over blue-and-green plaid pants. I spritz my hair with water, then blow-dry to sleek perfection. I apply a nude palette of makeup, just enough to give me a professional glow. Glasses or no glasses? Mm, let's stick with contacts. Voilà! Serious and studious. I can handle landing a campus job! And once I have that victory in hand and a cushion of cash for books and supplies, I'll feel ready to take on the rest of Dartmouth.

With a new energy in my step, I head outside and down the block. The chill wind gusts at me, tugging at my hair and blazer. The sky is dark, no stars, everything covered by clouds. An owl hoots. Like a warning.

I'm about four blocks from the store when the skies open up overhead—

And the rain pours down.

I charge several blocks down a street with my purse over my head before a storefront tells me I'm headed the wrong way. By the time I double back to Jones's Mail Stop, I'm soaked to my skin. I peel my hair off my face and squeeze water from its ends. So much for the blow-dry.

As I push open the glass door, I hastily wipe my cheeks on my shoulders. A slouchy guy in a starched dress shirt looks up from counting money at the cash register. A young guy in a T-shirt is breaking down boxes. He looks about fourteen.

"Hi, I'm John, the hiring manager." The slouchy guy takes my damp self in with a double raise of his brows. "You . . . must be Sophie?"

"Yeah." I'm out of breath. "Sorry I'm a little late." I catch a glimpse of my reflection in the windows. Oh my God. It's a drowned rat!

John frowns. "Interviews are important. Maybe you're not really ready for a job like this."

What? My heart lurches. "No, I'm ready. I'm sorry. I got turned around in the rain. If I could just have a few minutes to dry off . . ."

He doesn't budge. Then he juts a thumb leftward. "Bathroom's that way, but I've already cleaned it. Please be careful to keep it that way."

Ten minutes later, I'm seated across from him in a cramped back office. Dust or mold in the air makes me sneeze like Emma. The job is a staff job—take out trash, clean the bathroom after customers, close up shop. Late-night hours, not great, but they fit with my class schedule.

"My mom works in a hotel and I've helped her with the paperwork," I say. "I raised my four brothers and can do anything around the house—change light bulbs, glue broken toys back together. Whatever needs come up, I'm your girl."

I'm babbling. We've talked for about half an hour. But I can't shake that hesitant expression on his face.

Finally, John sets down his pen. "I think we're done here. I have other applicants."

Another bombed interview. What went wrong this time?

"I'm qualified." I'm begging. "I'll do a great job."

He rises and heads toward the main store. "We're *really* not showy people here."

"Showy?" I frown, hurrying after him. Why would he say that? "You didn't . . . happen to see my video, did you?"

John's expression grows resolute. "I don't want to get your hopes up unnecessarily. I don't think this is going to work out."

He saw the video. "But I work hard! I'm reliable!"

"You were late."

"But not usually!" The slouchy guy is gaping at me, but I can't seem to stop. How can I hope to succeed at anything at Dartmouth if I can't even get a high school kid's job? I grab John's arm, needing him to listen. To *believe* me. "I can mop up after students! You have to hire me!"

John wrenches free. In two strides, he crosses to the door and opens it. He's shaking. Literally *shaking*. A thirty-five-year-old grown man with a hundred pounds on me. And somehow, I've scared the shit out of him.

"Please just leave, Ms. Ha."

10

XAVIER

Club Pub is cranked up full force in a refurbished bank near Hollywood. Ear-shattering music and the scent of beer spill onto the sidewalk from the guarded doors. We get into a short line, and when we reach the bouncers, I flash my fake ID with the black card peeking out.

"Seven entries," I say.

It works like always—the bouncer taps a finger on my ID, then waves me inside.

I pay the cover for us with my card, and we all head into the main space. Strobe lights play over the dancing curves of hips and pale arms pumping in rhythm. The whole place reeks of cologne and sweat and freedom—yep, way better than hanging with the dean.

Tonight I'm shifting the tides of Harvard-Westlake in my favor.

I weave through the dancers to the bar, with about a hundred bottles of wine lined up behind it. I nudge aside a box of lime wedges and hand my card to the bartender.

"Drinks for my friends." I turn to the others, who've lined up. "What can I get everyone?"

"Thanks, X-Man. Pretty awesome of you." Damien squeezes my shoulder. "Mint mojito for me," he tells the bartender.

"Such a girly drink, Damien," says his lady, who gives me a friendly wink. She places her order, followed by Rob and the rest.

"Thanks, Xavier." Maddy's golden hair shimmers, and she runs teasing piano fingers down my arm. "Pretty great of you."

"You all can get me next time." I lift my brows at her, then I let her gaze go. Noncommittal, but not saying no to whatever it is she's suggesting.

This is a guy I know how to be.

Damien joins me with his mojito, waiting for his girl. "You're new to school, so anything you need to make life easier, I got you covered."

"Sounds like a plan," I say.

"There are sodas in the back closet in the gymnasium. It's for the staff, but no one's around in the mornings."

"Got it." So Damien knows *all* the hacks of Harvard-Westlake.

I order a beer and sign the tab with an X. Then I lean on an elbow against the bar. Rectangles of colored lights pulse over the dancing bodies. Lulu joins me, nursing a virgin piña colada she insisted on paying for herself. No favors. Sheer stubborn Yeh pride.

"What are you trying to prove?" she asks. She's a mini Ba with long hair.

"Just making friends."

She bites into her wedge of pineapple. "Guess it's working," she admits grudgingly.

A familiar hip-hop song comes on next. It played at Club Kiss in Taipei, the first night we all busted out clubbing. I feel a surprising tug of regret. I danced to this song with Sophie, and we ended up making out right there. Some guy said later that we were practically having sex on the dance floor. My body remembers . . . but chemistry was never the problem between us, and that was how our shitstorm began.

Anyways, all that's in the past.

"Hey, Xavier. Wanna dance?" Maddy shimmies toward me.

"Maybe in a bit."

She joins me, her dance-warmed arm brushing mine as she moves to the music. She sips her peach spritz, nudging me in time to the beat. I crack a half smile. She slides her hand up my back and into my hair, where her fingertips tease at my curls.

"I like the waves," she says. "I'm Maddy, in case you forgot."

"I didn't forget."

Lulu sets her emptied glass on the bar. "And that's my cue to leave. I've called my driver."

"Adios, cuz," I say as she heads for the door.

"Driver?" echoes Maddy. Outside, Lulu's guy opens the back door of a blue Audi for her.

"You people." Maddy smiles. "You didn't need a ride from us."

I shrug.

"You're an incredible photographer."

I don't really want to get into *that*. "I just shoot what I like."

"Maybe you can take my photos sometime?"

"Sure." She probably models. And models love photographers. I'm not that kind of photographer. Still, everything's falling into place.

Now maybe Harvard-Westlake won't be so bad after all.

"Sir? We've had another round of orders." The bartender points to Damien, who's dancing with his girlfriend, his tattooed arms raised like goalposts. "The guy there said you're covering."

I hand over my card, and the bartender swipes it on his machine. A blue glow illuminates the blades of his cheekbones.

He frowns at it. "One moment, please."

He slips toward a back office, taking my card. Whatever. I lean back and try to enjoy the music pulsing in my bones. The bar's getting crowded. Maddy lurches against me, shoved by guys on her other side. She laughs and winds her arm around mine, steadying herself.

"Maybe we should get out of here early," she suggests. Her light perfume tickles my nose. Then her lips graze my jaw, so slight it could have been an accident. "My parents are out for the weekend. We could head to my place if you want to crash."

She gives me a look I recognize. This part I'm used to.

No girls. No parties.

Right, Ba. Tonight I just want to pretend I don't have a silk noose tight around my neck.

"Sounds good," I say.

The bartender reemerges with my credit card in hand. And a pair of scissors. His mouth twists with embarrassment. He can't be more than a few years older than me.

"I'm sorry, but I've been instructed to do this."

He opens the scissors over my card.

"What the f—!" I yell, straightening. But it's too late. My card falls on the counter in two neat halves.

Everyone has gone silent, staring at me. Even the song's ended. He takes my glass from my hand. "Someone named Ba says you need to go home and study."

11

SOPHIE

I rap on Emma's door, but though her hallway reeks of pepperoni pizza, she doesn't answer. I knock harder, setting her cherry-blossom print swaying on its nail. There's no light under her door. She must be out with friends.

My shoulders slump as I head back out into the humid night. How did it get to this? No class, no project, no job. I am an utter disaster.

I wander the campus quad, past the silent old buildings and dorms leaking music, until my legs start to shake. Then I sit on a bench with a view of Baker-Berry Library and look up at the lopsided triangle of the Capricorn constellation. The clouds have finally rolled back, too late. Doesn't matter if I stay dry now.

A pit forms in my stomach as I realize I don't have a single friend within a hundred-mile radius.

I reach for my phone, but Ever's asleep by now. So is Rick at Yale—or out partying with his football team. My mom's probably up paying bills, but I don't want to worry her when she already has enough to juggle, not to mention if I hear another MARRYMESOPHIE comment right now, I'll die.

I start to text Xavier: Any chance you're free?

As my finger hits the send button, my phone rings with an incoming call.

Xavier's face flashes on my phone.

12

XAVIER

Sophie blooms on my screen. Her face is flushed. Softened, round. Luminous eyes. She's outdoors but dressed to give a speech to the United Nations. The purple silhouettes of trees blur in her background.

At the same time, her text chimes: Any chance you're free?

"Xavier?" Her eyes widen.

"Did you just text me?" I ask.

"Yeah, but then you called!"

"Weird," we say at the same time.

I'd called her on a whim. After my credit card fell in two halves, everyone took off. Again. Ba has a way of making that happen. I needed a friend tonight. A *real* friend. The kind who stayed in the airport when everyone else ran away. Because no matter how humiliating it was to have her see that, that's what it meant that she stayed.

"Where are you?" she asks.

"Griffith Observatory." I set my sketchbook on my bench and pan the phone to show her the domed building behind me, glowing white against the night. Then I return it to face me. "I had my driver take me here. I'm just . . . looking at Capricorn."

"No way. So am I." There's a hollow look in her eyes.

"Shitty night?" I ask.

"Yeah. You?"

"Yeah, but you go first. You look like you've had a rougher one."

She sighs. Her story pours out: her rejected proposal, then the failed interview with the store manager. "It wasn't a dream job or anything, but I needed it. And I dressed up! I told him I'd change light bulbs! I must have sounded so stupid." She buries her head in her hands in a flounce of black hair.

"What the fuck, Sophie," I say. "Why would you care what he thinks?"

"Because I need a job! People do, you know." She groans. "It was awful. The man was terrified of me. That was the *worst* part." She sighs. "I have so many hopes for Dartmouth. But I keep running into myself. I can be . . . a tornado."

"What do you mean?" I ask, but then I think I know. I experienced some of that tornado over the summer.

"I just get so . . . excited . . . about something. Then I don't even realize what else is going on around me. Like in class, I sat

98

in the front row with the TAs—and now the head TA thinks I'm a gunner. You know. Too ambitious."

"I don't sit in the front row, but that's not the worst."

"Yeah. But then there was this *video*." She fills me in on *that* and I pull it up on my phone. "I made it for *Ever*. How did it end up everywhere? I'm already, like, one of only ten girls applying for the class. It's a total bro-down in there. I looked so . . . unserious! I could barely go back to class after that."

"Two thousand views!"

"What? Oh, no!"

"Let me take a look."

"No, don't!" she cries, but I've already started to play it. Her brush glides a soft blue over her lid as she voices over. "The key is blending. Take your time. You have to be patient to get the shades just right. . . ."

"Turn it off!" she says, but it's really good. I watch it all the way to her kiss and flirty wink.

"It's great," I say truthfully. "You look great. That red's a great shade on you."

"I should just delete it."

"Fuck no. Post more."

"Post *more*?"

"Don't let them win. Don't let them tell you how to be."

A pause. She draws a shuddery breath. "Never thought of it that way."

"As for that manager tonight," I say slowly. "Honestly? He probably thought you were hot, and he's more afraid of himself stepping out of line than anything else if he hired you."

There's a pause on her end. "That sounds *horrible* . . . and it's presumptuous of me to agree . . . but you might be onto something." She sighs. "Note to self: don't grab random guys' arms."

I give her a wry smile. "So what are you gonna do now?"

"Well, if I can get an internship in Silicon Valley through Horvath, it would make up for a campus job ten times over, so . . ." She finger-combs her hair from her face. "What about you? What happened?"

"I went out with some kids." My impromptu night spills out. "It was going well. Then the bartender cuts my credit card in half. Everyone just . . . took off."

"Ugh. That can't have felt good."

"I was trying to prove I'm not a waste of space."

"You? Honestly, you don't need to win anyone over." She pauses, as if she's considering her next words carefully, too. "But you've sort of got this shell around you, you know? Maybe you feel alone because you don't let anyone in. To the real you."

I scoff. "No one wants to know the real me. They like the shell me better. The guy buying drinks."

"You can't pay people to care about you."

I frown. I said the same thing to the dean. "Maybe I was trying to prove to *myself* I'm not a waste of space." I've surprised myself. Telling her that.

"Oh, please. You're so not."

"You heard my dad." Maybe that's why I'm telling her. She stuck around. She's *still* around. "Everyone we went on

Loveboat with is now at some top-ten college. My cousins could host their own Ivy League tournament. They're trying to get on the Forbes 30 Under 30 lists. Then there's me. Who can't even. Freaking. *Read.*" I've never said it quite so bluntly to another person before. But with the dean knowing, my new teachers, Ever Wong, too, it just comes out.

"You never told me it was that bad, but I sort of guessed." She's not judging me. I wasn't sure if she would. "Yes, reading's important, but if you think about it, lots of people can read. Not many people can do what you can. Your art. It's like—a miracle."

"Ha," I deadpan. "Miracle" is over the top, but then again, so is Sophie. Then I laugh. "Haha, Sophie Ha."

"Do not take my name in vain! *Yeh* though I walk through the valley of the shadow of death, I will fear no evil!"

"You're so weird." I laugh again and lie down on my back. It feels good to laugh. "You crack me up, Sophie." She wasn't like this over the summer. Then, it felt like she was constantly posing—putting on a show. Making people see only the parts of her she wanted.

Kind of like me.

"You've probably heard this before, but there are also some really famous people with dyslexia, who say they're as awesome as they are because of it."

"Yeah, I have. It's just . . . my family's different about it."

My cut credit card spills out of my pocket onto the ground, and I reach down for the pieces and sit up again. "Well, all this just confirms I really need to get the hell out from under Ba's thumb. Take their stupid diagnostic tests. Figure out how to pass senior year."

My driver waves from down the driveway. Time's up. I grab my sketch pad and start toward him.

"Whatever shit hits the fan, I—I'm here, okay?" she says. "Anything I can do to help. Like all those assignments drowning you—maybe try to consolidate them."

"Thanks. Never thought of that."

"But I have to ask . . . is your trust fund worth going through your dad's hoops? Maybe it's stock or something you can't even use?"

"It's money from real estate. Nothing to do with Dragon Leaf. My mom's family's lived in the Taipei area since the 1750s. Back then, they owned a lot of farmland. They eventually built hotels."

"It must be worth a lot, then."

"I don't care how much. As long as it's enough to break free from Ba."

"It's just that . . . this doesn't seem like you. You could walk away from all of that. Create your art full-time. Build your life the way you want."

"Ba will send Ken-Tek and Ken-Wei in to drag me back. There's no escape. The only way out is through." My driver opens the back door, and I slip inside, onto the leather seat. I take a pastel to my sketchbook and draw those empty concentric boxes. "Honestly, Sophie, I can't let him keep my mom's money. She wanted me to have it . . . I think."

Though if she could see me now, would she feel the same?

"Of course she did."

"I wish I could ask her . . . so many things I never asked. And then, one day, she was just . . . gone."

"You need to be free of your dad. On your own terms." She opens her eyes wide. "And you should do whatever it takes to make that happen."

She gets it. That feels good, too. God, we are so much better at being friends than being together, and I'm glad we got here.

"That's the plan," I say. Then I draw a jagged line breaking out of the boxes as my driver starts back toward my apartment.

13

SOPHIE

This call . . . everything about it feels right. Xavier's dark brown eyes going from haunted to shades lighter. Me letting him into my shit and him letting me into his. Him escaping his dad. Me fighting my tornado. Him understanding what went wrong tonight more than I did.

And *post more*. In two words, he transformed my shame into something good. Something to fight for.

We're friends. Friends who have each other's backs.

Maybe that's why I feel ready to say, "By the way, I met an old pal of yours. Emma Shin. She's my classmate."

"Emma Shin? Whoa. That's a blast from the past."

"She said you were betrothed."

"Oh, yeah." He laughs. "Bringing two empires together."

"*Exactly* what she said. Cutest thing ever." A winged maple seed helicopters down onto my shoe. I lean over to retrieve it. Emma had wanted me to reintroduce them . . . but once I do, will he call *her* for *Hamlet* help and bartender disasters?

"Is she still into outer space?" he asks. "She used to want to be an astronaut."

"I don't know. She's doing her CS project on satellite imagery to predict climate disasters."

"She was always wanting to save the world. Like Lulu."

"I can see that about her." Emma is a really good person. The truth is, Xavier would benefit from reconnecting with her. The old Sophie would have tried to keep him to myself, wanting him to choose me so badly my heart couldn't bear any other option . . . but I don't want to be the old Sophie.

"I'll tell her you said hi and I can put you in touch again?"

"That'd be great. She's a good egg."

"And brilliant. Her dad went to Dartmouth, too."

"No surprise. Her family's really well connected. He's been to the White House for dinner and all."

An actual, modern-day princess, just without the tiara. "After meeting her, I couldn't believe *we* dated this summer."

D'oh. Hadn't meant to bring *that* up. Not when we're solidly on the friend track.

"I mean, barely," I add hastily. I twirl the maple seed between my fingers. "Listen, I should let you go. Your driver's probably about to pull up to your place and—"

"It wasn't all bad. We had fun. Sometimes." He pauses. "But

you were right to break it off."

"*I* broke it off? I just made it official."

"And it's all the better for world peace."

"What? Was it *that* bad?" I flash to the fight at the club, Rick peeling me off. I crush the seed in my hand, wishing I could erase that moment. Not to mention everything else that came after. "Okay, yes, it was. We were both figuring out our shit . . . chasing the wrong things. At least I was."

"I was, too. Probably still am."

"Well, then stop!" I say. He laughs. "All I know is, I can't be crazy like that again."

A beat. "So, I make you crazy?"

I roll my eyes. "Yeah, like right now!" I let out a breath and head toward the lights of Lord Hall. "Okay. I've got to work on my proposal. Stop bothering me."

He laughs. "Okay, Sophie Ha. Haha."

My name—there it is again. I hate how my heart lurches like it's a spell cast over me. I put it back to him, though I doubt it makes us even at all.

"Okay, *Xavier Yeh*."

I need to fall in love with a new project. That's all there is to it. On Sunday evening, Emma drops by to study with me and when I tell her Xavier said hi, her face lights up. I shoot them a text, linking them, and Emma sends him a separate note. It feels good, like I'm making all of us stronger. And burying the old Sophie away.

For the next hour, I chomp on a red bean mooncake and research applying deep learning to slides of cancer tissue. I check out Victor's recommendations about radiologists and ebola. I dip into the Red Cross's work creating virtual reality films to build empathy for the hardships of refugee camps.

"If I had millions of dollars, I'd give it to the Red Cross," I say to Emma, who's sprawled in my desk chair with her black hair bound by a pink band. "But I find all this stuff . . . really dry. I'd rather flip through *Vogue*. Does that make me shallow?"

"Of course not. But you might come across that way to certain people."

Great. I sigh and pull up the shell of my Mirror, Mirror app on my laptop. A dozen next steps leap out at me. I add more categories for my customer quiz, to capture more of the data Horvath was talking about. Length of body segments: arms, torso, legs. Shirt size, pants size, hips, waist, bust. He was right to push me on data. I work through the dresses on my Instagram feed, tagging them with qualities like designer, color, style, even types of sleeves, and before I know it, I've put in all five hundred samples.

I find myself swinging my legs and humming.

"Research going well?" Emma asks.

"I've been working on Mirror, Mirror," I admit. "Honestly, I can't imagine anything else I'd want to work on. I love playing with what textures go with what patterns and styles. It's like solving puzzles."

"You have a good eye." Emma squirts pear lotion into her

hand. "I noticed that about you right away."

She's so encouraging. We work for a bit in a cozy, pear-scented silence. Then I remember. "Xavier mentioned you wanted to be an astronaut."

Her eyes open wide. "Oh my gosh, I totally forgot about that. He remembers?" She smiles and gestures to her project, full of data from NASA and other places like it. "I'm still interested in space stuff."

Her project is made of intense calculations and seriously HARD-CORE science. I trace a finger around my baby-blue app with its breezy sketch of a girl. Next to Emma's project, mine even *looks* light and fluffy. But the more time I spend on it, the more I want to make it work.

Maybe there's another way to come at it for Professor Horvath.

I hop back onto the internet and search for fashion and artificial intelligence. Beautiful models in dazzling patterns, like watercolors, oil paintings, works of art. I could study them for hours: how this mermaid cut aligns with those boots, or the right necklace sets off that halter neckline . . . but now I'm looking with different eyes.

"'The fashion industry is one of the largest in the world, at over two trillion dollars,'" I read from an article. "'Large brands are applying AI to refine chatbots and reach more customers.' I don't get it. Does none of this matter to Horvath?"

Emma fingers her cherry-blossom bracelet. "My mom works

in venture capital. She says women's stuff always gets held to higher standards."

I frown. "So what do I need to do to get Horvath to take my proposal seriously?"

"Change projects." Emma laughs.

"Arg." I throw my pillow at her head and she ducks. "Fine. I'm going to the hive mind for help."

I jump onto the Loveboat chat, which has expanded to over a hundred of us.

> Sophie: guys I bombed my CS project proposal. I wanted to make a fashion bot but my professor dinged it. Any ideas for other bots to make?
>
> Marc: a writing bot
>
> Spencer: a bot to help you figure out which local candidates to vote for
>
> Pierre: I could use an app to help me find the best spring rolls in Virginia
>
> Rick: I'm doing a sports talent analysis to help managers build teams
>
> Sophie: Ahem. How is a sports talent analyst more legit than a stylist recommender?
>
> Rick: Never said it was

Hm. As an exercise, I google the value of the sports market. Highest I can find is $1.3 trillion.

"Half the size of the fashion industry," I say to Emma.

My phone pings.

> Debra: check out the Beauty Blog: "Digital Fashion—the Next Wave in Styling?"

Wait, isn't that what I'm trying to do?

Dismayed, I open the blog, which features a Taipei clothing boutique I love. Their logo—a gold hand mirror trimmed with the words "Magic Silk" in lilac letters—tops the page. I adore their clothes—elegant and playful shades, inspiring blends of textures and even hand-painted tropical fabrics. But I can't afford anything. I have my favorite stormy-orange dress from them, a present from Aunty Claire that I wore all summer. I even searched for their knockoffs in the Night Market but couldn't find any. They're too boutique-y for the piraters, I guess.

And they've built a top secret digital stylist called Magic Mirror.

We scan your body to determine the best fit for you. Choose from among thousands of items that fit, with just the click of a button.

"I'm too late," I say.

Emma looks up. "What?"

"Our Magic Mirror is in beta testing now," says Rose Chan, general manager. "We can't wait to unveil it to the world."

I show it to Emma. "Someone else is doing it already. It's even the same name."

"It means it's a legitimate project. I bet other people are doing it, too. And I like your name better. Mirror, Mirror."

"So it's real!" I pace my room, encouraged. "This is exactly what I want to do!"

"Why don't you show this article to Professor Horvath?"

I pause before her, frowning. "I could, but there's barely any information. Not even a picture of the app."

"You could call? Ask if you can interview them. Maybe they'd be willing to talk to a Dartmouth student."

"Is that how it works?" My mind buzzes with possibilities. "What if I *could* talk to them?" I scroll their website for contact information, passing models in basque-cut elegance. "It's Monday morning in Taipei, and their store is probably open. Oh my gosh! Maybe I can catch them."

Their number gets me to a robotic voice asking me to dial by name and need. Probably an AI-powered system. If it's half as good as their stylist, then maybe I'll get to who I need to. But none of the options include, "Can I interview your AI stylist bot inventor?"

I punch through a labyrinth of recorded answers. I'm about to hang up in despair when a woman says, "Wéi, nǐ hǎo?"

A real person! I switch to Mandarin. "Hi, I'm a student at Dartmouth. I read about your stylist app and was hoping to talk to someone about it."

"I'm sorry, I don't know anything about that. This is customer service."

"Do you know what department is working on it?"

"I don't. Try headquarters."

"Wait, don't hang up!" I say. "What's their number?" But she's gone. I sigh. Headquarters wasn't an option in the labyrinth.

"No luck?" Emma asks.

"Nada."

"Maybe you can message them on Instagram." She runs her finger over her phone screen. "Whoa, 1.2 million followers! Never mind."

My heart sinks and I pull them up on my Instagram app. "And they're only following ninety-nine people." I flop down beside her. "That's real social media power. Horvath will have to take this seriously."

I send a direct message via Instagram.

> I'm a freshman at Dartmouth researching deep learn-
> ing and fashion. I read about your stylist app and was
> wondering if I could interview someone about it.

"It's a super long shot," I admit . . . 1.2 million followers! But I cross my fingers at Emma. "Can't hurt to try, right?"

She gives me two thumbs-up. "Making it happen. Go, Sophie!"

I check my DMs obsessively for the next twenty-four hours, call Magic Silk's headquarters and get routed to customer service four times. I dig up an email address and send them the same message, but get an automatic reply. Xavier texts me a few questions about a diagnostic test he took. I send him an answer with a note: I've got a lead! Wish me luck!

Good luck! he answers.

"I'm running out of time," I say to Emma. I'm starting to feel not despair exactly, but close.

She twirls her pen in her hand. "This is like calling up Google or Facebook and asking for their secret algorithms. You don't have access to the right people. Do you know anyone who might know someone there? You need an in."

"I emailed my aunt in Taipei, but she just gave birth. I don't think she's checking right now."

"If you could get an exclusive interview, Horvath would eat that up."

Exclusive interview? Wow. She operates on a different playing field than I do. "If I could get *any* interview!" I check Instagram again. I've become a stalker. People stalk celebrities and crushes, but now I'm stalking a fashion bot. . . .

I'm becoming a nerd!

I click on the list of accounts they're following, on the off chance I know someone who knows someone who knows someone among the ninety-nine. I scroll past Oscar de la Renta and Louis Vuitton and Prabal Gurung.

I let out a short laugh. "Not a chance." I scroll past the prince of Morocco and Princess Asuka of Japan.

And then I come to the sketch of a purple dragon.

I don't believe it.

Xavier Yeh.

14

XAVIER

"Xiang-Ping. Dean Ramchandran called me." Ba's voice is terse through my phone. I brush hair from my eyes and squint against morning light, trying to catch up to Ba and wondering why I bothered answering in my sleep. "You failed—"

A roaring sound blasts my ear. I hold my phone away from raging voices in Ba's background. It sounds like a riot. Not that I can imagine one on the streets of Taipei. Ba swears a distance from his end of the phone. Something's wrong—normally, nothing ruffles him.

I'm curious, but not enough to ask.

He's back. "You did very poorly on your diagnostic tests."

I did? My heart sinks. "I thought I did okay." I showed up for them on Saturday, for starters. They're my first full set of tests;

114

the ones I did a few years ago were all on the downlow with a psychologist who didn't even get my real name. It was an oral assessment and lots of puzzles that made me feel like I actually had a brain. And I knew more than I expected, thanks to movies and YouTube. I even confirmed a question I wasn't sure about with Sophie and got it right.

"Your reading age is not even on par with an eight-year-old's!"

The pit I just clawed my way out of . . . turns out it's nested inside another one.

I sit up and throw back the covers. "Well, what did you expect?" I snap.

"I didn't realize it was this bad!"

"Now you do." And if no one knew how bad I really am, then everything the dean said about getting me through this year . . . is he just wrong?

"Dean Ramchandran says you refused to attend your specialist meeting at first."

Nice, Dean. "So did you."

His tone sharpens. "I sent Mike."

"I sent Mike, too."

Ba swears. Thousands of miles away, he's powerless to make me get out of this bed. Maybe when I'm more awake, I'll regret pushing him this far. He'll make me pay at some point. But for now, I can savor scoring a rare point against him.

"I've hired a second tutor to work with you every night."

"I don't need another tutor all up in my business."

"He is the world's leading reading specialist. Also, this weekend, you cannot afford the time to come for the Moon Festival. I'll tell Bernard not to pick you up. Besides, I'm dealing with company problems—it's not a good time for you to be here."

"Wasn't planning on going."

"Learn to read, Xiang-Ping! I know you have the brains to do it!"

"I don't get you," I say. "First you say I'm an idiot. Now you say I've got brains. You can't have it both ways, Ba."

"Chinese language is pictorial. It's *easier* for dyslexics, yet you still never learned your characters. You waste time. You lack *tenacity*."

He's ranted about time and tenacity before, but not about Chinese. I'm suddenly, sickeningly sure he's right. Other dyslexic kids seem to do fine with pictograms. Me—I'm missing screws. And with writing, too. I tried using dictation software last night to write the English essay, and I ended up staring at my empty screen for two hours. It's like I just don't have the muscles to do any of this. Writing one three-page essay will take me months. If I have to write two, might as well throw in the towel now.

"Dean Ramchandran will work with you," Ba says. "It's a good school, Xiang-Ping. You have had every advantage. I sent you to the States for the best education. It's a reflection on me that you have turned out so poorly."

"Sorry for making you feel shitty about yourself."

Bing. Sophie's sunny photo pops up with an incoming video call. Thank God.

"Gotta run, Pops. Awesome talking to you, as usual."

I switch before he can answer.

"Hey, Sophie."

"Hey, Xavier." She's backdropped by green mountains under a blue sky. It's a relief to see her. Like eating hawthorn candy after bad Chinese medicine. "Sorry I'm calling so early."

"No, I'm glad you called." I swing my legs off the bed and open my window blinds. I've been thinking about her since our last talk. Why exactly things didn't work out on Loveboat. She liked Xavier the persona, and I was okay with that. But then she started to push more. Maybe it was that tornado, but she got under my skin, and I guess I freaked out. She made a good point, though, about letting people in more. "What's up?"

"Don't laugh, okay? But can I ask you about something?"

"Why would I laugh?"

"I'm stalking a fashion company that's building a digital stylist bot. They're following you on Instagram. Do you know them? Magic Silk?"

"Don't think so. Let me look." I open my Instagram app. My number of followers has jumped to double digits. How did that happen? I've posted the squirrels and a shot of a woman selling churros, mostly for Sophie. I didn't bother trying to e-read the privacy settings, and now I wish I had.

"What's their icon?"

"A handheld mirror."

My followers and followings are both double digit now. So I can't tell which list is which, until I drill in. Sophie and my

117

cousin Gloria are in both. But most of the artists I followed aren't following me back. Which is fine. I wouldn't expect them to.

I back out of one list and check the other, until I come to the antique gold mirror: an oval circumscribing a slope-sided diamond, embedded with a smaller glass oval.

"My family owns them."

She sighs. "Of course they do."

"How can I help?"

"I, like, hate to ask for a favor," she says, "but would you be willing to introduce me?"

"To my family?" It doesn't compute for me—a demilitarized zone stands between my family and the rest of my world. One side doesn't speak to the other. "You've already met two dysfunctional Yehs. You want to meet more?"

"I want to build a personal stylist AI bot for my CS project," she explains. "I was hoping if I could interview the Magic Mirror app inventor, I could show my professor it's a real project. Maybe get tips on how to build mine."

"My aunt runs Magic Mirror," I say. "I, um, don't know her English name. I call her Aunty Three, and everyone else uses her Chinese name."

"Is it Rose? Rose Chan? She's quoted in the blog."

"Yes, that's right. My cousin Lulu's mom. My dad's third sister. She lives in Taipei. I used to go to their warehouse with my mom." Those memories are good ones. Warm cups of tea. Bright bolts of gold-threaded fabric in a cozy room while my mom and aunts gossiped about the family. I don't know Aunty

Three well myself, because I haven't visited in years.

"Maybe I could do a video call with her? I have so many questions! Like, how the Magic Mirror makes recommendations—how it actually figures out what goes best on a person."

"Got it." I wouldn't mind introducing Sophie to my aunt. It's so rare that I have anything to offer anyone, and I want to help her after all the help she's given me. "Let me think how this could work. Lulu sort of hates me and my aunt hates my ba. But then again, so do I."

Sophie groans.

"Sorry. My family's complicated." I grimace. "It might be a negative if I ask. Maybe you're better off calling them."

"I've tried. They have over a million followers."

"Way more than me." That's my family, too. Famous-y things. "The other problem is, I'm pretty sure my aunt won't talk about it on the phone. Not anything useful. It's Dragon Leaf policy. They meet in person. They've had internet and phones tapped by competitors before."

"Oh, no. Then I'm back to square one. I can't fly out to Taipei."

Bernard would fly her on the Yeh jet if I asked, but damn—I just agreed with Ba that I'm not going.

"Hold a second," I say.

I dictate a text to Ba:

I changed my mind. I need to come for the moon festival this weekend. I'll call Bernard and figure out the jet.

His reply chimes instantaneously.

Ba: Stay put and pass your tests.
Xavier: It's Ye-Ye's eighty-eighth birthday. It's the moon
festival.
Ba: We can appreciate the same moon from afar. You've
never cared to come. You complain to Bernard every year.

"Thanks for outing me, Bernard," I mutter. Although Bernard was probably trying to get me out of it.

Ba: Don't forget our deal. Graduate or you're not touching a cent of that trust fund.

This conversation is going nowhere.

"Hey, Sophie?"

"Hm?"

"I was supposed to fly to Taipei this weekend. For the Mid-Autumn Festival."

"Lucky you! Mooncakes are my obsession."

"Well, my dad just canceled my plane ride. I don't know if I can get it back. But if I can, you can come with me on the jet. We'd fly out Thursday."

"What? You'd do that? That's so generous!"

"Well, I have to get it back first."

"It's two days away! I'm on the other side of the country."

"I can ask our pilot to pick you up on the way over. He's

always flying family through Paris and New York. My aunts and cousins love any excuse to take their friends shopping." My family. How can we be related? "That part's easy. It's usually just me, a dozen seats, and Bernard. A total waste of fuel."

This is perfect on so many levels. And I'd get to see her again. My skin tingles with anticipation. I don't believe in second chances. I've never gotten back together with a girl after we broke up, and I've never managed to stay friends. I don't believe Sophie and I can have a second chance. But we *have* stayed friends, and that's something. And I want to see her again.

"But how will you get the plane?" she asks.

"My dad wants me to graduate. I need to tie being in Taipei to my grades somehow."

"Like my project." Her voice is doubtful.

I spin the dial of the combination lock on my bedside table. Ba's checkmated me at every step, but a plan is forming. A way to tackle the onslaught of assignments. A way to force Ba's hand like he's been forcing mine.

"Let me talk to my teachers this morning."

Her teeth flash with a grin. "You did not just say that."

I smile. But I do have a plan. "I've got a film assignment. I'll set it in Taipei."

"One project? Would your dad go for that?"

"He won't have a choice if it also counts as my history paper and my English paper on symbolism. The Moon Festival has symbols, and my family has plenty of history."

"Combine all three?"

"You gave me the idea."

I yank a shirt from my dresser. I've never made a film before, just little videos with my iPhone. But unlike editing a page of words, I can easily splice segments of video clips together. I can feel how the images should go together, what comes next, and next after that. It's more of an instinct than anything else.

Maybe that's why I'm confident I can pull this off, in a way I've never been confident before. I step into a pair of shorts. "I was supposed to come up with alternate assignments. This increases my chances of getting to the finish line."

She laughs. "Last Moon Festival, I prayed to the moon for a husband. This is definitely an improvement."

I laugh, too. Sophie Ha is never afraid to call herself out.

"If there's anything I can do to help you get your *freedom* . . ." Her voice catches. "I'll do it."

"I haven't done you the favor yet, but with the mighty brains of Sophie Ha behind my homework, I might have a shot at passing."

She snorts. "Nerd for hire. So *me*."

"Isn't it?"

"I don't know. It could be."

I've raised her hopes, and mine . . . and now I need to deliver for the both of us.

"Wish me luck," I say.

15

SOPHIE

"Emma!" The cherry-blossom print is askew on her door, which is ajar. I straighten it and rap on the wood, then push it open. "Hey, Emma! I reached the Magic Mirror—oh!"

Emma sits up on her bed, and a photo album slides off her cotton twill pants. She dashes a hand over her cheeks. They're damp. Her blue eyes are blotchy red. She's not at all her usual composed self.

Alarmed, I move toward her. "What's wrong?"

She hugs her pillow to her chest. One hand plays with her cherry-blossom bracelet. Then she lifts the album into her lap and opens it to a guy our age with a short black hedge of hair. He's standing behind a glass counter filled with jewelry. His smile is sweet. His plump hands are cupped, displaying the cherry-blossom bracelet on Emma's wrist.

"That's your bracelet," I say. "Did he give it to you? Who is he?"

"So remember I told you I swore off dating, too?"

"Yes." I squish in beside her. "I know why I did it, but I can't imagine why you would."

"I was dating him." She lays a slim finger on the boy. "Miles Chen. He wanted to be a writer." She flips to a photo of them sitting on a shoreline under an octagonal beach umbrella. Her yellow sundress flutters in a breeze. His T-shirt says NIETZSCHE IS DEAD. They're smiling into each other's eyes with a half inch between their noses.

"You look so happy," I say. "What happened?"

"He drowned. About a year and a half ago." She wraps her arms around her legs. Her soft hair falls over her face. "It was a boating accident. He would have been nineteen today. It's his birthday."

"Oh my God, Emma." How did she hide all this? "And here I come in yammering about my project."

"No, no, I want to hear about it. Stuff like that keeps me going. The planet keeps on spinning, right? My mom's been on my case about moving on, dating other guys. I don't know . . . I'm glad you stopped by. It's not a good day to be alone, but I . . . didn't have the energy to find a friend."

Who knew she had all this churning inside her? I put an arm around her and squeeze tight. "What was he like?"

A tear spills down her cheek, but she smiles. "Awkward in a charming way. He read dating books to up his game with me. I told him I liked him as himself, but he was constantly gleaning tips and using them on me."

I smile. "Super dorky. And the Nietzsche shirt?"

"Nietzsche said, 'God is dead.' Miles used to say God got the last laugh." Her smile fades. "Oh, Sophie. He was only seventeen."

"I'm so sorry."

She sneezes. "Ugh! I'm so allergic to New Hampshire." She wipes her eyes with a tissue. "He was always late, even for our dates. It used to upset me—like he didn't care as much as I did. Like he wasn't counting down the hours to be with me, you know?"

"Of course he was!" I study them backdropped by the Magic Kingdom castle at Disney. He's scooped her into his arms. Her mouth is opened in a surprised laugh. "You guys were adorable."

"We had something real." She runs her forefinger in a square around the photo. "I know it was real, and I'm glad for it."

Their radiant faces tug at a string deep in my chest. I don't think that kind of love is even in the cards for me. I may have escaped being the wicked stepsister this summer, but I am still only the stepsister. Unlike Ever or Emma, I'll never be the girl in the golden coach. But I shouldn't want that either. I've got my plan now.

Emma closes the album. "On the day he drowned, we were supposed to meet for dim sum. I assumed sailing had run late and he forgot to call as usual. I had a pile of complaints to drop on him."

125

"Oh, Emma."

"After something like that, nothing's ever that big a deal, you know?"

She must be an angel incarnate. Sent here to make me a better person by osmosis.

"Well, here I am going on and on."

"No, I'm glad you told me."

She smiles. "Me, too. But you came in so excited—what's up?"

A smile spreads over my face. "Xavier's family owns Magic Silk."

"No way!" She shakes her head. "Is there anything the Yehs *don't* own?"

I explain the connections. "He offered to fly me to Taipei this weekend. He still needs to figure out some things. But if he can pull it off, *I'm going to interview its creator. In person!*"

"That's amazing!"

"The timing is perfect—my deadline for Horvath is Sunday. If I can show him it's a real tech project by then, I'll have a really good shot at getting into the class. I'd get to figure out how to bring fashion and AI together. It would be so *fun*. And maybe he'd consider me for his lab and everyone can forget about my stupid makeup video."

"It's incredible Xavier's helping get you all this. Says a lot about him."

I'd been thinking that, too. In Xavier Land, is this a normal favor to do for a friend? Even a good friend? No . . . I can't let myself read something into this that's not there. I can't afford to.

"He'd do the same for anyone from Loveboat in my shoes." I really believe that. "He's generous. And it could help him, too . . . anyways, it's not a done deal."

"I hope it works out. Taipei during the Moon Festival is delish."

"Why don't you come?" I grasp her hand. "It's the perfect opportunity! You can reconnect with Xavier then!"

"Oh my God, really?" Her eyes widen and she squeezes me back. "Do you think he'll mind? Could you ask him?"

"Of course. He said the plane's a waste of fuel only carrying one or two people."

I pull up my phone and reply to Ever's post about her audition:

> Sophie: Hey, @Ever, @Emma @Xavier and I might be going to Taipei too!
> Sophie: for the moon festival and a project. Let's meet up!
> Ever: LOVEBOAT REUNION!

Emma's phone chimes at the same time as mine.

"Oops." I frown at the glow of my screen. "Didn't mean to post to the whole Loveboat community."

Replies are already coming in.

Marc: A reunion! I want to come

Lena: Wish I could! Classes Friday

Spencer: How are you getting there?

Sophie: Xavier's plane. If he can get it

Priscilla: Dibs on a ride

Bert: Me, too

Whoa. I don't even know some of these people.

Sophie: Hold on. I'll ask, but it's Xavier's family's plane

Bert: People can crash at my uncle's

Priscilla: My Loveboat roommates are in Taipei. They'd come

Priscilla: Let's have dinner in the Chien Tan cafeteria! For those of us who missed out on finding their special someone on Loveboat. #secondchanceromance

This is taking on a life of its own. I lower my phone and look at Emma. "If more people are coming, we could take a break Friday night. Why not?"

Sophie: Taipei 101 is better than campus . . . 88th floor!

Priscilla: Since you're so cool @Sophie, why don't you plan the reunion?

Ever: Ooo, @Sophie, you plan the best parties

"Wait, this isn't what I had in mind. I don't have time to plan a party in Taipei," I say to Emma. "I need to work on my proposal."

Priscilla: She's all talk.

Ouch. "Who's Priscilla?" I ask Emma.

"She was in my program," Emma says apologetically. "She's not that bad when you get to know her, but she trash talks and has no filter."

"Hm, okay."

"But a reunion!" Emma says. "Getting to see everyone again?"

Shopping together at Taipei 101, feasting our five senses on the night market—yes, please!

"It *would* be awesome." I'm already flinging my arms around Ever and Rick.

"This is exactly what I need right now." Emma tucks her feet under and picks up her phone. "I can get my family to sponsor a dinner."

"Are you serious?"

"Yes, if I tell them I want to throw a party for friends, they're cool with that. I don't do it that often, so they trust me."

"Wow, Emma. Nothing makes for a good party like free food. I can make reservations and plan the menu—I'm good at things like this. We'll put your family down as sponsor."

"They'll appreciate that."

I've gotten way ahead of myself, but I'm sure Xavier and I can pull this off.

I hop back onto the channel with the update.

Sophie: All right, folks. Loveboat reunion at the top of Taipei 101 Friday night, with dinner sponsored by the generous @Emma's family. I'll book the restaurant. Like this post if you're in.

Ever, Priscilla, Marc, and Bert like the post. Then another six people—three I don't know, plus Rick, Spencer, Debra. More than I was expecting. But I've got this. Sophie the eight-armed robot can pull off two projects in a weekend with her eyes closed.

"I'm so excited to see Xavier again!" Emma says. "I mean, now we're grown-up. Honestly, ever since I saw his picture in your room, I've been thinking about him. We were *so* close. How amazing that you're bringing us back together."

I feel a pang of wistfulness. She's from his world, the real deal. All summer, I only pretended to be. And maybe it's what she's been through that's made her as rock steady as she is— Emma would be so good for him.

And vice versa.

"You're pretty good friends with him, aren't you?" she asks.

Am I? Speaking to him, I've realized, calms and energizes me like nothing else. Even as he makes me, as I told him, crazy.

"I don't know. I think so."

"Is he dating anyone?"

"No, I'm pretty sure not. No one from Loveboat. And he just moved to LA."

"Do you think . . . you could feel him out for me?" She covers her face. "I have no idea how this works. To be honest, until this past year, I've always just *had* a boyfriend. I don't even know how you . . . signal? Ugh! I need your help."

My smile drops. *Oh my God, no.* It's one thing to reintroduce them, another to actively push them at each other.

But maybe this is what I need to fully untangle myself and move on. And her, too.

"Yes, I'll do what I can. I bet he'll fall for you in the first hour of just talking to you." I hug her, smoothing back her silky hair, and shove down the little claw of jealousy that cuts my heart. "So, how about we get that dim sum?"

She smiles. "Would love that."

16

XAVIER

"I'm not letting you waste my mom's time so you can impress some girl." Lulu slams her locker shut, scowling. She flings her black braid over her shoulder. "Forget it."

"She's not *some girl*." My voice sharpens. I'd expected resistance, but not flat-out refusal. And definitely not this dig at Sophie. "Sophie's a good friend. She has a real reason for wanting to meet your mom. She's a Dartmouth student."

Lulu, I heard from Mike, has her own heart set on Dartmouth. She could get pointers from Sophie. She could end up there with her. Lulu's scowl deepens, like she knows what I'm trying to do.

"I don't owe you favors," she says. "Especially after that lame Club Pub debacle."

She swings her red laptop bag onto her shoulder and strides down the hallway. I hurry after her. So Club Pub wasn't my finest hour, but how fucked up is this that I can't even get a meeting with my own aunt?

"Look, Lulu—"

"She can't talk on the phone about—"

"I know. Dragon Leaf policy."

Her brow rises, though her strides don't slow. The ghost of a smile flickers over her face. "When your family is too hard to explain, it's nice not to have to."

Okay. Making progress. "We'll fly to Taipei and we can meet your mom at headquarters."

"You know there's a ton of shit going on with Dragon Leaf right now, right?"

"Not really," I admit.

"You *do* have your head in the sand."

"Better than being 'a disgrace to nine generations.' Which is what Ba called me when the shit hit the fan at my old high school."

Lulu slows before her classroom. "I've got to go."

"Wait." I grab her arm. Maybe everything *would* be easier if I told her about my dyslexia. At least we could dispel this lazy-ass reputation. But the track record on stuff like that with my family has never been good, and my track record with Lulu isn't exactly a winning streak either. "What do you want from me? I swear to stay under the radar from now on and not embarrass you."

She tugs free. "That's the least you can do. And I'm not even sure you can pull that off."

I let out an exasperated breath. "Lulu, Sophie's brilliant. She's got a great sense of fashion and she's in touch with what younger people are wearing—she's a good talent for your mom to meet." That's not a stretch. And my family often says they're in the business of collecting talent more than anything else.

She frowns. "You're doing a lot for this girl."

Maybe I am. I'm not usually the guy people can count on. But I want to be different this time.

"This isn't just for her," I say. "I'm going for my assignments. It's part of my grades. Or at least, it will be."

"I don't even want to know what you mean." She pushes open her classroom door. "All right. I'll let you know what my mom says."

Yes! I smile. Halfway there.

Ms. Popov is the easiest to convince. Almost before I'm done explaining my Moon Festival film idea, she's out of her seat rummaging in her cabinet. She hands me a black video camera the size and heft of a puppy. "This used to be mine, but I donated it to the school—haven't found a student interested in using it before."

I slide my hand under its woven strap. My thumb fits snugly on a worn groove. Somehow, the world through its viewing screen is magnified. Brighter. It feels like an extension of my vision.

"Can I really borrow this?"

"Yes, the quality is wonderful. I haven't found a camera I like quite as much. If I were a musician, this would be my journeyman's guitar. So for the assignment, please be sure to include extended use of symbolism, as well as our grading rubric and . . ."

If I were Sophie, I'd hug Ms. Popov right about now.

One down, two more to go.

Ms. Castilla, my English teacher, is harder. She pokes a pencil into her frizzy beehive hair as I explain my idea.

"How do you see yourself incorporating our assignments?"

"We're studying foreign literature, right?"

"Shakespeare?" She blinks. "It's English language, but well, yes, it's not American."

"The Moon Festival is a big family holiday in Taipei. I can tell the story around it."

"Like a documentary?"

Makes it sound so formal. "Yeah."

"Are there myths around it? Traditions?"

"Some." Like Chang E flying to the moon, which everyone knows. "I'm not that familiar with most of them." Her face falls a bit and I add quickly, "I mean, I know what my family does. They sponsor a mooncake pavilion as part of an international festival. They give away a thousand mooncakes, and there's music and food trucks."

She's not biting. I rush on.

"Shakespeare wrote *Hamlet* in part because of the death of his son. He was inspired by Norse legends." Sophie told me that. Thanks to her, I sound like I know what I'm talking about. "So I'll make a film inspired by my family's story in Taipei."

"Yes, I like that. A story only *you* can tell. And cover two of the literary devices we're discussing in class—perhaps irony or metaphor?"

Shit, did I just promise to make my own *Hamlet*?

But she's on board, too. Maybe Sophie can lend me a fold of her brain to figure out what we actually film.

"Sure, Ms. Castilla," I say. "No problem."

I save Mr. Abadi, my history teacher, for last. Of all my teachers, he's been the least flexible. In his classroom, I find him with a metal coffee mug in hand, watching . . . a black-and-white documentary on the Rockefellers.

A powerful, dynastic family made up of captains of industry, full of wealth and privilege. I can feel the grin curl across my face. Maybe my ancestors are smiling down, not that I believe in that sort of thing.

Mr. Abadi hits pause and sets his mug between us as I tell him my idea.

"For the essay on key figures, I want to do a documentary

of my family instead." Funny how the more I talk about it, the more into it I get. How fun will it be to capture the energy of the street vendors, with sizzling octopus and smoke rising from griddles?

"It's a long trip for a school project. It's also not aligned with what we're doing," Mr. Abadi says. "We're focused on key figures in *history*. Not family."

This is why I came to him last. I've had to strategize my whole life to get through school, and now I play my trump card. The one I never use.

"My family has a long history in Taiwan. They've had books written about them." The words are like laundry lint in my mouth. I don't ever claim my family, and I *definitely* don't talk up their accomplishments. "In Taiwan, they're probably as important as, well, the Rockefellers."

He moves his coffee mug aside, opening space between us. "Tell me more."

"They've lived on the island for over three hundred years. My great-grandfather founded one of the oldest tech companies in Taiwan. My dad runs it now. Every year, they give away a thousand mooncakes to the community. I could do the whole documentary just on that."

"Living history. I see where you're taking this." He opens his drawer and hands me a museum postcard of the Rockefellers. "If you center your documentary around your grandfather, and you interview him and a few others instrumental to the business, I can approve it."

I look up from the postcard. "My grandpa?"

"And your father."

The joke's on me. I was trying to have it both ways—use my family to get the assignment I want, but not have to deal with them.

"I was planning to focus on the Moon Festival."

"The assignment is about key figures. How they leave a legacy. How individuals impact history."

No way can I survive a ten-minute interview with Ba. I imagine holding a microphone out to him.

How does it feel to be the patriarch of one of Asia's biggest empires?

Xiang-Ping, one day I will die and leave my empire to crumble in the hands of lesser mortals like you. How does that feel? Terrible.

Ba's the poison pill in this grand plan.

"I'm sorry." I rise to my feet. "I don't think that will work with my English assignment. Ms. Castilla wants a *Hamlet* story. Literary devices. Mooncakes—those are symbols."

"*Hamlet*, as I recall, is a story about fathers and sons itself. I'll talk to her."

It's a win, but with a bitter aftertaste. One assignment for three classes, a trip back to Taipei, a way to help Sophie . . . but now I need to kiss Ba's ass. Sophie better appreciate this. And by appreciate, I mean do half this project with me.

My cell buzzes with a text from Lulu. She adds a large yellow thumbs-up at the end. So Aunty Three's on board. Wow. It's all fallen into place.

I tuck the Rockefeller postcard into my pocket. So we're doing this! I just need to make sure Ba doesn't fuck this up for Sophie and me.

"I understand, Mr. Abadi. You won't be disappointed."

Xiao-Mei,

I'm coming to Taipei this weekend. I need to interview my dad for a school project that counts for three grades in three classes. He can call my dean if he has questions.

Can you get me on his schedule Friday around lunchtime? I'll be at the apartment for my grandpa's party.

Ten minutes is more than enough.

X

Getting on Ba's calendar. How far I've fallen.

SOPHIE

Dear Professor Horvath,

Thanks for your feedback on my proposal. I'm doing more research this weekend on the AI fashion bot and will have the proposal to you by the Sunday deadline.

Thanks for giving me another chance!

Sincerely,
Sophie

Sophie: HEY, LOVEBOATERS!!! Here's the sched (local times):

Party on the plane Thursday (six seats open, first come first served thank you @Xavier!)

Departing 5 a.m. New Hampshire (@Sophie @Rick @Emma)

Pick up in Cleveland 7 a.m. Thursday (@Ever)

Pick up in LAX 8:30 a.m. Thursday (@Xavier @Marc)

Taipei 101 88th floor 7 p.m. Friday night (thank you @Emma for sponsoring!)

International Festival 6 p.m. Saturday night (think . . . mooncakes!)

Jet home Sunday 11 p.m.

Rick: PART-AY IN TAIPEI

Bert: The entire Ocean campus is in!

Sophie: Seriously? How many?

Laura: Wish I could come!

Lena: Will you livestream the good stuff?

Sophie: Everything! 24-7!

Sophie: Like this post if you have a Taiwan or international license

Kelly: Hi, just joining this forum. A bunch of us from the third floor are just finding out about this. Why weren't we told there was a reunion? Why weren't we invited?

Sophie: OMG! Everyone's invited. Let me know and I'll up the RSVP.

Bert: That's twenty-three from Ocean

Sophie: WHAT?

Kelly: I wish we'd been told sooner so we didn't have to scramble

Priscilla: This seems a little disorganized

Sophie: Um, I'm not in charge! Just booking the restaurant

Joella: Is @Xavier coming? Can someone get him to go?

Debra: x2 see you all in Taipei!

18

XAVIER

It's not until I'm packing clothes into my backpack that the irony hits me. I'm busting my ass so I can get over the ocean to meet my family. For Ye-Ye's eighty-eighth birthday and the family circus.

I'm taking a ride on their fancy jet, like a freaking hypocrite.

But what this trip actually is is my farewell. Farewell to the fucked-up Yehs with their fucked-up problems.

Once I ace this project, I'm on my way to getting my trust back, and then Ba won't be able to touch me again. No more bodyguards forcing me to go anywhere or keeping a leash on me. No more hoops and cut credit cards. I'll set up my life where I want and how I want. I'll never have to go back to see them again.

The trip to end all trips.

Okay, deep breath. Wheels up.

19

SOPHIE
LEBANON MUNICIPAL AIRPORT, NEW HAMPSHIRE

Seven hours until I see Xavier. And I'm about to take my first private jet ride. And meet the Magic Mirror creator. The reunion's getting a bit out of control, but as long as I come up with some entertainment, I'm pretty sure the party can run itself.

There's so much to look forward to that I could erupt like a volcano, so I settle for taking a million photos for my brothers, all the way down the private runway. The small white jet is adorable: not much bigger than a school bus, sleek and gleaming under the harvest moon, as though bathed in warm buttermilk. It's exactly what I'd have expected for the Yeh family's travel needs: elegant, even artistic . . . and seductive.

"Hey, Ugly!" My big cousin in a blue Yale bulldog shirt is

144

jogging toward me from the airport. His shirt's half tucked into jeans. He's gotten a haircut: jet-black hair cropped close to his head. The sight of him is a big friendly squeeze.

"Rick!" I wave.

I drop my backpack as he reaches me, opening my arms for a hug. But he hauls me up and over his shoulder and spins, holding on to the back of my thighs with one arm while I pound his back, laughing.

"Put me down, bully!"

He sets me on my feet at last, and I swipe a lock of hair from my mouth and straighten my dress. "You're nuts!" He's always been playful, but dating Ever has put a new light into him. I'm glad.

Rick drapes a meaty arm around my neck, tucking me close as we head over the asphalt. "*Please* be careful this weekend," he says. "I don't want to have to scrape you off the ground and stuff you into your bag to ship home."

My cousin knows me too well, not to mention his front-row seat to my disastrous summer with Xavier.

I keep upbeat. "Where would my shoes fit, then?"

"Har."

But after feeling so steady with Emma, truth is, now that I'm here, I'm terrified. I'm hurtling on a nonstop trajectory toward Xavier. I want to help him nail his film project and escape his dad.

But I'm also afraid of how traitorous my own heart is. Not to mention the possible emergence of my tornado.

"Speaking of suitcase, where's your entourage?" Rick pretends to search behind us.

I jiggle the zipper on my backpack. If I keep playing upbeat Sophie, eventually she'll have to take over for real. "I'm proud to say I've fit this entire trip into two outfits, pajamas, and one pair of dance shoes." Unlike for my Loveboat trip, when I brought the biggest suitcase on the East Coast, and it still wasn't big enough. "Trust me, Rick. I'm the new Sophie Ha."

"I'll believe it when I see it."

I hip-bump him. "I'm spending this entire plane ride on my CS project. I want to finish the new proposal draft before we land in Taipei. Plus questions for Xavier's aunt."

"Cool. I can take a look if you like."

"Be careful what you offer. I'll have you working the whole time, too. How's it been apart from Ever?"

"Torture. I'm dying to see her. I didn't know it would be like this. I've never needed to be with someone so badly before. I was always so self-contained, you know?"

"And now . . . soliloquy!"

"Shut up." He grabs for my nose and I duck away, laughing. But then his smile fades. "She needs to get into Tisch again, near me, or I won't be able to survive the next four years."

"She will," I say. "No one deserves it more than she does."

"Amen," he says fervently.

We've reached the jet. LYNN is monogrammed on the side in gold script. A person? I snap a picture as a man in a purple cap steps out from under the metal stairs. His deeply lined face is shaped like a lucky square, and his brown eyes are bright.

"Bernard?" I ask.

"Yes, Ha Xiao Jie." He tips his cap. "Glad to meet Master Xavier's friend."

Master Xavier. Rick grimaces, but Xavier is so unpretentious that hearing the formal title is more funny than anything else.

"This is my cousin Rick. My friend Emma is on her way."

"Nice wings." Rick, at least, is polite. "How fast is the ride to Taipei?"

"From Los Angeles, eight hours."

Rick whistles. "Almost half normal flight time."

So not just any private jet, but an insanely advanced one.

"Who's Lynn?" I ask.

"Mr. Yeh's late wife," Bernard answers. "Xavier's mother."

"Oh! That's . . . sweet." Not what I'd have expected from that man at all.

We follow Bernard up a flight of steps into a cabin the size of a bedroom, with creamy leather seats in four rows, two per side. The seats have room enough to swivel to face each other over a square folding table. Woolly purple blankets sit in a stack in seat 2A. I move down the aisle toward two doors at back. The side one leads to a bathroom with a cobalt-blue marble sink and tiled shower.

"It's nicer than our bathroom back home." My reflection— black hair splashed over my purple sleeveless top—shrinks a bit. On Loveboat, we all slept in the same bunks and rode in the same cabs. Now here's a behind-the-scenes look at the life of Xavier Yeh, and he's exactly what he told his teacher . . . a Rockefeller.

Stop it. He's the same guy you've been talking to since Loveboat.

The second door separates the main cabin from a round chamber. Inside, a blast of air-conditioning hits my face. Two oblong windows hug two leather seats, reclined flat to form a king-sized bed. Fat feather pillows and a folded purple duvet wait at its feet.

"A private bedroom. Nice." I snap a photo and upload it to the Loveboat group chat.

"Wonder how many Yeh progeny have been conceived here." Rick pops a mint into his mouth.

"Stop." I put my hands over my ears. "We're two hours from Ever Wong. I don't want to know where your mind is." Rick grins.

"Would you like a snack as we take off?" Bernard asks from the minibar up front.

Rick and I join him and paw through American and Chinese treats. Prunes, which my brothers loathe but I love. Sunchips, another favorite. A box of fresh dragons' beard candy, still soft. Pineapple cakes. All my favorites, foods I'd eaten during Loveboat.

"Soy milk, shao bing, pork, and taro dishes in the oven warmer here," Bernard says.

I pick up a gold-foil-wrapped box of mooncakes and tug off its purple ribbon.

"I've had these ones! I used to wait in line an *hour* to get them."

"Master Yeh asked me to stock those for you especially," Bernard says.

"For me?"

I'm sure it's no big deal. Something Xavier mentioned to Bernard in passing. But his thoughtfulness is a dart in my chest. I open the box and shed the inner wrapper. The golden crust is the perfect crunch under the knife, and the inside has twin moons: the salted yolk and a smaller lotus seed—

I pop a sweet, savory bite into my mouth and die. "Oh my God! Just like I remember."

"The family makes them specially for the Moon Festival," Bernard says. "It's an old tradition."

Wait. My favorite mooncakes in the world—*these* are the ones Xavier's family makes?

A flutter of panic ripples through me. How can I spend two solid days side by side with Xavier, working on his project, working on mine, surrounded by a Loveboat reunion full of romantic hopefuls?

"Sophie? You here?" Emma steps inside, elegant in a sleeveless cotton dress perfect for travel. She waves, at ease. As if she's ridden in private jets her whole life. She lifts the back of one hand to her nose and sneezes, a dainty sneeze that doesn't ruin the effect at all.

"Allergies," she groans.

Emma. Emma is how I will do this trip. Emma is how I will keep my focus where it should be—on the work.

I hug her pear-scented person. "This is my cousin Rick." I introduce them.

"We're stopping in Cleveland first, aren't we?" she asks.

"Yes, picking up Ever. Then on to LA for Xavier and some other people, then Taipei!"

"So . . . I actually need to get off in LA," Emma apologizes. "When I told my mom I was going through there, she asked me to visit her old friend in hospice."

"Oh! That's so kind of you, but does that mean you're not coming?"

"I'm coming! I'll meet you at Taipei 101 for the reunion. And of course I'll say hi to Xavier at the airport in LA."

She takes my arm and tugs me out of Rick's earshot. Her eyes sparkle. "I've been texting with Xavier a bit. He's so fun! Everything you've said about him—I know it'll be like no time at all has passed. Thanks again for helping to set us up." She gives a nervous laugh.

"There's no more romantic place than Taipei 101 under the moon," I tease. "I've got plans for you two there." The path forward for them is clear in my mind. By the end of the reunion, they'll be inseparable.

And the sooner I see them together, the sooner my own heart will be free.

In Cleveland, Rick bolts out the door the moment Bernard unlatches it.

"Ever!" His roar practically ruptures my eardrums. Metal steps outside clank under his sneakers as I power down my laptop and hurry after him. My proposal isn't as far along as I'd hoped. I've put together a questionnaire to collect data from users, but I'm only about a quarter of the way through. I'll just have to keep at it the next few legs.

Across the jetway, Ever emerges from a doorway in the airport. Her long dove-gray blouse over tights shows off her slender dancer's body. Her hair is in a ponytail. Rick bolts across the asphalt toward her and she rushes him and they meet in a bone-breaking hug.

"Wow. *They* missed each other." Emma joins me at the base of the stairs.

"He's never been like this before." I'm happy for them. But as Rick gathers her face between his hands and kisses her, I can't help feel a twinge of envy. It's ironic. I was the one hell-bent on finding a guy on Loveboat. Neither of them was even looking for a relationship. But now they have each other. And I . . .

I have something better: a clear vision for my future.

"Hey, Sophie!" Ever is now rushing *me*, waving.

"Better brace for impact," Emma jokes.

"So good to see you in the flesh!" Ever squeezes me so hard I gasp—I'd forgotten how strong she is.

"I've missed you, too!" It does something good for my heart to be with her again. Like I can believe the tornado has no chance of spinning itself up when she's here. Because Ever has seen the best and worst of me, and she's still my friend.

Rick takes her hand, all his attention on her. I poke him in the ribs. "If Rick could have gotten out and pushed the plane along faster, he would have."

A scrawny guy in a too-tight plaid shirt and a leggy girl with glittery green eyeshadow are approaching. Bert Lanier and Priscilla Chi, the first to sign up for the free jet ride. Bert made his way to Priscilla yesterday so they could travel together. His dark-rimmed glasses are cool. Priscilla's hair gleams with brown highlights and shiny butterflies flutter over her black vintage baby-doll dress. She's a freshman at the University of Pennsylvania.

To be honest, she's been kind of a thorn in my side on the Loveboat chat group. Always with the negative comments. But now that we're meeting in person, I'm sure it will smooth out.

"Hey, Priscilla." Emma embraces the newcomers. "Hey, Bertie. How's RISD?"

"Aced my first assignment." He pulls out his phone and shows us a full-colored, exquisitely animated video . . . of a penis stiffening.

Everyone groans and I cover my eyes with my hand. "You're destroying my innocence!"

Emma laughs, but Bert smirks. "That's not what I heard."

Ouch. I open my mouth to suggest that *Bertie* shut his mouth when Bernard lays a hand on Bert's shoulder. "My friends, we need to take our place on the runway."

The penis gets put away. Thank God.

"Can I see the cockpit?" Bert asks, and he, Priscilla, Emma, and Rick climb the steps and disappear inside the plane. Spencer Hsu, yet another friend from Loveboat, arrives for more hugs, then he, too, vanishes into the cockpit.

Ever and I follow.

"How are your parents feeling about your dance school applications?" I ask. They'd resisted it for years, but over the summer, Ever found the courage to insist on doing what she really wanted to do.

"They've been incredible. Mom's researching dance schools for me. Dad videoed a few of my classes in case I need samples. He's happy with his new work gig." She lifts her periwinkle bag into the overhead compartment, and I motion her into my seat beside Rick's, taking back my laptop. "But now the onus is on me to make it work, you know? I mean, I had a full ride to med school. Dance school, believe it or not, is just as expensive, and it won't pay as well when I graduate."

"You'll make it work." I sink into the leather seat facing hers. It vibrates under me as the plane rumbles to life.

Rick drops down beside Ever and kisses her ear. "So what's the plan in Taipei, Soph?"

"We split up for the day. I assume you're going with Ever to her audition? As her bodyguard? Bag carrier? Devoted worshipper?"

"All of the above." He grins, and Ever rolls her eyes.

"I need to interview the Magic Mirror app creators, and Xavier's interviewing his grandpa and dad." I open my laptop to my CS proposal. "After that, Loveboat dinner at Taipei 101. Saturday, roam town—I'm trying to get us tickets for the zoo's baby panda exhibit."

"Even *I* want to see baby pandas," Rick says.

"That's because you're a baby panda yourself. Tickets are sold out, so we're on the waitlist . . . hm, story of my life!"

Ever laughs. "If anyone can get us tickets, it's you."

"This is harder than backstage passes to a Taylor Swift concert. No promises. Last on the schedule is the Yeh's mooncake pavilion at the festival Saturday night. I might be able to get the panda tickets for Sunday before we fly out."

"It's tight," Rick says. "I need to leave Sunday night, latest. I've got a test Monday."

"So do I," I say.

"Bottoms up, lady." Bert shoves a chilled glass of golden wine into my hand. We've hit cruising altitude.

"I need to work." I try to hand it back. "I'm only a quarter through."

"How often do we get a reunion in the sky? This is a thousand-dollar bottle of wine."

"A thousand *what*? I don't want to get Xavier in trouble."

"Pilot said to help ourselves. Look around, Sophie. That's real gold on those lamps. They won't care."

I glance at Rick for guidance, but he just shrugs. What the hell. It's not like I'll ever have the opportunity to be on a plane like this again. I take an incredible swallow and shutter my eyes briefly.

"That is . . . orgasmic," I breathe.

Bert whoops, "That's what I'm talking about!" He cranks up the music. Everyone starts to rise: Ever grabs Rick's hand and tugs him into the aisle. Emma cuts mooncakes at the bar and chats with Bert.

"Come on, Sophie!" Ever says. "Dance with us!"

My fingers cling longingly to my keyboard. But Ever is here. And Rick. We're together again. I can work after people go to sleep. I shut down my laptop and join them with my wineglass, shimmying all the way to the song's end.

"Oh, God, I've needed this break!" As an eighties song begins, I tilt back my head and sway, letting my hair swing free. In the last row of the cabin, Spencer and Priscilla are head to head, deep in conversation.

I elbow Rick in the ribs. "My reunion's working already!"

"And Spencer said he wasn't looking for someone."

"Maybe that's how the universe works," I say. "You get what you want when you're not after it."

"Like us!" Rick twirls Ever under his arm. Sweet, but do I want to vomit? You bet.

"So if I were to deliberately *not* look for love, it would happen. Except now that I've thought that, it won't."

"Like Schrödinger's Valentine," Rick says.

"I don't even know what that is," I say. "But yeah, probably."

An awesome Taiwanese boy band comes on next. I dip my shoulders, rock my hips, dance a loop—and find myself up close with a framed photo of Xavier's family on the wall.

His grandparents in red clothing are the central figures on a loveseat. But my eyes go immediately to ten-year-old Xavier, nestled between his mom and dad, all surrounded by aunts and uncles and cousins. Xavier's dad has a hand on Xavier's mom's shoulder, who clasps Xavier's hand in hers.

His smile is crooked. By this point, he would have been struggling to learn to read. Even so, there's no mistaking the affection in his mom's eyes. He's a little old to be holding hands with her by American standards, but not so much in Taiwan. Did she hang the photo here? Did his dad ever consider taking it down after she passed away? Because it's still here, every time someone takes this plane and walks toward the minibar ... and I've been lost in it for several minutes.

I turn my back to it, facing the cabin of my friends.

This is fine. I'll be fine.

Once I see him in the flesh, smell his cologne, I'll remember everything I *dislike* about him. His habit of clamming up in group settings. How he'd kissed Ever a day after I broke up with him, as though our relationship had meant nothing. How he'd obsessively drawn Ever's picture the whole time I was throwing myself at him—*there*.

That is the memory I needed. Heart frozen.

What would his kisses have felt like if he'd actually wanted *me*?

NO MORE! I can't—

"You okay, Sophie?" Ever's hand on my arm makes me jump two feet into the air. I wrench myself back to the present.

"Yeah. It's just, I haven't seen Xav . . . everyone. In a while."

"You seem tense."

"Lots going on. And we only have two days."

She cocks her head at me, then grasps her elbows. "Do you remember when I was planning the talent show dance with Rick? Debra was worried we'd break up and ruin it?"

So she caught what I didn't say. "Rick already warned me— too much is riding on this weekend. *I* need to blow my CS professor away. Xavier's entire trust fund is at stake. He has to get free of his dad. You should have seen—" I stop there. *What his dad did to him at the airport.*

"Xavier and me . . . that part's fine. I'm setting him up with Emma." Over by the bar, Emma dips with a laugh, along with Spencer and Priscilla, a princess holding court. They're completely charmed. "I've got a whole plan for them at Taipei 101. It's the perfect venue to match them. I've thought it all through."

"Emma? She seems great . . . but for *Xavier*?"

"Like you're one to judge," I snap, then clamp my mouth shut. I hadn't meant to bring up their history. "Sorry. You're right. I'm too wound up."

Her face reddens, but she lifts her chin. "I screwed up with Xavier. I know I did. That's why we're not close now. I didn't even know he was back in school. I thought he was doing an art gig this whole time." She leans past me and sets her fingertips on his family photo, then lowers her hand. "Not like you and him."

"Oh, um, we're not *that* close." Or are we? How do I even measure something like that? I wish I could talk it out with her and unravel all the knots of confusion inside me. This whole trip he's making possible for me. How I can feel so good talking to him and yet know we can't be?

But I can't. Not about Xavier. Not with Ever.

"I just can't help wondering if part of the reason you're working so hard to set up Xavier and Emma is to manage your own feelings."

She's striking too close to home. I set my glass down. "Look, I can't talk about this anymore." *Or I'll drive myself batty.* "I promised the Loveboat gang I'd livestream everything. I think this is the official start."

"Okay, Sophie." Ever gently rubs my back as I begin typing on my phone. Then she rejoins Rick.

Sophie: Hi, gang! Going live on my Instagram, so follow us there!

I aim the phone camera at my face and tap the live button. People start to join immediately. I wave. The group has tripled to over three hundred, and their energy radiates into this cabin. It's awesome.

"I'll stream everything from here on out," I say. "All the good, the bad, the ugly, like you were here with us. So fasten your seat belts!"

"The plane has a camera." Bert points to the round eye set into the wall over the closed cockpit door. "I'll connect it so they can see all of us." He crowds against me, pushing his sharp face into my screen's view. "Watch and weep, suckers!"

Bert hands me a long black cable for my phone, and in a few minutes, the alumni following on Instagram Live are treated to a bird's-eye view of the cabin, all the way to the door of the private chamber. Fifty-seven people are following along. Comments start rolling in.

> Wish we were there!
> Represent!
> We love you guys!
> Can we get matched up? Even if we're not there?
> Yeah @Sophie, count me in!
> Me too! I missed out last summer.

"Hold on." I'm pairing up Emma and Xavier, but the rest of them? "Who said anything about getting matched up?"

"It's Loveboat!"

Which sounds exactly like something the old me would have said.

"I'm busy with my school project," I say to the camera. "You all figure out your own matchmaking."

"Come on, it'll be fun!" Bert says. "Especially with so many of us here in person."

Any time a good idea gets planted in my head, it sprouts fast. Easy enough for me to group people into tables and virtual rooms. But also easy to get it wrong.

"Let me think." I climb onto a stool and adjust the camera to pan the cabin from side to side. Everyone waves and toasts glasses and beer cans. No wallflowers here. And all the people following along—the sheer energy is *intoxicating*. I can do this if I keep it simple.

"All right." I point the camera at my face, which fills the screen. "I'll pair up folks coming to Taipei 101. Any of you back home who wants to get matched for tomorrow night, DM me by morning and I'll put everyone into virtual groups."

I'm in!
Let's do it!

Bert snaps the tops of two beer cans, then punctures a hole in the bottom of one. Cold beer sprays my body through my dress as he holds it out to me.

"Hey! I'm wet!"

"Chug it, fearless leader. I'll race you."

He punctures the bottom of the second can, fits his mouth to the hole, and throws back his head. His Adam's apple undulates.

A chat rises in the cabin. "Chug. Chug. Chug. Chug!"

"I don't even like beer!"

"Chug. Chug. Chug!"

Bert's still drinking, and my damp dress clings like a lover to my body. I'm about to see Xavier in the flesh and set him up with Emma. I'm somehow "in charge" of an unofficial international reunion. And while all this is going on I need to bust my butt, trying to land myself the most coveted spot at Dartmouth.

So screw it.

I raise the bitter geyser to my lips and throw back my head as the chants break into cheers.

20

XAVIER
SANTA MONICA AIRPORT

"This is a new Xavier." Bernard's smile is teasing as I near the *Lynn.* "Normally, you don't pay attention to things like stocking the cabin for guests."

Bernard is possibly my favorite person in the whole Yeh household. The only one who calls me Xavier instead of Xiang-Ping, but speaking Mandarin, helping me bridge my two worlds. He takes my backpack, and out of habit, I let him.

"Last time I rode this plane, I was a prisoner." My hand closes around the lock in my pocket.

"Not a prisoner."

"What do you call two bodyguards forcing you to go somewhere?"

He sighs. "Your father is far too hard on you. I'm worried about him," he confesses. "Last few flights, he's had some difficult conversations with his investors. There are problems with employees. Perhaps you should help him."

"Help him? He thinks I'm *báichī*." An idiot. "I don't know anything about my dad's stuff."

"You're older now. Kids your age are already apprenticed to their families."

Tell me about it, Bernard. Oh wait, Ba already has, eight million times.

"Yeah, well. It's . . . not me, okay?"

Bernard squeezes my shoulder and I head up the stairs.

As I step into the cabin, a chorus of voices blasts me.

"Xavier, my man!"

"Awesome jet!"

"Thanks for the lift!"

What? The plane is jammed with so many people that at first I can't pick out faces. The seats in the front row are swiveled around to face the second row, tables laid with ivory mah-jongg tiles and go boards with stones. Sophie did ask about offering the extra seats to Loveboat alum, but . . .

"Best toothbrushes ever!"

"Ohmigod, the *wine*!"

So, a rager then.

Ooo-kay.

"Say hi to all our friends getting left behind!" A scrawny guy

163

points to the video screen, where a grid of squares each contains a moving person. Tiny hands wave like in the storefront of an antique clock shop.

The faces in the cabin begin to sort themselves: Spencer with a girl I don't know, Marc with a guy in the window seat Ma always took, to keep an eye on the ground. Weird to see all these strangers—and friends—in my family's cabin and yelling in English.

I force myself to raise my hand. "Hey."

"These socks are awesome." Spencer wiggles his toes in the woolly purple socks given to guests as a souvenir. "Like walking on clouds."

"Glad you like them," I say as Bernard presses a new pair into my hand. The golden Yeh crest is embroidered on the tops of each foot, and they *are* the best socks I've ever worn. I'd normally hate the crest on principle, but someone in the empire did right by it. Thick brushstrokes form the Yeh character that means leaf. The lean dragon loops around it. Although I don't get how fragile leaves and tough dragons go together.

A glass descends before my eyes, in the hand of the scrawny guy.

"Your *dad* . . ." He bumps into me. "Has the best fucking taste in wine."

"Let him breathe, seriously." Sophie bounds toward me from the back hallway. Sleek black locks curve down the side of her face and tumble over the shoulder of her plum top. Her eyes are bright with that inner fire I've forgotten, that wants to blaze out of her. "Xavier! You're here!"

My voice doesn't quite sound like my own. "Hey, Sophie."

A memory nags at me. As though I've seen her more recently than at the Taipei airport. Not just on video chat . . . but . . . at the tip of my pastels.

She stumbles and trips partway to me. Whoa. I dart forward and catch her, and she throws her bare arms around my neck. Her skin heats mine. Her familiar scent breaks over me: citrus and floral, overlaid with . . . beer breath.

Video chatting did nothing to capture the real Sophie Ha.

She tips back her head and flutters her eyelashes up at me. "My brothers would *flip out* if they could see this plane," she slurs.

I try to right her. "Sophie, maybe we—"

She grabs hold of a blue-eyed girl. "Xavier! Meet Emma! Again!"

Emma Shin smiles at me ruefully. "Hey, Xavier. You probably barely remember me."

I smile. "Of course I remember." She hasn't changed much—still the same round cheeks and pointy jawline of the girl I used to run wild with.

"You two were a thing from the cradle!" Sophie crows.

"We must have thought betrothed meant partners in crime," Emma says.

Memories flash. Good ones. "You climbed onto the counter in the kitchen to get the sugar cones—"

"While you sat on the floor and ate them."

"It worked out for me." I smile sheepishly. "I don't think the cook ever recovered from walking in on us. You dangling from the top cabinet."

"I was so busted!" Her eyes sparkle. It feels like another lifetime, scrambling to catch up to the present.

"See, you're already talking more than you ever do!" Sophie nudges me so hard I stumble back against Bernard. "Emma has to leave now—family something in LA. But she'll be at Taipei 101 for beef noodle soup, and you guys will fall in *luv* all over again." Emma laughs as Sophie yanks me down the aisle. "Meet more new friends!"

"Bye, Sophie! Bye, Xavier!" Emma calls. "We'll catch up in Taipei!"

I wave as she slips out the door. Then I turn back to Sophie. I want to talk to her about this trip. How I want it to be different from last summer in Taipei, because *we're* different. Although I don't know yet what that means.

"Um, Sophie, can we—"

Sophie halts before two girls eating shao bing and drinking dou jiang. One with a shorn haircut and black blouse sets her foot on her seat. The other, in a bright red vest, twirls her finger through her ponytail. They remind me of the king and queen in a deck of cards.

"This is Jasmine and Joella. They're sisters, and their family's like yours but in Hong Kong. They were at Ocean this summer—we all just met!"

"Hey, Xavier!" they chorus.

"Hey," I say.

"Emma is meeting us in Taipei." Sophie rests her chin on my shoulder, her arm curling around my back. Her body warms my side, and her face is inches from mine as she gazes up at me through gently curled lashes. She pats my chest. I pull my head in to focus on what she's actually saying. "Don't forget Emma, okay? She's your princess. But you can sit with Joella and Jasmine the first few hours. We need to share the wealth."

"Um, what?"

"I'm setting you and Emma up!"

The next thing I know, Sophie's detached herself, grabbed my shoulders, and plunked me down in the chair opposite them.

Joella unbuckles herself and moves beside me, sloshing ginger ale onto my pants. "Oops, sorry. Our dad's company supplies glue for your dad's company." She giggles and leans in, baptizing me again. "He will not *believe* we rode your plane!"

Jasmine yawns pointedly. "I've ridden a private jet before." She catches my eye and adds, hastily, "But this one is nice. Great soap."

Sophie tousles my hair like a puppy's. "So we're rotating seatmates for takeoff and landing, and in between, we'll sleep and party. Enjoy!"

She starts back up the aisle, swaying and balancing herself between the chair backs on either side.

I look at Joella and Jasmine. "Great to meet you. Will you excuse me a second?"

I dart after Sophie and grab her arm. She turns, surprised.

"I'd rather sit with my old friends," I say, low. "With you. We have a lot to catch up on."

Sophie rises on tiptoes and puts her mouth by my ear. Her lips brush my lobe, setting it on fire. "Better to start with them, because you and I," she whispers, "are stuck with each other all day Friday for interviews. Speaking of which." She pulls back to gaze up at me. "I've been thinking . . . you don't have to see your dad if you don't want to."

I blink. "My teacher didn't really give me a choice."

"Also, did I mention it's really really *really* generous of you to set up this ride for all of us and I'm SO sorry I didn't do a better job of screening people."

"What do you mean?" I ask, but then Rick taps her shoulder.

"Sophie, Aunty Claire's arranged to pick the three of us up at the airport." Rick's hanging on to Ever's hand.

"No need for a ride!" Sophie wraps an arm around Ever's waist, same way she was hanging on to me just a few minutes ago. "I got us free scooters!"

"Free mopeds?" Ever asks. "How?"

Sophie's head drops onto Ever's shoulder, smiling, and Ever lays her own head against hers. It's a photo moment. If my hands wouldn't shake when I tried to film it.

"I found a new shop that needs to get word out," Sophie says. "I told them we were coming to town with a few hundred people following us on social media, and they said we could have up to twenty scooters for the weekend if we tag them on our posts."

168

"Could you bring about world peace, too?" I ask.

"Ha." She rolls her eyes with a dramatic flick of her neck. "*But please.* You own this plane. I just made a phone call."

"Aunty Claire wants us to drop off our bags so she can feed us properly," Rick says. "Ever, too."

"Does that mean fatten me for slaughter?" Ever grimaces. "Your family *hates* me."

"I'm not letting you stay anywhere else, and they don't hate you." Rick kisses the tip of her upturned nose. "Not anymore."

Ugh. I drop my gaze to Sophie's blissful face.

"I can't wait to meet Aunty Claire's baby! To my new cousin, Finn!" Sophie raises her can and drinks to him. "I bought him a Dartmouth onesie. I bet she's so happy she's lighting up all of Taipei—when Fannie and Felix were born, she loved on them so much she could have eaten them up. Hi, Xavier." She lurches against me and belches. "Oops."

A smile twitches at the corner of my mouth. I reach out to steady *her*.

Only Sophie Ha could make burping cute.

Ten minutes later, we are airborne. Sophie won and I'm seated across from the sisters in black and red. I've managed to forget their names, but I can't let on and make them feel bad. They're talking about a deceased historian I've never heard of.

"The *Atlantic* was spot-on," says the girl in red.

"I thought the *New York Times* piece was more nuanced," says the other.

I'm lost. I've never read the *Atlantic* or the *New York Times*. And . . . everyone here is a college student.

But me.

Sophie shrieks with laughter up front. I lean into the aisle to see better. Two bottles of champagne are spraying Sophie, Rick, and Bert, who has stripped to boxers and socks. They're drenched.

Bert grabs the handle of the exit door. "Let's spit into the wind!"

"What the fuck?" Alarmed, I unbuckle and bolt toward them as a girl screams, "No, don't!"

Rick yanks Bert back by his shirt. "If you'd opened that door, we'd all have died!" he yells.

"I wasn't really going to do it," Bert protests.

"This isn't your plane," Sophie says. "We should have left you on the runway. Try showing some respect!"

Ever lays fingers on Rick's arm. "Maybe we should cool it with the drinks?"

"We're international." Marc slicks his milk-chocolate hair back behind both ears. "Drinking age is back to its rightful place of eighteen."

"This party is all about the drinks!" Bert says.

All eyes turn toward me. I've come to a stop in the middle of the aisle.

Weird. I'm in charge. Sophie nailed it—Bert is acting like a dick and trashing Ba's plane. Yes, it's annoying, but then again, this is what Ba would expect from me, right? I'm glad Rick is here, and now that Bert's blocked . . . in my humble opinion, he's not entirely wrong. Everything is less awkward with drinks.

"Fuck it," I say. "Let's celebrate."

Marc whoops and cranks up the music. Sophie climbs onto a chair, barefooted, and raises her glass to Rick, Ever, Marc, and me. "To the best friends a girl could ask for!"

I don't know how long we drink, dance, drink, and sing terrible karaoke. But at some point, when the lights dim and the chamber's pulsing warm and everyone's stripped to bare minimum for the pajama party of the decade and my brains start leaking from my ears, Sophie grabs my hand.

"Dance, Xavier!"

And we do.

Sophie is undeniably hot. Her hair is all the colors of water under a moon at night, and it flows and plays around the curves of her face. Her eyes are like black pools, catching glimmers of the cabin lights. Her plum top tightens against her curves, and she hangs on to my arm and swings and shakes her head, so wild and free.

"I see you, Xavier Yeh," she crows. "In my crystal ball, I see crowds come to witness your art and they leave *transformed*. You piss them off on behalf of forgotten peoples. They do more. They live more. They *love* more."

"I see you on a throne," I say. "Running the world. Organizing the impassioned. People like your stupid professor bow down and kiss your toes."

"Ha!" She sways against me.

"Sophie, maybe you should take a break," Rick says, but she pushes his hand away and a bubble of laughter escapes her lips. Her shoes are long gone, and now so are mine. We keep dancing. Dancing off school projects and asshole parents. Her heated skin glides against mine. My hand goes around her back and her heavy arms slide up around my neck and we writhe to the beat, hips in sync, her black hair flying in every direction.

The citrus, floral scent of it—I can't inhale enough of her. Our bodies meld together and we move move move in time. Her head falls back, eyes half shut and a smile on her lips. It's like the first night we went clubbing together on Loveboat. That fire between us was there then, too, and all the reasons we shouldn't have kept going, but none of those matter right now.

I don't know who makes the first move, but suddenly, our mouths are moving together, too. She tastes like lotus seed and sugar. My fingers thread into her hair, pressing her closer, breaking our edges as she arches against me, the freaking best kiss ever attempted at this altitude.

Sophie smiles dreamily up at me. Her arms tighten and her entire weight yanks me sideways. Some remote part of me is telling me to stop and that we'll regret this in the morning, but the rest of me . . . I bury my nose in the hollow of her neck and bite at her scented skin.

And then we're stumbling toward the back room. Fire burns through my body. It needs to be quenched, and by her, all of her.

We tumble into the empty space, and bump against the king-sized bed. Sophie releases me and grabs the door. The last things I see, before she slams it shut, is Priscilla glaring after us, her mouth angry, opening and closing with words I can't hear—and Rick's worried gaze.

And then she and I are locked together again: the curves of her body fitting into mine, her nails digging into my flesh, our mouths on fire . . . and none of them out there matter anymore.

21

SOPHIE

It's the stillness that jolts me awake. No more vibration. No more hum of the engine. Just the quiet of the cabin, the weight of Xavier's leg over mine. A familiar humidity stirs in the air. Morning sunlight stabs into my head, and I wince and shade my eyes with my hand. The oblong windows frame a mercilessly white-blue sky.

Taipei. We've landed.

I sit up, and pain slices through my brain. My head weighs about a hundred pounds. It wants to fall off my neck. The night comes rushing back: our bodies tangled together, arms and legs, the taste of red wine on his mouth and the heat of his lips on my skin. . . .

Oh my God! Did we—?

He's still asleep, lying on his stomach with his face turned toward me, half buried in his pillow. His black shirt is rucked up to expose a pale sliver of his back. His pants are still on. I pat myself down. Blouse, bra, skirt. All where they should be. Thank God, we must have passed out before things got too out of hand. But my skin tingles with the scrape of his stubble on my cheek, his hands exploring . . .

How did I let this happen? What was it? The seductive private jet? Seeing him in the flesh? *Dancing?* Just coming into his orbit again brought back a rush of so many feelings I thought I'd massacred.

And now one night, and I completely lost it.

I slip off the bed. Xavier stirs, rustling the duvet.

I grope for my phone on the floor to text Ever and Rick, only to find it dead and unresponsive. Story of my life. I head into the main cabin, but it's emptied of our friends. Two cleaners are collecting beer bottles and snack wrappers, and a third vacuums. Yellow sunlight pours through the open doorway. As I head toward it, the air warms by several degrees.

Ever's voice floats my way. "Well, I'm going to wake them up. We're late—oh, hi, Sophie!"

I grasp the open doorjamb and find myself bathed in warm sunbeams, standing at the top of a red-carpeted ramp leading down to Ever. Everyone on the pavement behind her is paired with luggage and backpacks. Two workmen are refueling the plane from a large silver tank. The muggy air, like a warm blanket, is less fierce than it was over the summer. But everyone's faces, upturned toward me, make me shiver.

How long have they been debating the best way not to interrupt us?

Priscilla folds her arms over her shiny butterflies. The stiffness to her shoulders shouts louder than words.

"Nothing happened," I say. "We just . . . um, drank too much." My swollen brain pulses against my skull. "We passed out."

A mosquito pricks my arm and I slap it away. No one answers. No one believes me, and why would they? Now on top of facing Xavier, I have to face all of them, too.

I let out a moan, which only makes my head swell to bursting. I put fingers to my temples, trying to hold it in. The one thing guaranteed to complicate everything, and I did it.

The tornado strikes again.

"Please can we all just pretend this didn't happen?" I beg. "I'll get Xavier," I say, and turn back into the cabin.

Xavier sits up, tossing back the silk duvet when I enter the chamber. His wavy hair is disheveled, falling into his eyes. His fingers move to rebutton his black shirt. I pull my gaze from his bare midriff, grab a pillow off the floor, and hurl it at him. It thumps his face with a satisfying smack.

"We shouldn't have done that!" My voice trembles. I tug my purple jumpsuit from my backpack. I need to get out of this beer-and-Xavier-scented blouse. I need to get away from *him*.

He runs his thumb and fingers over the sprouted shadow on his jaw. "I'm sorry."

He looks as terrible as I feel, but a part of me still wants to shut the door, make a flying tackle at him, and pick up where we left off.

"I don't even want to do this project anymore," I say, which isn't exactly what I mean. I want to meet his aunt about the Magic Mirror. And I owe him help on his film. "I don't want to do it with *you*."

His head hangs. "I . . . got carried away."

The regret on his face makes me ache inside. He got carried away . . . so did I . . . we were stupid and horny. And this time . . . if that wasn't real, I guess I don't know what real feels like. Only that hooking up isn't love. And I can't let these feelings screw up my weekend and turn me into a basket case once I fly back to Dartmouth and he flies back to LA and we're three thousand miles apart again.

I fold my arms and glower at his bare feet. "For the record, I don't believe in second chances."

He doesn't answer.

"And we both need to nail our projects. I didn't get anything done on the flight!" After all my plans . . . nothing. "*I* need this class. *You* need to get free of your dad. So we're going to interview, film . . . and go home. Last night didn't happen. Okay?"

"Okay." He looks at me at last, blasting me with the shock of those dark eyes that see so much. "Sophie, honestly. The most important thing to me is being your friend. I don't ever want to hurt you."

But that does.

"Same here," I say stiffly, then head into the bathroom to change.

Three adults in business suits have gathered on the asphalt outside the *Lynn*. Camera eyes point in our direction as we descend from the plane, and I spot a vaguely familiar logo on a video camera hoisted on one man's shoulder.

"The press?" I ask.

"They're always around," Xavier says.

A bit panicked, I rake my fingers through my hair tangles, but Xavier takes it all in stride. Par for the course when the ruling class lands in Taipei? My aunt was always in tune with his movements last summer—this must be how.

"Shit, not again," he swears.

I follow his gaze, not toward the press, but the airport. My heart sinks. A familiar man in a navy sports coat is striding toward us, a little girl hanging on to his hand. He's followed by three others this time: a bodyguard, a man in a purple Dragon Leaf pilot's cap, and a woman in a lime-green suit, hurrying in high heels with a nervous hitch.

Xavier swears again. "Why the hell's Ba here now?"

22

XAVIER

I wasn't supposed to have to deal with him until I got to the apartment for our interview. For ten minutes, max. Now he's in my face again—same lethally sharp haircut and hawkish black eyes. As he comes closer, I feel every last scrap of color being sucked out of me. I need to stop him before he tries to send me home or poisons my trip.

The world's moving too fast this morning. After a night when everything felt right, only to wake up with Sophie gone, and realizing she and I had run off the rails after all, when I never want to do anything to risk our friendship. Then there's landing in Taipei, where the humidity and green mountains feel weirdly like home, but not really. Not since Ma died.

And now Ba. The worst part: he's as calm as if he were

strolling on a beach. He's holding Alison's hand—Bernard's four-year-old, who's hugging a Mickey Mouse as big as she is. His bodyguard, Ken-Tek, a second pilot, and an executive form up behind him.

I crouch warily, readying to fight if it comes to it.

"My press friends." Ba opens a hand to them. "Thank you for keeping tabs on my son. I'd like to have a word with him and his friends in private."

"Sir, can you at least give us a statement?" asks a man.

"I have no statement," Ba says.

The woman in the lime-green suit snaps her fingers. The press people shoulder bags and cameras and head toward the airport. They're followed by the plane cleaning and refueling crew. His word, her snap, it's their command. I'm back in his world, where he holds more power in his little finger than the average emperor.

Ba clasps Bernard's shoulder with a fond old-boy squeeze.

"Bernard, you've done more than your duty as usual. I've booked you and Alison a suite at the Magic Kingdom resort in LA. She's excited to go. Take her to the *Star Wars* theme park for a long overdue vacation. Gao-Li will fly so you can sleep."

The man in the pilot uniform shakes Bernard's hand.

"Wait. What?" I say. A low alarm rings in my head. We're scheduled to fly back in two days. "Right now?"

Bernard slides his purple cap off his head and wrings it between his hands. "Lao Yeh, you are too generous." He glances at me. "Lao Yeh, these young people—"

"Don't worry, I'll take care of everything." Ba flips his watch, checking the time. "You should head off so you land in Los Angeles at a decent hour."

"I want to ride in the cockpit!" Alison races up the ramp, Mickey Mouse bouncing, and Bernard and Gao-Li climb after her.

"Ba—" I begin, but he sets a silencing hand on my arm as Bernard pushes away the ramp and shuts the door. The reporters vanish into the airport. As the plane taxis away, he turns toward me.

"You are out of control," he says.

Faster than lightning, Ba grabs my ear and yanks down. Fire flares through my head. Polished black cap-toe shoes gyrate before my eyes.

"Leave him alone!" Sophie yells.

With a roar of rage, I wrench free. No fucking way he's humiliating me in front of everyone again. Not this time. My face twists into a mask of hatred as I charge him. But Ken-Tek panthers forward and blocks me. He comes at me and I dance back, fists doubled, drawing him from my friends.

Sophie's hands are clenched, as if she's getting ready to take Ba out herself. Ever clutches Rick's arm, wide-eyed with horror. My ear burns and I feel a trickle of blood run down my neck, but I refuse to give Ba the satisfaction of acknowledging it.

"Fight me yourself!" I spit at Ba. "Sitting on your throne's making you soft."

"Jane." Ba straightens his navy jacket with a deft flick of his wrists. "Please show Xiang-Ping and his friends what your team found early this morning."

I don't lower my fists. I keep one eye on Ken-Tek as the woman holds up an iPad. A video plays: a scrawny, shirtless Bert, dancing on a chair with a bottle of merlot—then he yanks down his pants, and his big round hairy ass fills her screen.

"Bert!" Rick groans.

Sophie grasps at her pocket. "The livestream!"

Jane must be Ba's head of PR. The second most important person in the Dragon Leaf universe. A second video pulses with music: Sophie glitters in her purple top, her pale arms raised and pumping to the beat. Someone online screams, "We're riding billionaire class!"

Then Sophie and me, bodies knit together like a pair of lover statues in Paris, grinding to the rhythm, not PG-13, but full-on rated R. Everything we regret from last night, right here under Ba's nose. The stuff Instagram privacy policies are made for.

Then Bert again, wrestling with the plane's door handle before Rick yanks him back, yelling, "If you'd opened that door, we'd all have died!" Bad enough then—and now, under Ba's gaze, raw stupidity.

"You could have died," Ba repeats slowly. "All of you."

"He wasn't going to do it," I say. But I know it sounds lame. Bert himself has vanished, hairy ass and all. "It's my fault."

"No, it's m—" Sophie begins.

"Of course it is," Ba cuts her off. "Videos were cropping up all over the internet. *Scribe Asia* printed a front-page piece. 'Prince of Taipei Returns in Style.'"

"Who cares about *Scribe Asia*?" I say.

"I care about any press coverage that has no business being in the world!" Ba thunders.

"I'm never here. No one gives a damn who I am!"

"And we want to keep it that way! We spend millions making sure the reputation of the family and the company is as stainless as a communion altar. We stay out of the press unless our people are controlling the message. And you blow it on one joyride."

"We're in the papers?" Priscilla whispers, thrilled. Ever glares at her. But God, I wish I could just be Priscilla myself—I wish all this was someone else's shitstorm.

"You're not in the papers," Ba says. "Thanks to Jane's team. Five people spent the last three hours scrubbing all traces of the article and photos from the internet. Including Instagram."

"Any additional mentions will be deleted off the Web immediately," Jane says. "We've put out a piece on the latest therapeutic drugs from our cancer research center. Any internet searches for your name or the jet will pull that first, followed by similar stories."

"How'd she do that?" Priscilla whispers.

Scrubbed clean, everyone redirected. If I wanted to convince the world I exist, no Google search engine would help me now.

That's me: the Buried Yeh.

"I'm afraid Bernard will be gone for the week. Which means

my plane," Ba stresses the possessive, "won't be available for your return flight."

A gasp goes up behind me. But it takes a beat for this to sink in.

"I can't afford a ticket home!" Priscilla says. "I have tests Monday."

They all do. This is the real humiliation. Not yanking my ear off or siccing Ken-Tek on me.

But forcing me to let everyone down.

"You told Bernard you'd take care of it!" I yell.

"I *am* taking care of it. There are consequences to bad behavior. It's time you learned them. You'll all be finding your own ways home, because I certainly am not footing the bill."

"No one here can afford a thousand-dollar ticket."

"Hell no." Priscilla's near tears.

"You should have considered that before throwing your friend's rear end onto the screen."

"Mr. Yeh, we're sorry about the videos, but they're gone now. And I don't think that headline made your family look bad," Sophie says. "People look up to your family. Prince of Taipei isn't a bad label."

"Next time, young lady, you'd be better served remaining in the main cabin with your seat belt fastened instead of riding my worthless son."

Sophie chokes, and my vision goes red. I hurl myself at Ba, and this time, I break past Ken-Tek. Ba's eyes fly wide with

184

surprise. He raises his arm to block, but I claw it aside, and my fists connect with his chest with a solid double thump. He stumbles back a step, arms flailing against the air.

It's a fleeting victory. Then Ken-Tek's hand is at Ba's back, breaking his fall. He comes between us like a wall of iron.

"Keep the fuck out of my life," I snarl at Ba.

My dad's breathing hard, eyes narrowed. He jerks his jacket back into place. Jane lays a hand on his arm before he can reply.

"Sir, we need to get to the racetrack now."

Another PR thing—a car race with him driving a Porsche fast means Dragon Leaf outpaces its competition or some other bullshit. I don't care as long as he's fucking out of my face and Sophie and I can get on with filming in peace.

"Yes, let's take care of Xiang-Ping first." Ba's already brought his breath under control. "You twisted my arm to come all this way for your school project. You said it counts for three grades. So we must ensure its success. Fortunately for you, your cousin arrived an hour ago. So I've asked him to supervise."

Lulu? But no. Him—Ba said *him*?

Ba calls toward the airport, "Lin-Bian, where are you?"

Shit, no way.

The Douche Lord emerges from the airport, a younger version of my dad in a blue dress shirt and perfectly side-parted hair. The last time I saw him was at their home in Taipei, years ago, when he set fire to my shoes. He's only a year older, but unlike me, he's skipped grades, not repeated them. The poster

185

child of the Yeh dynasty, apprenticed to the business since he was in diapers.

"I don't need supervision! Especially not from *him*."

"Wait . . . Victor?" Sophie's bewildered. "You're *cousins*?"

23

SOPHIE

"What's going on?" Victor says. "It's my girl, Cha Siu-Bao Face."

"*Cousins?*" I repeat.

Victor holds out a hand for a high five, which I return automatically, dazed.

A million emotions swirl my already-addled heart. Xavier's fight with his dad, the stupid videos, his dad flinging what happened between us into our faces like a porn film . . . and now . . . Victor and Xavier?

These weeks I've been texting and talking to both, and didn't have a clue. It seems impossible . . . but they have the same lean build, fine bone structure, wavy jet-black hair. Victor's shed his hip-nerdy student look for a silky blue shirt, closer to how Xavier dresses. They even speak with a similar warm timber, from voice boxes built from the same DNA.

But Xavier slouches, while Victor stands like a soldier. And there is one giant difference between them. Victor is all Dartmouth TA calm, and Xavier is an angry bear. His face is contorted with fury. A forked vein pulses in his forehead.

"I don't need him fucking up my stuff," Xavier rages.

"Stuff?" For the first time, his dad's voice softens. "I'm glad your mother isn't here to see you like this. It would break her heart."

Xavier's face drains to white. He falls silent as his dad heads off, followed by Jane and his bodyguard. I want to go to Xavier and wrap him in my arms and comfort him, but won't that contradict everything I said to him on the plane? The other kids, with an uncertain glance at Xavier, start toward the airport, leaving the cousins and me on the asphalt.

Then I notice the trickle of blood drying on Xavier's neck.

"Oh, Xavier, your ear."

I pull a tissue from my purse as he swipes at it. "I've dealt with worse."

"I'm sorry." I daub at the blood. He flinches but doesn't pull away as I wipe it clean. "About the party. The livestreaming. It's my fault."

"It's not your fault he's a freaking control freak."

"A ton of shit's going down with Dragon Leaf. He's managing it all right now," Victor says.

"Oh, you're still here?" Xavier says sarcastically.

"Like your old man said. I'm supposed to make sure you show

up for your meetings. No more antics, no more headlines: 'Black Sheep Returns with Brat Pack.' Your timing couldn't be worse. Do you have any idea what's been going on with the company?"

"I don't, and I don't care." Xavier starts after the others and we follow.

"Dragon Leaf's stock price is tanking," Victor says.

"Ba's getting poorer? So he can only buy the world over, like, what, twice now? I feel for him."

"Oh, Xiang-Ping. This is exactly why I'll be glued to you like a barnacle all weekend. We have so much to catch up on. How long has it been since we've seen each other? A year? Two?"

"Four."

"You've learned to count."

"You've learned to tie your shoes. When'd you stop using Velcro?"

Victor's so smooth, and Xavier's all raw fury, and yet both of them are saying the same thing—they'd gouge out each other's eyes if they could.

At the runway's end, the *Lynn* takes off. Victor shades his eyes to follow the white jet into the blue sky. "You know, I flew United here, like the average mortal. I spent the flight preparing a speech I'm giving for the family at our mooncake pavilion tomorrow." He returns his gaze to Xavier. "So forgive me for finding it ironic that the worst thing that's happened to you is that you've lost your party plane."

Xavier breaks into a jog and speeds ahead.

"And why are *you* here?" Victor asks me. "My cousin's a train wreck. How did a smart girl like you get roped into his circus?"

I really don't want to talk to him, not when he's on Team Xavier's Dad. Not until I have a chance to understand from Xavier what's going on. I pick up my pace, too.

"We're friends from Loveboat."

Victor's brows rise into his forehead. "Tell me he wasn't your Mr. Mistake."

Heat flushes my cheeks. "Not your business," I snap. Crap, he's Horvath's *TA*. I can't afford to get on his bad side. "How are you related?"

"My dad's his dad's younger brother."

"Edward?"

"You know the family tree." He's not surprised. They're all pretty well-known. Like the Windsors. Still, it comes across like conceit.

"When you said you were working for your family after you graduated, I didn't think you meant this one." No wonder he's so secure. *He's* set for life, although their family dynamic is much more complicated than the fancy department stores and private islands they own.

"Yep, that's the reason I'm here. For the speech—thousands of people will be at the Moon Festival. It's my announcement that I'm returning to Taipei after graduation. I'll do my four months with mandatory conscription, then on to Dragon Leaf. I'm sure I'll start at a modest position. Vice president of emerging tech. Something like that." He gives me a wolfish grin.

"I'm actually here to meet your family for my CS project," I admit. "Rose Chan."

"For CS?" He frowns, confused. "My aunt runs . . . a *clothing boutique*."

He sounds like Horvath. Not in a good way. "She has a stylist bot app that uses AI. She agreed to talk to me. I figured if I could show Horvath why a company as big as Dragon Leaf thinks this is a good idea, he might come around."

"He's one of the most respected CS professors at one of the oldest academic institutions in the States. Getting his judgment and advice is why you're there. Why challenge him?"

I bite my lip, stung. My tornado at work again? Is this entire trip an insult to Professor Horvath? Would he be angry if he found out I was working so hard to prove my idea was worthwhile, despite his advice?

"Please don't say anything to him," I beg. "I need time to figure this out."

"I'd only mention it if you want me to put in a good word, Sophie."

He's never given me a reason not to trust him, but there's a reason Xavier hates his guts.

We're closing the gap with the other passengers. The girls are talking. Priscilla's face is tight with anger. "I got on that plane because I expected to be riding it home."

"We all did," Joella says.

"Oh, no," I groan. "I need to deal with this."

191

"Say their names," Victor says.

"What?"

"It's the first rule of charismatic leadership. I read it in a book. The sweetest sound to anyone's ears is their own name."

I flash back to all the times Xavier's said "Sophie." Which was *a lot.*

"Does your whole family do that?" I ask indignantly, but he just squeezes my arm.

"I better run ahead. I gotta babysit my cousin. You still owe me boba. Ciao." He gives me a two-finger salute and charming smile, Dartmouth TA again, and breaks into a jog after Xavier.

"So you hook up with one Yeh heir, and now you're after another?" Priscilla asks. "You are something else."

My mouth falls open. "No, he's . . . my *TA.*"

"Even worse! You are *constantly* flirting. Honestly, how can you stand yourself?"

My chest tightens. "I'm not flirting. Look, there's a lot going on, in case you haven't noticed."

"Sophie did all the work to organize this trip." Ever falls back to join us, Rick in hand. She loops her arm through mine reassuringly. "You glommed on. So why don't you show some appreciation?"

My eyes sting as I cling to her—it's never the hate that makes me want to cry. It's this.

"Yeah, thanks for nothing. Now I'm stuck in Taipei." Priscilla storms after Victor.

"I should have said her name," I mutter.

"What?"

"Nothing." I brush moisture from my eyes. "*Am* I constantly flirting? I don't mean to."

"You're beautiful," Ever says. "You smile at a guy and he goes weak at the knees. You're friendly, and you want to make people feel good. It's not your fault and you shouldn't feel guilty about it."

"Sounds like a weird problem to have."

"But it's real. I've been trying to explain things like this to Rick. *He* doesn't have to deal with it." She frowns at him.

"What the hell," he says. "How do you think I win so many games? I smile at the linebacker, he goes weak at the knees, and then I run him over."

We all laugh. "I needed that," I say.

Ever presses a kiss to Rick's cheek, then turns back to me. "It's unfair to hold it against you, really."

"Okay." I smile, grateful for the momentary reprieve.

Ever's tone turns serious. "Poor Xavier. His dad—I knew it was tough, but . . ."

So much for keeping it under wraps. "This is why he needs to nail his film project," I say. "He's trying to get his trust so he can get out from under his dad. He can't even just take off—his dad will send guards after him."

"He's so trapped," Ever says.

"It explains a lot," Rick says.

"Yeah. So, anyways, we should figure out the plane ride on our own. We all need to be back in classes Monday. Will the dance scholarship help you?" I ask Ever.

Her nose wrinkles. "No, they canceled my ticket when I told them I was riding with friends."

"We're screwed," Joella says.

"We're here already," I say. "Let's not waste the trip. We're visiting family, dance auditions, interviews. The rest of you, I'm pairing up for a day around town—go have a blast. Can I borrow a phone charger, please? I'll ask the alum for help."

"What can they do?" Joella asks, but she passes hers to me.

My phone slowly comes online. It's not quite eight in the morning here—still early. Hopefully jet lag won't hit until tomorrow. I check social media first for the incriminating livestream videos. They're gone without a trace, just as Jane said. Creepy. I didn't know anyone could edit someone else's posts. No wonder Xavier can't escape.

A text from Emma pops up, sent eight hours ago.

OMG. Xavier is GORGEOUS! Who would have guessed he'd turn out so hot? And as sweet as I remember. I haven't felt this excited about a guy in so long. Can't wait to meet again at the top of Taipei 101. Thank you, my friend!

Oh, man. What have I done? I was supposed to be setting them up and then I . . . he and I . . .

I open the Loveboat alum group.

"Whoa, it's growing like crazy. Five hundred more people!" My Instagram followers have shot up by almost as many—alum from the past few summers following our wild weekend getaway, private jet party and all.

Comments have popped up on my Instagram feed.

Trina: was that her screaming "billionaire class"?
Alexandra: She's not even pretty. How could she be dating Xavier Yeh?
Melody: gold diggers are so passé . . . yawn

Who are these people? They must have seen the videos before they were stripped from the internet—so the Dragon Leaf PR machine isn't completely leakproof.

And now, on top of everything else, I have a bunch of stranger haters.

Priscilla: She's flirting with his cousin now, too. It's disgusting

Like I said.

We're just friends, guys! I want to write. Like that'll help. And even worse, that traitorous part of me wonders . . . why *didn't* something happen last night? Guys *don't* hold back with me.

So why did Xavier?

I shake my head. The tornado is spinning. But everyone is

looking to me. Maybe I can harness the power of it and keep us going. I pretend I'm not reading any of that crap, and that they aren't either, and write:

Sophie: Mayday, gang

Sophie: Scheduling conflict with our plane ride home. Any ideas? Private jets? Commercial planes? Cash? We need to get home Sunday night.

Lena: That sucks @Sophie

Jillian: My aunt's a flight attendant for Singapore Airlines. I'll ask her

David: I'll ask around. My dad knows people at United

Laura: Represent us at the reunion! Wish we were there!

Bless the Loveboat alum who are still my friends.

"Can anyone help?" Joella peers at my phone.

"Let's give them time, okay? Someone might have a lead." Buoyed by the hive mind, I head toward the immigration counters. "Come on, we only have two days! Let's make the most of it."

24

XAVIER

"You never told me you were hanging out with my cousin at Dartmouth," I say to Sophie on our way out the airport. All this time I've been calling her from LA, she's been with him. He even had some cutesy nickname for her. "When did you guys meet?"

"Start of classes." The wind blows her hair across her face as we step outside again. "He's a TA for the AI class I'm trying to get into. I had no idea he was your cousin, honestly."

Of course the Douche Lord would have made a beeline for Sophie. Complete with thousand-dollar Dior Homme sunglasses or some other status symbol.

"You should stay away from him."

"I can't afford to blow him off," she says. "He's the TA."

"Did he offer to get you in with your teacher?"

She flushes. "Yes, well, he *did*. Why'd your dad sic him on you?"

"He's a kiss-up. To everyone he wants something from. And now we're stuck with . . . the *Douche Lord* . . . all weekend!" I'm pushing too hard, I know. And calling him the name I slapped on him ten years ago is not the most mature. But I want her to tell me she sees through his fake little shell, too . . . . but she's not saying anything like that.

"Bao-Feng?" A guy across the street tucks a blue motorcycle helmet under his arm and waves. "I'm Li-Fan. We emailed."

Sophie darts toward him, and I follow.

"Taipei Rides?" she asks.

"All here." He gestures proudly to a rainbow of two-wheelers with gleaming hubcaps. Bert is already running his hand over shiny red chrome, talking with a few people—fifteen more Loveboaters have joined us from other gates and flights, shaking hands, two talking with Australian accents.

"Hi, everyone. I'm Sophie Ha. Wow, our ranks are swelling!" She's poised in hostess mode, but I can tell she's nervous. She's talking faster than normal, one hand tightly folded behind her back. "Loveboat friends from Chien Tan, Ocean campus, last summer's program—meet each other. Everyone who wants to get matched up tonight—online or virtual—I've posted a group dating app in the Loveboat channel. Please download and fill in your information.

"Everyone coming to Taipei 101 tonight at seven, dinner is

198

being sponsored by the generous Emma Shin—HOWEVER! To gain entry, bring a box of mooncakes to exchange with a dozen people. Or another party favor."

"Brilliant," Ever says.

Sophie takes the blue helmet, upside-down, from the Taipei Rides man.

"We can't possibly experience all of Taipei in a weekend, so we'll have to live vicariously through each other . . . so post away on social media! And now—here are your rides for the weekend!"

"What? No way!" Priscilla says.

Sophie glances at Li-Fan, who has moved down the row of scooters. She lowers her voice and says sweetly, "It took me four phone calls to pull this off . . . so no more hating on me, please?"

Priscilla frowns.

Sophie shakes the blue helmet so we can hear the rattling of keys inside. "Everyone pick out a set, and that's how you'll find your ride partner. Any pairs without licenses, switch partners or take a tandem bike. For photos, tag hashtags #TaipeiRides and #LoveboatReunion!"

"Rick and Ever." She tosses Ever a set of keys.

Rick straps their bags onto their rack, and Ever climbs on behind him. "Text us when you guys head to Aunty Claire's, and we'll meet you there," Rick says, and they motor off.

"Xavier, you and I have our own scooters since we have a lot of ground to cover." A blue scooter beeps twice, and she hands me its keys. I set my backpack into the attached trunk, slip on a helmet, then straddle the bike. As it rumbles to life beneath my legs, the gunning of a larger engine makes everyone turn. The Douche Lord pulls up on a sleek black Yamaha motorcycle he bought to impress his first girlfriend.

"Xiang-Ping, where to first?"

"Headquarters," I say shortly.

"Then my aunt's," Sophie says.

"We're supposed to stick together," he says.

"What'll you do if I don't?" I ask. "Arm wrestle me?"

"There aren't enough scooters," Priscilla says.

Sophie frowns. "I'm sure I didn't miscount."

"Bert took off on his own," Marc says dryly.

Sophie meets my gaze, then glances away. "We can share," I say, but she doesn't want to. It's too classic couple—exactly why she set it up for everyone else and not us.

The Douche Lord gives us a cool smile. "Maybe you'd rather ride with me?" He guns his motor like the show-off he is.

She slips her orange helmet over her head.

"We need to figure out the film plan on the way," I say. Totally legit. "We're behind."

"Okay." Sophie nudges me. "But I'm driving."

"What? I'm ready to go." I don't budge. I need to feel the wind full on my body, blowing through my shirt and hair and blowing away all the crappiness Ba dumped on me. Pretending I'm in charge of the road, since I'm not in charge of anything else.

Mostly, I can't be holding on to her and having her hair

blowing in my face, making me think about how it felt to hold her while she slept last night, with her breath warming my neck and her heart beating against my chest.

She nudges me harder, furious. "Just because you're the guy."

"Hold the rails."

"I'm driving the next leg!"

"Fine."

She throws her leg over the back of my seat and grasps the handrails at her sides. I can't help feeling it's a good step for both of us that I'm not letting her overwhelm me, or being afraid of her overwhelming me, even if I don't know what that means yet either.

"Make sure you stay with me," the Douche Lord says. "Your dad said—"

I gun the bike forward, hanging a hard turn out of the lot.

"Wait!" yells the Douche Lord. My cheeks tighten with a grin. Even on his motorcycle, the Douche Lord doesn't have the balls to move this fast. As the light ahead turns yellow, I put on a burst of speed, shooting through as it turns red. A car honks. The Douche Lord yells again, but his words are lost as our scooter eats up the blacktop marked by large white characters. We lean so far to the side we're in danger of raking skin off our legs.

Sophie's arms cinch around my waist. "What the hell, Xavier?!"

I smile into the wind. I know it shouldn't, but even more than Club Pub, all of this feels more like me again.

The blue-green spear of Taipei 101 dominates the skyline as we near the city.

Once on a drive with Ba, he pointed out the ways the family has shaped that skyline. Two buildings eastward built by my grandpa, another to the south by my dad. I'd sat on his lap in the car and felt a sense of pride—still feel it now—but the memory only goes to show how much has changed since. The Family and its Reputation are exactly the reasons I'm such a disappointment. The reason they keep all mention of me buried. To keep me from taking them down with me.

We pass a ten-story hotel that belongs to Ma's family.

"I want to visit my mom's grave," I say into the wind. "I meant to over the summer."

"Where's she buried?" Sophie seems to have forgiven me now that we're squarely on the road.

"Yang Ming Shan."

"In the mountains?" Her arms shift lower on my waist. "It's a little far—"

"About an hour. My family's tombs are up the road from Sun Yat-Sen's son. We can go tomorrow. It won't take long." Ba's voice echoes in my head. "I can't believe Ba used her against me. Although he always does."

"I'm sure she'd be proud of you."

I just want to know she wouldn't be disappointed in me. She didn't keep a journal, as far as I know. There's no way I could know what she wanted from me or how she'd feel about me today. Only what Ba's telling me.

"I wish I *could* know." I recognize the turnoff for Dihua Street and veer toward the green exit sign, 出口—the "mouth" that's easy enough to read. "I mean, her trust fund is the only reason I'm even here. . . ."

I trail off. There's Sophie's project. I wouldn't have come for the Moon Festival, but I think I would have for her.

The light changes, and we pour off the highway with a hundred other scooters and mopeds in every color. The energy fuels me with more hope and I turn onto Dihua Street and motor by a two-story row of historic redbrick buildings: a first-floor corridor formed of three archways per building, topped by second stories with three eight-paneled windows . . . all forming an endless block down the road.

"So much character," Sophie says. "I love this place."

"It's the oldest street in Taipei." I slow to a stop, then pull my video camera from my backpack and hang it around my neck. It's early morning, so many of the shops are still shuttered behind rosewood-paneled doors. "Headquarters is down the street. I want to film all of this."

"I assumed we were headed for a skyscraper."

"Nah, we've been here forever. My family started out trading in fabrics, which is why they're here, close to the water. To meet the trade ships." It's something else I like about Dragon Leaf. The beginning. Before the diversification and holding companies, the acquisitions and strategic investments. Once upon a time, the Yehs did one thing. We had a trade. "This is a great place to get footage."

As we continue down the street, I film shops selling dried everything: mushrooms, white fungi, teas, plums, mangoes, halved figs with pink hearts. Braids of purple garlic hang from a rope. Musty, sharp scents tickle my nose.

"We're just a block from the Dadaocheng Wharf," I say. "I used to feed ducks there with my mom. An old city wall gate's still standing. My family used to ship fabrics from the dock all over Asia."

"You sound proud when you talk about stuff like that," Sophie comments.

"Yeah?" I'm a little embarrassed. I'm no spokesperson or anything. Clearly.

Then, headquarters comes into view: a quaintly historic building at an intersection, the second-floor corner cut flat like the edge of an octagon. I've always liked it, as well as the impressive Dragon Leaf logo that hangs there, with the pearly black dragon encircling the Yeh character. But magnified like that, the resemblance to the dragon I painted this summer is unmistakable, down to the clawed feet and leafy scales. Ba wins again. I'm not even original.

The entrance doors are rosewood carved with more dragons and scenes from the wharf's history. But my view is blocked by a crowd of chanting men and women crammed into the covered sidewalk between the brick columns. They fill the intersection to the opposite buildings.

"What's going on?" Sophie asks. "Must be a few hundred people here."

"I don't know." Cardboard signs bob over their heads. "They sound angry." I frown, lowering my camera. "I can't film with them here. Now what?"

I park the scooter at the crowd's edge. "We'll have to go through them to get inside, too. Here, come on."

I put an arm around Sophie's shoulders, protecting her from the crush of bodies and jabs of elbows as I push toward the doors. She presses tight against me.

The chants grow clear: "Take him out! Take him out! Take him out!"

"Take who out?" Sophie whispers.

"No idea!"

I squeeze us under the archway. A blue wooden police barrier blocks the carved rosewood doors, buttoned in their centers by two brass knockers. "1912," the date of Dragon Leaf's founding, is engraved into a green-gray stone placard. The entryway is decorated for the Mid-Autumn Festival with red paper banners, spidery ancient script across their tops and down either side—but I can't film any of it with this crowd jostling my back and three guards in uniforms blocking the way.

Craning my neck, I glimpse one of the signs.

Ba's face, like a decapitated head, crossed out with a fat black X.

A queasy sensation twists my stomach. It's his public portrait: dark suit, chin lifted, dark eyes steady and oblivious to the X slicing through his nose.

"What do those say?" I ask.

Sophie pulls free to look. "'Oust him.'"

"The CEO makes millions a year," someone shouts. "He races fancy cars. He can spare my salary. I need to feed my family!"

"Fi-re *him*!"

Are these employees? The shouts are drilling holes into my skull. Ba *does* race cars, but he also prides himself—to an obnoxious degree—on treating his employees well. All these people hating on him doesn't feel . . . I mean, I don't know how to feel. In the long history of Dragon Leaf, I've heard about backstabbing business partners and troublemaking customers and murderously angry family members. But I've never seen anything like this.

I shake my head. Whatever this mess is, it's his problem, not mine. I just need footage for my documentary and to get Sophie in to see my aunt.

I step around the barrier.

"Stay back!" A guard's in my face, wooden baton out. "No farther!"

He shoves me in the chest so hard I step on Sophie's foot. The Dragon Leaf logo flashes gold on his breast pocket. Sophie grips my arm.

"You okay?" I turn to her.

"Fine," she says tightly. "Let's figure this out."

I pull out my passport. "I'm Xiang-Ping. Um." I hate to say it. "Chairman Yeh's kid."

As the guard opens the book, two guys behind us say, "The son? It's the son?"

"Yeh is a common name." The guard squints at my photo, then my face. "I'm not aware the chairman has a son. He has a nephew."

The Buried Yeh strikes again.

"I'm his *son*," I say.

"Your badge?"

"I don't have one."

More of the crowd is listening in. Muttering. The second guard flips through my passport. "You look like Mr. Yeh," he says dubiously, but the first says, "We can't admit anyone without a badge or authorized escort."

Something heavy hits the back of my head. "Ow! What the fuck?"

"Hold fire!" a man in the crowd shouts. "This is a peaceful protest!"

"A sandbag." Sophie picks up a black sandwich-sized bag tied with twine.

I'm getting nailed for Ba's sins—can this get any more ironic? Another bag whizzes by my ear.

"Can we talk about this inside, please?" Sophie urges the guards.

"We aren't letting anyone in right now."

"We're here for a school project," I say. "Call my Aunty Three—Rose Chan."

"She's tied up managing this emergency."

Another bag hits the barrier and explodes in a cloud of sand. Another grazes my shoulder and I set a hand to Sophie's back, maneuvering her in front of me and out of the line of fire. Clearly, there's a lot going on with Dragon Leaf . . . but we only have this weekend.

"Can we call my aunt?" I ask urgently. "She's expecting—"

One of the doors cracks open behind the guards. The Douche Lord appears, hair damp as though he just rinsed his head in a sink, a succulent half-eaten starfruit in hand.

"It's all right, gentlemen. They're with me."

"Lin-Bian." The guards' faces relax a fraction. "Apologies, we didn't realize."

The Douche Lord is the master of smirking without actually smirking. Having him bail me out is like snorting silt from the wharf. Which I'd rather do than accept his help.

"Ow!" Sophie says. "Get 'em!" someone yells.

Sand bags are flying everywhere. I shove her ahead of me as another bag bruises my back between my shoulder blades. Then the back of my head. A volley of them flies.

"Go, go, go!" I yell.

25

SOPHIE

What the hell have I gotten myself into?

I rub the sore spot on my shoulder. We are in an outdoor courtyard, with the anti-Xavier's-dad chants reverberating through the closed doors.

All I wanted was to nail my project proposal so I could impress Professor Horvath and get into his CS class. Now I'm halfway around the world, smack in the middle of some family feud AND social unrest . . . all because I'm chasing my crazy idea for a fashion bot.

And Xavier couldn't even get into his own family's headquarters! Anyone else would have thrown a shit fit, but not him. And now what? He can't film with these protestors in the way, and I can't meet his aunt if she's tied up with them—but of course his family has much bigger fish to fry than two school projects.

"Who are all those people?" Xavier asks, rubbing the back of his head.

"They were fired from Dragon Leaf last week," Victor says. "Mass layoff."

"Why? Dragon Leaf is a gold mine."

"You're so naive, Xiang-Ping."

Xavier's nostrils flare. "Whatever. We just need to find Aunty Three."

"Let's get inside." Victor leads us toward a sleek black building trimmed with red beams. It's jarringly modern in the middle of tradition, like an iPad in a hand-carved antique trunk. But I like it. I'd snap more photos if we weren't in the middle of outrunning this storm.

Inside, a high-ceilinged lobby is lit by white globes. Three oil portraits of men hang on the wall, probably Xavier's great-grandpa and grandpa, with Xavier's dad at the end. Two receptionists on headsets wave from behind a granite desk.

"This way." Victor leads us past them, through an archway.

We step into a hangar-like museum. Chic red lanterns, square bottomed with plump cloth sides, sway from the black ceiling, like a field of poppies with glowing hearts. Below them, futuristic vehicles are parked in roped-off squares: a sleek three-wheeler with a glass roof and an enormous front wheel. A red vintage-style electric car.

"This is the showroom," Victor tells me.

Much more what I expected of Dragon Leaf. I just hope

everything's okay. Xavier's trying to ignore it, but that's getting harder. I can still hear the crowd.

"Is Aunty Rose here?" Xavier asks. I look for a woman who could be her, but only see a few men probing a machine. So much amazing tech. I can't wait to see the Magic Mirror app.

"If she's around, she'll be in her warehouse in the back. Let's head there."

"Xavier, should we film this?" I ask. As much as I can, I need to keep his project on track, too.

"Yeah." He seems distracted but lifts his video camera to eye level. A small green light shines. "This is the stuff Dragon Leaf shows off to VIP guests," he says.

"How many minutes of footage do you need?" Victor asks.

"It's for a six-minute film," Xavier says. "I don't know yet."

"You need a plan," Victor says. "A list of shots, how X minutes of footage translates to this much for the final cut, that kind of thing."

"I don't know yet, okay?" Xavier says heatedly. "That's why I'm here. I'll film whatever makes sense. Symbols. Mooncakes."

"I'd say it's your funeral, but unfortunately it's mine, too," Victor says.

Xavier ignores him and points his camera at the cars.

While he films, I open Instagram to update the others. A flood of #LoveboatReunion posts have swamped my notifications: Ever and Rick toasting bubble-tea cups, Spencer and Priscilla at the Taiwan parliament—the gang is hitting up all of Taipei: the zoo, the markets, even the Chien Tan campus.

Another thirty alum have flown in from Europe and Asia for the gathering at Taipei 101, which has jumped to 110 people. Whoa, that's a lot of people to keep happy. I make a mental note to up the reservation numbers. I hope we haven't passed the cap.

But overall, I love the rush of energy. I go live on video, and a hundred people tune in immediately.

"Hey, gang! I'm here at the *incredible* Dragon Leaf showroom and—"

"Um, Sophie, you're not allowed to video here without permission," Victor says gently.

"I give her permission," Xavier snaps.

"Um, right." Lovely. A hundred people listening to me getting busted and the cousins fighting. "Well, we're going to hear some secrets about their fashion tech, so I'll have to shut this off, but if I can swing it, I'll try to get you some inside looks."

I shut off the livestream. A comment on my feed jumps out at me:

What cheap clothing. She can't be his girlfriend.
Aw, I think they're cute together.

Wait . . . me?

I open a collection posted by Bert. The top photo is innocent enough—the thousand-dollar bottle of wine—probably how he slipped through the PR scrubbing machine. But the photo behind it, sure enough, is of me dancing with Xavier. His hand is on my waist and my arms are draped around his neck, and we're pressed together in a way that makes my body remember that moment too keenly. He wanted me then. I'd felt it.

I shiver and tear my eyes away.

Sophie: Hello! I'm not his girlfriend!

"You okay, Sophie?" Xavier asks.

And why must he always pick up on my moods?

"It's the feed—" I break off as another line jumps out at me.

This reunion better be worth it. I'm paying a lot for my plane ticket. Counting on you, @Sophie!

Ugh!

"Nothing's wrong." I pocket my phone, but despite all the heartwarming #LoveboatReunion posts, a bad taste lingers in my mouth. I try to push the zingers from my mind as Victor points out a metal pod with bat-like wings.

"This is a personalized aircraft. It actually flies."

Xavier lifts his camera. A few exhibits down, a group of men gather around a hospital bed. Long robot arms operate on a life-sized dummy.

"Lots of cool inventions underway," Victor says, "but Dragon Leaf has been selling the same electronics, gaming, and health-care tech for fifty years. Competition is catching up. Hence the layoffs."

"This is why Ba was so pissed about bad PR?"

"It's not just *bad PR*." Victor's scathing again. He's turned into a guy who *would* throw a shit fit if the guards didn't know him. If I hadn't met him first as the super-helpful TA, I wouldn't recognize him now. "These days, anyone can be taken down because of one bad tweet about a customer treated badly in one of their stores. You fly in like a Roman emperor on a bacchanal while our former employees are out in the streets. We're facing hundreds of bad tweets, even with Jane playing whack-a-mole. Now a private equity firm, the Crusaders, is trying to take over the company."

"The Crusaders?"

"Like their name. They conquer and destroy."

"Ba will never sell," Xavier says. "Dragon Leaf's been in the family over a hundred years. He's run it since he learned to crawl. I played here when I was a kid."

"You really are so stup—"

"Stop it," I say. I don't care who Victor is. "Seriously, Victor. Enough."

Victor glances at me, surprised. Xavier touches my elbow briefly: *thanks*. I'm in his business again, but maybe it's okay this time. He'd do the same for me.

"It's, uh, not only up to your dad," Victor continues in a less-asshole tone. "Grandpa and your dad hold a chunk of Dragon Leaf, our aunts have tiny stakes, the rest is held by distant cousins and random people who've bought shares over the years. They can sell to the Crusaders and walk away with money in their pockets. By themselves not a problem, but all

214

their shares combined in one fist controls the company."

"What about your dad?" Xavier asks.

"*My* dad?" Victor's jaw clenches again. A divot appears at its edge. "Did you see *his* oil portrait in the lobby?"

Xavier frowns, thinking. I'm not sure either—was it there?

"Forget it. Point is, the family's entire legacy is at stake," Victor says. "And all you care about is your keg party in the sky."

Xavier flushes. "Don't you have something better to do than babysit?"

"Unfortunately, your dad gave me strict orders," Victor says. "Don't let you screw up your little high school report, or he'll extract a pound of flesh—from me."

Victor yanks opens a door in the far wall. The door itself is plain, but a delicate perfume wafts from a magical kingdom inside, of bright clothing hung on a hundred racks. For a moment, all I can do is gape with my mouth open. Is this real?

"Magic Silk warehouse," Victor says. "If Aunty Rose is around, she'll be here."

26

XAVIER

Sophie's face is like a kid on Christmas morning as she moves into the warehouse. She picks up a pair of boots, a fur shawl, a beaded dress. The space is one story high, snug, with one wall all made of shelves, loaded with bolts of embroidered cotton and Thai silks, hat boxes, funky leather boots. A maze of clothing racks disappear around a corner.

It's a workspace, a storage space for inventory, not a show-room set up for the public. But Sophie turns in an awed circle, taking in the antique handheld mirror logo painted on the wall, the rows of high-heeled shoes, purses, folded sweaters, and all the dresses hung everywhere.

Hearing her defend me against the Douche Lord was a bit surreal. I've had to block his darts on my own my whole life. It's one of those things that wears you down to the point you can't keep fighting. Maybe this was what Ma meant when she said none of us were meant to go it alone.

And now my mind is spinning with all the stuff going down with my family: the protests, Ba's face on the sandbags, the Crusaders. I had no idea. Head in the sand is probably fair. I've always assumed Dragon Leaf was untouchable. Unbreakable. Then again, it's never been my business.

"Did you say you used to play in here?" Sophie turns to me.

"Yeah. Weird to be back. It's been so long." I pan the room with my camera. All this footage could be useful. A woman points a scanner gun at a tag on a scarf. Another sorts through racks of clothes organized by colors and materials: reds, creams, pastels, prints, silks, faux furs. A sewing machine hums somewhere in the back. "I used to pull the fabrics over my head to turn the world different patterns."

I home in on Sophie as she pulls out a pink T-shirt with a graphic of a chocolate-chip cookie. "'You my love have eyes like a cookie, nose like a cookie, and ears like a cookie.'" She laughs. "What is this?"

"I actually remember that," I say. "It's their bad stationery T-shirt collection. It was supposed to be a big failure, but people loved it. Guess they're still selling them."

"They're funny." She pulls another one out: a sketch of chopsticks holding a dumpling. "'You and I go together like dumplings and soy sauce.' Ha! This place is truly magic. Anything's possible."

I follow her with the camera as she runs her hand along a row of satin ball gowns. Sometimes bright colors around a person can wash them out, but with Sophie, they bring her to life. I capture the clean lines of her profile. The bursts of energy that propel her from one space to another.

She faces me, then jumps, eyes widening. "Oh! I didn't realize you were filming me." Even more coral coloring infuses her cheeks.

"Keep going. You're a natural at this."

"At admiring clothes?"

"No, dork. Being on camera." I try to find the right words to explain. "You wear all your emotions on your outside. It's like . . . sunbeams. Spilling out."

"Sunbeams?"

Ugh, now who's the dork? "Sorry, I suck at words. That's not exactly it."

Sophie's mouth twitches. "You don't suck at words. And I actually kind of love it." Her smile makes me think again of last night. No matter what she said, it isn't something I can just forget . . . even if I know I have to.

She points to an automated bagging machine sheathing cocktail dresses in clear plastic. She puts on her formal voice: "Fashion meets tech. Check it out. All state of the art." I swing the camera to pan the robotic arm moving the bags to a rack.

"Where are those going?" Sophie asks a girl with purple pixie-style hair and a jewel-studded coat.

"To the docks. We're shipping them to customers."

"Where?" I ask.

"Japan, Singapore, a plane to Europe. Everything goes from here to the world." She drops a note into a box of printed silks.

"And what are those?" Sophie asks.

"Scarves from a woman's cooperative in Peru. Ms. Chan has us send them out with our merchandise. Trying to help get their names out."

"That's great." Sophie glances at me. "Your PR folks should get *that* out."

"I'm just the floor manager."

"Do you know where Ms. Chan is?" I ask. Sophie gives me a quizzical glance, but I'd rather not identify myself if I don't have to.

"She's managing the crisis outside, but if I see her, I'll tell her you're looking for her." The girl heads off with the box.

"SO incredible," Sophie says. "I can't wait to talk to your aunt."

"She must be here somewhere." We move deeper in, searching until we come to a balcony railing overlooking a small living room below. A spiral staircase leads down to blue silk couches patterned with large magnolias. It's a little oasis for guests. Ma used to sit here with cups of tea when we visited.

To my surprise, my great-aunts are down there, snowy-white hair, in matching lavender and turquoise kimonos that remind me of a pair of slippers. Great-Aunty Two is seated at a table, drawing a calligraphy brush over a long scroll half full of inky characters. Great-Aunty One has fallen asleep on a chaise with a woolly white blanket drawn to her waist.

My throat aches with an unexpected sense of loss. I've been so focused on Ba and Aunty Three that I hadn't expected to run into them here. Although come to think of it, they were almost always here. They were close to Ma. I remember lotus seed cakes, the scent of white flower oil, silk softness against my cheek. Mostly, a gentle presence. I haven't seen them in several years, and only now do I realize that I've missed them.

"Who are they?" Sophie asks, hushed.

Great-Aunty One lets out a snore and rolls over. Her white blanket slips, and Two sets down her brush and retrieves it from the floor.

"My grandpa's sisters." I raise my camera as she draws it back over One. "The sleeping one is Ako and the other is Yumiko."

"Japanese names."

"Yes, nicknames, but everyone uses them. They must like hanging out here if they're still coming."

"They're so elegant."

Yes, that's exactly what my great-aunts are. Love and pride well inside me as I snap another photo.

"Let's go meet them. I'll introduce you—"

"Xavier, you're supposed to be filming for your project," says my cousin. "It's already nine thirty. You need to get to your place by eleven thirty to interview Ye-Ye."

Great, the Douche Lord is back, rolling his sleeves to his elbows.

"It's none of your business what I film." And maybe I am

filming for my project. I don't know yet.

The Douche Lord turns to Sophie. "Did he tell you about our booth at the festival when we were little?"

I know exactly where this story's going. "Fuck you," I say.

"No," she says, confused.

"People joke about tiger moms, but they don't know what it's like to have a tiger grandpa. Ours insisted every grandkid contribute to the family booth at the festival. So little Xavier shows up with his arms full of photos he's taken with his new camera, and he expects people are going to fall over their feet buying them—"

"I did not—"

"—and all weekend, with thousands of people coming through that booth, he sells . . ." He holds up a finger. "One."

I'd come back eager to see my sales, only to face the Douche Lord so puffed up with glee he could have floated to the moon. I'd wished he would and never come back.

"What would *you* film here?" Sophie asks him.

Who cares? Does she really want to know?

"I *wouldn't* film here for a Yeh documentary, that's my point," he answers. "Here, look."

I make an impatient noise as the Douche Lord opens Instagram on his phone. He flicks his fingers through a carousel of asshole photos: him in a silver vest at a Dragon Leaf gala with Taiwan's President. Him on a grassy golf course with a sharply dressed woman in white.

"You know the dean of Dartmouth?" Sophie looks impressed,

221

which is exactly why the Douche Lord takes those photos.

"Dragon Leaf is a major donor at Dartmouth. Xavier could take photos like these, too . . . but he doesn't."

"Why would I want to take photos with deans?"

He growls with disgust. "Your brain moves a hundred miles per hour in the wrong direction. I can't even explain. Watch this. I'll go live for a minute."

He films himself in English, then, for good measure, translates to Mandarin. "Hey, guys, I'm in Taipei babysitting my cousin. Yeah. I'm sweet that way. I'm also here with my Dartmouth friend Sophie Ha. Say hi to her, will you? Follow her on Instagram."

He pans his camera in Sophie's direction, and after a startled pause, she waves.

"Hi," she says.

He points the phone back to himself. "I'll be giving my speech at the Moon Festival tomorrow night, so check in then if you can. Night all." He shuts it off. "A thousand people watched that ten-second clip. More will overnight."

"A thousand?" Sophie's awed.

"All right, kids. I need to prep for my speech. Xavier, find Aunty Three for Sophie. You need to leave here by eleven." He heads off. Hopefully to flush himself down a toilet.

"His Instagram is perfect," Sophie says.

So she's Team Turd now? "Well, I have better things to spend my brainpower on than plotting my next pose."

"I didn't mean it that way. It was perfect—like the Yeh image. But . . . cold? Distant?"

222

Oh. So maybe she does see through him. "Sophie, I should—"

"Don't say my name," she snaps.

"What? Why not?"

"Xiang-Ping, my darling." Great-Aunty Two is coming up the spiral stairs toward us, smoothing her lavender kimono. She wraps her light arms around my neck, smelling of a delicate ointment. She gives my cheek a light pinch. "Xiang-Ping, you look like your father."

I catch Sophie's eye. Every kid probably hates to be told this, but I have to believe I hate it more than anyone else. But Great-Aunty Two took Ma under her wing, and so I don't have the heart to contradict her.

"I caught some photos of you and Great-Aunty One." I show her the screen on my camera.

"Do I look that young?" She runs a hand over her white hair. The skin under her eyes is soft and wrinkled, but her gaze is bright.

"It's exactly you."

"That is the nicest photo I've seen since my hair went white. May I have it?"

Why can't the rest of my family be like my great-aunts?

"Sure, I'll send it to you."

She smiles at Sophie. "Great-Aunty One and I always said this one was a charmer without trying. Even at three, he was the only grandchild who wasn't afraid of my kisses." She pinches my nose and plants a kiss on my cheek. Hilarious—she's trying to impress Sophie for me. Sophie silently laughs at me with her

223

eyes, and I grin back. Somehow I don't mind her seeing me like this. "But don't waste your charms on me, Xiang-Ping. I don't have any power to help you. You need your ba for that."

Must she remind me?

"Your ba is a good man," she says, reading my mind. "He looks out for your old aunties. Not everyone in our family does."

Right. A good man who smacks his kid around in front of all his friends. How does that fit with the guy she's talking about?

"Who's your beautiful companion?"

Sophie's cheeks pink. But it's a gentle reminder of my bad manners. She used to do that when I was little, nudges I didn't mind, *Xiang-Ping, come greet your Ye-Ye. Xiang-Ping, shake Uncle Pei's hand.* So different than yanking off my ear.

"This is Sophie. We're here to meet Aunty Three. Sophie, this is my second great-aunt, my grandpa's younger sister."

"I like your slippers," Sophie says.

Great-Aunty Two flexes her tiny foot: lavender silk, close-toed like ballerina flats, embroidered with white blossoms.

"Thank you, dear. That's my big sister downstairs. She's very tired." Great-Aunty Two smiles at Sophie. "Please help yourself to anything here you like."

Sophie's eyes widen. "Really?"

Great-Aunty Two is already toddling back down to her sister.

"She's shy around strangers," I explain. "My grandpa sort of overshadows everyone. But yes, she's serious about helping yourself. These are floor samples and can't be sold. My aunts

224

give a shopping pass to employees of the month, and they get to come pick out two items."

"How do I get a job like *that*?"

I snort. "You can get any job you want. *I'm* the one who can't get a job." I sober, that odd hollow ache now in my chest. "My great-aunts loved my mom. They care about me. But I've been in the States all these years. And until now, I never—"

My voice trails off. I'm not sure what I'm trying to say. The picture I took says it all.

"Xiang-Ping, there you are."

We both jump. Aunty Three is powering toward us, her wavy reddish-brown hair floating like a short cape behind her. Her rosebud-themed jeans, under a matching leather jacket, make her look even younger than Lulu. But her face is unfriendly. Not a good sign. I take a step toward her, trying to close a gap that feels too large to cross.

"Um, hi, Aunty Three. Thanks for meeting us."

"Lulu asked me to take the meeting." She stops an arm's length away and wraps her hands around her elbows. "I have a packed day, but I understand this is for a project at Dartmouth. How can I help?"

After my great-aunt's warmth, her prickliness is a splash of cold water. Sophie doesn't seem to notice.

"Hi, I'm Sophie." She pumps Aunty Three's hand up and down. "I'm a *huge* fan of the Magic Silk clothing lines. All the risks you take with patterns and *shapes*, like the Empress Cloud last year with those layers of silver tulle—the clothes *danced* on your models."

"Yes, the Empress Cloud was quite the sensation. What can I do for you?" Aunty Three is slightly less hostile. Sophie working her magic.

"I came to ask you about your AI stylist app. I'm trying to make one myself. I was hoping I could ask you questions and get a demo. It's only for school. I mean, I'm not going to steal your secrets." Sophie pulls out her phone and hands a blue icon to Aunty Three. "This is the shell of my Mirror, Mirror app. I'm just getting started."

Aunty Three flips through Sophie's app. "Nice design. You have a real eye for color."

"Thank you."

"But our Magic Mirror isn't an app." She hands her phone back.

"It's not?" Sophie's smile goes out like a storm has passed overhead. "Did I misunderstand?"

Aunty Three crosses to two blanket-covered pieces of furniture against the wall. They're wardrobe-sized—taller than her. She catches hold of one blanket, carefully unsnagging it from the wood beneath.

"It's right here," Aunty Three says, and tugs it off.

27

SOPHIE

Xavier's aunt seems wary of me. She probably has a lot of people wanting her attention, and maybe she's not sure she can trust me, or even Xavier, with all the bad blood in their family. But I'm already in love with the world she's created inside these walls—stylish, warm, and exciting all at once. Her outfit is jarring and chaotic—the boxy mauve jacket over pants with rosebuds floating on blue the color of the Caribbean Sea, a paisley scarf holding back her wavy hair. The effect is like the buzz of electricity from an eel.

I want her to like me. I want her to *trust* me.

At her tug, the silk blanket parachutes down to reveal chrome bars forming an open box like a small elevator. Purple velvet curtains hang at each corner. A pad on the floor with two gold footprints tells the user where to stand, facing a screen that forms the box's back wall.

She tugs the second blanket off to reveal . . .

A three-way mirror.

Three identical panels framed by intricately wrought steel. The pattern is familiar: the Dragon Leaf dragon undulating among festive moon lanterns.

"Wasn't this my mom's mirror?" Xavier's wondering expression grows larger in the three panels. He runs his thumb down one dragony edge. "She had it in her room."

"It was originally your grandmother's—your father's mother. She and my aunts designed it, and the dragons inspired the Dragon Leaf logo."

Xavier frowns. "I didn't know that."

"They stay out of the spotlight," Aunty Three says. "But everything lovable about Dragon Leaf, down to its logo and the shade of lighting in every store, was designed by them. They've been the tastemakers behind the scenes for the last fifty years."

"No wonder they blend into the operation." I smile. "They *are* the operation."

"*That* explains why I like the logo," Xavier says.

"Your ba gifted this mirror to your ma for their wedding. Shortly before she passed away, she bequeathed it to me for my project."

I approach the mirror. My own tripled reflection, in my purple jumpsuit with the cowled neckline, gazes back at me.

"There's a lag," I say. "This isn't a regular mirror."

"Sharp eye," Aunty Three says. "I've been trying to get rid of the delay." She points to a tiny lens hidden against the curved body of a dragon in the middle panel's top frame. Then to another lens on each side and at the bottom. "Four cameras interpolating. May I introduce . . . the Magic Mirror."

She doesn't sound like a proud inventor at all. More deflated. But a surge of excitement courses through my body.

"How does it work?"

"First we scan you in this kiosk." She runs a sturdy hand down a chrome bar. "Sixteen infrared cameras create a digital avatar of your body. Once the system has your measurements, it generates your three-dimensional image. The tool will identify which clothes in our system fit your body, and reduce your selection from tens of thousands to hundreds. You pick what you like, and the tool shows you what they look like on your body, without the effort of locating and changing physical clothes. If you like something, add it to your wishlist or order directly."

"So your customers can try on your clothes, and you don't even need them in stock."

"Yes, and only clothes that fit. Saves them time."

"Amazing!"

"Can Sophie try it?" Xavier asks, and I shoot him a grateful look.

"Oh, yes! Could I?"

"It's not ready for public use . . ." Aunty Three begins, but then hands me a large alligator hair clip. "Here, tie your hair back. Best if you remove your clothes to scan your body."

I twist my hair into a knot and pin its weight on my head. Xavier snaps a photo—um, why does he keep taking my picture? I step into the box, and Aunty Three draws the four curtains shut around me, darkening the space. My reflection mimics me removing my jumpsuit to reveal my black bra and panties. And Xavier's right on the other side of this flimsy curtain.

I gaze at my nearly naked self. "Do I, uh, take off . . . everything?"

"You may leave on your underwear. Hand me your outfit." I pass it through a slit in the curtain, feeling vulnerable inside here. "Now follow the instructions."

Two glowing red dots appear to either side of my reflection. A robotic voice says, "Raise your arms and touch the circles."

I lift my arms until my reflection's hands hit the circles. They pulsate. A whirring noise sounds, and a horizontal beam of light runs down the mirror from my head to toes.

In place of my reflection, a charcoal-gray avatar appears. Like a plaster cast of me, with my exact form, every curve visible. It could have been creepy, but it's so well designed that it's more like a lovable doll.

"It's done." Aunty Three hands me my jumpsuit, and I climb swiftly back into it. I'm still zipping up when Aunty Three draws back the curtains to expose my avatar.

"Nice," Xavier says, and I snatch the curtain back to hide it from his view.

"Not for the film!"

"Whoops, sorry." He flashes an apologetic smile, lowering

his camera. But the mischievous gleam in his eyes makes a curl of pleasure unfold in my spine. "This is really something."

"Do you have an occasion to plan?" Aunty Three taps an electronic tablet in her hand.

I finish yanking up my zipper. "We're going to a party at Taipei 101 tonight." And now that I've seen this warehouse, I realize how woefully underdressed I will be. Thanks to my tiny backpack.

She hands me the tablet, which glows pale green with a smart, front-drape dress. "Here's our special occasions collection. Pick out whatever you'd like to try."

"She'll never leave. This is like a candy store for Sophie," Xavier says.

"Fashion is art that you wear," I declare.

"I buy that," he says.

I scroll through the delicious outfits. "These are all *real*?"

"Yes, there are over fifty thousand pieces in the catalog."

A robin's-egg-blue gown embroidered with a garden's worth of flowers jumps out at me. It's more girly than what even I wear, but it's a serious work of art.

"Go ahead," she urges.

"This one." I tap the select button. "This one." She has me choose from among woven metal belts, Tahitian pearls, pendant necklaces, crystal brooches, and more styles of footwear than I knew existed.

"That should be enough." She takes the tablet back. "Let's run it."

I reposition myself before the three mirrors. "I look better in the glass than in real life."

"I've added enhancers," Aunty Three says.

My images blur, and then . . . I'm wearing the embroidered blue dress over black snakeskin boots. Silvery tassel earrings dangle from my ears.

"Whoa," Xavier says.

I span my waist with my hands. "It fits *perfectly*. The tones don't match—the blue is cool, the brownish undertones in the boots are warm, but they're *to die for* . . . this is truly magic!"

Aunty Three smiles. "It started as a school project for me, like you."

"Really?"

"My father wanted me to go to a girls' finishing school. But I wanted to go to the National Taiwan University of Science and Technology. Xavier's father convinced him to let me go."

"*My* dad?" Xavier's surprised.

"Yes. Your ye-ye thought it was a waste, so your ba paid my way." She raises her tablet. "Ready for more?"

For the next half hour, I model dozens of the outfits I'd picked. A black floor-length gown with white organza cutting an elongated triangle into it from shoulder to toe. A juicy blue trench coat over pants leaping with jungle animals. A crimson shirtdress bleeding threads, with a slightly undone effect. Xavier snaps a photo of every new style while keeping his video camera rolling. I don't see how this will be helpful to his film, or even if his secretive aunt will allow any of it to be used, but since

I can't buy any of these dresses myself, at least I'll get to drool over the photos.

"It's working," Aunty Three sounds pleased. "It's been a while since I tried it on a new person."

"So can it find *new* looks for me?" I ask. "Clothes I haven't picked out?"

"No, but the catalog reduces your choices to outfits that fit you. Measuring the inventory was hard work."

"And you can do so much more!" I say. "Instead of having your customers flip through the catalog, you can use AI to learn what they like and make recommendations. Here, let me show you."

I open my app on my phone. It's basic—nothing compared to hers—but I demonstrate the concept. "It figures out what qualities flatter your body type, like a square neckline versus high collar. Then it scours shops on the internet for matches. It could even recommend changes—adding cap sleeves, an empire waist—if someone wants to customize clothing."

"That's a very ambitious school project."

"Yes, well . . ." Does she mean unrealistic?

"But achievable," she adds quickly. "Very much so."

I smile, encouraged. "It might take longer than one term to reach the final version."

"And some teammates."

"Yes. And the goal is, you won't have to find clothes that fit and flatter you—those clothes find *you*!"

"I love that." Aunty Three's eyes have brightened. "For us

especially, since we source clothing and accessories from thirty different countries, Thailand, Mozambique, India—and we have so many seamstresses and tailors who could customize. We have infinite combinations, and the hope has always been for this Magic Mirror to help these dressmakers get discovered." She types rapidly on her tablet. "Let me have the system make random recommendations based on fit, for starters. Let's see how it does."

In the Mirror, new looks cycle over my body. A sophisticated sarong of Indonesian batik. A black catsuit with a slinky silhouette. A flirty silver gown pouring down from V-shaped shoulders, embedded in the otherworldly empress cloud of silver tulle that I admired online. Summer Sophie. Goth Sophie.

I catch Xavier's eye. "What are you smirking at?" I demand.

His smirk deepens, dimpling his cheek. "Watching you try on one ridiculous outfit after another."

"They're not ridiculous." A puffy pink mesh dress marshmallows onto me. "Okay, this one is."

He laughs and snaps a photo. I give him a mock scowl.

"Which do you like best, Sophie?" Aunty Three's smiling.

"The turquoise Taroni silk gown, with the hand-painted dragons. It's ethereal and romantic and strong all at once. But not with the pumps—with the snakeskin boots. They work thematically. The blue brings out the orange in the boots."

"Nice," Xavier says.

"I like it. I'll order them drone delivered." She taps on her iPad.

"Oh, thank you!" She's like Xavier, impossibly generous. "I'll be super careful and have them cleaned before I give them back, of course."

"They're yours."

"Oh! I couldn't!" Several thousand dollars worth of fabric and workmanship, not to mention it's *Magic Silk*.

"You're helping me with my project, Sophie," Xavier says.

This is more that I can ever repay, but I have no willpower to resist.

"Thank you," I say. "Xavier, what about you? You need something for the reunion." I grin. "And you *definitely* need an avatar."

I half expect him to refuse, but he powers down his camera. "Yeah, can't refuse that." He disappears into the curtained box.

Ten minutes later, Xavier's three images are blurring in the Mirror with randomly generated outfits:

#1 Formal Xavier, black tux with tails: "I'm going to my own funeral."

#2 Bad-boy Xavier, moody leather jacket over skinny jeans: "Trying too hard."

#3 Stylish Xavier, electric-blue jacket framing a white ruffle shirt: "How the press team would dress me. No thanks."

I can't stop laughing—both at how badly it's getting him, and his running commentary.

#4 is . . . regal. A navy suit with a high mandarin collar cut by a row of gold buttons.

Now it's my turn to snap a photo.

"Prince Xavier," I tease. He quirks his royal brow at me. I blow him a kiss.

Oops.

I drop my gaze. It's so weird. No matter what pact we agreed on, no matter how I mean to keep my distance, we just fall back into this easy flirty banter that's almost more intimate than we were last night. I'm glad when his outfit blurs and changes again, bringing us back to the task at hand.

#5 Another Xavier I haven't seen before. Silvery-lilac pants and a powdery-white shirt under a satin beige overcoat. Muted but artsy. A color palette for eyeshadow, the opposite of the silvery-black he wore all summer, with a touch of mystery—I like it.

"I'll take this, Aunty Three," he says, surprising me. So he likes it, too.

"Excellent." She runs her finger down her tablet and taps twice.

"This is seriously a miracle," I say. I prop myself on the edge of a display table. My mind races with the data we would need to help it make better recommendations—the hard data Professor Horvath wants: clothing categorized not just by measurements, but by body types, styles, color, even how it makes you feel. I could build a program to go through reviews for key words and phrases, like "This outfit makes me feel strong," and tag them. Horvath will be blown away. "I'll send you my questionnaire for your system. But for it to *really* work, it should be able to read us. Our mood, our personality, even the different sides of us."

"That would be the holy grail," Aunty Three says.

"Ms. Chan?" The purple-pixie-haired girl hands a clipboard

and pen to her. "The accountant dropped off the papers."

"Thank you, dear." Aunty Three signs, then fishes in her Prada purse for a soapstone chop—round like a tube of lipstick. The girl unscrews a pad of red ink, and Aunty Three stamps a red square beside her signature.

"You sign with a chop?" I ask as the girl heads off.

"In Taiwan, we are still old-fashioned like this." She tissues the ink off the chop's end.

"I used to go with Ba to the bank." Xavier frowns, like he'd rather not remember. "He always stamped his passbook there."

"Yes, that's how it's done. And you accompanying him. It's part of our culture, for our children to be part of the family business. Lulu has sat in on meetings since she was eight, learning to entertain business associates."

"Hey, Xiang-Ping, wrapping up yet?" Victor is moving toward us, another starfruit in hand. I turn to face him, a bit wary. I don't want any more fighting, especially not in front of Aunty Three.

"We're stopping by Sophie's aunt's first," Xavier says shortly. "To drop off her stuff."

"Better hurry. It's almost eleven." His eyes flit over the Mirror. "What's this?"

"It's a styling mirror," I say. "It lets you try clothes in any combination—seriously, pure genius."

"Maybe it can pick an outfit for my dad." Victor pops the last bite into his mouth. "He could use fashion advice."

Aunty Three gives a short laugh and sets down her tablet.

"We all know Edward's not interested."

In a line, he's managed to rob all her joy. I frown at Victor. "This isn't a joke."

"Sorry, Sophie." He's sincere. "Didn't mean it that way."

But is that how Professor Horvath will react? A pat on the head, but . . . no thanks?

"You're right to be skeptical. It's a gimmick." Aunty Three throws the silk blanket back over the Mirror. "We may be shutting it down."

"What? But why?" I ask, dismayed.

"We're shutting down all of Fashion." All the light has gone out of her, and her face is grim again. "Those people outside were my employees in my warehouse and stores. Another twenty-five hundred entrepreneurs in thirty developing countries, the ones who provide all our materials, fabrics, buttons, zippers, clasps, accessories, jewelry. Fair trade—they're being cut off, too."

Xavier lowers his video camera. "Ba's shutting you down?"

"Oh, no. Fashion falls under your Uncle Edward. He made the call."

"Dragon Leaf is outdated." Victor crosses his arms. "My dad says trees need to be pruned to let other parts flourish. The Crusaders—"

"Want to demolish this historic building," Aunty Rose says.

"Every other global business has moved to Taipei 101. Better yet, they've got a *view* of Taipei 101. We're still here by the wharf, like peddlers."

"I love it here," I say. "It's amazing to have modern businesses rebuilding here."

"Our family has been on this wharf for two hundred years, even before Dragon Leaf was formed," Aunty Three says. "Side by side with rice, then tea and textiles. If you think about it, my little unit is the only part still carrying out our original business in the fabric trade." She lays a hand on the box's edge and looks sadly at it. "Two decades of work. Edward told me it was a fairy tale, like its name. I should have listened."

Aunty Three starts to throw the second blanket over the avatar box, but I seize hold of it. "It's not a fairy tale! You were ahead of your time. You're *still* ahead! I can't even imagine the technology you had to bring together to make it work. Cameras, computer vision, augmented reality, motion detection—"

"I appreciate your enthusiasm, Sophie." Her smile doesn't reach her eyes. "You may share this interview with your professor. I'll have my assistant give you written permission. Secrecy no longer matters."

"Let me help." My fingers tighten on the cloth. "I can prove the Mirror matters."

A knock sounds on the door. "That will be your order." Aunty Three crosses to it while I exchange a frustrated glance with Xavier. She returns with a shallow cardboard box.

I open my mouth. "Aunty Three, please let me—"

"Your new clothes." She sets the box in my arms, ending the conversation. "Enjoy your evening, dears."

A storm rages inside me as Aunty Three escorts us outside into a back alley, where our scooter has been moved to avoid the protestors. Birds circle madly overhead, and in the distance, the chants of "Oust him!" still echo off the bricks. Xavier's face is sober—and as for me, I've gotten my story, but it has an unhappy ending. Horvath will not be convinced by a fashion project shut down by its own company.

Victor slips past us toward his motorcycle. "I'll head over to your place, Xiang-Ping. Jane is going over my speech with me. Don't be late."

He climbs onto his seat, and the motor grates to life. As he disappears down the alley, I turn to Xavier. "I came all this way."

"It's a letdown, isn't it?"

He thinks he's not good with words . . . but how does he always nail just how I feel? A half step ahead of me, too.

"You can still write it up for your proposal." He gives my shoulder a comforting squeeze. "And we still have reunion. Trip's not a total loss."

I groan. "Reunion is out of control. We're up to a hundred fifty people now." But then an idea strikes. "Wait. Maybe we could do something there."

His eyes hold mine. "Show off the Mirror? Make-your-own avatar?"

"Exactly!" We're on the same mind beam again. I run back to the door and pound my fist on it. "Aunty Three!"

She opens it so suddenly that I fall into her, scratching my nose on a metal button on her jacket. She catches me by my arms and rights me again.

"Did you forget something?"

"We're trying to do the same thing," I blurt. "I'm trying to prove to my professor that this technology matters. You're trying to prove to Dragon Leaf that the Magic Mirror is worthy of resources. Why don't we work together?"

Her brows furrow. "What do you have in mind?"

"If you'd let us borrow the Magic Mirror for our party at Taipei 101 tonight, we have hundreds of people coming and following on social media—they'll be excited to support it. And we'll get all kinds of body types to train your recommendations. A hundred people, ten outfits each, liking or disliking the choices—that's a thousand samples right there."

"My family won't want the publicity. Even on social media."

"PR again! Don't you have any say?"

"The Fashion division is the smallest in Dragon Leaf. Less than a quarter of Healthcare and even smaller than Electronics. So when PR speaks, we listen."

"Tell them you had nothing to do with it," I say. "You lent it to me. I went rogue."

"I'd have to be the one to go rogue," Xavier says. "I'm not letting you get in trouble with them. It's what the family would expect anyways."

Aunty Three's brows have climbed into her forehead. "You two want me to subvert our own PR?"

"We could sell clothes!" I say. "Wouldn't that show it's working?"

"Even five sales would be a great beta test." Cautious optimism creeps into her eyes. "Xiang-Ping, you said your friend was a talent . . . you were right."

A talent? Xavier puts his hands in his pockets, and his foot scuffs the ground.

"I know the lead anchor for Taipei TV," Aunty Three continues. "I'll ask her to attend. I can't myself, as I have another engagement, but my assistant will arrange delivery and pickup. But please be careful. The Mirror is quite fragile."

"Perfect. I bet it's one of the most valuable pieces of tech in all of Dragon Leaf." Impulsively, I wrap my arms around her. Her body is warm, but she remains stiff, and I release her quickly. I've overstepped. Again. "Um, okay, great. See you later," I say awkwardly.

She nods, neutral. "Yes, come by after the party. Or in the morning. I'll be here."

I head toward the scooter with Xavier, who ties our clothing box onto the front rack.

"Hope I didn't offend her," I say. "Hugging her."

"My family doesn't hug. We've burned each other so much over the years that I'm surprised we didn't smell smoke when we drove up. My dad and my uncle control billions of dollars, but when Lulu's dad lost his job, she had to leave her private school for a year. No one offered them a loan, and they were too proud to ask. Everyone keeps their distance."

"Yet your dad sent Aunty Three to technical school, against your grandpa's wishes. "

"Surprised me. Same with the Mirror being a wedding gift for my mom."

"That was sweet," I admit.

"Was it real, though? When she defended me, he'd yell at her, too. Not the kind of thing you forget, you know?"

"Yeah. I don't know if my dad loved my mom and it just died, or what. I've accepted I don't have a dad. But yours . . . I'm not sure if . . ." I trail off. I don't want to make Xavier feel worse. But he picks up my train of thought.

"If it's worse to have him or not," he says grimly. He lifts his helmet onto his head. "I don't know either."

Our eyes lock a moment. His are dark, defiant. A bit of blood from his ear has stained the edge of his collar. I feel a pang in my chest. He came all this way for me. Will this trip be good for him, too? I want it to be. But his dad, his cousin, the protests and company pressures—it's such a tangled mess, and now he's being dragged into it.

"I don't want to do anything to make things worse for you," I say.

"How would you?" he asks grimly. "I just need to nail this film, get my trust, and get the hell out of Yeh-dom."

"Your aunt was cool, though." My phone buzzes with a text. "It's Aunty Three's assistant." With arrangements to meet me at Taipei 101 tonight. "Give me a sec. I'm going to give our friends a preview of Magic Mirror, too."

"Sure. I'll check the footage so far." Xavier lifts his camera while I open my Instagram to upload our Magic Mirror images.

A few pings have come in from the Loveboat chat—

> Jillian: Sorry, @Sophie, no luck with Singapore Airlines
> Lena: Can't help with flights, but here's the harvest moon in South Carolina! Love from here!

Oh, no. What if nothing comes through?

> Sophie: Let's keep trying.
> Sophie: Awesome! Post moons everywhere! It's the same moon!

I post the Magic Mirror photos from me and Xavier, write a quick explanation, then: Which would you choose?

I text Rick and Ever:

> Sophie: On our way to Aunty Claire's. See you there.
> Ever: Okay, we'll head over. Got forty mini boba teas for tonight!
> Sophie: YUM can't wait!

Emma's sent a photo of her blue-eyed self, white traveler's dress, nestled in a roomy plane cabin that looks half the size of Xavier's family jet. She's holding up two fingers and a glass of wine. I feel another surge of guilt about Xavier and me . . . but what can I say to her? He and I have our pact. And now that I've seen the complex world Xavier lives in, the kinds of pressures he's facing, I know she's exactly what he needs.

Even if it hurts to accept that.

"Emma's on her way," I say to Xavier. "She's excited to hang out with you again."

He fits his helmet back over his head. "Hope I don't disappoint her."

"Of course not! You'll pick up right where you left off."

I text Emma back.

> Emma, the Magic Mirror is awesome. I'm showing it off at the reunion tonight. I can't wait to share it with Horvath. And Victor is Xavier's cousin—did you know? I was so surprised!
> Xavier's excited to see you again!

Replies to my Magic Mirror post start coming in:

> I vote for the blue gown
> Those earrings are cool!
> Wish I could use it—I need a stylist!

My heart gives a little lurch. Even #TaipeiRides is getting flooded with new Loveboat customers, as I'd hoped. My plans . . . maybe they're already working.

With renewed confidence, I snap a badass photo of Xavier throwing his leg over the scooter and send it to Emma with a note:

Can't wait for fireworks to go off! :)

28

XAVIER

The bristly fronds of banyan trees swing aside as we zip by on the scooter, heading toward Sophie's aunt's place. She's driving, and her scent blowing in my face is taking my mind in all the wrong directions. Which, I have to admit, was also happening while I watched her in front of the Magic Mirror. But I kept focus. Because I know the project is the most important thing to her. And I'm going to do everything I can to get her to the finish line, which means helping Aunty Three, too.

I can see how Aunty Three's fashion avatar wouldn't get more than a few eye rolls from Uncle Edward and others in the bigger divisions of Dragon Leaf. So the fact that my dad's supported Aunty Three was surprising, but also not. Not surprising because my dad obviously saw what Sophie does—that fashion can be a serious moneymaker. Not to mention a business that our family's fortunes are rooted in. But Sophie's idea to help the Magic Mirror could be a real game changer. And getting Sophie and Aunty Three together? I made that happen.

If they actually can make magic together, it would mean I helped Dragon Leaf.

Not that it matters. But it's not something that's ever been a part of who I am. I don't know what that means, except that maybe, even by Yeh standards, I am not a total waste of space.

"So besides the interviews, what else do you want to film?" Sophie asks, breaking into my thoughts.

"I need to find symbols."

"Well, it's the Moon Festival. So . . . the moon?"

"What do you have in mind for it?"

"My mom says it symbolizes happiness, wholeness, and completion—that's why the Mid-Autumn Festival is the most perfect night ever. Mooncakes . . . I don't actually know what they symbolize, but I'm sure they symbolize something."

"Well, my family makes their one thousand mooncakes at my place."

"Ooo . . . let's shoot how they're made! That would be awesome on film."

She takes a wrong turn. "Other way," I say, and she loops a U-turn. "Sorry. Not trying to back-seat drive."

"It's fine. I don't know the roads. How do you?"

"Landmarks. I've always had to remember them. As a survival tactic." Street names are meaningless.

"I bet you have a lot of those. I could definitely use some pointers."

There's a different energy between us now. Not just because of the hookup. But maybe because, like she asked, I'm letting her in. And vice versa. To the real me and the real her.

Now I point to a red pagoda roof peeking from the greenery. "That temple there. We passed on the side of the street close to it on the way here. I keep track of stuff like that. And the view of Taipei 101, the angle changes as we—" My phone buzzes in my pocket. "Hold on." I fish it out. It's Jane, probably to adjust the schedule. "Hello?"

"Xiang-Ping, I'm with your father leaving the racetrack." A mash-up of voices in her background makes it hard to hear her. "He's been in an accident. We're headed to the hospital."

What? I can't absorb what she's saying at first.

"Ba doesn't have accidents." His world is too tightly managed, down to owning only the same black socks so he'll never have a mismatched pair. "Was it a racing accident? How?"

"He lost control of his car. We're not sure why. He'll need surgery. Please do not mention this to anyone. We don't want the news to pick it up. I'm struggling to contain leaks."

"Why would the news care?" I ask before the answer dawns on me.

"His good health is critical to Dragon Leaf," Jane says. "If the Crusaders get wind of this, it would be more ammunition to spook our shareholders into selling. He won't be able to meet you at home with your grandfather, but I'll be there. You can interview your father in the hospital tomorrow. He asks that you bring a portfolio from his home office with you."

Some part of me wonders why Ba didn't call me himself if he was alert enough to pass all this information to Jane. But what would I say? He's been in an accident. He's headed into surgery. I should be worried and upset, but I'm honestly not sure how I even feel. . . .

And he knows that.

"Okay. I'll ask Ye-Ye for Dragon Leaf's history—"

"Your father's calling. I have to go." She hangs up.

"Wow, hope he's okay." Sophie sounds way more worried than me.

"He's invincible." That much I know. I pocket my phone. "And now he and Jane won't be breathing down our necks for the film project."

"That's a relief." She puts her foot to the pedal and speeds past the traffic light.

My mind whirls with possibilities too amorphous to see yet.

"You have no idea, Sophie."

29

SOPHIE

The wind sweeps through my hair as we motor toward Aunty Claire's. Now we're hitting up my family, and I grow more nervous the closer we get. Our last visit over the summer ended in disaster. Rick and Ever got busted for fake-dating, and Xavier and I broke up. But this time, everything is the way it should be: Xavier and I *aren't* dating, and Rick and Ever are.

In fact, returning reminds me of exactly why we broke up, and how that reason is still like a block of ice between us. . . . Xavier just wasn't into me. Even now, he's hanging on to the rails behind me, as distant as he can be on the same scooter. But in some ways, it was simpler (although a disaster) to just be chasing Xavier for my family's approval. That was safer for

my heart. Now it's more complicated, my feelings more confused . . . and dangerous.

As we motor up the driveway toward the green-shuttered
mansion, I inhale a calming breath of freshly mown lawn and
rosebushes. I find myself pushing hard on the throttle, eager to
reach my aunt. I need to talk to her. I want to ask her how Xavier
and I can have such good energy together, and yet be so wrong
for each other. Just speaking to her and holding her new baby
will help to anchor my world again.

We stop before the slate steps that lead to her double doors.
Rick and Ever pull up beside us. "Perfect timing," I start to say,
but they're deep in a heated conversation.

"But why London?" Rick tugs his helmet off. His heavy black
brows crouch low and tense on his forehead. "We'll see each
other once a year at most."

Ever dismounts with a graceful swing of her ballerina leg.
"I may not get into Tisch again. I have to cast as wide a net as
possible. We don't have to talk about this now. Who knows if I'll
even get in over there?"

"We need to come up with other options!"

They're both so intent on each other, Xavier and I might as
well not be standing here.

"Um, guys?" I say. "Everything okay?"

"No," Rick says, at the same time Ever says, "We're fine."

"Ooooo-kay. Maybe you should, like, try to work it out before
we go in?"

Too late. The front door opens. Ever's shoulders rise and fall with a deep breath, and we fall silent as Aunty Claire's butler appears.

We follow him into the air-conditioned foyer, where orange-and-white carp glide through the pond built into the marble floor. Aunty Claire descends the curved staircase, cradling a swaddled baby. Her drape-like floral duster flutters around her bare legs, so different from her usual tailored outfits. Her hair flops in an uncharacteristically sloppy ponytail and her usually vibrant face is drawn.

But the baby in her arms has the most darling squashed-tomato face I've ever seen.

"Finn!" I dart forward.

"Welcome, sweetie." Aunty Claire kisses my cheek. "Here's my new prince."

"Hello, Aunty! And hello, cuz!" I rub my nose against my baby cousin's fine head of hair. "Oh my God, Aunty Claire. He smells so yummy."

"And here's my girlfriend," Rick says. "For real this time."

Ever gives a nervous laugh, but Aunty Claire takes her into her arms. "My dear. I'm so glad it turned out to be true, even if it wasn't at first." She laughs. "My new-mom brain. No one would understand what I just said, but there you go."

"I'm glad, too." Ever's smile is like the sun as she returns my aunt's embrace.

Five-year-old Fannie races down in a lacy pink gown, juggling a stack of mooncake boxes. She's trailed by Felix, who is giddy under his pomelo-skin cap carved like a flower. A Moon

Festival tradition I used to do, more because I liked smelling the citrus than because I wanted the luck. I pretend to rumple his hair. "Nice hat!"

"Pick one!" Fannie holds up her boxes. "We got so many kinds!"

I laugh and sweep my youngest girl cousin into a hug. "Which is your favorite?" I ask.

"This one. No, this one! They're all good!" She piles them into my arms and I laugh again.

"Can I hold your new brother?"

"Yes!" she yells. Xavier takes the boxes from me, and I fling Finn's baby blanket over my shoulder and take my newest cousin into my arms. I lay him chest down against my shoulder, gazing at the soft folds of his eyelids.

"He's like a hot-water bottle." I feel a fierce rush of love toward him: a whole new person forever connected to me. I press my nose into his soft cheek, inhaling his clean baby scent. "Hi, little guy, I'm your cousin Sophie. And you have four other big cousins waiting to play in the States."

Unlike the last trip, when I spent every waking moment trying to impress Xavier, this trip, I can just enjoy my family: Felix tackling Rick, Uncle Ted doting on Aunty Claire. Their marriage was what gave me hope when Rick's family and mine fell apart.

I catch Xavier's eyes on me, then we both glance away. A bit of heat creeps up my neck. What was it he'd said at the warehouse? Sunbeams. My emotions spilling out. It actually hit me harder than I let on. He was talking about that tornado in me that over-whelms people, like the print shop manager near Dartmouth. I never thought that tornado could be something beautiful about me, but Xavier somehow made it that way.

Finn burps against me. I smile down at his sleeping face, grateful for *his* anchoring presence. "Aunty Claire, you and Uncle Ted must be so happy."

"Yes, of course." But Aunty Claire's smile doesn't reach her eyes. She must be exhausted from breastfeeding, poor thing.

"You should let other people help you." She's always been the kind of person to do it all herself.

"Don't worry about me. I've plenty of hands to spare. It's just the sleep that's hard—Finn's waking and sleeping at all hours of day and night."

"Which room is Ever's?" Rick asks. "I'll bring her bags. Her audition is this afternoon."

"I can carry them—" Ever begins, but Aunty Claire inter-rupts.

"Oh, let Rick do it, dear. You're our guest. And I have break-fast in the dining room. A congee bar, twelve toppings—all the favorites, black century eggs, roasted pork floss. My maid just picked up some sweet baozi shaped like pink bunnies for the holiday."

"Oh, that sounds wonderful," Ever says.

"Come see my terrarium." Fannie tugs on Ever's skirt.

"How's your frog?" Ever asks, following her.

"He died," Fannie says calmly, and they disappear around

the corner with Rick and their suitcases.

"I love how Fannie is so fierce and princess-girly at the same time," I say. "I hope that never changes."

"Well, she'll have to grow up at some point," Aunty Claire says vaguely. "Hello, Xavier." Aunty Claire's smile cools a bit. "My husband, Ted, is in his study. He's hoping to speak with you. Would you mind?"

"Um, yeah." Xavier glances at me. What does Uncle Ted want with Xavier? I hope Uncle Ted behaves.

"We can't stay long," I say. "Xavier and I need to head to his family's place to interview his grandpa and film mooncake making."

"Well, you must eat before you go. Xavier can chat a few minutes with your uncle, and you and I can catch up."

A maid leads Xavier toward the study. I watch them go, my brow furrowed.

"We're not dating anymore. Uncle Ted knows that, right?"

Aunty Claire frowns. "I think so. He's so busy these days, it's hard to know what he's absorbing. Were you at the Dragon Leaf showroom?"

"Yes. I interviewed Xavier's aunt," I say.

"How nice," she says distractedly. She removes her hairband from her ponytail and ties it back up. "Let's go to my room. I have presents for you, besides the mooncakes, of course."

"Aw, don't worry about me." Typical Aunty Claire. Gifts are her thing—every time I see her, she finds a way to slip me something. I move Finn expertly into the crook of one arm and loop my other through hers as we walk. "I brought a onesie for Finn, but I should have brought *you* a present," I say. "Isn't your birthday Sunday?"

"*You* remembered, at least." The sad fall to her voice surprises me. Aunty Claire is so adored. Shouldn't a celebration be in order?

"Everyone's probably distracted by this little guy." I kiss Finn's head.

Aunty Claire doesn't answer. She pushes her door open into bright sunlight illuminating the bed made of *ji tan* wood densely carved with ancient goddesses. It's heaped high with luxurious white linens, her side turned back. Last time I was here, I was sobbing my eyes out about losing Xavier. Now I'm embarrassed just remembering how I acted.

I didn't even know Xavier then. Not the real him. So what was I crying over? My inability to lock down my MRS on an advanced schedule. Getting my pride trampled.

And Xavier saw right through me.

Aunty Claire enters her walk-in closet and frowns at a few scarves. I run a hand down the raised designs on a silk brocade gown. All of Aunty Claire's clothes are fit for an empress. "I used to play dress-up in here when I was little."

"You and Rick. He tried on my clothes, too." She pulls out an eggplant-colored dress with a fitted bodice and bell-shaped skirt. "This was his favorite."

I laugh. "It really was."

"How is your mother? And the boys?" I fill her in on ice

skating and coding, on Mom's new office job at the hotel. "And with Xavier? You aren't dating, but . . . you're still friends?"

"Yes. I'm here for my research project. Xavier helped me." I explain the project, and what I learned from his aunt.

"Ted told me Dragon Leaf is in trouble. A lot of people lost their jobs. But they just made another donation to a cancer research center, so everything must be fine."

I groan. Jane is a powerhouse. I wonder how much of my aunt's perceptions of the Yehs has been molded by her over the years.

"But you're talking to Xavier's aunt?" She frowns. "I've never heard anything about the sister. Only Xavier's father and uncle. I didn't even remember there was a sister until you mentioned it."

"Actually, there are several sisters, I think."

"They must be very private people. I've never heard a word about them and we've been visiting their pavilion at the festival since before you were Fannie's age." Aunty Claire pulls a bottle from a basket of essential oils, then pushes aside a few slip dresses, searching for something. I open my mouth to pour out my worries about Xavier, when, to my surprise, she sniffles.

"Oh, Sophie. I'm so miserable. I haven't slept in weeks. And I'm afraid I'm never getting my figure back."

Wait. What? Here I was about to blabber about my problems, and I didn't even realize she was upset. I suppose she *has* gained weight. Her face has swollen to an oval. It's more striking because she's always been incredibly petite; even when pregnant, her enlarged belly was the only thing that stood out from the rest of her figure.

"You'll get back to your normal self in no time. You did with Fannie and Felix."

"I have hypothyroidism." She sniffs again. "I'm on medication. Oh, I don't want to be so vain, but I did love all my beautiful dresses, and now I can't wear them."

"It doesn't matter," I insist. "Uncle Ted adores you." My perfect Aunty Claire has always had the perfect life. I've wanted to be just like her since . . . since always.

"That's just it, Sophiling." She twists the platinum ring on her finger, with the diamond as big as a pea.

"What's wrong?"

"Could just be postpartum blues." She touches my cheek and smiles. "School is your concern. Tell me about all the eligible boys you're meeting at Dartmouth."

No. No, not this again. Not for me.

"I'm excited for my CS project." My voice sharpens. "I know that doesn't sound like me, but it's true." There's a ghost I need to exorcise. A stubborn one that has refused to let go. "This whole family has always expected me to be a wife. I realized over the summer that I'm going to be more than that."

A vertical line forms between her brows. "Of course you are."

I gaze around her room at the blue jacquard drapes, the porcelain vases full of fresh-cut flowers, the duvet cover embroidered with chubby-cheek kids. So many lovely things. And Aunty Claire herself, unfailingly lovely. And so sad.

Is this what happens when loveliness is your entire focus? When it's all you have?

"You told me once that if I kept giving boys a hard time, no one good would want me. Like Ba leaving . . . all of us. But do you still think that's true?"

"Oh, sweetie." Aunty Claire presses my hand to her lips. "You shouldn't be with anyone who isn't big enough for you. Anyone who hasn't earned your respect." She puts her arms around both me and Finn, resting her cheek on his back.

Sometimes the simplest, most obvious truths are the hardest to realize. But hearing her say it aloud . . . a weight comes off my shoulders. I stroke her hair, but I'm also fighting tears that I don't understand. I want to be this new me. But maybe that means there will never be anyone for me.

"I'm worried your uncle is having an affair." Aunty Claire's voice is half hidden in Finn's shirt.

"What?" I blink down at the crown of her thick black hair. She did not just say that. My stomach cinches with foreboding. "What makes you think that?"

"He hasn't taken me to the theater for the past few performances. He disappears from his office a few hours every week. My maid, Kai-Lin, spotted him and followed him once, thinking she could catch a ride home. But he went somewhere else."

My blood in my veins feels cold. I grip her arms. "Where?"

"To the Dragon Leaf showroom. Kai-Lin saw him meet a young woman with purple hair. He went inside with her."

I gasp. "I saw her! I talked to her!"

Her face whitens. "So she's real."

"You think he's having an affair with *her*?" The purple-haired girl suddenly has a new dimension. "She's almost my age!"

"I didn't want to think that. But . . ." Her voice trails off.

I swear. Does a curse run through my family? Uncle Ted always doted on Aunty Claire—was it simply for her beauty after all? I love my Uncle Ted. He's been kind to me. And generous. But if he is cheating on Aunty Claire, I will personally castrate him.

I rise and stomp around the room, still hanging on to Finn. "Why is every guy such a jerk? If I could find one good man on this planet . . ."

"Rick is a good boy."

"Because he had us to train him." I rush to her and sweep her into my arms with Finn. She clings to us. Her heart hammers against the side of my rib cage. "I'll be going back to the Dragon Leaf showroom later tonight," I say. "I can find out more."

"No!" Her hand tightens on my arm, pinching my flesh. "Please don't interfere. I don't want him to know I suspect. I can't afford to lose him. Not with the baby. The children. I'm not like your mother—I don't have you to help me."

I stare at her. "But how can you live like this?"

She gives me a sad smile. "I had the arrogance to believe I was different. But as it turns out, I'm like any other woman." A small laugh slips from her. "He actually *measured* my waist the other day. With a tape measure. I didn't even know he knew what one was."

"That's awful."

She buries her face in my shoulder. I cling to her, stroking her sweat-dampened back. She's so smart and has such good taste and is so incredible with people—what would her life be like now if she'd gone after her own plans instead of being well married?

"You're not just any woman, Aunty Claire." I grip her tightly to me, taking care not to crush Finn between us. I will be discreet, but I *will* get to the bottom of the purple-haired girl. "You're a Woo woman, same as me. And we come out on top in the end."

30

XAVIER

Our reflection on the scooter follows us in the store windows: me in black and Sophie in dark petal purple, her pale arms encircling my waist and her head angled down, lost in thought. We're heading toward my home to interview Ye-Ye.

It was surprisingly painful to be back at Sophie's aunt's home, having to relive my least finest hours from the summer. Last time I was there, I really screwed things up. She said I made her crazy, and I can see why now. I didn't have to treat her as badly as I did.

And something's wrong with Sophie now. She's freaking out and holding it in . . . although I'm pretty sure it has nothing to do with me this time.

"You okay?" I ask.

"You were quiet during breakfast."

She stirs against my back and her arms tighten around my waist. "What did my uncle want? I hope . . . he didn't give you a hard time?"

"No, he asked me about the Dragon Leaf Crusader thing. Whether it's slowing things down. I didn't really have answers. What happened with your aunt?"

We breeze past a bus covered with cartoony ads. Its measured beep fades behind us. Then words come pouring out. Aunty Claire's suspicions. Uncle Ted's too-obvious behavior.

"They have three kids together! It's so . . . *ugh*!"

Hard to think of the man I spoke with in his office cheating on his wife. He had a photo of him, her, and their older two kids on his desk. But then again, I don't know the guy, and my family's weird about this, too—Ba's never remarried, and the family has declared he can't date anyone more than ten years younger than him. It's actually not a bad rule, as far as rules go.

"Maybe there are no happily ever afters." Sophie sighs.

"Rick and Ever seem happy."

"Rick and Ever were meant to be," Sophie says. "I'm not so sure the universe has the same plans for me. The women in my family are cursed. My mom. Rick's mom. Now Aunty Claire."

"You're not cursed."

"Flattery will get you everywhere," she says, and I smile. After a moment, she says, "You know, we're different than we were on Loveboat. I noticed it going back to my aunt's. How much we've changed."

"I've been thinking that, too. We were a shitstorm. Now we can accidentally hook up and still talk about it afterward."

She laughs. But I mean it. I've never had conversations like we've had . . . with anyone. It's always been easier to hook up and then run away. Or just run away. Not the most mature, looking back now. But cleaner. For me, at least. Secrets kept. Heart protected. Exoskeleton thick and intact.

"Yes, true, and that we're still friends. And you can be dating other people, like Emma. And I'm okay with it. That's growth, isn't it? For me, at least."

I don't want to be dating other people.

The truth of that hits me. I don't. I want to be talking to her. Making her laugh and feeling her sunbeams. And when our projects are done, *could* we try again? Should we? I want to ask her about it. I want to say the words. They're right there, ready to bust out of my heart.

A car honks behind us, and I swerve out of its way.

God, I'm still the same selfish bastard. Sophie told me in super-clear terms what she wants. And she just said it again— *you can be dating Emma.* In a tone of voice like what she'd use to order coffee. I need to be her friend. Show her the respect she deserves, listen to her, and just. Be. Her. Friend.

I squash those other words in my heart.

"Yeah," I say.

Taipei 101 rises into the sky just ahead of us. It's a modern super-tall pagoda made of gleaming blue-green square tiers. We reach its main entrance a few minutes later, and I take the turn into a roadway away from it, leading to my family's apartment complex. Our building's shiny black front is broken up by a ladder of wooden balconies overflowing with leafy plants, all the way to the penthouse.

"Wait, you live *across* from Taipei 101?" Sophie asks.

I sort of hate where we live. It was bought to impress guests, but I don't like the gap it puts between me and other people. The plants do breathe life into the walls, though. And it does look all kinds of cool.

"We moved here when it was built. I got to go to the movie theater a lot," I say, which is true.

"And here I was bragging about getting reservations for dinner at Taipei 101."

"It's not like *I* did anything to make this happen." Why can't I just let her be impressed? The Douche Lord would. "Unlike you—you're organizing the entire reunion up there. The view of the moon will be awesome. My uncle complains that Taipei 101 blocks our view." I slow the scooter. "Honestly, Sophie. I'm here to film the mooncake making and interview my grandpa. Then once I film some B-roll of the festival tomorrow, I'll be golden."

The air cools slightly as we enter the shade of the portico. Eighty-eight birthday balloons blow in the breeze. Sophie removes her helmet, letting her black hair spill down her shoulders. She steps toward the view of Taipei 101, folding her arms as she stares out at the tower and the ten flags waving on their poles before it. But she doesn't take out her camera, and when she turns back, all she says is, "Nice plants."

"You could have scratched the chrome, you fool!" My Uncle Edward is charging out the glass front doors toward the curb. Oh man, here we go. He's younger than Ba by four years and nearly twice his weight—a two-hundred-plus-pound wall of muscle that strains against his pinstriped dress shirt. In the flesh, he's even more snarly than I remember.

Uncle Edward glares at Kai-Fong, our ancient butler and Bernard's older brother, who straightens up from the Ferrari, a rag and green plastic bottle in hand. "You've been here how long, and you still don't know how to mind a car? My brother should have retired you years ago."

Kai-Fong's thin shoulders hunch. He shrinks back as Uncle Edward snatches the bottle from him.

"Uncle Edward, back off." The sharpness of my voice surprises even me. Uncle Edward turns, and so does Kai-Fong.

"Master Xiang-Ping. Welcome home." Kai-Fong gives me his gray-haired bow. He's dressed in a softer Yeh uniform, one I associate with the staff who've been around for years: a charcoal-purple suit, matching tie, and starched shirt. Instead of a golden Yeh brand over his breast, he wears it as a discreet lapel pin.

"So the prodigal son returns." Uncle Edward comes toward me, eyes narrowing in his moon-shaped face. "How dare you speak to me like that?"

Uncle Edward, Ba, the Douche Lord . . . right now, they're all the same to me: angry noises hating on me.

I raise my chin and let my expression say it all.

He glowers back. "Just give me a reason to—" He breaks off as a black limousine pulls up. His mouth spreads in a scarily authentic smile, and he slips past me. "Your Excellency, welcome. Good of you to come."

I leave him shaking His Excellency's hand.

"With him for a dad," I mutter to Sophie, "no wonder my cousin's such a . . . well, Douche Lord."

Her lips twist wryly. "Lovely man."

"May I take your bag, Master Xiang-Ping?" Kai-Fong asks.

"I've got it." I can probably bench-press Kai-Fong. But he insists with such frail dignity that I don't have the heart to refuse. Not after how my uncle treated him. I fall into step beside him. I never thought I'd feel this way, but, even despite my uncle, Kai-Fong makes it feel good to come home. I'm glad I was here to tell Uncle Edward off, but I wonder how many other days he's made himself an ass.

"How's Jessica?" I ask. Kai-Fong's granddaughter, who Ba discovered has a gift for physics and sent to Kyoto University. It's ironic, of course. Ba's staff's families have gone to college thanks to Ba, but he can't get his own kid there. But I'm glad for Jessica.

"She is well. Sophomore year. Big course load." Kai-Fong ushers us into the entrance foyer, which is framed by a double set of curved stairs and lit by the chandelier overhead. He shows me Jessica's photo on his phone, of her waving from between two brick pillars. "She loves it there, but she may have to leave if the company is sold."

"Really?"

"Her scholarship is funded through Dragon Leaf. Your ba isn't like other employers, you know. Not many would treat us the way he does."

"Yeah. I'd rather be his employee than his kid."

Kai-Fong takes hold of my arm. "Xiang-Ping, your father needs your help. We all do. Your ba is a good man, but he doesn't know what he doesn't know."

Why do they all look to me like I'm some proper heir? "The family doesn't want me messing around in Dragon Leaf business. They don't even expect me to attend these parties." Guests in tuxedos are crowding one of two open elevators, more leaders who control billions of dollars or rule millions of people. I shake my head. "But don't worry about Jessica. I'll talk to Ba." Don't know if I can make a difference, but for Kai-Fong, I'll try.

Kai-Fong gives me a short bow. "You are so much like him."

That again? If there *is* anything similar, I want to cut it out with a knife. I've been in Yeh-dom too long, and it's messing with my head. I just need to get out of here as fast and painlessly as possible.

One elevator door closes over its guests. Kai-Fong presses the penthouse button in the next elevator, hands me my backpack, and gestures for Sophie and me to enter. The doors shut, and for a moment, we're alone. An image of me pressing Sophie against the padded wall, my mouth to hers, flashes through my mind.

"You guys have a lot of servants," she says.

I close my hand over my bag strap, steady myself. "My

grandpa lives here. And one of my aunts when she's not in London. Some of the staff, too. Like Bernard. After his wife died giving birth, Ba brought him and Alison here so he wouldn't be alone."

"Amazing. They've worked for your family that many years?"

"Yeah. Ba treats them better than he does me."

She smiles. "So do you."

"What?"

"Also it's better than the reverse—spoil the son and traumatize the servants."

I frown. "He wouldn't do that."

"It does say something about your dad that his people are so loyal."

"Not the protestors outside headquarters."

"Yeah. But those are your aunt's people. And your uncle fired them, not your dad."

More of Sophie's skewering insights. I've never had anyone outside the family come into it, and having her eyes on them makes me feel weirdly . . . less alone.

The elevator doors part, and we step into a foyer full of sculptures and paintings.

"These are incredible!" Sophie runs fingertips down the framed painting of an orange tiger pacing in its canvas. "Even the National Palace Museum doesn't have pieces like these. No wonder you're such an artist. Your whole family is into art."

For a moment, I see it, too. The whole room is eye candy, full of tasteful works of genius. But then I shake my head. I point to the three bright red stamps decorating the side of the tiger painting. "This is the part Ba cares about. This stamp is the artist's. This one's the grandson of Puyi, the last emperor of China. He was the first owner. This one's my grandfather's, the second owner. It's a challenge. Who will you be that your mark belongs beside the mark of emperors?"

"The most expensive piece of art we own in my house is a clay elephant my brothers made in camp."

"Bet it's better than all this stuff combined." I study the painting with her. "This tiger's my dad. The world itself is too small for his ambitions." How can Kai-Fong, anyone, think I'm like him?

Sophie tilts her head. "He doesn't look happy stuck in that canvas."

"Exactly. And now Ba's stuck, too. His accident. His company under fire."

Sophie lays a hand on my arm. A simple gesture, but I can feel everything she means by it. "How are you feeling about it?"

I look away, at a framed portrait of Yeh firstborns: my great-grandfather, grandfather, and father my age, standing together. Matching noses and jaws. Ye-Ye's hand is on Ba's shoulder. Ba's chin is raised and he looks directly at the camera, confident and strong.

"Honestly? I can't help feeling a little sorry for him. He never rests. Now he's being forced to. He's never *not* in control. And now . . ."

I imagine him lying on a surgery table in some hospital he

funded, a nurse telling him to count backward from one hundred. His vision darkening to a tunnel of light. His cage getting smaller. . . .

I shift, and my reflection in the glass over the portrait separates from Ba's image. I was superimposed on him without even realizing it. Now I've put myself into the portrait in line with them, the fourth Yeh man. And it looks real.

But it's *not* . . . or is it?

So many conflicting feelings and memories bubble inside me. Uncle Edward telling Ba I needed to be lobotomized. Getting shipped off to the States. Those years away that I could have spent getting to know my great-aunts and vice versa. And now the staff is looking to me and today I tasted what it could feel like to not be a waste of space. Like connecting Sophie to my aunt.

I came to say goodbye. But is that really what I want?

Sophie lifts her nose, sniffing the scent of baking cakes. "What smells so good?"

I step away from the photo, pulling myself from the lineup.

"That's the mooncakes for tomorrow's giveaway." The work goes on, side by side with the party. That's also the Yehs.

"So fun! Let's go film," Sophie says.

"I'm supposed to interview my grandpa." I've got my questions teed up. *What was Dragon Leaf like in its early days? How did it become the empire it is today?* With Ba in the hospital, I need Ye-Ye on film—and my history teacher won't let me get away with anything less than a Rockefeller-like interview.

"Where is he?"

I frown. A receiving line for Ye-Ye is already winding through the living room and up the staircase. "He must be upstairs on the terrace, greeting guests. How and where am I going to interview him? I don't know what Jane has in mind."

"Well, maybe we cover the mooncakes first, while the line dies down?"

"Okay." I take Sophie's hand and tug. "Kitchen's this way."

The kitchen Emma and I used to sneak into to steal ice-cream cones is as big as the living room. Pots and pans hang from ceiling racks. Two giant stoves blaze with blue-orange flames, and an entire wall of ovens is loaded with cakes.

Aunty Four, wearing a purple Dragon Leaf apron over her leopard-print dress, kneads a large lump of dough at the counter.

"Xiang-Ping, there you are. Lin-Bian mentioned you were on your way." She greets us with a reserved smile. Formal but kind, that's her. Even with her apron covered in red bean handprints. "Come in. We're finishing the last batch."

An assembly line of men and women in hairnets and smocks also knead dough on two long tables. Others roll out circles, and spoon out sweet taro, lotus, and mung bean fillings.

"How many aunts do you have?" Sophie tugs her hand free as we enter. I hadn't realized I was still hanging on.

"Um, four. Don't let the flour and apron fool you. She runs Dragon Leaf's European operations and her daughter Gloria runs the London office."

"Power ladies. These mooncakes don't stand a chance."

"Sometimes I think Ba wishes I was a girl."

"Xiang-Ping, wash your hands and make a mooncake." Aunty Four rips her ball of dough in half and sets half aside. "You used to make the loveliest cakes. Such intricate designs."

Nice she remembers it that way. "I need to film," I say. "Sophie can make one."

"Oh, I don't want to interfere with a family thing," Sophie says.

"Not at all, Sophie." Aunty Four pats the spare lump. "Come."

Sophie joins her, and I lift my camera to my shoulder and film them side by side.

"Most mooncakes are made by machines now," Aunty Four says. "But our family, we still do everything by hand."

I zoom in on Sophie's flour-dusted hands as she wraps a circle of dough around a spoonful of bean paste. I zoom out for a long shot. Her skin glows against the black fall of her hair. Her plum jumpsuit draws out the other purple in the room: the tiles behind the stove, yams on a tray, the ribbon on a box of mooncakes.

Aunty Four brushes her nose with her sleeve, adding instead of removing a smudge of flour. "Here, taste a fresh one." She offers a platter stacked with a pyramid of golden mooncakes, all marked with the raised Yeh crest.

"I don't actually like mooncakes," I admit.

"Blasphemy!" Sophie's eyes widen, mid-bite into one.

"They're too dense. Also I don't like the salted yolks."

"That's the best part!"

Aunty Four laughs, setting the platter aside. "I like your friend."

More of her magic, winning over everyone around her. Even my reserved aunts.

"I like her, too," I answer, and Sophie flashes me a smile.

"What do mooncakes symbolize?" Sophie asks.

"Their roundness means completion," says my aunt. "Eating mooncakes during the festival week means the completion and unity of family."

I lower my camera. I must have known this, which is why I never wanted to come. The Yehs were a circle that shut me out—at least, it felt that way from across the ocean. But right now, with Sophie and my aunt grazing elbows as their hands knead dough, I feel a weird regret—

"What are you doing?" At Jane's voice, I jump. The PR queen stands in the doorway, lime-green suit freshly ironed, a hand on her hip. "You were supposed to be here a half hour ago to interview your grandfather. Now he's tied up with guests."

I must have missed that, even with the Douche Lord pounding it in. "Sorry."

"I need you to manage yourselves. We're struggling to contain news about the protests. A crowd is on its way."

"Here? Now?" Through the kitchen window, the flawless blue-green Taipei 101 rises against the sky. Oblivious to any riots coming. "I thought you had the press in your pocket."

"It's like trying to contain a double fistful of sand. Security is prepped, but my team is maxed out. For your project, please send us the originals when you finish. And destroy all copies."

What? Destroy . . . ?

"Jane's scrolling through her phone."

"Fine," I say stiffly. "I won't need it after I get graded."

"Greet your grandfather, then arrange to interview him after the party." I open my mouth to ask how Ba is, but she says, "And don't forget to pick up your portfolio from your father's office," and ducks away.

Sophie washes off, then we head into the living room. "Good thing she doesn't know our plans for the Magic Mirror tonight," Sophie says. "We'll be one of those grains of sand slipping through her fingers."

"Right," I say. But Jane's instructions are sitting like stones in my stomach. All this footage . . . and I'm supposed to just delete it all after I get my grades?

We join the end of Ye-Ye's receiving line, near the staircase to the rooftop terrace. Waiters in black tailcoats offer us shrimp cocktail and tiny eggrolls. Sophie hands me a satay stick, but I shake my head. I'm not hungry.

"The Douche Lord's right." I put my hand in my pocket and spin the dial of the combination lock there. "None of the stuff I'm filming matters. My grandpa will be annoyed I'm interviewing him. They'll shred my film when it's done. I'm a *risk* to them."

Only now do I realize . . . I thought my film *would* matter.

I wanted it to matter.

"You don't film what other people film," Sophie says. "Maybe that scares them."

"If I do, it's because I'm missing a layer up here." I tap my temple.

"No you're not, Xavier! Stop it. Seriously. Look—I went to your family's festival every year and never knew all this went on behind the scenes. Your PR people should have shown *this* to the world. That kitchen! Your aunt! Chaos and fresh mooncakes. It's human! It makes me fall in love with your whole family. It's . . ." She chews the inside of her cheek. "Sorry." She frowns. "Too far."

"No, you're right." There's a kind of magic to her words, how she puts the complicated mess of my feelings into a box, in a way that makes it possible for me to breathe. I gaze back at the yellow warmth of the kitchen. "I was feeling that. My aunts aren't like Ba or my uncle. . . ."

"You okay?" Sophie gives my hand a tentative squeeze.

I've trailed off for several moments.

"After my mom died," I say slowly, "I got disconnected from . . . all of this. I had friends in Manhattan, but they didn't stick around. When it mattered." Like Ma's birthday every year—the most important day to me, but not the kind of thing a guy can share without making his friends uncomfortable. "I spent a lot of time on my own. But that's also my fault. Like you said, I never let anyone in. I tried to take off first."

Her lips press into a tight line. When she speaks, finally, her voice is raspy. "You can count on me, Xavier," she says. "I don't know if that means much. But it's true."

My insides feel swollen. "It meant a lot to me that you stuck around at the airport. On our way home this summer."

Her brows twitch in her forehead. "I wasn't sure you wanted me there."

"I didn't at first. But . . . later, I was glad."

She squeezes my hand again. "Then I'm glad, too."

She's the kind of friend I haven't had before, who knows me, because no one's had the chance to really know me in a long time. And is still here. The kind of friend I want to learn to stick around for, even when things are rough. Even if my feelings maybe go beyond that.

A guy in a white tuxedo two people ahead in line turns around. Damn. It's the Douche Lord.

"Xiang-Ping, you made it." His tone is as neutral as the white gift box in his arms.

Okay. So maybe we're better now, too.

In the spot ahead of him, my cousin Lulu turns too, a small brown-paper-wrapped package in hand. Victor motions for the couple between us to move ahead.

"I heard you met my mom?" Lulu's also much less hostile. I introduce her and Sophie, and Lulu shakes her hand. "I figured if Xavier was going out of his way to help someone, she'd be pretty special."

Sophie blushes. "Oh, um, no! I mean, uh, thank you. I'm grateful you set me up. I love your mom—she's like my fairy godmother."

"Haha! I'll tell her you said so. She was really jazzed by your meeting." Lulu smiles at both of us, friendly in a way she's never been. "I haven't heard her that excited in a long while."

"Oh, I'm glad! I'm showing off her Magic Mirror tonight at a party."

"Thanks for helping." Lulu's gaze softens. "I've always told her she had great inventions. But she's never been bold enough to push them forward."

"Well, she should be!" Sophie glows. "I hope we can help! Want to come tonight? You can run the Magic Mirror."

"Oh." Lulu blinks, surprised. "Yes. I'd like that."

"Victor." Jane rushes up to us, her face lined with tension. She grips his sleeve. "Ambassador Chiu wants a word with Xiang-Ping. Prep him."

"Me?" I panic. Jane's already crossed the room to intercept an elderly man headed our way. She shakes his hand, smiling as she speaks. They both head straight for us. "What am I supposed to say?"

"Tell him we've never felt more confident in our investor support," my cousin says.

"What does that mean?" I ask, but Jane's back.

"Xiang-Ping, this is Ambassador Chiu."

"Former ambassador. I'm a private citizen now." He grips my hand. "Xiang-Ping, I met you when you were waist-high. How you've grown. I expect you'll be returning to Taipei soon yourself?"

My cousin gives an imperceptible nod.

"Yes," I say. "We have never felt more confident in our investor support." I'm parroting the Douche Lord—how did this happen?

"Excellent." Chiu smiles. "You'll fill your father's shoes in no time."

"Hi, Ambassador. I'm Victor." My cousin nearly drops his box trying to extend a handshake. "Great to meet—"

"Congressman Wu, a word with you, please." Former Ambassador Chiu lifts his fingers at a gentleman by the piano. He moves on with Jane.

My cousin lowers his hand and shrugs. "Oh, well."

I exhaled. "He seemed satisfied enough."

"He wants Dragon Leaf to continue on," my cousin says. "We do a partnership with his holding company, and his net worth doubles. He was feeling you out on the Crusaders and the future of the company."

So did I just lie straight up? "Whether I come back or not doesn't make a difference to Dragon Leaf."

"You're your dad's heir. It's a signal."

"How do you . . . know stuff like this?"

"I've been in the trenches my whole life." He hitches his box higher in his arms. "Where's your present?"

"Present?" I scan the line heading up the stairs. "No one else has gifts."

"I do." Lulu holds up her package.

"Just go on being yourself." The Douche Lord smiles. "You make me look like the good grandson without me even having to try."

"I should have thought of gifts," Sophie says.

"Not you, you're a guest," Lulu says. "But, Xavier, you better come up with something. After Victor and me, Grandpa *will* be insulted you didn't bother."

"He can afford whatever he wants."

"It's the thought that counts."

Crap, now what? Not that I care whether the Douche Lord looks like the good grandson. I've never been in the running. But I do need to interview Ye-Ye, so I shouldn't start off in the hole. I scan the crowds, searching for ideas among the dresses and suits.

Lulu waves to someone by the fireplace. "Can you hold my spot? I want to say hi to a friend."

"Sure," the Douche Lord and I say together.

Our eyes meet, both annoyed. Lulu darts off. The Douche Lord sets his box down on a pearl-inlaid table. He unslings his Apple watch from his wrist and shoves it into my hand.

"Here. Give him this. It's trendy, at least."

It's generous. Not just the cost, but the last-minute rescue.

"But—"

"It's right out of the box. I bought it today."

I frown at the watch. "I thought you wanted to look like the good grandson."

The Douche Lord rolled his eyes. "You've got ten minutes to wrap it."

"Wrap it?"

"Presents get wrapped, Xavier! Go! We'll hold your spot."

281

I race the hallways to my closed bedroom door and burst inside. The blue gauze drapes billow into the open window. Two years later and my room is the same—a four-poster bed heaped with a matching blue duvet cover Ma embroidered with little dragons. A painted conch shell from a family trip, still on my bedside table. My desk is clear. I never used it. I preferred to work sprawled on the wooden dining room floor, where the stained-glass windows spilled patches of colored light.

I suddenly see Ba as I used to here, after Ma had read to me and tucked me in and the lights were out. Sometimes he'd come in and stand in this spot. Just listening to me breathe. One time he came close and put his hand on my forehead. I forced my breath steady, pretending I was asleep so he wouldn't leave too soon, but I was secretly watching his shadowy figure, the wrinkles on the hem of his untucked shirt. After a minute, he slipped back out, leaving the warmth of his hand on my head.

The memory is jolting. It belongs to another Xavier and another Ba from a time long ago. I shake it off and cross to my dresser and yank open a drawer of a weird mix of things: stamped pennies from museums, wooden toys, and gold. My aunts were always giving me gold: brooches, necklaces, rings, solid wealth that wouldn't vanish in a stock-market crash—all of which I'd shoved in here and promptly forgotten.

I dump a necklace from a velvet pouch and slip the watch

into its place. It's a nice watch, but modern—will Ye-Ye even like it? I want him to feel good about my gift, but maybe my cousin will let him know he had to bail out my sorry ass again.

As I start for the door, my eyes fall on a long rectangular box leaned against the corner. The familiar white patch of a peeled-off sticker gazes at me like a dull eye. I'd carried that very box into the National Theater this summer.

My heart jolts.

I bought it to spare us the shame.

The lean green creature fluttering across the stage. He bought it, and then shoved it away here, safely out of the sight of all those eyes.

Shame scorches my chest. I exposed myself in that auction. I exposed the whole family. Then when he bought it, I was so . . . *puffed up.* I had something over him, I thought. When all along, he was just cleaning up after me. Deleting the film to black.

I cross to the box and rip off its top. I want to set a lighter to the whole rolled-up rice-paper sheet and watch it crumple into black carbon.

But instead of finding the parchment, I stare down the empty square tube to its bottom, flecks of forest-green still speckling the cardboard.

Ba, always a step ahead, already beat me to it.

31

SOPHIE

We emerge onto a rooftop terrace, with Taipei 101's pagoda-like shaft spearing the sky right before us—amazing. This has to be one of the nicest views in all of Asia. The line to meet Xavier's grandfather stretches all the way toward it, to a vine-covered trellis at the edge of the roof.

"Those are the Lee siblings, by the wall of plants," Victor says.

"The who?" I ask.

"The famous YouTubers with over ten million subscribers. And that guy scratching his nose over there runs Taipei's start-up company scene, but you wouldn't know from looking at him."

"Um, wow."

"Xavier's family's not flashy in general," Lulu puts in. "No gold-plated toilets, like Victor's house."

"Only in our guest bathroom," Victor says.

"But they know a lot of talented people," Lulu finishes.

"That's Princess Asuka who just went downstairs," Victor says.

"Wow, a *princess*." I'd admired her simple, silvery dress.

"Remember how she used to chase Xavier into the trees trying to kiss him?" Lulu asks. "Super annoying."

"Well, we all make errors of judgment," Victor says smoothly.

It's still unbelievable to me that this is just Xavier's life. Everyone crammed onto this rooftop is dressed for a coronation. Waiters balancing trays of raw oysters slip in and out among them. And Xavier's penthouse apartment, ten rooms plus this terrace, is more spacious than most houses in New Jersey.

All this was what I thought I wanted when I came on Loveboat. But what actually goes with it—family, whichever form it takes—that's the part that means something, and that has nothing to do with the view.

And for Xavier, it's even more complicated. It's the father who flings him around by the ear. The aunty with the warm hands and flour on her nose. Can he survive one and thrive on the other? Is that even possible? I hope so. For his sake, for his *heart* that he keeps so locked away, I hope so.

"My dad over there is talking to the editor of *Vogue Asia*." Victor gestures to the man of the sensitive yellow Ferrari, a heavyset guy with a moon-shaped face. Also impeccably dressed in an indigo suit and gold tie, a nod to Dragon Leaf colors.

"Shouldn't your mom be talking to *Vogue*?" I ask Lulu.

"Only Xavier's and Victor's dads are allowed to talk to press."

I frown. "Isn't she the fashion expert?"

"That's our family. The girls keep a low profile. Even me—my mom has yet to admit to Ye-Ye that I'm a black belt, not to mention I've placed in world championships."

"Wow."

"Ye-Ye wouldn't approve." She scowls. "We all know our parents' weaknesses, don't we? It's always jarring for me to come home and see how my mom still defers so much to the patriarchy."

I think of my own mom and Aunty Claire. "Do you think we should try to help them change?" I ask.

"It's not our place." Victor gives me the look he gave me when I suggested I was challenging Horvath. Which, I am ready to admit, I am doing. So I should give it my best shot. I pull up my proposal on my phone, and as the cousins talk, I draft an email to my professor about the Magic Mirror.

"How do you like Dartmouth?" Lulu asks as I near its end. "I'm hoping to apply."

"Oh, great," I say. "It's hard, but I'm hopeful? I can look over your application if you want."

"Oh, thank you. That would be amazing."

"It's the least I can do after your mom."

"You're helping her, too, Sophie."

The entire Yeh family really does say everyone's name, like a forever roll call.

"Well, she's ahead of her time. Her technology could propel Dragon Leaf into the next century. It could change the way people shop forever." I write that into my draft email as I say it. "Speaking of which, I better check on progress for getting out word on the Magic Mirror."

I open the Loveboat account to check my Magic Mirror post—four hundred likes and climbing! And a text from Aunty Claire—the zookeeper will bring baby pandas tonight!

To our party!

I didn't even mean to organize this thing, and look at me organizing the hell out of it.

I can't wait to tell Xavier.

I give directions to a few newcomers, clarify there's no cover charge, add another twenty people to our reservation, then text the restaurant: the pandas are coming! I put the zookeeper in touch directly to sort it out.

I peek at the #LoveboatReunion feed on Instagram— Loveboaters riding the Maokong Gondola, hiking Elephant Mountain, eating deep-fried crabs on Fisherman's Wharf. Photos of moons in Paris, Singapore, Moscow, San Francisco, Melbourne, Johannesburg.

I smile, loving the sense of the world coming together. The Loveboat alum are literally everywhere.

The only thing left to do is find a ride home.

"How's the proposal for Horvath?" Victor asks.

"I'm feeling pretty good about it, actually. Will you take a look before I send it?"

"Sure."

I hand him my phone and explain as he scrolls through. "He wanted a more data-centric project. So I'm collecting data on clothing styles, body types, moods. Plus, if you like a style, the AI interface can crunch your measurements and tailor it to make it the most flattering." I'm chattering like a chipmunk, but to my surprise, Victor's nodding.

"It looks great." He hands my phone back. "I didn't realize how rigorous the algorithms were. Aunty Three never talks about tech."

"Who'd listen?" Lulu asks.

"Add more specifics about how it can be used," Victor says.

"I'll get those tonight. We're showing the Magic Mirror at the party."

"Cool. And nice work."

TA stamp of approval! The project can't get much stronger than that.

Victor glances over my shoulder. "All wrapped?"

Xavier holds up a red velvet pouch. "Yes. Thanks," he says shortly. His fist at his side is white and clenched. A sheen of sweat glistens on his neck.

I frown. "You okay?"

"Yeah." He averts his gaze. "Yeah. Fine."

He watches Victor approach their grandfather, a white-haired man in a black tuxedo, with a narrow face like his sisters and Xavier's dad. He's seated in a velvet armchair, backdropped by Taipei 101. On a covered table to his left, a wheel-sized birthday cake is set with a zillion candles.

Victor takes his grandfather's gnarled hand. "Ye-Ye, I'm honored to be giving our family speech tomorrow. Thank you for the privilege."

"It's time we pass on the mantle of leadership," his grandfather says. "The festival is our night to connect with Taipei. A strong reputation leads to strong business partnerships."

"I will make the family proud." Victor places his white box in Ye-Ye's lap and tugs the red ribbon free. "Ye-Ye, may I present the original masthead from your legendary dragon boat race, restored to full color."

Ye-Ye lifts out a green dragon's head roughly hewn from wood, lovingly painted. Its gold eye glares and its forked tongue samples the air.

"Reminds me of your mural," I say to Xavier, but he doesn't answer.

"Wonderful!" Ye-Ye runs his gnarled hand over the dragon's crested head. "All I wanted was for this snout to cross the finish line first."

"You told me, Ye-Ye. I remember."

"I am deeply touched by your thoughtfulness."

"Take a picture with me." Victor puts an arm around Ye-Ye's shoulders and snaps a selfie, then gets Lulu to take a photo with the Taipei 101 backdrop. "Landscape mode, please."

They look great together: the black tux and the white one,

the revered elder embodying history and tradition beside the bold next generation. Victor is many things, but he definitely has a knack for presenting a powerful image.

My phone chimes. Emma's sent a photo of herself in a car with creamy leather seats. Her black hair is clipped back, showing off the cherry blossom earrings dangling at her cheeks. She's adorable, even after a ten-hour flight.

> Sophie, I've landed. I just heard/saw what happened with you and Xavier on the jet. Why didn't you tell me you guys dated on Loveboat? I thought you were setting him up with me?

Oh, no, this is exactly what I was worried about. Of course she heard about it. I text her back.

> Emma, I'm sorry I should have told you.
> And we only dated for like, two weeks.

Marc posts a photo of a group inside a karaoke taxi, belting their hearts out.

A moment later, Emma's text chimes.

> I was so excited to come. Honestly, Priscilla warned me she heard you'd stab your friends in the back, but I thought she was wrong.
> Now I don't know what to think.

Wait wait wait. What? No.

Oh, God. I cannot, *will* not, lose a friend fighting over Xavier. Especially not Emma. I'd rather stick the knife into my own side first.

I text:

> Sophie: You're right. I should have been honest with you, and I do have your back. The plane ride was a big mistake, but it showed me I truly am over him.
> Emma: I'm headed to my family's apartment to drop off my stuff and get a facial. Let's talk at the party.
> Sophie: Yes, of course. I'm sorry I've confused everything.

She doesn't answer. The conversation is over until tonight. But how do I fix things? I do the only thing I can think of—I shove her photo at Xavier.

"Emma's here."

"Great." He lifts his camera to his shoulder. "I'm excited to see her again."

Is he? I can't tell. But I need to double down on making sure they have the perfect evening, if it means serenading them myself.

"Wai Gong." Lulu has knelt before her grandfather. "A gift from the States." He shells its paper wrapping to a bar of dark chocolate from Trader Joe's.

"Fair trade." She beams.

"I *love* Trader Joe's." Ye-Ye grins, showing off perfect teeth. "What a fantastic little company. That one got away from me."

Lulu laughs. "We have plenty of stores here for you to buy."

"Not like that one."

"I see where the Yeh charm comes from," I say to Xavier.

Xavier's smile doesn't reach his eyes. Ye-Ye pats Lulu's hand. As she moves on, he extends a hand toward Xavier.

"Xiang-Ping," he says. "You've been gone too long."

"Let me film for you," I say quietly.

Xavier grimaces but hands me his camera. I can feel the nervous tension in him as he steps forward and takes his grandfather's hand.

I lift the camera to eye level and let it roll.

32

XAVIER

"Ah, Xiang-Ping." Ye-Ye rubs my hand between his gnarled ones. His tan skin is rough and papery, and reminds me of his many many years ahead of me. They're weirdly comforting. Like I've got time to figure things out. "Xiang-Ping, Yeh means 'leaf.' It's a good name for our family. You bear it. Never forget."

Ye-Ye often says this to me, like a ritual. I usually nod and move on. But this time, I can't help noticing he didn't say it to either of my cousins.

"Why is it good?" I feel about three years old. "Aren't leaves fragile?"

"Leaves are numerous. Always growing. They are all over the world. Like the Yehs."

Is he trying to be profound or funny? "Gotcha."

"You are not here often, Xiang-Ping." Ye-Ye's still holding my hand. "Do you not like us?"

I tug free. "I'm here now."

"I was your age when I started Dragon Leaf. You are not a child anymore."

"That's not how Ba sees it. Anyways, I brought you a present, too."

"Xiang-Ping, thank you." His smile deepens with genuine gratitude. "What a surprise."

I hand him the pouch with my cousin's watch inside. I feel like a fraud.

Ye-Ye's eyes are unexpectedly misty as he picks at the knot on the pouch strings. He's more frail than I remember, closer to brown than the crisp autumn leaf he was a few years ago. I feel a surge of guilt. Maybe I've been wrong to force this gap between us. He used to take me and Lulu out in his boat. One time when I was sick, he made me rice porridge with roasted pork song, which is like mac and cheese to most American kids. Comfort food. Even though he didn't usually cook. He has servants to cook for his servants.

Ye-Ye spills the silver watch into his gnarled hand.

His body stiffens. His hand jerks, and the watch falls to the concrete floor with a clunk. Is he hurt? Sick? A shout of alarm rises to my lips, but then his face sharpens like a fox's.

"Edward," he barks.

A meaty hand clamps down on my arm. "How *dare* you." Uncle Edward growls in my ear. His coffee breath wafts over me as he hauls me away. Smoothly, so no one notices but Sophie, who's lowered the video camera, her eyes wide with confusion.

No one but Sophie ... and the Douche Lord, whose predator's grin is the last thing I see before my uncle hauls me downstairs.

Whatever the Douche Lord did, I was stupid enough to fall for it.

Uncle Edward drags me into the teal-papered guest bathroom and slams the door. He shoves me against the sink and a bowl of potpourri Ma made herself shatters on the floor, sending up their scented chaff.

"You trying to give him a heart attack?" he demands.

"I don't even know what I did!"

His fist knocks my head sideways. I plant my foot on his fat stomach and shove, sending him sprawling on the toilet. The salty taste of blood rushes my mouth. I flex my jaw, feeling for damage. My cheek feels cut open, and my eyes pick out the platinum ring on his finger.

We are in private quarters instead of before an audience of my friends. But this blow feels worse. No one at Harvard-Westlake or at my old school in Manhattan would have raised a finger against me. But in my own family, I have so little status that anyone can break my jaw. Better yet, they'd get a standing ovation for it.

"I need to talk to him," I grate. "I can explain!"

Uncle Edward heaves himself to his feet. "You clown on your own time. Not when it risks his health. I told you to give me a reason to kick you out on your ass."

"You seriously think I want to hurt my own grandpa?"

Worse, does *Ye-Ye*?

"I'll give you exactly two minutes to take your little girlfriend and go before I have the guards throw you both out."

"Don't bother," I say as he grabs the doorknob. "I'm leaving."

Then he's gone.

"You," he says outside. "Find a broom and clean up in there. It's a pigsty."

I rub the pricks from his fingernails in my arm. In the mirror, a red slash is bleeding on my cheek. By now, nothing my family does should hurt. Just like a prank from the Douche Lord shouldn't have caught me off guard.

But it does.

Because I'd let him in. Them. All of them. Deep down, I still thought of them as my family, and I allowed the tiniest little crack in my shell.

And they slipped in a box of explosives.

I wipe the blood off my face. I need to find Sophie and get the hell out of here.

"A watch, Xavier?" Lulu grabs my arm as I step from the bathroom. Her eyes are bright and furious. "What were you thinking?"

My jaw clenches as I start toward the terrace steps. "What does a watch mean?"

"It means his clock is ticking. That you want him to die as soon as possible. It's bad luck to give as a present."

Fuck the Douche Lord. This is worse than I thought. "Does Ye-Ye believe that?"

"Are you kidding me? They *all* believe in bad luck." She gestures at the luminaries filling the room. "Nothing can touch a billionaire *except* bad luck."

She's right. The entire place is decorated with good-luck charms from every culture, including golden horseshoes and even a crystal crucifix, though none of the family is Christian. Years ago, when the flat was being built, Ye-Ye brought a feng shui expert to advise where doors should go and stuff, the sort of details I don't pay attention to.

And my Ye-Ye believed I'd try to curse him. Ye-Ye who made me rice porridge with rou song. . . .

My own grandfather doesn't know who I am.

"I thought you didn't have a present!" Lulu says.

"You-know-who gave it to me."

"You're just . . . too trusting, Xavier." She frowns. "Why has he always been so out to get you?"

"Ask him. Let me know what you find out." I start up the stairs, which has emptied of guests. "I needed to interview Ye-Ye, but all I got on film was your chocolate bar and a story about *leaves.*"

"Xavier." Sophie is coming toward me, my camera bag slung over her shoulder. She falters. "Your cheek."

I touch the back of my hand to it, coming away with another smear of blood. "When have you not seen me bleeding this trip?"

"I can't believe Victor. Your uncle. I can't believe he just . . ."

"This is why your dad sent you to the United States," Lulu says somberly. "It was safer."

I frown. "I've never heard that. It was because Ma died. Ba didn't want me around with no supervision. If I'd gone to school at Kang Chiao like the rest of the family, all of Taipei would've known I'm a dumbass."

"You're *not*," Sophie says. Her eyes glitter fiercely. "I tried to catch Victor, but he took off. What he did was beyond shitty. There's not an excuse he can give that could ever make this okay. We still need your grandpa's interview—"

"It's fucked." I head for the front door. "My grandpa's not talking to me. And I basically swore in blood I'd profile him. So my project's fucked."

So now what? I halt at the sight of two Dragon Leaf security guards coming my way, guns swinging discretely in holsters at their hips. Lulu shoves me toward the west wing. "Go around the back way. Don't give Uncle Edward the satisfaction of throwing you out in front of the entire party."

Part of me wants to see them try. Make a scene at long last, the Buried Yeh. But the guards coming at me aren't Ba's regular security. It's like Uncle Edward's not just disciplining me, but disciplining Ba.

Something feels wrong, and I'm not going to be a pawn in anyone's game.

I grab Sophie's hand and weave away from them. We dodge around a Japanese ambassador and the CEO of the biggest

Taiwanese electronics superstore.

"But what about your trust?" Sophie says.

"I'm not getting it," I say tightly. "I'm done jumping through Ba's hoops. So be it."

I round a corner. Down the hallway, one of Ba's personal guards is standing outside the carved doors to Ba's office. Haru. Plain navy uniform. Ba's always had a guard there, since a guest tried to get into Ba's safe. Haru's friendly to me, but if Uncle Edward's told him to chuck me out, he might try, and I am leaving on my own terms.

"I don't understand," Sophie says. "How can your dad just take your trust if your mom gave it to you? Something's not right."

"There are a lot of things not right with my family."

I can't go back through the living room, so I start toward Haru.

Then Ba's office door swings open. To my surprise, Aunty Three comes out. "It's *not* a hobby business." She tugs off her paisley scarf and lets her hair tumble around her angry face. "I made more money than Healthcare last year, even with you starving my teams. Try pruning the fat there first."

I tug Sophie into the recess of an inlaid door, just out of sight.

"The public protests are undermining Dragon Leaf." The open door frames Uncle Edward sitting in Ba's big purple chair like it's his: feet in gold-toe black socks propped on the desk. "We need to send a strong signal to our investors that we're taking them very seriously."

Two men in dark suits, toupees combed in opposite directions, stand beside my uncle with their arms folded.

"Who are they?" Sophie whispers. She presses against me, her warmth comforting. I put an arm around her shoulders, needing her to steady myself. What would this visit have been like without her? I wouldn't have stood a chance of surviving it.

"They're Ba's cousins. From Singapore. Twins. They own a good chunk of Dragon Leaf." I frown. "Weird they're meeting without Ba while he's in the hospital."

"So my team takes the fall? You already fired three-quarters of my people," Aunty Three says. "They've been with me for over a decade, some of them two."

"Two thousand uneducated women in shitty little countries send you cloth by *ship*. That's not the kind of workforce we should be employing moving into the twenty-first century. And you're overpaying!"

"I pay them what they're worth! My fashion division already has the smallest budget—why can't you leave the rest of my unit alone?" She pounds her fist on the door. "Honestly, I don't blame the protestors. I'd get out there with them if I could."

"We don't want company resources wasted on things like your Frankenstein project. Victor tells me you're showing it in Taipei 101 tonight. Ridiculous."

Sophie swears softly under her breath. "Traitor."

"Selling Dragon Leaf to the Crusaders might be the most responsible move we make as a generation," says one of the twins. "Sometimes family companies need new blood."

"If it does, that's because all of you have poisoned it. And if the body is dead, it doesn't need new blood."

Aunty Three slams the door and storms down the hallway. I press Sophie back. As my aunt passes us, the stiff anger on her face crumples. She covers a choked sob with her hand. Then she's gone.

"It's so unfair!" Sophie whispers.

I squeeze her hand. She cares. So much. "We're going to save her business," I say. "We're going to save the Magic Mirror tonight."

She chews on her lower lip. "We *have* to."

The office door swings open again. Uncle Edward emerges with Ba's cousins and a guy in tweed, like a twelve-year-old with a mustache. I frown. Who is he? Bad enough for family to be in Ba's office without him, and that guy's not even family.

"We'll announce the sale at the mooncake pavilion during tomorrow's festival," Uncle Edward says. "My son is speaking. He's graduating from Dartmouth this year and coming back."

"Fantastic venue," says a cousin. "Thousands of people and influencers. Nice painting here, by the way."

"Can your station cover it?" Uncle Edward asks the kid in tweed.

"Yes, we can televise live."

So he's press. Is Uncle Edward going rogue, getting ready to sell off Dragon Leaf? Ba's devoted his life to it. Pretty sad the minute he goes under the knife, his own brother's scheming behind his back. At this rate, he'll wake up from surgery and find out he's lost his company.

As they head off, Haru closes the office door. But for a moment, I have a direct line of sight to the closet where Ba keeps his safe. A memory returns: me as a kid, kneeling beside Ba as he spilled his chop from its pouch into his hand. Me pressing the chop onto his paper book, leaving the inky mark behind . . .

And an idea strikes. Ba's chop. The emperor's seal of power.

That's what I'll need . . . to get my trust from the bank.

I make my choice. One I should have made when Ba first forced me into Harvard-Westlake.

I'm getting back my trust. On my own terms.

I grab Sophie's arm and spring forward. "Come on."

Haru turns, startled to see us.

"Haru, I need to pick up something. Jane sent me." All true.

"Yes, Master Yeh." Haru swings the door open. Sophie slips in after me. Stained-glass windows shine colors down on a carved dark-wood desk that belonged to Prince Gong, sixth son of Emperor Dao Guang. Fancy pens sit in a row on its glass top.

Behind the throne-like chair hangs Ma's portrait: her black hair twisted up off her neck, hands folded in the lap of her lush purple dress. At her throat gleams a small seashell on a red cord that doesn't match this commissioned painting—the clumsy necklace I made for her. But that was Ma; I remember the look of pure love on her face when I gave it to her.

Sophie gives a soft whistle. "Your dad worshipped her."

I don't want to hear it. I turn from Ma's watchful gaze. Ba's marked a brown-paper-wrapped package on the desk with the letter X. It's heavy, like a big book. I am not at all curious what it is, but I shove it into my backpack.

Sophie lays her hand on a silver canteen of coffee sitting on the table, etched with the Crusaders' sword-and-shield logo.

"Still warm," she says.

"My uncle might be back for it," I say. "We have to move fast."

I move the chair aside and reach under Ba's desk, feeling for the hidden hollow. My hand comes away holding the little black key.

"What are you doing?" Sophie whispers.

"Ba's safe's in here." I unlock the closet, then kneel by the gray metal box on the floor. It's the size of a small refrigerator. And heavy—it would take a few sticks of dynamite to smash it open. It has a dual lock: a fingerprint scanner and a combination lock built into its door.

Its smug little pug nose smirks at me, but I fight down the usual panicky sensation. "Sophie, I need your help."

She kneels beside me. "What's the combination?"

"My birthday. September ninth." I give her the year. "If he hasn't changed it." What does it mean that my birthday is—or was—the code? He thinks of me every time he opens it? I doubt it. "My fingerprint works for the scanner."

Sophie's own fingers are nimble on the dial. I press my thumb to the dark glass scanner. We're like the two sides of a pair of scissors, in sync . . . then she tugs the door open with a soft click.

So it *is* still my birthday. It reinforces something I don't like to think about. If Ba wants to pass his legacy to his bloodline, he's only got me. And as far as I know, only he and I have access to this safe. And maybe that actually means something to him.

Two cardboard boxes sit stacked inside, covered in a pile of velvet drawstring pouches. I tug out a familiar yellow pouch and pour the rectangular block into my palm. A simple green vine adorns its surface.

"His chop?" Sophie's eyes widen.

"Yes." I rub my thumb over the characters carved into its bottom, smearing a trace of red ink onto my skin. Even though I can't read it, I know it says Yeh Ja-Ben. "The bank will need it."

I shove the chop and pouch into my pocket, then I pull out the worn passbook, the paper booklet that keeps track of the account's transactions.

"You're going to stamp for your dad?"

"Yes." I shove aside a curl of guilt. I have no idea what the penalty is for using someone else's chop, but I bet I'm not the first. "I'm taking my trust funds."

I start to close the safe door, but Sophie grabs my hand. "Wait. Your trust papers are probably in here." She tugs out the boxes. "They could be helpful."

I exhale. "Papers. I can't—"

"I can't read them either. Look, they're in Chinese." She pulls out her phone and takes a snapshot of the top document. "Google Translate."

Brilliant again. But we need to get out of here before my uncle comes back for his mug. Get to the bank before anything else comes between me and my trust. But she's right. We'll need the papers. I open the second box and lift out stapled Chinese documents and a few in English.

I pull out my reader pen, and run it over the top lines of one. "Recording requested by the State of California," says my pen. I read further, and get the gist: ownership papers for the apartment building I live in in Los Angeles. I read the rest of the titles—all deeds to properties in the United States and Europe.

"I think this is it!" Sophie whispers excitedly. She's halfway through her stack. "Your trust. Your name is here, and so is your mom's. Lynn Yeh."

She hands the thick Chinese document to me, and I flip rapidly through the pages to a delicate signature like mine: scrawly, but balanced. The faded red square of her chop.

It's like a friendly little wave from Ma. She's still watching us from the wall. Approving? Disapproving? If she were here . . . I can't even imagine what my life would be.

I turn back to the trust's last page. One stamp. One signature.

"Is this all of it?" I ask Sophie.

"That's everything."

"But Ba said his lawyers changed it to cut me off. Shouldn't there be an update, signed by him?"

She voices my next thought. "Maybe he thought you'd never read it?"

Footsteps in the hallway reach my ear.

"Shit. We have to get out of here." I shove the trust papers into my backpack, and she jams the boxes into the safe while I slip the key back under the desk.

The footsteps draw closer. I brace the office door shut, holding my breath. I grasp the pouch in my pocket, the one thing I can't lose, no matter who comes through this door.

But then the footsteps pass and fade away.

"Come on," I whisper, and swing open the door.

A huge framed dragon hits my eyes, hung on the opposite wall. It's so long it spans the entire length of the hallway.

"What the hell?"

I pull up short and Sophie rams into me.

In my rush inside, I hadn't even noticed it hanging there: a long green creature that was never there before. Clawed feet and scaly crest that I spent hours getting right.

"That's *your* dragon," Sophie says, confused.

The scales in every shade of leaf and moss. All those days and nights kneeling over them.

"He told me it sucked." My voice cracks.

"And he hung it here?"

He hung it here. He freaking hung the family freak show where every royal guest would pass by going in and out of his office, and the whole time he let me think it was just another stain of shame on the family altar.

What the hell did he tell me that for?

Something oily black and lethal detonates in my chest. It blasts me at the frame and I rip it free, letting the whole thing clatter to the floor. I raise the frame high, ready to let loose, smash the frame, the glass . . . everything.

"Master Xiang-Ping!" Haru hurries nearer. "Sir!"

"Don't!" Sophie grabs my arm, locking it upright. "You'll regret it."

For a moment, her steady dark eyes are all I know.

"Please don't," she says. "I love that dragon."

Another moment later, I let my painting slip from my fingers. There's only one path from here. There's only ever been one path.

My voice is tight as wires. "Let's just go get my trust."

33

XAVIER

The sun is low in the sky by the time we arrive at the bank. Three tellers have shuttered their windows. One is counting blue NT bills. A man in a navy suit, gold pin gleaming on his lapel, comes to meet us.

"I'm sorry, but we're closing in five minutes. Can you please come back on Monday?"

No, my man. I cannot.

I stretch my hand out, Ba style. "I'm Xiang-Ping Yeh, son of Chairman Yeh. I've been studying in the States, so that's why we haven't met yet. Thank you for all the ways you have served my family."

I can feel Sophie silently laughing. Some of the stiffness in my shoulders fades.

Okay, maybe a little too Prince Xavier.

"Ah, yes! We've met." The man grasps my hand in both of his. "Pleasure. I'm Chin Pei-Wan. President of this branch. I remember you coming with your father when you were this high." He flexes his palm at his waist. "How can I help you?"

The good thing about being the Buried Yeh is that no one knows how little power I have.

I pull out Ba's chop. "I'm here on family business."

Mr. Chin springs to attention. "I'm at your service, Master Yeh."

"This is my associate Sophie."

"Hello, Mr. Chin."

"Pleasure as well." He shakes her hand with equal warmth. He has it down to a science. He's probably dealt with a hundred Douche Lords eager to step into their father's shoes.

"Please, let's chat in my office." Mr. Chin gestures toward glass-enclosed rooms at the back. "It's always a pleasure to work with your family. Your uncle was here just this morning."

Uncle Edward? Sophie and I exchange glances as we follow Mr. Chin. She leans against me.

"For your trust?" she whispers.

"I don't know. But he handles stuff for Ba. This is why I need to take it now."

"Could be about the Dragon Leaf sale."

Maybe. I frown, but then we enter Mr. Chin's office, and a wave of memories hit. "I remember this place," I say, not acting for the moment. "I always had rabbit candy here. The furniture was different, but in the same positions."

"Not much room for creativity with banker's decor," Mr. Chin says dryly.

So he has a sense of humor. This is the same coffee table I stamped Ba's passbook with the chop. I'd felt so responsible and grown-up.

Now I just feel reckless.

"Please, take a seat." Mr. Chin gestures to a soft blue couch. "Tea?"

"No thanks," I say. "We're in a hurry." I set my ankle on my knee, Ba style again. "Mr. Chin, I live in Los Angeles now. I want to move my trust to my bank there."

"Ah, you wish to transfer funds?"

"Yes." I hand over my passport, my ID, my account number in LA, and Ba's passbook.

"Typically trusts in Taipei don't vest until the age of twenty. Sometimes thirty."

Really? My stomach dips. That makes sense by Taipei standards, but I'd always remembered Ma saying it would vest when I turned eighteen. I glance at Sophie for help. She pushes my trust document across the table.

"Xavier's went to him a few weeks ago."

Mr. Chin flips through the pages, brow wrinkled. "How unusual. The trust *is* to be distributed to the beneficiary at eighteen. Trusts are rare here, and I assumed . . . well, your mother had enormous faith in you, young man."

I can't quite take in what that means. But it's all there in black and white with her handwriting and her chop. Not waiting until thirty, or twenty, or until Ba said so, or even until I learned to read. Ma decided I could get it at eighteen, no strings attached.

"An amount that size—there will be reporting requirements on the US side. It will take a few days to complete."

"A few days?" By tonight, when he comes out of anesthesia, Ba will bring everything to a screeching halt. I can't show weakness. I have to channel him. "I'm afraid that won't work. I'll need the funds sooner."

Um, right. You buying the Eiffel Tower tonight?

Mr. Chin wrings his hands. "If we'd had more notice . . . my apologies, but it's a regulatory requirement for amounts this large." He's not questioning that I actually need the money now. "I told your uncle the same thing."

So Uncle Edward was *also* trying to transfer a lot of money?

Mine? Or his? And for what?

I need to move fast, before I get outmaneuvered. I lean in.

"Mr. Chin, I am positive that urgent situations like this one are exactly why my family continues to bank with you." I let it hang there. I'm the next generation. And if he wants to keep our business, he needs to keep me happy.

Mr. Chin pages slowly through my trust document again, as if trying to find instructions there. Then he stands, gathering my papers.

"Give me a few minutes," he says.

Once he leaves, there's no telling what he'll do—call Ba, security, the military. I want my papers back. But Sophie clears her throat. She folds her hands calmly in her lap. Message received.

Mr. Chin heads back out into the bank and Sophie expels a breath.

"You were a pro." She smiles. "Like—"

"Prince Xavier?" I say at the same time she does.

I groan. "I just know how my family works. Better than I understand Harvard-Westlake or even my high school in Manhattan." My smile fades. "Hope he's not calling my uncle."

"Well, he's cooperating so far." She drums her fingers on her knee, as jittery as I am. "It's funny. *This* is the guy I thought you were when I first heard about you."

"A rich prick?"

"Totally my type."

I smile. "I'm glad you realized it wasn't." My smile fades. "I just want my freedom."

"But you're feeling differently about your family now, aren't you? I mean, your aunts love you. That's not something a trust can replace—you said yourself you can't pay people to care about you."

"You can care less whether they do or not," I shoot back. But I feel a stab of anxiousness. She's right that I'm just reconnecting with my aunts and great-aunts. Do I really want to cut them off again? I shake my head. "Why couldn't Ba just say he was proud of my dragon?"

"What would you have said?"

I spin the dial on my combination lock in my pocket. "Something sarcastic," I admit.

"Maybe he doesn't know how to say how he feels. Or can't. It's too . . . vulnerable? I mean, your family's entire PR system is set up to make Dragon Leaf look as perfect as possible. Unbreakable. Maybe after your mother died he—"

I don't want to feel sorry for him. "Sophie, I—"

"Don't say my name," she snaps.

"What's with you and that? Why can't I say it?"

"It's the first rule of charismatic leadership."

"I don't know what you're talking about."

"Victor told me," she says. "It's in some book. And your whole family says everyone's name, all the time. I've been observing this trip! It's manipulative. You guys are *deliberately* seducing people."

"My grandfather always says everyone's name," I say. "I doubt he read some book that told him to. It's just his way. Maybe everyone else picked up on it."

She frowns. "Hmm."

I raise my brow at her. "Are you saying I'm seducing you?"

"No!" She swats my arm, scowling. "I'm just saying. I don't want you to be fake."

"I don't think I can be fake with you." I stretch out on the couch, letting my legs hang off the armrest. I lay my head in her lap, and her fingers close on my hair. She lets out a soft breath, but doesn't speak. It's restful. I just want to stay like this, her and me and the world shut out.

I gaze up at her upside down.

"What happened on the plane ride over," I say. "I think . . . I just missed you. And I guess you, you know, got under my shell."

She flushes a cherry shade. I'm pushing her. But I want to. I want to talk about us, and what might be after this terrible and magical weekend. Her throat bobs with a swallow.

"Why didn't we ever . . . go further, then? Why did you always stop us?"

I frown. "Whatever I say isn't going to make me look good."

"Didn't you . . . want me?"

Is she serious? "Is that what you're worried about? If that was all I wanted, it would have happened already. I've . . . hurt a lot of girls. I'm not proud of it."

"You're saying you've slept with a lot of girls. Which I already figured."

Does she judge me? I wanted her to know the truth. No lies or hand-waving.

"I *never* want to hurt you again," I say.

Her fingers play with my curls, stretching them out. I close my eyes, savoring her touch, but then she pulls away. I want to grab her hand and put it back into my hair and ask her to keep going.

Then she touches my wrist. "Why are you carrying that around?"

I lift the combination lock. I'd been fidgeting with it. I sit up again, and catch the relief that passes over her face. She shifts away. Ouch. I shouldn't have pushed her.

"A lock?" she says.

I spin the dial. "When I was nine, the Douche Lord locked me in a shed behind our complex with a lock like this. He left the code on it, and I could reach the lock. It was his idea of a joke, knowing I couldn't open it."

She sucks in a breath. "What happened?"

"I yelled and banged on the door and by the time Bernard got to me hours later, I was so upset I couldn't even explain. I'd even pissed myself."

"No wonder you hate Victor so much."

"The feeling's clearly mutual." I spin the dial, then hold the lock out to her. "Show me how?"

Her brow wrinkles. "What do you mean?"

"How you can follow the dial around that many times and keep track. Why don't the numbers switch places on you?" I grimace. "My family is building things that do the impossible, but the simplest things in life are impossible for me."

"You're doing the impossible, too." She takes the lock. It's a relief to pass its weight to her. "And you're not the only one whose head's a mess. I told you. I never know when the tornado will blow up and scatter everything in my brain. It's why I need to hyper focus when I want to get something done."

"Well, whatever you're doing is working." I fish the crumpled code sticker from my pocket and she smooths it out. "This code is pretty simple. Nine, twenty-seven, thirty-six."

"Why is it simple? That's a real question."

"The numbers are in ascending order. They're all factors of nine."

"Honestly? I can't remember the order. I can't remember if it's right-left-right or left-right-left. And even if I could, I can't actually tell left from right."

I have suspected for a while now that my dyslexia is worse than other dyslexics. I've never let anyone in to how my brain works and doesn't work. But I want her to understand. I want this part of me known by her.

Sophie's cheek twitches, and she presses her fingers into it.

"If it was a song, or colors, you'd remember," she says.

"What? Never heard of that. No such thing."

"Well, why *can't* we have a password that's based on colors? Or tones? Why can't more desks and doorknobs be made for lefties? Why can't lefties write from right to left so they don't smudge the ink? Same thing. What if locks were made of complex shades that only people with eyes like yours could distinguish?"

I frown, considering. "A lock where all I'd have to do is pick out the right shades of color? I could do it. But it doesn't seem fair to make everyone else use a lock like that."

"Neither is making *you* use a combination lock. Why not have different locks for different people?"

Yes, what would it be like if the world were built your way? Or at least, not built against you? A whole layer of rules and resistance . . . just gone.

"It would be a game changer," I admit. "I guess my whole life,

I've just found other ways to get around the locks. Hiring kids. SparkNotes. Landmarks instead of reading street signs."

She places the lock back into my hand. "Try it."

I give the dial a spin.

"Other way. If you can remember which way you started, maybe you can do it the other way if it doesn't work?"

Step by step, she talks me through the steps. The scent of her hair as she leans into me is comforting. Her voice gives me a direction to hang on to. After three attempts, I yank open the clasp.

"No way! First time ever!"

"You don't mind me teaching you?" she says.

"Why would I? You got me to open it."

She purses her lips. "I can be overwhelming."

"I like how you overwhelm me."

"Ha. Whatever."

"No, really. People get inspired by your energy. It's how you got fifty people to come to Taiwan at the drop of a hat."

"A *hundred* fifty, actually." She smiles, smug.

A rap on the door makes us jump. "Apologies for keeping you waiting," Mr. Chin says.

We'd shifted closer, her knee pressed against my leg. Now I sit back as Mr. Chin takes his seat across from us. A trickle of sweat glistens on his forehead. He types furiously on his laptop while I relock my lock and nervously spin the dial.

"There will be a fee for the overseas transfer," he says finally. "I'll need you to authorize me to override controls. Normally, these are in place to protect large accounts like your family's." He peers into his screen. "Ah, very good."

I pull Ba's chop from its pouch. All the times I stamped his passbook with him . . . only now he's not in the chair behind me. If he were, he'd change every possible code and lock to keep me from doing this.

But taking my own trust is completely legit. If Ba did try to stop me, *he* would be in the wrong. Not that that's stopped him yet.

I hand Ba's chop to Mr. Chin for inspection.

"Ah, Master Yeh, we don't need your father's chop. We need yours."

"Mine?" I stare at him blankly.

"Yes. This trust is fully within your control, as you said. Your father's mark is no longer needed. We will register yours."

Mine.

I sit frozen for a moment. Then I dig into my backpack for the chop I carved into soapstone over the summer. I feel Sophie's eyes on me as I ink its end with the red stamp pad, set the seal over the clean page Mr. Chin holds out to me, and press down.

And when I lift it, my dragon gleams back up at me.

I stamp a few more papers for the bank files. I ask for enough money for ten plane tickets home, and it's so easy. He hands me a fat envelope containing the cash for the plane rides. "The balance of your funds are being transferred now to your account in Los Angeles. As I mentioned, it will take a few days."

He pushes a thin-sheeted page toward me. I don't need to be

able to read to understand that there are a lot of digits. I hand it to Sophie. Her eyes widen and she gives me a nod.

My voice shakes. "It's done?"

"Yes," he replies. "We look forward to seeing more of you for your other family matters, Mr. Yeh!"

My phone buzzes. It's Jane, probably with some PR emergency. I shut it off, still too stunned to respond. Sophie looks equally dazed, like she's spun about a hundred circles on the ice and just come to a standstill.

Only now does it hit me. Ma left it all to me; she trusted me. She wasn't expecting me to live up to some bar first. She already believed I'd lived up to it. She loved me with no strings attached.

And because of her, that's how I get to live now—with no Yeh strings to yank me in every direction like a puppet. Just like she wanted.

Checkmate, Ba.

34

SOPHIE

He did it. Xavier set out to get his trust, and he got it. A crazy lot of money.

And you know what? It doesn't matter to me.

I've seen him get his ear yanked off by his dad, and his cheek pinched by his great-aunt. I've watched his cousin smack him down with a humiliation he can never recover from, and I have seen him stand back up and take control of his future.

I've seen how much the people who've known him all his life like and respect him.

I've watched him struggle with his dyslexia and his family's shame.

I've seen him shine when he captures the world he sees, in drawings, photos, or film, in the way only he can.

And I love all of that about him.

But now . . . how can I tell him now?

Hey, Xavier, now that I've toured your museum and mansion and seen the many millions in your bank account, I've changed my mind. I want you to lay your head on my lap and look up at me every single day.

How could he trust me? How could I trust *myself*? He's never been closer. He's never been more out of reach.

"Ma'am?" The hostess touches my arm respectfully, bringing me from my reverie. I'm standing at one of the wide windows that encircle the eighty-eighth floor of Taipei 101, on eye level with the reason all of Asia is celebrating this weekend. But what was supposed to be a brilliant view of the largest moon of the year is a smoky haze of clouds.

How fitting.

"Ma'am, shall we bring out the appetizers?" she asks for what might be the third time.

"Um, yes. Please do. Thank you."

A clock on the wall reads 7:01. Behind her, Loveboat alumni are pouring out of the elevators dressed in iridescent glamour and grit. Spencer and Priscilla scrub flecks of fluorescent paint from their hair. Debra takes charge of the influx of mooncakes, unwrapping boxes and party favors: fans threaded with red ribbons, mini boba teas with fat bamboo straws. Folded white paper lanterns, small ones left over from lunar new year, but it's the thought that counts. They're all going fast, so I snag a lantern for Xavier. We split up to change an hour ago, and I haven't seen him since.

Around the room, couples are pairing off at standing tables, sharing drinks in giant crystal goblets. Others nestle into lime-green couches filled with red pillows, positioned for a view of the elusive moon. Debra dances with a group to a K-pop band blaring from speakers. Two girls are making out in the corner.

I smooth my turquoise dress, which fits as perfectly as the Magic Mirror promised. The hand-painted dragons are iconic, and the snakeskin boots aren't just striking, they're loving on my tired feet. This is one of the qualities I love about clothes—how the right outfit can transform you into your best self. And tonight, that best self has a job to pull off: managing people trying out the Magic Mirror, navigating Taipei TV, and getting our #LoveboatReunion followers to support.

Focus, Sophie. No tornados tonight.

Aunty Three said selling five outfits would help make her case for the Mirror's technology—I want *ten*, to blow this victory out of the park. Dragon Leaf will *have* to take notice. Then there's the reunion itself—simple food: dumpling appetizers, a classic bowl of beef noodle soup, and a Moon Festival dessert of sweet osmanthus rice wine and sesame mochi, but complicated by a hundred sixty-one guests . . . and the most important goal, getting Xavier and Emma together.

"Amazing party, Sophie!" Debra calls. "You've done it again."

"I didn't mean to do any of it," I admit. "But glad everyone's happy."

I begin a livestream on my phone that also plays on several large wall screens. "All right, Loveboaters, we've got a big scene here in Taipei 101. Music, matchmaking, and a very special Magic Mirror demo, not to mention baby pandas!"

Dang, two hundred people have already dialed in.

"We have over ninety pairings online and another fifty live pairs here . . . for a total of three hundred participants tonight."

"Three hundred?" Rick chokes.

"That's the Sophie we know and love!" Ever calls.

Where's Xavier? I don't see him anywhere. I force myself to focus on the sheer energy of all these people. I'm actually in my element in moments like these. Getting everything and everyone moving to the same drumbeat.

Comments start popping up in my thread.

Can I sign up?
How do I sign up?
Here's the moon in Madrid!

I smile and reply:

I posted a dating app on the Loveboat channel this morning. It assigned everyone to a table here or in a virtual chat room. If you missed the sign-up, find people on the chat and meet on your own. We'll get started in ten minutes, so make your way there!

"Hey, I don't have a table assignment." Bert looks up from his phone.

"Oops." I smile sweetly. "Animated penis, mooning hundreds of people, trying to open a plane door thousands of feet over the earth . . . maybe the dating app thought you weren't ready for a mature relationship."

"Ms. Sophie?" The Taipei TV crew is heading toward me, shouldering video cameras the size of torpedos. Seriously hardcore—fantastic! A petite woman in a soft blue blazer holds out a hand. "What a crowd! I'm Sheryl. Rose Chan sent us—"

"Yes, so glad to have you!" I swoop down to hug her, then link arms and tug her toward the Magic Mirror, which Aunty Three's team has set up on a dais by one of the windows. Lulu's manning the digital scanner, teaching each person how to make their own avatar. A second line has formed before the Magic Mirror itself.

"Sophie!" Ever calls. "This mirror is incredible!" On the dais, Ever in a crimson skirt is dancing with three Ever Wongs in the panels, swirling in a pearl-white ball gown that outshines the shy moon just beyond her. She nailed her audition today, although she won't hear results until later tonight.

Rick hangs back, beefy arms crossed. The only unhappy face, as far as I can see.

"Don't like the gown?" I ask.

His eyes are on Ever. "It doesn't seem right, that two people who've finally found each other can't be together."

A lump forms in my throat. "No. It's not right. If Ever ends up in London, I'm going to miss her, too. But it's her future."

He looks at me. Then his arms unfold. "Yes, I don't want her

324

to regret not giving her all to her applications, because I was holding her back."

"She wouldn't see you that way."

"Yes. But *I* might." He hands me a glass of white wine from a passing tray. "And with you—I tried to stop you on the plane with Xavier, but then I realized the same thing. It's not up to me. You two are going to make your choices, and I'm here to support you. Even if that means waiting for her for four years. Or stuffing you into that suitcase and giving myself a hernia carrying you home."

"Ha!" I slip an arm around his rib cage and squeeze. "You put on a good front, but inside, you're a teddy bear."

"So are you." He smiles. "I just hope you don't both leave me behind."

"Never," I tell him.

Three Evers pirouette in a beautiful and bizarre metallic dress, its spiky necklace flaring in a circle. I capture her on video as it transforms into a severe, throat-choking suit made from the American flag.

"Seriously?" she groans.

Laughing, I post her flag outfit on my Instagram, and it immediately gets a few hundred likes and climbing. I whoop and show Rick. "How about that?"

"George, get a shot of that long line," says the reporter. Her cameraman pans from Ever to the people waiting for the Mirror, to Lulu's line of Loveboaters making avatars.

On Instagram, comments come in from our viewers marked #LoveboatReunion.

> Beautiful outfit!
>
> I want, I want
>
> Wish I could try that mirror. Someone fly me to Taipei?

I type into the comments. If you like what you see, order directly from the store and say you saw it on the Magic Mirror!

I won't know how many outfits have sold until I see Aunty Three tonight, but I'm already dying to find out.

Ever steps off the dais and shoves me toward it. "You go now."

"I've already tried it," I protest.

"Yes, but now you have us to heckle you."

"Ha! All right, I can always use more fashion advice." I set down my glass of wine and step into place. My image blinks as the Mirror registers my avatar. Aunty Three must be doing some work in the background, because it automatically starts to make recommendations.

My clothes swap out in rapid succession: a candy cane–inspired crop top over vertical-striped pants, showing off a midriff and belly button that—to be honest—are not as good as my real ones. An aquarium-blue pantsuit, complete with a red stripe down each leg, a matching red jacket exploding with big blue dots, and a fedora hat tied with a ribbon. Then a prim black dress with a fat gold zipper suggestively running down the front of my entire line of symmetry. Definitely not Dartmouth CS-class appropriate.

Marc whistles from the crowd. "*Hot*, Sophie!"

I put my hand to my tilted head, strike a pose. Whoops fill the air. "Go, Sophie!" Debra calls. My face in the Mirror stays radiant, but as a ruffled Victorian dress whirls onto the outside of my body, inside is a tug-of-war.

Who am I, really?

Am I this sexy girl who, I admit, enjoys catching eyes—or the strong, powerful woman who wants to rule the world? The truth is, I like feeling beautiful and bold in exciting clothes. I love doing things like tonight's event, galvanizing people around a plan and bringing them together. I love having a big idea, digging deep, making it work. Showing that I have a vision—one that shouldn't be dismissed.

Can I be all of those? Have all of those?

"Sophie!" Emma comes toward me, waving. Effortlessly blow-dried hair frames her face, and a cherry-blossom sprig is tucked into the sleek blackness. Her sleeveless rose-colored gown hugs her ribs and accentuates her slimness, skimming the tops of dainty pink sandals. She sparkles as though covered in stardust.

"Some party!" She's graciousness incarnate. But her blue eyes are cool.

"Emma!" I leave the Mirror to meet her, grasping her arm. My words tumble over one another. "It's so amazing your folks could sponsor us tonight. And I'm so glad you still came. I mean, I knew you were coming to reconnect with Xavier. That's still the plan, I *swear*."

"Yes, we should talk." She frowns. Even angry, she's calm and well-spoken, scented with an expensive Jean Patou fragrance. "Why didn't you tell me you'd dated him before? I gave you every chance."

I look down at the toes of my snakeskin boots. "I didn't want to get into our whole history. After a while, it seemed weird to bring it up."

Her chest rises and falls with a long breath.

"Anyways, I've put you two together for the experience of a lifetime. The zoo is bringing baby pandas, and I got authorization for you and Xavier to hold them. For a photo shoot—it'll be so fun!"

"That's amazing." Her arms unfold and her frown diminishes. "I suppose I didn't tell you about Miles upfront either." She sighs. "I don't *own* Xavier. It's just . . . I didn't want to think you stabbed me in the back. I believe you didn't mean any harm."

I'm relieved she's mollified, although a tiny part of me can't help feeling . . . well, *thanks*. Because she's right. She *doesn't* own Xavier. . . .

My phone chimes as another comment pops up on the feed:

@Sophie I bought the black dress! That gold zipper! Oh my!

"Hey, someone bought off the Mirror!" I say. "It's working!"

"Already? That's fantastic. Did you tell Horvath about it?"

"Not yet. I wrote an email and wrapped up the proposal just before the party. But I've been too busy to send it."

"Send it! I can't wait to hear what he says."

"In the middle of a party?"

She laughs. "Why not? Want me to proofread it for you?"

"Yes, please!"

Emma reads over my shoulder as I pull up the email on my phone:

Dear Professor Horvath,

I've had the chance to interview the inventors of a digital stylist in Taipei. They've created a virtual avatar system that could change the way people shop for clothes in a $2 trillion industry. My plan is to build in an enriched set of data to help their system make better recommendations for outfits, based on data like size, color, style, occasion, even mood. Eventually, I would like to expand the set into harder-to-quantify characteristics of personality so that an outfit not only reflects its wearer, but enhances the person in all their complexity. The project incorporates both deep learning and reinforcement learning, which, as you noted in class on the first day, is where many exciting developments lie.

I'm attaching my revised proposal.

Thank you for giving me another chance.

Best,
Sophie Ha

"I like it," Emma says. "Why don't you include a video of people using it?"

"Great idea." I add in a line: "Here's a video of happy customers." I attach Ever pirouetting in her metallic dress, the crowd cheering.

With a nervous shiver, I hit send.

"You'll crush it," Emma says. "Horvath doesn't have anything like this in his class. He'll get to say one day that you were his student."

"I hope you're right."

"Selfie?"

"Why not?" I hold out my phone and she leans in. Her in pink, me in turquoise.

"Looking good." She smiles.

I open Instagram to post our photo. A comment on my rules of the road speech leaps out at me:

She's insanely bossy.

UGH!

With three words, I plunge from towering heights to black depression.

I lower my phone. "I should delete my account. They hate me." I turn the phone toward her.

"Are you kidding? That's one jerk out of hundreds. You can win this person over, or ignore them. Either way, don't let them upset you."

A waiter presents sparkling champagne flutes. My wineglass is gone, so I follow Emma and take one.

"Cheers," she says, and we clink our glasses. In this moment, I couldn't care less whether champagne gives me a headache. I want to believe Emma. But I am pretty sure Emma could be in charge of the world and no one would accuse her of being bossy.

"I vote for ignore. Thanks, Emma." I hug her. "And there's Xavier." I finally spot him at the bar, barely visible through the dancers on the floor. The back of his head, with his pile of curly hair, is toward us. His satin overcoat shimmers under the lights.

Emma takes a huge gulp from her flute, then threads her hand through my arm. "Okay, let's go!" We head to the bar. "I'm shaking," she gasps.

I'm shaking, too.

"You're old buddies," I say, for her as much as me. "Once you start talking, that connection you've always had will be right there again."

"Emma, you're here, too?" A girl in a strapless black dress flings her arms around Emma, who laughs and gives me an apologetic smile.

"You go ahead," she says. "I'll catch up in a few."

She seems relieved for the reprieve.

Honestly, I am, too.

Xavier's black video camera is slung at a casual angle on his shoulder. He's surrounded at the bar by Bert, Joella and Jasmine, Rick and Ever—everyone from the jet. He hands his phone to Joella, who gives her passport number to a curly-haired woman on a video call, then passes the phone to Rick. Xavier lifts his camera and aims it at the bartender as he shakes a frosted metal canister. A television screen overhead broadcasts a soccer match with players racing over astroturf.

I haven't seen Xavier this relaxed in a long time. His soft silvery-lilac clothes give him an elegant, artsy look that's 100 percent *him*.

I scoot in beside Priscilla, who flips her hair back. She fixes me with an acid stare.

"You really know how to make other people's money go a long way, huh?"

Priscilla, my friend again. "Sorry, what?" I ask warily.

"This whole party—you're not paying a cent, but you get all the limelight. And a free trip—I mean, yeah, we all got to bum a ride, but you—you're here for a school project. It's really generous of Xavier to help you out. Says a lot about him."

"Yeah, it does," I say. "I'm really grateful."

To my alarm, Xavier's hand grips my shoulder. He glares at Priscilla. "My aunt's project was stuck under a blanket for twenty years until Sophie came and unstuck it. So if anyone's benefited, it's my family."

"Sure, Xavier. Sure." Priscilla's not convinced but slips off.

"Hey," Xavier says to me.

I can't quite meet his gaze. Priscilla knows I'm not in his class, and I can't bear to see that same knowledge in his eyes.

"Hey." He grips my jaw in his hand and forces me to look at him. As our eyes meet and I see only concern in his, I have a sudden sense of my anchor being cut, of being a tugboat tossed on open waves. "You okay?"

"Yeah." I fight for calm and control. I'm more okay after he releases me. "Thanks . . . for that."

"It was all true. I can barely help myself under normal circumstances. You got me moving. That says a lot about *you*."

Where did this guy come from? I smile through the pain in my chest. "How are you feeling now?"

His eyes are bright. "Free. I'm finally fucking home free."

His jet-black curls blow in a breeze. The imprint of his hand is still on my chin, warm and assured. Will I always feel this pull toward him? Maybe I just need to accept that my heart may never cooperate with my head.

I shove the paper lantern at him. "Best party favor here."

He examines the tiny waxy candle. "Cool, thanks." He glances sideways at me. "That dress is great on you, by the way."

"Thanks." Dress compliments I can handle.

"I knew you'd pick it."

"What? How?"

"I just did." He smirks. "Although it makes you look more like a Yeh than I do."

"Whatever. It's the dragons." I trace a finger along one delicate painted ridge. "Now that you have your trust, do you . . .

333

think you'll talk to your dad at some point?"

His eyes go flinty. "Not for a while. If ever. He doesn't deserve my time."

"I just . . . can't really see you cutting off the rest of your family."

He falls silent. After a long moment, I touch his video camera. "You're still filming."

"Not for the assignment," he says. "For me."

I smile. "Can I peek?"

He takes his camera into both hands but doesn't show it to me just yet.

"My mom used to read me a story about a magic paintbrush, where everything painted with it became real," he says. "I used to imagine painting a whole zoo of animals and letting them run around my bedroom."

"I want a brush like that."

"So did everyone in the story. Especially the evil king. So the painter was careful not to make the powers known."

"How?"

"He never finished his paintings. He always left out one last brushstroke. Until one day, a drop of paint accidentally fell from the tip of his brush, making the eye of a rooster. The bird flew off the page, and the painter was caught."

"How amazing would it be if a painting actually came to life?"

"I sort of figure that even if I don't have a bird literally fly off the page, that should be the goal. Paint so well, or take a photo that's so real, that it feels like it does." He laughs. "Okay, now I've raised the bar sky-high."

He hands me his camera. As I scroll through the footage, he spins the dial on his lock, fidgeting. He's landed his trust fund and has more talent than anyone I know—and he's still nervous showing me his footage.

"The colors are good enough to eat," I say. In the showroom, the cherry of the vintage car, the blueberry of Victor's shirt, and the purple of my pantsuit pick up highlights in the aircraft his dad invented. My head is turned at the same angle as Victor's, my mouth open with a laugh, my hair draped like a heavy black curtain over my shoulder. Xavier's captured a moment of wonder—and more amazingly, infused it with his own.

"How do you do this? Everything is more real than reality."

"It *is* reality. I just caught it."

I advance to a clip of the jagged Taipei skyline against the afternoon sky. I point to the clouds. "Like these. They're not white. They're blue, purple, lavender, rose. How did you do that?"

"It's what I see," he says. "Everything is colors."

I look up and our noses bump. "Oh, sorry," I stammer. My face warms, and I drop my gaze from those unfairly long lashes. "What colors am I?"

"Orange and purple."

"Like a bruise?" I frown.

"No, dork." His laugh warms me. "Like a sunrise."

I look back down at the clouds. He sees everything, every*one*, so clearly. But instead of feeling afraid, this time, I can't help feeling how much easier it is to be myself *because* he sees me so clearly. A sunrise.

"What is all this?" Victor pushes through the dancers, toward us. He's changed into a blue-striped blazer over maroon pants. Honestly, for all that he's dismissed the Magic Mirror, I have never met a better-dressed guy. I should be swooning over him, but for so many reasons . . . no.

Xavier puts his camera away. His lips press into a thin line.

"Xavier's buying our plane tickets." Priscilla flashes Xavier's phone, all wide smiles. "We're on hold with the agent."

"No, I mean where did the press come from? Only authorized people—"

"That song is getting old." Xavier takes his phone back. "And you have some nerve showing up here."

"That watch trick was low, Victor," I say. "I didn't think you were like that."

"I didn't think he was stupid enough to fall for it," Victor snaps.

"Hello, Xiang-Ping?" The curly-haired agent is back. She delivers an enormous quote for all our plane tickets.

"Great," Xavier says. "I have the money here. Stop by any time tonight."

"Xavier, we should pay you back," I say, but Priscilla throws her arms around him. "Thanks, Xavier! Huge relief. Now we can party in peace!"

"We all owe you," Ever says.

"No need. It's my celebration gift."

"Where did you get that kind of cash?" Victor asks, suspicious.

Xavier smirks. "It's mine."

"You're supposed to be on a tight leash. For everyone's good."

Xavier straightens. "You know, I looked up to you when we were kids. Even after you laughed at me for only selling one photo at the festival, and for not being able to tell left from right—I still looked up to you. And you shit on me every time . . . until I finally realized I didn't need to stick around to let it land on me."

Victor's face pales.

"I don't have brothers or sisters, and neither do you," Xavier continues. "You should have been the closest I had to a brother. But instead you've always had it out for me. Why is that?"

Victor's hands clench. I'm afraid he'll deck Xavier right here in front of everyone.

"Victor, we're having a party," I say.

He glances at me, and his fist opens again. But his eyes flash as he grates, "My dad always made it clear that no matter how good I was, I was going to be your lackey."

"I've never asked for that."

"I'm giving the speech of my lifetime tomorrow. I need to prepare. I need my head clear. But I land in Taipei, and the first thing I get is a text from your dad saying to wait for you to arrive. I'm a TA for the hottest professor at Dartmouth. You can't even graduate from high school. You screw up everything and don't care who you hurt."

"What the fuck—"

"Then suddenly, it's MY JOB to make YOU look good? Your dad didn't think twice before asking me to babysit your project. Jane had me *spoon-feed* you lines for Ambassador Chiu. And in case you missed it, that's what my dad's done for *your* stupid dad for thirty years. After your dad forced mine out of Dragon Leaf."

"What?" Xavier's genuinely stunned. "Your dad is Ba's right-hand man. He heads up a division."

"That's what it looks like, doesn't it? My dad runs a small division now. Barely any shares. No portrait at headquarters. Not a factor in the equation."

"Why would Ba do that?"

"To model how to treat family? The usual boring reasons? Money and power?" Victor's fists clench again. "But all of that— it's ending. Very soon." He lobs his glass at the bartender's sink, halfway down the bar. It shatters inside with the sound of splintering glass.

"Hey!" says the bartender.

The space around us grows silent. Victor storms for the exit. He bumps into a tiny waitress, sending her careening into Debra, but doesn't even stop to apologize.

"He better not cause trouble," Xavier says darkly.

"Give me a moment." I run after Victor and grab him by the arm.

He turns, scowling. "What? You're on his side. I get it."

"What's wrong with you? You're nothing like this at Dartmouth."

"At Dartmouth, people know what I'm capable of. My role isn't predetermined by birth."

"Look, I get that your dad has beef with Xavier's, but what you did at the party? That wasn't just hurting Xavier. That was hurting your own grandfather. Why are you leaving disaster in your wake just to screw with your own cousin?"

His mouth works. "There's so much history you don't know."

"Your dad hasn't exactly been a model citizen himself. Instead of being caught in the middle, why don't you take charge of your own destiny? Why don't you decide what *you* believe, and act on that? You *don't* have to accept the role they assign you. Just like I didn't have to roll over for Horvath. Fight for your own path. You're better than this."

His sullen expression doesn't change.

"Fine," I say, resigned. "I'll see you at Dartmouth."

I leave him at the elevators and weave back toward the bar. I reach Xavier and the others just as Emma arrives from the opposite direction.

"Sophie! Xavier! Hey!"

"Hey," Xavier says. He's still troubled, but smiles. "Emma. You made it."

She holds out a little gold-and-ruby ring on her palm. "Do you remember this?"

He picks up the ring and his smile widens. "My mom helped me buy this for you."

She laughs. "We got engaged in the garden."

"By the orchids. Turns out you were allergic to them."

"Yes! But not the ring. I still had it in my vanity table at our apartment here."

Some of the stress leaves his body. That's what a good old friend can do for you. And he gave her a *ring*, with his mom playing along. And he remembers it. All the details.

But a hollow pit is opening in my stomach.

No, no. This is exactly what I planned. I slip away to give them space. I hide in my phone, checking that the virtual rooms are up and running. They are. The #LoveboatReunion hashtag is flooding with photos of couples. People drift toward their assigned tables, which rotate by courses. I've engineered it, of course, so Xavier and Emma are together for every rotation.

A spotlight shines on them. She's talking to him, her head tipped up. He leans on an arm on the bar, looking down at her. They don't need enhancements to look like the royal couple of the century. The silvery-lilac of his outfit blurs with the rose of her dress.

All their hues run together, so beautiful it hurts.

"I knew they would hit it off again," I say to Ever, who's propped her elbows on the counter beside me. It's not just their history together or that they're both über-wealthy Taiwanese American parachute kids. Or even that they've both lost someone. They're both authentic human beings.

And right now, they're lost in each other.

Ever tucks her hand through my elbow and squeezes. "You threw this entire party for us. With nothing in it for you. That's your MO."

"MO?"

"Modus operandi. Reason you do. Everything."

"I just want everyone to have a great time." It's true, even if another part of me is bleeding. Everyone's a couple.

"That's what I mean."

She hugs me, and suddenly I'm fighting tears.

The zookeeper enters the restaurant cradling a baby panda the size of a sack of flour in his arms. A woman in sage overalls pushes a stroller. The hostess is swooning as I reach them.

"You can stay right here the rest of the party," she declares. "No need to go in."

In the carriage, a soft heap of black-and-white fur rises and falls with breath.

"OH MY GOD THEY ARE ADORABLE!" I squeal. I can't take my eyes off them. "I wish my brothers could see them. I'm Sophie. We spoke on the phone."

"That's Lang sleeping." The zookeeper holds up his panda cub. "This is Ling." The little guy sneezes, then gazes at me from droopy black circles.

"I hate to say it, but he's as cute as my baby cousin," I say. "I'm *dying* to hold him."

"Only two people can hold pandas tonight," he says. "For their safety. Are you one of them?"

"Oh. No, that's my friends, Xavier and Emma. It's for a photo shoot for the press. We're trying to get word out on the Magic

Mirror here—come on, this way."

I turn to call the others, but I need not have bothered. Ever, Xavier, Emma, Rick—everyone is barreling down on me, and soon the zookeeper and his helper are surrounded.

"Baby pandas in Taipei 101?" Rick asks.

I grin. "Since I couldn't get us tickets to the exhibit, I got the exhibit to come here!"

"I heard you could only hold baby pandas in Chengdu."

"How did you ever manage this?" Ever says. "There must be rules—"

"I'm disappointed in you both," I scold. "Did you learn nothing on Loveboat? I can pull off anything."

"You are unbelievable." Xavier laughs. "Only you, Sophie Ha."

"I'm gonna let you say my name that time, *Xavier Yeh*," I tease. "Let's move over to the Magic Mirror. We can have it in the background for the photo shoot."

By the Mirror, the zookeeper gives Emma a smock to wear over her dress, a huge squirt of hand sanitizer, gloves, and a mask. The Mirror reflects Emma's back as she takes her baby panda into her arms, cooing with delight. Taipei TV is filming live, slipping through Jane's fingers. I hang back with Xavier, holding my hand to my chest and willing my heart to still.

"How perfect is this?" I say. "After all these years, your trust, now you two back together?"

He gives me a sidelong glance. "Why are you trying so hard to set us up?"

342

I swallow hard. "She's from your world." I train my gaze on Emma as she swoons over her baby panda like a new mother.

"When have I wanted *my* world? Don't you know me?"

Even in the midst of this crowd, a bubble of stillness surrounds us.

"Xavier?" Emma calls. "There's a panda here purring your name."

"You should join her," I say.

"Yeah." But his eyes on me hold a question mark.

"Go," I say, and as he starts, I say, "Xavier?"

He turns back. "Yes?"

I'm not even sure why I called him back. Except to keep him with me one more beat. Before he goes to Emma. Because no matter what he says about wanting to rebel against his family and turn his back on his world forever, I don't believe he will.

"Never mind," I say.

"Let's talk more later," he says, then joins Emma before the Mirror. The zookeeper robes him in smock, gloves, and mask, then places a baby panda in his arms. Xavier hitches the cub higher, awkward and adorable. Emma moves closer, and the baby pandas paw at each other.

A collective sigh goes up. "So cute!"

"Loveboat king and queen! Let's crown them!"

Cameras flash. Behind them, the Mirror dresses them in matching black and white. On Instagram, dozens of black-and-white pandas are flooding my feed.

Along with a running list of complaints:

I didn't get put into a room.

Our virtual link is broken. Hello? Anyone listening?

Why did I get grouped with people from my summer?

Makes more sense to match me with people from
another summer.

This reunion seems disorganized.

I got turned away at the door! They said it was full, fuckers

Can't even see the moon from there

Who's the #bossy girl?

What a cow. Too many xiao long bao, lol.

The comments keep going. Hundreds of them.

What the hell? A last-minute party, free food, baby pandas, and at least a *chance* at the best view of the big fat moon—seriously, I can't make these people happy.

Sophie: Guys, FINE.

Sophie: Please grow up, take some initiative and have
your own party.

I shut off my phone. Brilliant. I've made myself about two thousand haters.

Ever and Rick, arms locked around each other, are swaying together on the dance floor. Xavier, cradling his panda, is leaned over Emma cradling her panda, forming a protective box that encloses them in their private world. The camera crew shifts closer, lights flashing, playing with angles.

Emma leans toward him, speaking, laughing.

My heart jolts.

It isn't just that Xavier makes me crazy. He also makes me bigger. That expansion throws me off balance, yes, but it also lifts my feet off the ground. And when I think ahead to returning to campus, to going about my days without him, life feels . . . ordinary. But maybe this is reality, despite these romantic shots we're taking of Emma and Xavier. Maybe life isn't rushing romance and pounding hearts. Maybe life is just what it is: work, friends, eating, playing. Getting up every day and going about your business.

Business like my CS project.

I open my email inbox like I'm trying to find answers there. Maybe I can send Horvath a photo of the pandas in the Mirror.

The title of the email in my inbox is bolded—Horvath wrote back already! Wow, he's fast. Eagerly, I open his note.

> Ms. Ha,
>
> Virtual avatars have been around for decades and never taken off.
>
> I think it's best for you to try another course. There's a start-up company class and a design class that might be better fits.
>
> H

Try another course?

Try another course. . . .

But virtual avatars are beside the point . . . so I'm out?

I glance up as the zookeeper and his helper take the pandas from Emma and Xavier. Emma offers Xavier a sip of her osmanthus tea. The ruby ring sparkles on her little finger. He removes his mask and leans down to take a sip—such a simple, yet intimate gesture.

Oh, God. I've made a terrible mistake!

Two thoughts hit me at the same time.

First, I want to be Cinderella, too.

And second, a question—is this why I came all this way?

Have I been fooling myself, convincing myself I was coming for the Magic Mirror, the new Sophie Ha after her MBA . . . when all along, there wasn't anything to chase. . . .

After all my swearing off dating . . . after telling myself that it was ambition sending me halfway around the world, did I come all this way for . . . a BOY?

The zookeepers, Xavier, and Emma are heading toward one of the private rooms. Pandas, camera crew, and all follow along. And I realize . . .

I am incapable of friendship with Xavier. Not if I want any chance at a normal, healthy, happy life at Dartmouth. Because I'm in too deep. My heart too connected. Friendship is too tight a sleeve for what I feel, squeezing what is uncontainable into too small a space.

Rick passes me, headed for the bar. "Rick, hold on a sec?" I grab a napkin and print a quick note to Xavier, then fold and hand it to him. I'm fighting tears. "Can you give this to Xavier when . . . he's done?"

"Sure, but what's wrong? Where are you going?"

It's all I can do not to implode on my poor cousin—who warned me, didn't he?

"I just need some time. Give it to him for me, okay?"

Rick tucks the note into his breast pocket. "Sure," he says, and I'm so grateful I can trust my cousin to deliver. Even if I can't trust myself.

I turn to go but freeze as my eyes fall on Bert strutting before the Magic Mirror, a glass of beer in hand.

"When did I get so handsome," he slurs. He peers closely at his enhanced image. A familiar T-shirt appears on his body: YOU AND I GO TOGETHER LIKE DUMPLINGS AND SOY SAUCE. "I wonder how it would clothe the family jewels."

Oh, God, he's completely wasted.

He tugs at his pants, and people begin to yell, "No! We don't want to see it!"

Taipei TV is standing by, cameras lowered. The anchor-woman looks horrified. Penises in the Mirror—this isn't the news story they were looking for!

And worse.

I rush forward as what is about to happen whales me in the face. Booze and kids and fragile technology in the same unsu-pervised room. All along, my tornado was at work, and only now am I seeing the devastation it's caused.

Bert lets out an enormous belch.

He topples forward.

"Look out!" I yell.

Then Bert crashes face-first into the three-way mirror, and along with him, the whole thing topples off the dais.

35

XAVIER

The zookeeper's helper lays Lang's warm heft gently in her stroller as I train my camera on her black-and-white fur, catching the quick dips of her breathing. She's parked by a window with a view of the patch of paler sky that should have been the harvest moon.

Over in the far corner of this private suite, Emma and Ling are surrounded by photographers for a last few shots before the pandas go home.

An arm brushes mine. It turns out to be connected to Ever Wong, snapping a panda photo. She's dressed like a ballerina: tights, crimson tulle skirt, a matching sweater crisscrossing her waist, fully embracing her dancer identity.

"Hey, Ever."

"Oh." She's startled. "Hey, Xavier. How's it going?"

"Going great."

"I'm glad." Her expression is carefully neutral. She turns to go, but I say, "Ever?"

"Yeah?"

"I've been getting closer to Sophie." I want her to know. Not because of our history, but because she's Sophie's best friend, and I want her to know what Sophie has come to mean to me.

Ever smiles. "Yes, I know. I'm glad."

I'm glad she's glad. "She's . . . she tackles life. Head-on." Am I really trying to explain what it is about Sophie that's so . . . her? The words keep wanting to try. "For a long time, I've been hiding from life."

Ever lays a tentative hand on my shoulder. "We're all growing up, huh?"

"Yeah," I say, and she slips away. I watch her go, swaying slightly to that inner soundtrack of hers. I'm glad our lives intersected on Loveboat, even if only for such a short window. Even if I wish we'd done things differently, since she'll never look at me with anything other than that carefully neutral expression. But she opened a door to art for me that had been welded shut before, and for that I'll always be grateful.

I sink onto the blue couch, filming the glow of the moon, hoping for an actual view, but it's still stubbornly hiding. The combination lock digs into my backside, and I tug it out and give its nose a spin. Even juggling pandas, I've been trying to sort through the blowup with my cousin. Ba pushing Uncle Edward out, never making any statement about it . . . that's Ba. I wish I could say I feel sorry for Uncle Edward. But he's an older, fouler version of the Douche Lord. Taking Uncle Edward out is actually a smarter move than I expected from Ba.

I spin the dial, trying to retrace the steps Sophie walked me through . . . but it stays firmly shut.

Then Emma drops down beside me, removing her mask. "Those pandas were *to die for*! I didn't want to let go."

Beside her, the zookeeper snuggles Ling and smiles. "He likes you, too."

"Thanks for trusting us." I pocket the lock for now.

"You both were great. Be well now." He replaces Ling in the pram with his sibling. The crowd follows them out, still cooing and snapping photos. I scan them for Sophie, but she's not here. Probably catching up with all her friends.

"What a night." Emma lifts her arms overhead and rolls her neck. She smiles at me. "I'm surprised by how easy it was to hang out together. You and me."

"Yeah. It's been so good." We condensed ten years into an hour—my mom, our moves to the States, her boyfriend's death, my struggles with Ba, and her trying to figure out the meaning of her life. We've both been through so much heartache, almost parallel journeys. I even told her about my dyslexia—"That makes *so* much more sense," she said, and I said, "Really?" and wondered what she'd noticed.

But it was like finding the last puzzle piece that had been

missing for a while. She's my oldest friend, and she saw those parts of me that never quite fit together. Hearing her validate that is a final bridge between my past self and who I am now.

Emma crosses her legs, letting her pump dangle from her toe. "Remember how we hid from the cook under the bushes? You got scratched so badly your mom thought we'd had a fight. That I'd scratched you! As if!"

"And you got hives—"

"I'm still allergic to everything." She laughs.

I lean back against my elbows and gaze out at that hazy patch of hidden harvest moon. For the first time, my life isn't just staying afloat, it's hurtling 100 percent in the right direction. My trust. This kickass party. A real friend. Friends, plural.

"So do you still want to be an astronaut?" I ask.

"I'm *so* impressed you remembered." She gazes moonward with me. "I think in my heart, I want to touch the sky. But in reality, I'm okay keeping my feet on the ground."

I smile. "Lots of ways to fly."

"So true." Her hand falls on my arm, warm and steady. "I'm glad we're back in touch."

"Me, too." So solid—that's Emma. I'm grateful Sophie brought us back together. I'm not good at keeping people in my life. But Sophie—she gathers up everyone in her wake.

"Can I ask you something serious?" Emma says.

"Aren't we already serious?"

"Yes." She smiles again, then her hands twist together in her lap. "How long did it take you, after your mom died . . . ? I'm sorry. I don't even know what I'm asking."

"How long did it take me to accept it?"

"Yes. That's it."

I look back at the moon. If the clouds would get out of the way, I'd be able to see the rabbit my mom told me lived there. I used to think Emma would get to meet it if she became an astronaut.

"Honestly, part of me still hasn't. Maybe we never do. I just had to keep on living."

"You can't get them back. You can't go running to their room when something reminds you of them."

"Or call them."

"But the planet keeps on spinning."

"It changes everything when you lose someone. And nothing. In the worst of both ways."

We fall silent a moment.

"So what are you going to do now that you have your trust fund?"

"Everything." I stretch out my arms and legs. "Help my Aunty Three and her Mirror. Draw and paint. Buy a museum, if I want to get ambitious."

"Have a few princesses on your arms," she teases.

"Or just one." I smile. I glance over my shoulder at the closed doors. Sophie's probably seeing off the zookeeper, loading him down with extra food. Always two steps ahead of everyone. I admire that about her, and I wish I could at least keep up, if only to keep her company.

I turn back. "Actually, this might sound cliché, but I was thinking I could help kids with dyslexia. Like maybe I could give money to schools to buy everyone reader pens or something."

"That's a great idea, Xavier."

Sophie will have better ideas. It was something she'd do, I think. And I want to, too.

Moonlight gleams off the zipper on my backpack. My bag is partially open, and I glimpse the package I'd picked up from Ba's office. A book? A photo album? I haven't even had a chance to be curious.

"What is that?" Emma asks as I tug it free. The paper lantern from Sophie comes with it, and I tuck it back.

I remove the brown paper wrapping to find a soft book, stitched and bound with silk cords.

"It's a . . . a scrapbook," I say, surprised. "My dad gave it to me." She leans in as I flip through thick paper pages laid with my baby photos in cute frames. "My mom must have put this together." Sophie once said I'd gotten my eye from Ma—she's right. Something about the colors, the layout on each leaf. It's her, but also me. There are photos of me and her and Ba. Mementos: my first footprint, handprint, crayon drawings. Even as a five-year-old kid, my drawings had a sense of style and proportion.

So Ba wanted to give this to me . . . for my film? The collar of my shirt suddenly feels too snug. I tug on it as I flip to a collection of familiar photos.

"No way," I say. "These are the photos I tried to sell at my family's mooncake pavilion years ago." The big fail that gave the Douche Lord more stones to throw at me. A man frying octopus street food. A woman and her daughter pulling smoking incense sticks from an urn. All preserved here in this paper book.

"These are amazing!" Emma leans against my arm to see better.

They're not as bad as the Douche Lord made them out to be. At seven, I was capturing images that, even now, make me feel something. I turn the page to another collection of photos I'd taken at the same festival we're attending tomorrow. My camera finger had been trigger-happy back then—point and click, point and click—capturing everything I liked seeing. I flip through the pages: a knobby crab in a tank, matcha-green mochi, a glittering street performer.

Then my eyes land on a young girl in an orange dress, backdropped by my family's pavilion. She's pointing to the floating moon, and her face is filled with awe.

I remember her. Even though I was seven when I took this photo. "Is she the moon goddess?" I'd asked Ma, because she was so full of light. Eleven years later, I still recognize the kinetic energy radiating from her body. That boundless enthusiasm for all things wonderful.

And the sight of her now, like back then—is a bright glow in the night.

She's Sophie.

"They're beautiful," Emma says. She takes hold of my fingers and shifts to face me. She's no longer looking at the album. We're completely alone—everyone else followed the pandas.

Emma tilts her head.

My throat itches. Wait. Does she want to . . . ?

Her fingers wrinkle her gown on her thigh. "Xavier, I wanted to say . . . I mean, I need . . ."

She leans in. Instinctively, I move my head aside, and her lips fall on my jaw.

A curtain of hurt falls over her face and she drops my hand and slides off the couch. She starts for the doors.

Damn.

I set the scrapbook down and hurry to catch up. A sprig of cherry blossom falls from her hair. I rescue it and offer it to her.

"Emma, I'm sorry."

She doesn't take it. "It's Sophie, isn't it?"

I open my mouth to deny it on instinct. But that would be a lie.

When exactly did I fall so hard for Sophie Ha?

Emma crosses her arms and looks out the window over the city. She rubs her cheek with one small hand.

"Emma, I'm sorry—"

"Hey, uh, Xavier?" The door opens. It's Rick, who doesn't talk to me if he can help it. Something's wrong. His eyes stray to the cherry blossom in my hand, to Emma, then back to me.

"Sophie asked me to give this to you." Rick hands me a folded note.

"Sophie?" Why would she give me a *note*? "Why didn't she come talk to me herself?"

He frowns. "She left a while ago."

"Left?"

"The Mirror broke."

"Seriously? How?"

"Bert strikes again. We're taking care of it." He glances at Emma, misunderstanding. "You don't need to come back in yet."

I open the note. Sophie's printed it for my reader pen. Her handwriting is graceful and strong. So much like her that if I'd had to pick it out of a sample of notes, I'd have known it was hers.

I want to believe she's just upset about the Mirror, but my spidey sense tells me she wouldn't run off if it were just that. She'd have felt responsible, not that I blame her at all for the wild card that is Bert.

"She didn't say where she's going?"

"She wanted to be alone." Rick's grimace reminds me he's never liked Sophie and me together. But something's wrong. I need to find out what and why. I need to talk to her.

I hold the blossom out to Emma. "Can we please talk in a bit? I need to make a call."

Emma smooths her skirt, then takes the sprig. "Yes. I'll be in the other room."

They both slip away, and I call Sophie's cell phone. My call goes to voice mail.

"Sophie, it's me. We're done with the shoot. Give me a ring."

I dig into my backpack for my reader pen.

Dear Xavier,

I would have told you this in person if I could bring myself to. In just a weekend, I've had a chance to see so many sides of you. With your family especially. I'm glad I got to see you so happy and loved and at the top of your world.

I'm going to find my own way home and need some time and space to focus on things at Dartmouth. Thanks for everything you've shared with me. I'll be rooting for you.

Your friend,
Sophie

She's gone? A cold panic is spreading through my veins. I dial her again, but go straight to voice mail. I swear and hang up. Why is she calling it my world when she fits into it better than I do? Does she think all I needed was her help with my trust? Because that's just wrong—and she didn't even give me a chance to say goodbye.

I rush down the hallway and back to the main party room. Loveboat kids are dancing to music before the bar, no signs of Sophie's party ending anytime soon. But also no Sophie.

My phone rings in my hand. My heart jolts wildly in my chest—but it's only Jane. I'm about to press snooze when, on the television screen hanging over the bar, I glimpse the news with an image of . . .

Ba.

That edged haircut, head cushioned on the white pillow of a hospital bed, a tube under his nose.

I stride toward the screen with my phone to my ear. "Jane, what's going on with Ba?"

"Xiang-Ping, there have been complications with surgery. Your father hasn't woken up."

"When was he supposed to have woken up?"

"Several hours ago."

I frown. "So what does that mean?"

"The board will have to vote on a succession plan, but it may never get to that if the investors decide to sell Dragon Leaf to the Crusaders."

"No. I mean—why isn't he waking up?"

"The doctors aren't sure. They're trying to figure it out."

"He'll wake up. He . . . he has to." Ba's invincible. No one knows that better than me. I wanted to kill him myself, and I knew it was impossible.

Two news anchors are holding a conversation: a woman in a canary-yellow blouse with her hair in a tight bun—and the twelve-year-old mustachioed guy in tweed. The one in Ba's office.

He gazes directly at me through the screen. "Dragon Leaf

chairman and CEO Jasper Yeh is in the hospital in critical condition," he says. "His reps were not available for comment. Do you think they'll sell now?"

"Yes, they have no choice," says the woman. "Dragon Leaf has been struggling to move into the present. The offer to cash out is too compelling for their investors."

"Who votes the CEO's shares if he is incapable of making decisions for the company?"

"His brother, Edward Yeh."

"Does he support the sale?"

"My sources tell me he does."

"Seems like a done deal then."

What the fuck?

"Xiang-Ping, what are your thoughts?" Taipei TV's news anchor thrusts her mic at me. Wire mesh scrapes my nose.

"Me?"

"Aren't you Jasper's only son? Dragon Leaf has always been tight-lipped about succession plans and you haven't been in the spotlight much, but haven't you been groomed for a moment like this your entire life?"

No, I haven't, actually.

"The Crusaders are going to take down the Dragon Leaf logo from your family's building. The empire your great-grandfather founded and your grandfather and father built could end while your father's in a coma—can you make a statement?"

Jesus, she won't let up. I turn from her and weave through

the crowd, but she follows on my heels. On the screen, the kid anchorman is still going strong.

"These family-run companies need new blood. With so many protesting, it's pretty clear the employees and public agree."

"Xiang-Ping?" Taipei TV's anchorwoman jumps in front of me. "They've drowned out my coverage of tonight with this news. What do you have to say?"

"I have no statement," I say, then push past her and head for the doors.

36

SOPHIE

Evening celebrations for the Mid-Autumn Festival are in full swing, despite a slight drizzle. It's past nine o'clock, but up and down the sidewalks, families crowd flaming propane grills, turning slabs of pork and rows of pale shrimp blushing orange.

I barely see them as I run by. I've been running for almost an hour, but can't seem to outrun myself. A fat tear splashes on my phone as I pull it out to dial Ever.

I've missed two texts and a call from Xavier.

> We're finished with photos, where did you go?
> Got your note call me

Heartache isn't a figure of speech. It's a real thing.

Another text from him chimes: Sophie, please call me back.

I call Ever instead.

"Sophie, where did you go?" Ever asks. "The restaurant's finished cleaning up the Mirror."

I can never, *ever* face Aunty Three again.

"Can you meet me at Boba Guys? Just you? Please don't tell Xav—anyone I'm there."

"Sure. Hold on a sec." She goes silent, then, "I'll be there in five minutes."

We hang up. My head throbs from the champagne. With a small sob, I pull up my entire text thread with Xavier—thousands of words of conversation—and his phone number.

And I hit delete, erasing him from my life.

At the bubble tea shop, I have no choice but to sit under a lantern made of a hundred rosebuds, each shining with a tiny light inside. Symbols of love and joy are everywhere.

I open my emails, but can't even begin to compose a note to Aunty Three. What can I say? So instead, I write:

Dear Professor Horvath,
I took your advice and changed my project to making graphic images look like photos.

I'll see you in class Monday. I still want to try for your waitlist.

I sit back and reread the email. It's useful work. And life isn't a fairy tale. It's getting up every day and working. Not yearning for ridiculous happily ever afters.

But I don't want to believe that.

I don't.

I want to feel like I'm flying. I want life to be heart-pounding amazing.

I want the prince. I want the world-changing AI career.

I want it all.

Greedy Sophie Ha. That's me. A greedy, sucking tornado.

"Sophie!" Ever lands on the table with both hands, making it shake. "You won't believe it. I won the dance scholarship! It's a full ride to any dance school I can get into!"

"EVER!!! I'm so happy for you!" I throw my arms around my best friend. Cinderella incarnate. "You deserve it!"

Then I burst into tears. Ugly stepsister tears.

"Sophie!" As I drop my face into my hands, her arms go around me. "What's wrong?"

"I've lost . . . everything." I gulp air as I fill her in. "The Mirror was Xavier's aunt's lifetime of work and Xavier convinced her to meet me and I convinced her to let me show it tonight and I promised to take care of it."

"I know it's not good Bert broke it. But from what I understood, the Mirror was getting shut down. Xavier's aunt took a risk to save it."

I scrub at the dampness on my face. "People *hate* me, Ever. Have you seen the Loveboat hashtags? Maybe the reason there's disaster all around me is because . . . *I* am a disaster. *Me*."

"You're a trailblazer," she says. "Seriously, Sophie. Look at all you did! The people you got to come out to Taipei for a weekend! In the middle of school! You inspired Emma to sponsor a huge dinner. You inspired Aunty Rose to take a bet on herself and go public against her own PR. And you brought *baby pandas* to the top of Taipei 101—who does that? No one."

I smile through my tears. "They were the cutest."

"And you make everyone feel good about themselves—that's such a gift! I never feel beautiful and I don't know how to do anything with clothes and makeup, but you show me how to bring out the best parts of myself, and you make me believe I *am* beautiful—and that matters."

"It's what the Magic Mirror was for."

"Yes. You're doing things no one's done before, so there will be people who don't understand you. Like Horvath. But you're miles ahead. They have no chance of ever catching up."

I shake my head. "I want to believe you. But all I was supposed to do this weekend was this project! *Ace* it. Not be . . . stupid about Xavier."

"Stupid?" Ever's lips twist into a wry smile. "Stupid because you weren't just thinking about the project . . ."

I squeeze my eyes shut, hiding from hers.

"I knew it!" Ever gasps. "You're in love with Xavier. Like, actually in love with him!"

"No." I shake my head. "No, no, no, no, *no*. I swore off guys!"

She falls quiet, holding my hand. My rock of a friend.

Her gaze is steady. Seeing the truth I've tried to fight.

"FINE," I admit finally. "Yes, I'm in love with him. Ugh! Why am I such a *girl*?"

"Because you're human? And real, not a robot. I'd rather have a human for my friend any day. And he cares about you."

"I told myself we were different than we were over the summer. I told *him* that. But it was a lie. It's me tornadoing after him—MARRYMESOPHIE—just like last time."

"No, not at all." She tucks a strand of hair behind my ear. "Then all you saw was the Xavier Yeh from your aunt's magazines. The one your family wanted you to have. For all the wrong reasons. But do you think you know the real Xavier now? What you love about him?"

My heart spasms in my chest. Yes. Because he trusted me enough to let me in and share himself with me.

Ever listens patiently as I try to explain. He says people's names because he sees them. He's managed to grow up, for the most part, unspoiled by the world he lives in . . . and still see the people in it. And when I'm with him, I feel so *right* . . . that's the hardest part to untangle.

"He puts words to how I'm feeling. 'Post more! Don't let them tell you how to be!' Or even just 'What a letdown,' because *God*, it was! When I don't even realize how I'm feeling. Sometimes it's an image he's taken. It gives the chaos of how I'm feeling . . . structure? And then I can find a toehold and take the next step forward. I don't even know what I'm trying to say."

She frowns, thinking hard. "He's your emotional outlet?"

"Partly. Not exactly."

"He helps you name it and tame it? Sorry, lame. My social-emotional learning teacher used to say that."

"That's closer. I'm such a mess no one's ever . . . gotten it before."

She smiles. "You're one of a kind, Sophie. I don't think most people can keep up with you."

"I'm a freak?"

"No. I know you forget this, but you're . . ." She searches for the word. "Indomitable. Any guy strong enough to hang next to you would be so lucky. But you always want to *do* things for people. We all benefit from it. Sometimes I wonder, when you turn all business, if that can be a front to hide how you really feel. A shell."

"*I* have a shell?" I laugh, mystified. "I told Xavier he had one."

"Maybe his is more obvious? But yours—if you didn't do anything, if you just . . . *are,* we'd still love you. I think you over-estimate your number of haters and underestimate how many people fall for you without you even trying. Can you believe that? Can you trust that about yourself?"

I laugh. "I think you have magic powers of persuasion."

Because I'm hearing her. That tornado I'm fighting causes destruction, but it also does good for the world. Would I lose one to get rid of the other?

And what does this mean for Xavier and me? I told myself I couldn't be friends with him. Because my tornado won't let me, not when I'm in love with him. But isn't that Letting the tornado win? If he means as much to me as I just explained to Ever, how could I give up his friendship, even if he doesn't love me back?

How could I do that to him?

I don't have answers, but the convoluted snarls in my heart are starting to untangle. I wrap my arms around my best friend and squeeze, so grateful for her.

"What about you and Rick? You seem better—but how are you handling next year?"

"We have to wait and see." She sighs. "This weekend together was . . . everything. Thinking about being apart for four years . . ." She massages her hand with a thumb. "It won't be easy."

"You'll work it out." I really believe that, too. "You guys love each other. What are you doing tonight?"

She turns the shade of the rosebud lantern. "Do you even have to ask?"

"Oops." I smile. "I should let you go. I'm ruining your night together. Here, I'll text him you're on the way and it's my fault."

I open my phone. "Oh, not again."

I've been tagged in two dozen posts in the Loveboat feed.

Then some lines catch my eye.

Guys, we need to stop complaining
She didn't have to take any of this on for us
It's not easy being the leader.

No way. I sit up and read more closely.

Did we make the mirror break?

I might have egged Bert on—feel pretty bad

We should help

Why don't we get more eyes on the Magic Mirror? That's what she was asking for!

Yes, @Sophie, can we help get word out?

We're 2000 strong. Plugged into 1500 schools in 23 countries

Right, here's the harvest moon in London!

Well, they're trying at least. I'm no longer angry as I write back:

Thanks, guys. Unfortunately, the Mirror broke.

I shut off my phone, smiling for the first time since then.

I'll never get to Xavier's level of not caring what others think of him, to a fault. Maybe it will always hurt when I get pilloried, my amygdala warning me into fight-or-flight mode because sharks are swimming . . . but that's because I'll always be putting myself into those kinds of waters.

I'm not stopping because of a few haters.

And now I want to call Xavier. But I need to figure out what to say first so I don't take him on a roller-coaster ride. I guess that's growth, too.

I squeeze Ever's hand. "Go have fun. I'm going to see Aunty Three. And apologize."

The Dragon Leaf guards let me into Headquarters with surprisingly little fuss. The protestors are gone, hopefully celebrating the Moon Festival with their families. Inside, I find Aunty Three in her rosebud pants, shiny black hair caught up in a clip, sewing a button onto a wool coat.

"Sophie, you're back sooner than I expected."

"I broke the Mirror," I blurt. "It fell and the glass shattered—I'm so sorry. All your work—"

"You're not hurt, are you?" She bites off her thread.

"No, um, no. It was someone else. He's fine, too."

"I'm glad. Thank you for applying all your energy to helping us. You've been a great encouragement to me." She gets to her feet and moves deeper into the warehouse. I follow her toward a door in the wall. "I hope the frame itself is still intact? They made things well in my grandmother's day."

"Yes." My eyes widen. "Can you rebuild it?"

"Certainly. The software system is in the cloud."

She opens the door to reveal . . . a three-way Mirror. Not with the ornate frame of Xavier's mother's mirror, but a plain chrome frame, showing off four camera eyes, one at each coordinate. My three images in turquoise blur, then a fuchsia dress sheathes my body, matching ribbons waterfalling down its sides.

"It's the Mirror!"

She smiles. "Did you really think we'd only have one? And of course, the real magic is in the software, which you've been training all day." Her smile widens. "From your party alone, we got over a hundred orders."

"A hundred!" My knees give way. I collapse onto a sofa behind me. "A hundred!"

"Are you okay?"

I am, but my head is spinning. "Aunty Rose, I have so many *ideas*! How to make the Mirror portable with an app version so anyone anywhere can use it." I may not land a spot in Horvath's class. But I still believe in the Magic Mirror. "And it needs more variety. Not just Magic Mirror clothes—sorry, but most people can't afford these high-end designer dresses. Open your catalog to other stores, up-and-coming brands, so they can get their stuff out. It could be *so* exciting—"

Aunty Three's phone rings. "Hold on, dear. I want to hear more, but I need to take this."

I head back to the Mirror. I want to prove to myself it's the same. It styles me in a peach ball gown beaded with pearls and armed with puff sleeves. Cinderella Sophie at last. Yes, it's the same Mirror.

"But you don't really understand me." I sigh. I should be dressed in mourning black. "You can only see what's outside."

My image changes to a mourning-black dress, black tights, and black pumps, with black sunglasses covering half my face.

Huh? Is it learning already?

My reflections change again. But this time, the Mirror does something it's never done before. Instead of three identical Sophies, the left is studious Sophie in a sensible cable-knit sweater and jeans; the middle, in my favorite stormy-orange gown, is sexy Sophie; and the far one, in a pinstriped pantsuit, is powerful Sophie.

"What are you saying?" I ask. "Am I supposed to choose?"

"Angie, thanks for meeting me this late." Uncle Ted's voice, from around the corner, startles me. What's he doing here? And at this hour on a Friday night?

A dark cloud of dread shadows my moment of sunshine. I peer around the corner. Uncle Ted's salt-and-pepper hair is neatly combed. His favorite light jacket with the fraying sleeves is unzipped. A swath of yellow chiffon hanging from a clothesline is blocking my view of his face and the woman he's talking to.

"Claire's birthday is tomorrow," he continues. "I wanted the dresses ready by then, but with everything facing Dragon Leaf, I wasn't sure if you'd be able to finish them."

My brow wrinkles. If Uncle Ted's cheating on Aunty Claire, buying her dresses would be the last thing on his mind.

What's he up to?

"I think you'll be happy." Angie leads him away from me. "We finished stitching the layers onto the Bella gown. The set is ready to go."

I run after them on tiptoes and swipe the yellow cloth aside—then crash into a cart that careens into a naked mannequin. The clatter of metal fills the air.

"Sophie? What are you doing here?" Uncle Ted's standing with the young woman with the purple pixie haircut. She's pulled a sea-green qipao from the rack, identical to the one Aunty Claire wore over the summer.

"Sophie?" Uncle Ted's surprised, but not as dismayed as if I'd caught him cheating.

"Um, I'm here on an errand." My eyes wander over the rack, packed with jewel-toned satins, delicate organza, soft pleats, and romantic Thai silks. Fearlessly elegant dresses to swirl onto your body. The kind Aunty Claire has always had in her closet.

"Please don't tell your aunt." He frowns. "I don't want to spoil the surprise."

I come closer. "But what is it?"

"It's for her birthday. She's been feeling so down since Finn was born. I wanted to do something to cheer her up."

"You picked all these?"

"I have terrible taste, but fortunately, Angie here doesn't."

I hold one of the silk dresses to the light. "She'll feel right at home in these." I tug at the waist. "Are these larger sizes?"

"Your uncle asked for specially tailored clothing—so your aunt can feel more comfortable with her new body."

"Do you think she'll like it?" Uncle Ted looks as nervous as a little boy who's unsure whether the birthday cake he baked will be accepted.

"Oh my God." I press my hand to my mouth. "You measured her *waist*."

All this time, Aunty Claire was worried that her new figure was driving Uncle Ted to sneak around behind her back. And she was right.

373

"When are you showing them to her?" I ask.

"Tomorrow?" He looks terrified.

"Oh, Uncle Ted." I fling my arms around him, then Angie. "Thank you for restoring my faith in the universe." I pile the silks into his startled arms. "Take them home *now*. You have to show her right away. She'll be over the moon!"

Uncle Ted looks confused but happy. "Well, I'm glad you think so."

I was wrong about every guy being a jerk. I snap a picture to share with Aunty Claire later, then head back toward Aunty Three with a new lightness to my steps. I nearly collide with her by the Mirror.

"Sophie! I was coming to find you."

I glimpse myself in the Mirror. "Oh, look!"

The three different Sophies have appeared once again.

Aunty Three gasps. "What's this?"

"It happened earlier, too!" Studious Sophie and sexy Sophie again. But this time, the far Sophie in a sultry green-striped suede jacket over an iron-armor-weave pair of pants. The jacket's slipping off my shoulder and it's wild, pulsing with the energy of a comet. She can only be described as badass Sophie.

"Ah." Aunty Three draws closer. "I made some adjustments earlier, after you talked about different sides of your personality. I didn't mean for this to happen, but I rather like it."

My three images dip and laugh with me. "I don't know which is the real Sophie."

"Why can't they all be you?"

I smile. "I'm starting to feel that way." And Aunty Three really must be my fairy godmother. I say that to her and she smiles.

"I feel the same way, dear. You are a romantic, hopeful visionary—exactly the kind of person we need among us. You see potential where others see obstacles and barriers. That's why you are going to touch the stars."

Impulsively, I give her a hug, and this time, her arms close around me. I put all the Yehs on pedestals—Victor, Xavier, their aunts, dads, and grandpa, even Emma. But they're people, too, with insecurities and flaws and fears and strengths and hopes and dreams.

And among them, as it turns out, I can hold my own.

I pull back from Aunty Three, but keep hold of her. "We can't let the Crusaders destroy Dragon Leaf."

"The investors want to see the path for Dragon Leaf's future. How it can make a comeback."

"The Magic Mirror," I say. "That's Dragon Leaf's comeback. I have an idea, but we need Xavier." I reach for my phone to call him . . . but it's dead. Of course it is. And even if I power it back up . . . I've deleted him.

"I don't know if you've heard, but Xavier's dad hasn't woken up from his surgery yet," Aunty Three says. "It's another reason the investors are spooked."

"Oh, no! I didn't know." How is Xavier feeling? I should go to him. It's not a hard decision at all, whether to stay away any longer. Supporting him is what a good friend would do. "Do you, um, have Xavier's phone number?" I ask. "I lost it."

She frowns. "No, but I could ask Lulu."

While she tries to reach Lulu, I pull up Xavier's Instagram account on my laptop. I don't know if he checks his Instagram messages, but I can try him there.

He's added a few more photos since I last checked. A panoramic view of the party at Taipei 101. The zookeeper with the insanely adorable Ling and Lang under his arms.

And an image I haven't seen before. A seven-year-old girl at a festival, pointing to the glowing moon.

How could this even be possible, but . . . she's me!

How did Xavier get this? Does he even know it's me?

And then I read the caption, and I know he does.

It says:

Call me.

37

XAVIER

My taxi pulls up to the hospital Ba founded almost ten years ago. I've tried to reach Sophie in every way I could. She promised me she'd stick around, and I'm going to hold her to it. Because she'd do the same for me and I'd want her to.

But now I'm here. Why, exactly, I'm not sure. Except that I need to see Ba for myself.

A woman in a white coat, speaking to a nurse by the reception desk, makes eye contact.

"Sir, your father is down the hallway to the right. I'm Dr. Lu, one of his attendees."

So she recognizes me?

"Will he wake up?" I ask as she shakes my hand.

Her expression is sober. "He's stabilized. But it could be weeks, months."

If ever. She doesn't say it, but it's there.

"I can take you to him," she says. "He was telling me about you just before his surgery."

About me. Before he went under the knife.

A knot cinches inside me. "Thanks, but I'd like to see him on my own."

She bows slightly and gestures to the corridor. I head down it, trying to ground myself with the sharp scent of antiseptic. Orderlies in blue rubber gloves pass in the opposite direction and when they are gone, I see Ken-Tek and Ken-Wei at the hallway's end, along with another guard in uniform. Bodyguards again. I thought the first thing I'd do with my trust was hire my own against Ba's, and now I don't need one—the enemy I've fought my whole life is suddenly knocked out cold.

Ken-Tek motions with two fingers for the others to let me by.

"He's the son," he says, and I nod thanks.

Ba's room is a studio with an empty lounge. A late-night show plays on a screen, volume turned low. In case Ba can hear, I guess.

Because there he is.

Blue gown, eyes closed. A tube snakes into his arm, and another is looped under his nose. A nurse rises from his bedside with a sharp-needled syringe in her hand. She greets me, then steps out, leaving me alone with Ba with a million machines attached to him, controlling whether he breathes or whether his heart keeps beating. He runs an empire of machines, and now they're running him.

This isn't the Ba I know. His ties are sorted by color. His drivers pre-calibrate his car mirrors and seat adjustments. He tried to yank my ear off just this morning. He's the tiger pacing its canvas, and the world a cage too small for him.

But this man is frail. Clinging to breath.

Come to think of it, I don't remember the last time I saw him lying down.

I pull a chair to his bedside and drop into it. Ma's framed photo sits on his nightstand, wearing a brightly patterned orange dress Sophie would like. She smiles out at Ba, tilted so he could turn his head and look into her eyes. It's the only personal item here, and it surprises me, how much Ba still needs her. She was special to both of us, and maybe there's not anyone else for him either.

A tic pulses in the pouch of skin under his eye. But how do you feel sorry for someone who's been a knife in your heart for years? How do you mourn someone you never planned to see again?

"Why did you lie to me about my painting?" I hear myself asking.

No answer.

"You liked my art. But you couldn't say it. You had to make me feel like a piece of shit. You supported my film project, but all you said was I better not screw it up. You never told me you sent me to the States to protect me from Uncle Edward. You gave me Ma's scrapbook. . . ."

Why? Why do I have to feel now—now of all times—like maybe he cares?

Maybe Sophie's right. Maybe, after all those years of fending people off, he's built a shell even thicker than mine. For a lot of reasons, he's had to hide all the parts that made him human.

I stand, looking down at Ba's strangely relaxed face.

"It's too late." My voice is sharp. It echoes off the walls, rising in pitch. "It's too late for you and me. Do you hear me?"

Blue veins spider under the thin skin of his hands as they rise and fall on his chest.

Can he hear me?

Has he *ever* heard me?

"You told me I was a disgrace to nine generations!" I shout. "You said you should have beaten me harder to beat it out of me!" I lift my chair and slam it down, sending a piece shooting under the bed.

His guards stick their heads in, then back off. The door closes. My hands ball into fists.

"But today, Ba, I took my trust fund. And I could do it—I talked to the banker, I got him to do what I needed. I got rides for all my friends after you left them in a jam. And I did all of that without you—and now I don't have to stick around and deal with this dysfunctional crap! Can you hear me?"

I kick the chair aside. "It turns out *you* were the stupid one,

Ba. Because *you underestimated me.*"

A knock on the door makes me jump. My throat is raw from shouting. The Douche Lord steps in, still dressed in his blue blazer. "Uh, you okay?"

Somehow, I'm drenched in sweat. I glower at him. "Get the hell out before I put you in a coma, too."

He glances past me to Ba. His face pales, but he lifts his chin. "We have to talk. You were right." He closes the door behind him.

Those words from the Douche Lord do not compute. "What?"

His eyes stray past me again. He seems to be wrestling whether to speak, not typical Douche Lord.

He gestures to Ba on the bed. "My dad's always talked about how important family is—and the moment his brother is in a place like this, he's looking to sell the whole family out. He'd do that to his own brother. Well, I've decided. I don't want anything to do with it."

More words that don't compute.

"I found out my dad was embezzling funds from Dragon Leaf. To pay off gambling debts. Your ba didn't want it leaked, so he paid. And he punished my father himself. That's why he pushed him out. But never said why. He was protecting my dad, all these years. Even *I* didn't know."

All the sound and fury has gone out of him, like a deflated balloon. I'm surprised to find I feel sorry for the Douche Lord, trying to be a loyal son. Must be pretty horrible to find out the person you hero-worshipped is actually the villain.

"The things he's said to Aunty Three." He shudders. "The way he treats the servants. We don't have to be like them, Xavier. We can choose our own path. I—I'm sorry."

I'm too stunned to answer. I walk around Ba's bed and retrieve the chair's broken foot on the other side. Then come back around and drop it on Ba's table.

"Okay." I continue to eye him suspiciously. "You've said all that, so . . ." I gesture toward the door. "Bye."

"There's more."

"How can there be?"

"The takeover," he says. "The Crusaders promised to make my dad CEO, in exchange for help from the inside. That's why he's been stirring up trouble. Like firing Aunty Three's people."

"Exactly the family drama I never want to get involved in."

My cousin tugs Ba's blanket higher over his chest. "This was my dad's chance to seize control. But I have a friend who works at the Crusaders. I talked to her tonight. She says they're double-crossing my dad. Cutting him out. They'll break Dragon Leaf into five companies and sell them off. All of it will be gone." He glances at the television screen. "Damn, we're on the news again."

The kid anchorman gloats at us. In his window is a shot of the Dragon Leaf historical building—the logo over the carved panel doors.

"Here with me is Crusaders' CEO Morris Lin, who has launched an offer to buy a controlling share of Dragon Leaf."

"I hate that kid," I say.

"He's not a kid. He's thirty-five."

"He looks twelve."

"He shapes what half of Taipei thinks."

The screen cuts in half to display a Taiwanese businessman in a home office, backdropped by a wooden bookshelf. The Crusaders' logo, sword and shield, hangs on his wall.

"Dragon Leaf had its heyday," Morris Lin says. "But they're out of touch. They're still down by the wharf, clinging to the ways of their ancestors. The business is too insular. Too many divisions run by family riding on old coattails. It's time to end a dynasty that's outlived its relevance."

The screen goes blank as the Douche Lord turns it off.

"They don't know our family at all." I pace the room to the door and back. "Ba doesn't let anyone ride anyone's coattails. I know that more than anyone."

"I wish we could help."

I pick up Ma's photo. Her smile is crooked, like mine. What would she think of all of this? What would she want done? Two hours ago, I wouldn't have considered trying to do anything about it—me, the Buried Yeh. No one's ever asked me to take charge of anything. Even now, no one in the family would think to say, *Xavier, why didn't you stop your dad from losing his company?*

This is not my thing.

I can walk away and let the chips fall where they fall.

But the thing is, if I say I'm not like my dad, then I have to be different from him. I have to allow people to be who they are. I have to see them for who they are. *All* of them.

Because as much as I don't *want* to see Ba for who he is—a guarded fortress, ignorant about dyslexia, impatient, an asshole . . . but at the same time, a guy who protects the staff, cares for their families, supports my aunts, is forever in love with, and maybe forever brokenhearted about my mother . . . and in the end, human. . . .

I see it all. With Sophie's help, I see it all now.

And I can walk away.

Or I can be different.

I turn back to my cousin, who is staring at Ba's immobile figure.

We can both choose our own paths.

"Your speech at the festival. It will be televised and broadcasted, right?"

"Yeah. Jane's arranged everything."

"So the investors will hear it, too?"

"I wouldn't be surprised if they come in person. My dad invited them all. Everyone will be there—Ye-Ye included."

"I need you to give me the slot."

He must have been preparing for this speech for months. It's his debut. His chance to show Taipei how good he is. But all he does is raise a brow. "You're giving a speech?"

"Words aren't my thing, you know that."

"No, I don't." He snorts. "You're the smoothest talker in the family."

Another surprise, coming from him. And it might be true. I've had to talk to get around reading or writing. Maybe I need to revise that.

"Well, I have something else in mind."

"What?"

I sling my camera bag onto my shoulder. "I want to show my film. This is the last thing I'm doing for the Yehs."

"Your school project? Jane will never agree."

"You could convince her."

He shakes his head no. "This is the family's signature event. Thousands of people will be there. Even if I wanted to, I couldn't get it past PR."

We made some progress tonight, but I can accept he's gone as far as he can. "All right." I head past him for the door.

"Wait. Xiang-Ping. I never understood. Why the poor little rich boy thing? Why so angry? Why all the getting in trouble and failing out? It could have been so easy for you. Why did you make it hard?"

I shake my head, amazed at how little we all know of each other. By our own choices. I tap my temple with my finger. "I didn't make it hard. My brain did. Your dad would have had me lobotomized. But I'm pretty sure that doesn't help dyslexia."

"So you really can't . . . ?" He's not scornful. Just quietly curious. More progress.

385

"Read? No." It's no longer hard for me to share. "Maybe we're all outsiders in different ways, Victor."

It might be the first time I've spoken his real name in over a decade.

He shakes his head. "Wow."

It doesn't make up for years of torture. But it's something.

"What are you going to do now?" he asks as I open the door.

"Find another way to open the lock," I say. "That's what I've always done."

I park the scooter at the gate leading to my family's mausoleum. The Yeh tombs sit on the highest terrace of a city of tombs, set into the mountainside of Yangmingshan.

The marble lions guarding the entrance glare as I pass between them and under the flat roof. I shine my phone light on black marble sarcophaguses inscribed with gold lettering. Lush, leafy plants hug the tombs from all sides: banana-plant leaves and birds of paradise. The colors under the cloudy moonlight can't be captured, but I lift my camera and try.

Victor didn't say yes to giving me his slot, but he didn't say no either. I'm hoping he'll come through. But either way, as I said to him, this is my last act of service to the Yeh family. Bittersweet as I'm just rediscovering my aunts and great-aunts, but everything else that comes with them . . . I'm here to finalize the film, and say farewell.

Farewell to the Yehs.

I grope along the wall for a light switch but come up empty-handed. Then I remember Sophie's paper lantern. I pull it from my backpack and shake it open. I light the waxy candle with my lighter, then attach it to the base.

Then I let it go. I follow it with my camera as it floats toward the ceiling, lighting the tombs as it rises: the marble trapezoidal blocks that house my great-grandparents, my grandmother with a blank oval for my grandfather's portrait when he eventually joins her. More marble tombs sit to either side. I walk the row, filming my fingers trace over the gold-etched characters. The nine generations. The earliest six were brought here from the east and reburied when my grandma was buried.

My Asian American friends have said they don't have a sense of their own roots. That being immigrants, they sometimes feel as though they spontaneously appeared as a family in the middle of the country. No heirlooms, no family history. Me, I've always known I come from a long line of people whose lives began and ended before I ever took a breath on this earth. It's always been a burden.

But as it turns out, it's my uncle who disgraced the nine generations. Not me.

I double back past my grandma, passing a marble altar to my ancestors, to Ma's tomb.

Lynn Noel Yeh.

And in Chinese: Chun-Hwa. Morning glory.

It doesn't feel that long ago that we brought her here.

"Ma?" My voice is swallowed by the night. "I got what you wanted for me. I wanted you to know."

A wren hops forward, chirping. It stares at me with a beady eye.

She'd have been proud of me. That was what the trust fund was about. Her letting me know. And way more than the money, her faith is what sets me free.

"Xavier? Are you here?"

"Sophie?" Here? I turn toward the door. But how did she find me? I set my camera on my great-grandparents' tomb and start toward the entrance. Rain has begun to fall.

Sophie bursts in from the black night in a splash of moonlit hair and turquoise satin. Her face glows as she brushes raindrops from her cheeks with impatient hands. Her heels echo on the marble floor as she darts toward me.

"You're here!" Her eyes shine with an amber intensity.

In three strides, I cross to her, grab her by her arms . . .

And kiss her.

Her mouth is hungry and eager, tasting of lemons and sugar cane. My hands slip into the warmth of her thick hair, cupping her head closer. The heat of her body seeps through my shirt. I can't stop tasting her, drinking her, all my buried feelings for her roaring to the surface.

A rustling noise in the trees brings us back to our senses.

"Mountain lion?" She laughs shakily. Her eyes take in the mausoleum. "I think this is sacrilegious."

"I don't care." I kiss her mouth, her nose, her cheek, her chin, but then she puts a hand on my chest, holding me back. We're both damp with rain now. Droplets sparkle on her lashes as she looks up at me. Black makeup is smudged at the bottoms of her eyes, but she's never looked more luminous to me.

"Your heart," she murmurs. Her hand is still on my chest. "It's . . . beating so hard."

I wrap my hand around hers, holding it to the pounding there. "How did you find me?"

"I heard about your dad—I'm so sorry. I dropped by the hospital and Victor said you'd just left. I figured you'd come here."

"*I* didn't even know I'd come here."

She smiles wryly. "You mentioned it this morning." She sobers. "How are you feeling?"

My hand tightens on hers. "Like I'm looking at a photo in the dark. All I can see are shadows and shapes. But the sun is starting to come up."

"I feel it, too."

"Did you see your photo on my Instagram?"

"Yes, at the Moon Festival! Where did it come from?"

"Believe it or not, I took it. Years ago."

"That was the last Moon Festival I went to with my dad." Her eyes shine with wonder. "There must have been hundreds of people there, and you saw me? And you took my picture?" She shakes her head. "I bought a photo there."

She shows me the home screen on her phone: the glowing white lanterns rising into the sky.

"Wait, *you* bought this?"

"In a booth. There were postcards on sale everywhere, but this photo . . . it captured the magic of Taipei for me." She touches it with a finger. "Even now, when I look at it, I feel . . ."

"Lighter?" I say with her. We laugh.

"So, you're not going to believe this but . . . it's mine," I say. "I mean, I took it in Pingxi during the lantern festival and put it into the family booth. Victor mentioned I only sold one photo, and this was it." All those years ago. "I always wondered who that sucker was who bought it."

She holds the picture to her chest. "*I* bought *your* photo? We were seven."

"What's wrong?" I ask. "I've upset you?"

"*I* saw you," she whispers. "Before I knew who you were."

Before she knew anything about trust funds and empires, she means.

"It doesn't matter—"

"It does to me."

"If you *were* after me for money, I'd spend it all to keep you."

She laughs. "That's just it. *I* needed to know."

Her skin is cool and silky under my fingers. Peach and gold. I trace her cheekbone, her jawline, down her neck. She shivers and closes her eyes. We can never fully capture the colors of the real world on a camera or in a painting. I'll never be able to capture hers.

But I can see myself trying for the rest of my life.

I bend my head toward hers . . . then her eyes snap open.

"What about Emma?" she asks.

I give her a steady look. "I think you know me better than that, don't you?"

She swallows. "It's just that . . . I'm a tornado."

I brush her hair back from her face. "You don't know your own worth," I say. "And I want you to. I want you to know how important you are. To everyone. To me."

She trembles. "Why me . . ."

"*Only you.*"

Our mouths meet again. Her lips part under mine and my body presses hers against the marble wall. Her hands on me are feverish. The sound she makes deep inside unlocks something in me. I want that storm in her unleashed on me, with nothing holding her back anymore.

But the need for air makes us break apart.

"Woof," she says, and I laugh. We're both panting. Her lips are as shiny as her eyes. I want her, more than I've wanted anyone, I want her. My body's giving me away and her eyes tell me she can feel it.

But I force myself to steady.

"Something good is happening here," I say. "Let's not fuck it up." I crack a smile. "Literally."

She smooths the wreck I've made of her hair. "This trip—we could be on a high."

We're not. *I'm* not. But I need to be careful with her. I can't

afford not to. "Let's go home, well, and if you still . . . want . . .
me . . ."

"If *you* do—"

"We can decide then. How to be together."

She tilts her head. "I think we just decided not to sleep
together. For now."

My body rebels. "Another brilliant pact."

"The Sophie tornado tamed."

"The Xavier tornado tamed."

After a startled pause, she laughs. "Maybe a tornado isn't
always bad?"

"For sure." She pulls my lapels, tugging me back to her, and a
few minutes later, we are verging on reneging.

Then my phone rings. Her eyes are mischievous as we break
apart again.

"Oh crap, it's the—Victor," I say. "Hello?"

"Meet me beside the stage before my slot. I found a way to
get you on."

I let out a breath, fighting to get my body under control. "So
now you think I know what I'm doing?"

He laughs ruefully. "No. But I know my dad screwed up and
the world knows you're the heir. We need to save Dragon Leaf.
So if we're going to take a bet, let's go big. Screw PR."

His voice grows loud in my other ear. Sophie's fingers fly
up the unbuttoned buttons on her dress. Then my cousin steps
through the doorway, wiping rainwater from his face.

"My dad's shares plus your dad's aren't enough to give the

Crusaders fifty-one percent." Victor lowers his phone to his side. He glances curiously between us. "Sorry, Sophie said you'd be here. Am I interrupting?"

I exhale. Sophie says, "Go on."

"If we convince the twins or another investor not to sell, we can still save Dragon Leaf."

"And the Magic Mirror," Sophie says. "Aunty Three deserves her chance."

"Yes," I say.

Victor holds out his wrist, letting the light catch his Apple watch. "I called Grandpa and told him the truth. I owe you . . . an apology."

After so many bloody years between us, this feels like an impossible victory.

The wren cocks its head at us. Maybe at the strangeness of three humans making way too much noise in a vault of the dead. I wonder how long it's been coming here, whether its ancestors came, too, keeping the Yehs company through the years. Whether its descendants will one day keep company with Victor's grave, and mine, another in the long chain of Yehs.

Because that's just it. No matter how I've tried to escape it—

I am a Yeh.

And I'm not ready to be buried yet.

I grasp my cousin's hand, which is the same size and shape as mine. It feels right to shake on it.

"We'll save Dragon Leaf," I say. "If there's one thing being Ba's son has taught me, it's that no one tells a Yeh what to do."

Victor's grin matches mine. "Amen."

One last thing to do. I turn back to face my ancestors' final resting place. "If you need something to remember me by . . . ," I say.

With a smile at Sophie, I fish the combination lock from my pocket.

And leave it on their altar for them to figure out.

38

SOPHIE

Xavier and I arrive at Aunty Claire's past midnight. It's been an impossibly full day, adrenaline still pumping, and jet lag only now catching up to us. With Finn's erratic sleep schedule, we are just in time to catch my aunt dazzled by Uncle Ted's birthday present. She can't stop kissing his sheepishly grinning face, in between modeling her roomier dresses before her bedroom mirror.

"You look like poetry," I gush.

Her smile is impish. "Next time, Sophiling, we'll use your special Mirror to do this."

I laugh and lean over my cousin's crib to kiss his sleeping head. "Yes, let's make it easier on Uncle Ted next time."

I sleep deeply in the guest room, uninterrupted by dreams. In the morning, Xavier and I head toward Magic Silk to work on the film for tonight's festival. The sky pinkens as we motor by men and women washing wide pails of raw chicken, ginger, bamboo shoots, green onions, and cucumbers. But Dihua Street is boarded up, still sleeping as we speed toward headquarters.

Lulu meets us inside the warehouse with a platter of pineapple cakes. "Thanks for everything you're doing for my mom," she says. "I never thought I'd see something like this happening."

"This is for all of us," Xavier answers. "Sophie included." He smiles at me, eyes crinkling, and the nice thing about a guy who never bullshits is you know he's not bullshitting now.

"I thought Xavier was just trying to impress a girl." Lulu pours hot water from a porcelain teapot into cups and hands me one. "It worked. *I'm* impressed." She hands a second cup to Xavier. Her smile turns rueful. "So much better than Club Pub."

He laughs.

No more punches?"

She laughs, too. "No more punches."

We work the next hours with Aunty Three and her staff to replace the Mirror's broken screens and film more key moments around the warehouse. Xavier spreads out on an orange couch with his laptop connected to a few larger screens. He gazes with ferocious concentration, feverishly splicing segments of video together.

Victor, as it turns out, has access to Dragon Leaf archives of family footage going back to black-and-white photos of Xavier's great-grandfather on his mom's side, a straw hat on his head, farming lands that are the Zhongshan District today.

"No wonder Ba wanted you to help me." Xavier rubs his eyes.

Victor looks up from the credits he's editing. He frowns. "My dad won't lose graciously, you know. If the Crusaders' offer falls through, he'll get other investors to back him."

"Aunty Three, why don't *you* get a bunch of investors to buy Dragon Leaf?" I ask.

She's stretching a soft tape measure along the Mirror's edge. "Thank you for the faith, dear, but I'm a no-name. No investors want to back me."

"Did you hear from Horvath, Sophie?" Victor asks.

"I'm withdrawing from the waitlist," I say.

"What? Why?"

"I realized I'll never convince him. But I want to do this project. So I'll find my own way. He mentioned a class for start-up companies."

"Don't throw in the towel yet. Let me talk to him. Sometimes you need an advocate."

In some ways, it would be easier to walk away and not put

myself through any more trying-to-win-over Horvath. But Victor's right.

"Okay," I say.

He's already pulling out his phone as he steps from the room.

"Sophie, here's a bit on the Mirror. Need your permission," Xavier says.

"Permission?" I join him at his workstation. "Why—"

"The key is blending," says my voice on his laptop. A familiar close-up of a soft brush spreads a sky-blue shadow on my eyelid. "Take your time. You have to be patient to get the shades just right."

"Wait, what does this have to do with your—"

The image cuts to my mascara wand brushing up the length of my curled lashes. It pans out to show both eyes, my nose, my mouth, my whole face. It pans out to show my entire reflection in my purple jumpsuit within the steel frame of the Magic Mirror, then me in triple, then the actual me standing before it, my hands on my hips. He's joined the video segments so seamlessly that, even knowing where they came from, I can't believe they were taken from two different times and places.

I can't breathe. I put my hand on my stomach. One Magic Mirror outfit after another swaps over my body's reflection, so rapidly their shades *do* blend together, until they come to a stop on the dragon-print turquoise dress.

Then the dragon-print dress is on my body, facing three identical images of me.

Sophie on video strikes a sexy pose.

"I didn't know you were watching me then," I murmur.

Cut to another close up of my face: wink and kiss. "'They won't be able to ree-zeest you.'" Only this time, in the film dream he's created, I'm saying it to the Magic Mirror.

It's a fifteen-second slice of perfection.

I meet Xavier's grinning eyes. "How did you come up with this?"

"Do you approve?"

"It's *genius*—but you can't put me in your film!"

"Why not?"

Honestly, he can be so clueless. "The film is about your *family*."

"The film is whatever I want it to be. And the Magic Mirror is *from* my family, and *you're* making it look good. Or should I say, *irrree-zeest-able*."

"Shut up!" I beat on his shoulder, but my face burns with a hundred-watt smile.

Then Victor's back, pocketing his phone. "Bad news, Sophie. I just talked to my head TA. Horvath accepted one person off the waitlist. Oliver Brooks."

"Oliver? He was my seatmate. He bombed his proposal. He was going to drop out."

Victor's brows crouch deeper on his forehead. "His dad works at Microsoft and just agreed to fund Horvath's lab at Yale."

It takes a moment to sink in. "I never had a chance, did I?"

It's the feeling I had when I found out Emma was a legacy kid. Only I don't feel helpless anymore. No matter what happens, I will still be able to bet on myself.

"I think he intended to give you a chance but couldn't turn down the opportunity to build the next billion-dollar private AI lab," Victor says. "But it's not right. We're working on it. Stay tuned."

Emma drops by around noon, a black bottle of herbal medicine in hand. Xavier and I are snuggled back-to-back on the couch, each working on our laptops.

"Hey, Emma." I unfold my legs and rise.

"Hey," Xavier says.

I give her bottle a quizzical look. "For my allergies," she explains. "I will never sneeze again."

Leaving Xavier on the couch, I head with her into the back of the warehouse for privacy.

"So you and Xavier are together again?"

There's no more denying. "Yes. I wanted to believe it was over. It *was* over. But something special happened this weekend. Taipei magic." I take her hand. "I'm sorry."

"You shouldn't apologize." She squeezes me back. "I *was* upset at first, but I was also the one who pushed you to set us up. And this weekend . . . even if it didn't turn out the way I hoped, it was what I needed. Talking Miles over with Xavier, being with him, all helped me realize it's okay to move on. But also . . . it's okay if I'm not dating someone."

"I came to the opposite realization. Swearing off guys wasn't the right path either." I hug her. "I'm glad we're okay. I'm excited about our friendship."

I hop onto the Loveboat feed and post a photo of the new Magic Mirror.

> Sophie: Hey gang, you said you'd help get word out.
> Sophie: We're showing a special film at the mooncake festival.
> Sophie: It will help the Magic Mirror and Xavier's family.
> Sophie: And we need your help
> Sophie: Worldwide
> Priscilla: Who put you in charge?
> Sophie: I put myself in charge, but thanks for asking
> Joella: Dang, girl
> Joella: #OwnIt

I smile. I'm not going to win over the whole world. But that's not the goal, is it?

> Sophie: All right. Here's the plan, team.

I lay it out. I ignore Priscilla's next barb.
And I sign off: #bossgirl

The international food festival stretches over a grassy space outside the Taipei Nangang Exhibition Center. A row of white square tents shine with lights, filled with food, crafts, and tech samples from dozens of countries. Families gather around rough wooden tables, tying Chinese knots from silken cords and folding origami.

A village of cameras on tripods point toward the pale glow in the night sky, waiting for the moon to cooperate.

"I hope we see that baby before we leave Taipei," Xavier says. "What's a Moon Festival with no moon?"

"Right?" Xavier slips his fingers through mine. It's somehow unexpected. "Sophie." He smiles. "Can I say your name?"

I smile back. "Fire away."

"Sophie Ha. What do you need from me to know I'm here for you?"

He's talking about life after Taipei. Only Xavier would even think to ask. "If you tell me, I'll believe you for a day or two. Then my insecurities will kick in and I might start to doubt you."

"How can I prove it?"

"I don't know," I confess. "Don't just say it? Do it?"

His eyes are thoughtful.

"What about you?" I ask.

His fingertips run down my jawline, then his lips brush mine. "I already know," he says.

A long line of people has formed at the Dragon Leaf pavilion for the free Yeh-stamped mooncakes. The golden brown stacks in geometric pyramids fill four tables. Nearby trees glow with white globes, and everything feels festive.

But waving over the crowds are those cardboard signs with Xavier's dad's crossed-out face.

We make our way toward the pavilion's stage, where dancers are finishing a modern number. A crowd is seated in a half circle on the grass with others standing, eating fruit on sticks. Two large screens on either side display the dancers, magnified to triple size.

Victor is already waiting beside the stage. No tuxedo. Just a red shirt loose over white pants. Less slick. More genuine. He looks good.

"Ready?" he asks Xavier.

"No, but I don't have a choice." Xavier's jittery. The Magic Mirror is already at the back of the stage, covered by a sheet. Victor's speech slot isn't for another fifteen minutes, but that's part of the plan—give it before Uncle Edward and Ye-Ye arrive. Xavier's aunts and great-aunts, guarded by security, are already seated with Lulu on the opposite side.

Xavier puts a foot on the stage steps.

"Xiang-Ping!" From behind, Jane knocks me aside. She seizes his arm. "What are you doing?" she cries in a low voice. "This is Victor's speech."

"It's under control, Jane," I say.

"Jane, hold on," Victor says. As she turns, releasing Xavier, he snaps, "Xavier, just go! Now!"

But Xavier remains on the step. Then he turns to Jane, whose face is a mask of panic.

"Jane, Ba's in a coma and our family is about to lose our company. I don't know how much you know about all that. But I'm here now because I'm not letting that happen. I've worked on this with Victor and Sophie, and my aunts. So I'd like to keep going with your blessings, but I'll do it without your blessings, too."

Jane takes a shuddery breath. Then she bows her head. "You're his heir."

"Thank you, Jane, but you don't bow to me. Seriously." Xavier holds my gaze a moment. "I'm doing this. And it will make a difference. Right?"

"Is there a word that's the opposite of destruction?" I ask. "The concept of inflicting, *unleashing*, great good on the world in a powerful burst of energy."

Xavier smiles. "You're asking *me* for a word?"

"I don't think there is one, but that is what we're about to do." I return his smile with pride of my own. I think of the magic brush folktale. "It's time to put the last drop of paint on the rooster."

Xavier climbs onto the stage and takes the microphone. "Good evening. I'm Xiang-Ping Yeh, the son of Dragon Leaf's Chairman Yeh."

His voice booms out over the field in perfect Mandarin. More people start moving toward our stage.

"It's the son," says a man.

"We never hear anything about him," says a woman.

"A lot of ugly stuff about my family has been in the news lately," Xavier continues. "Some true. My dad is in a coma in the hospital. Dragon Leaf fired five hundred people last week, and the Crusaders are trying to buy the company." A ripple of voices rises from the crowd.

"As for me." Xavier's shoulders tense. "I'm in the United States, repeating my senior year of high school. I can't read much, and the reason is, I'm dyslexic. Pretty severely, it seems."

The audience has gone silent. He wipes his palm on his pants and glances at me, then back to the crowd. A smile tugs on his lips. "I'm still figuring it out, but even though I've never been good at putting words on a page, I'm really good at making pictures."

He yanks the sheet off the Magic Mirror. Except for a small dent in its side, it's good as new. The video cameras project the Mirror onto the two large screens on either side of him, and my phone on a stand is livestreaming it to the world.

"My art teacher has a quote on her wall, 'A picture is worth a thousand words, and a video a million.' Here's my attempt at a few hundred thousand."

The audience falls silent as the Dragon Leaf logo appears in the center panel of the Mirror: first the golden Yeh character, then the purple dragon, from head to tail, coiling around it. Xavier steps back down the stairs, still holding the mic.

"This . . . this is the Yehs."

39

XAVIER

The film opens with a splash of colors, like a mirage, shifting and dream-like. The colors grow more defined and crystallize into the shape of my hand, my real hand holding a pastel. It sketches on a creamy page on fast-forward. A golden-brown mooncake appears. Identical to the ones in so many hands in this square.

This is the Yehs. The perfect, golden-crusted Yeh family. Like the Rockefeller postcard: elegant, wealthy, tasteful. The Yehs that Jane and Ba and even my teacher want the world to see. But that's only the surface.

My hand paints the Yeh character onto its top. Stroke after brushstroke. It's the magic paintbrush. With the last downward stroke . . .

Everything comes to life.

The mooncake dances off the page and floats into a sky of deep dark purple. It glows, golden-orange. Purple and gold and light—the colors of the Yehs.

A sharp knife slices the mooncake in half. As it opens, revealing twin moons, a little green leaf flies out. It dances a spiral on the screen, then darts off—a bit of animation that Sophie got Bert to do, working all day as his penance for breaking the Mirror.

More than speaking, showing my work like this is terrifying. Like baring my soul to the arrows of an oncoming army. It's hard to make a film. It's not just about capturing incredible footage or even selecting the best cuts. It's putting them into a cohesive story with a beginning, middle, and end. It's making people care. I don't know if I'm going to accomplish any of this.

But what I do know is that those infinite boxes I drew at the beginning of the school year are no longer emptiness inside emptiness, but full of things that are important to me. All the things I've put into the vast rectangle of this film.

The leaf flits through a black page with white words that Sophie's voice reads aloud:

"Meet the Yehs."

Music begins. The leaf flits over a black-and-white photo of two young sisters growing larger on the screen. They're stylish but comfortable. Two girls who could be friends with anyone: rich, young, old, destitute.

Sophie's voice narrates. "Two centuries ago, the Yeh family

opened a small fabric shop by the wharf."

The film pans through more black-and-white images: from the Dadaocheng Wharf up a dirt road. Inside a wooden building to a small room holding two old-fashioned sewing machines and hung with fabrics.

"Over the next hundred years, that textiles business grew into a fashion boutique."

Aunty One at a table, sketching the bristly Yeh logo with a charcoal pencil. Aunty Two sketching the handheld mirror that has since become the iconic symbol of Magic Silk.

The video pans back to Sophie, backdropped by the modern-day warehouse. "These women turned an old warehouse into the home of a fashion line that has graced the covers of major fashion magazines, all based on their love for fabrics, colors, and style—and most of all, each other."

Sophie stirs beside me. "Tens of thousands of people are watching," she whispers.

It's freaking unbelievable. Everything that's been in my head, now framed by the Taipei night.

The film cuts to present-day Great-Aunty Two, covering her sleeping sister with the white blanket. There's only sweetness in the angle. The audience sighs.

"These women have been the silent tastemakers behind every major Dragon Leaf design. And as Dragon Leaf exploded into the empire people know today, these ladies have never stopped creating themselves."

The video cuts to a re-created shot of Sophie in the chrome

box as the infrared scanners measure her body. Her PG-13 avatar, then the clip with her makeup video, her figure in the Mirror as a series of Magic Silk clothes swap out over her body.

Then the long lines at the reunion, all our friends posing with their avatars and trying on Mirror clothes.

An envious sigh rises from the crowd. "Amazing. Can we try it?"

"This is the future of shopping—and we have big plans!" Aunty Three says.

"You won't have to look for clothes," Sophie says. "The clothes will find *you*."

The leaf travels beyond the historic Dihua intersection.

My voice-over: "My family has been on this wharf for two hundred years, and plans to be here for at least another two hundred. I hope this film gives you a taste of the great things that lie ahead. And now I'd like to introduce the most important part of Dragon Leaf. In my humble opinion."

The leaf flits through a montage of images. Things too humble for Jane or PR to consider highlighting:

Aunty Four kneading dough for mooncakes, a smudge of flour on her nose.

Lulu's bar of fair trade chocolate.

Kai-Fong's granddaughter, waving from her classroom in Kyoto.

Bernard at Disneyland, with Alison riding his shoulders.

Ma's grave, and the tombs of my ancestors under the hazy moonless sky.

Then the empty Mirror. It grows to fill the screen. Each of the three panels populates: Great-Aunty One, Great-Aunty Two, Aunty Three. The three segments duplicate, one above the other, then triplicate, quadruple, each panel hosting a different Yeh woman: Aunty Four, and cousins Gloria and Lulu.

The men of the Yeh family appear next in a row below, their sleek public images that are all they ever allow to be shown.

Then every image flips like a coin, as if the Magic Mirror has taken a pass over the entire grid of photos.

Now no one is as the public has seen them before. White-haired Great-Aunty One preening before a mirror. Great-Aunty Two laughing so hard her red face puckers like an apple. Black-belt Lulu, bare foot flying at her opponent's face.

Ba at Ma's grave, his hand on his temple and his head bowed and weeping.

Victor freaking out when he spots his avatar, accidentally created, in the screen behind him. The real Victor, beside me, shifts uncomfortably. But as a supportive chuckle ripples through the audience, a smile touches his face.

A clip of Victor in the showroom, holding up two fingers. "I'll be back here after I graduate from Dartmouth in June. Looking forward to working with you all then."

Cut to Ye-Ye, who pats my hand with his gnarled ones. "Yeh means 'leaf.' It's a good name for our family. . . . Leaves are numerous. Always growing. They are all over the world. Like the Yehs."

"Why are you doing this?" Jane chokes beside me.

"These are the best parts of my family," I say. "Even if they don't know it."

The family crest makes sense to me now. Frail leaves. Dragons of power. Even in weakness, there is strength. For me, dealing with not being able to read, always feeling like an outsider—that also gives me the eyes to see others.

On the film, my voice-over: "The leaves of a tree—there are so many because they need to do the work of sustaining a bigger enterprise. Like the tree."

Onscreen appear images of all the people who make up our world: Kai-Fong enjoying the Night Market, Bernard and Alison, Haru, Angie, the security guards, and even Jane, who sucks in a breath beside me. Then the hundreds of employees who, until a week ago, were part of Magic Silk. A ripple moves through the audience as people recognize themselves. Lastly, photos of the thousands of women cloth makers around the world, some with goats, others with looms, sent to Aunty Three at her request.

Dragon Leaf isn't just Ba or Uncle Edward or Ye-Ye. It's a living breathing community of people who've worked so hard and loved so much.

"All of these are the people who make up the Yeh family."

The images coalesce into a mosaic that dives into the mooncake from the opening image. The insides turn from pixels of photographs back into mung bean and lotus seed filling. Then the mooncake closes. A seam of light glows brighter, then vanishes, leaving the single perfect mooncake with the Yeh crest in place.

"This is the Yeh family you never see," says my voice offscreen. "But this is who we are. This is what is most important. And this is the future of Dragon Leaf."

The image fades to black.

A silence has fallen over the audience, which now stretches past the edges of the lawn. I find I'm hugging Ma's scrapbook to my chest.

All I can hear and feel is the frantic beating of my own heart.

40

XAVIER

As the applause rings out over the grounds, Uncle Edward pushes through the crowd toward us. A blue vein pulses in his forehead. His entire moon-shaped face is a dark red.

"What the hell do you think you're doing?" he snarls. "No one cares to see the great-aunties! No one cares to see that old butler and the *pilot*! On vacation! You wasted everyone's time and made us look like we've been squandering company resources. How dare you!"

His arm draws back to strike me. But Victor grabs his wrist with what I'm now recognizing as Yeh reflexes.

"Actually, Ba, I gave him my spot."

Uncle Edward's eyes open wide with shock. "Why would you do that?"

"It was mine to use." Victor releases him. "I thought what Xavier had to say was the right message."

"You were right." Sophie gestures to the still-cheering audience. Lulu, as planned, leads my aunts and great-aunts onstage. Their beautiful faces glow under the lights.

"And this is what I want for Dragon Leaf," I say. "This is the future of Dragon Leaf."

"*Báichī!*" The veins on Uncle Edward's forehead threaten to rupture. "We always knew you had no sense. This is exactly why I needed to save the company from your idiocy. Both of you, *get the hell out of this pavilion*! As of tonight, I've taken over Dragon Leaf. I don't want to see you set foot on its property again."

"Sorry, Uncle. But that's not what I want for Dragon Leaf."

"You don't have that right." A grim satisfaction settles into the lines on his forehead. "I just bought the controlling shares. I saved Dragon Leaf from the Crusaders."

"No, you haven't. I have." Aunty Three joins us. "And it never needed saving until you undermined it from inside."

"My lawyers are closing the deal now. The twins want out. They're selling."

"They sold." Aunty Three flashes her phone at him. "To me."

"You?" For the first time, uncertainty flickers in my uncle's eyes. "You're lying!" He grabs her phone, his face darkening. "You can't afford their shares. You run a hobby business."

"I told you before it wasn't a hobby business," she says. "And you're right that I couldn't afford it all. Xiang-Ping chipped in."

"Xiang-Ping?" Uncle Edward turns on me. I smile.

"Quite a bit, actually," Aunty Three says. "He owns more of Dragon Leaf now than you ever did, not counting his father's shares, of course. So he had more right than anyone else to give tonight's speech, and if you ask me, he . . . how do you kids say it now? He crushed it."

"But he's . . . you're . . ." Uncle Edward's expression is wild, like he's looked down to find only air under his scrambling feet.

"An idiot?" I supply. "It's true I don't understand a lot of things. But I'll learn over time. And what I do know is that Ba trusts Aunty Three. And so do I."

"Thank you, Xiang-Ping." Aunty Three firmly tugs her phone out of Uncle's Edward's hands.

"We'll bring Aunty Three's digital avatar into the rest of Dragon Leaf," I say.

"Healthcare can use it for fitness and remote surgery," Victor says. "Electronics for virtual reality gaming."

"This is just the beginning," Sophie says.

Aunty Three smiles. "So you see, we have big plans, and I'll need every last one of my people and more to return." Her smile fades. "Now get out of our pavilion. I don't want to see *you* after what you've done to our family."

Uncle Edward glares at Victor. "We need to talk."

Victor flinches. It's the only time I've seen him struggle for words. But he lifts his chin. "We don't have anything to talk about."

It's Uncle Edward's turn to flinch. A shadow passes over his eyes: shock, uncertainty, defeat. Then he spits on the ground and stalks away.

Aunty Four beams at me. "Your film may have been the most memorable statement to the world that Dragon Leaf has ever made. Our PR machine, those sanitized articles, hours of spotless blogs—they couldn't do what you did tonight in six minutes. You gave us a heart."

I smile at Sophie and take her hand. "We did it together."

Ma was right. We can't go it alone. And I don't want to either.

"Xiang-Ping . . . join us," Great-Aunty One calls from the stage. Both my great-aunts are beckoning to me, smiles creasing their faces. Beyond them in the audience, sitting by their seats, Ye-Ye raises his hand and waves at me.

And beyond them, the hazy glowing threads of clouds part to reveal the fattest harvest moon that's ever smiled down on Taipei.

"Finally!" Sophie sighs.

The audience is clapping in rhythm. Their chanting has changed.

"Yeh Xiang-Ping. Yeh Xiang-Ping. Yeh Xiang-Ping."

"Go." Sophie nudges me. "You're the filmmaker."

"Come with me." I grab her hand. "I couldn't have done it without you. I wouldn't have."

"I'm the brains behind the tech operations. Or I will be. This one's yours." She pulls free, smiling.

"Yeh Xiang-Ping. Yeh Xiang-Ping. Yeh Xiang-Ping."

This was supposed to be the trip to end all trips. My last time on Yeh grounds. Instead, for the first time, I feel proud of what my family has done with its small slice of history. And for the first time, I have a place among them. Tonight, instead of me bringing down my family's reputation, the opposite has happened.

People have fallen in love with my family . . . because of me.

Handing Sophie my scrapbook, I step onto the stage with them, and into the spotlight.

41

SOPHIE
DARTMOUTH COLLEGE
DECEMBER 1

The clerk at Jones's Mail Stop slides a large padded envelope toward me. He's the same guy who was breaking down boxes when I was last here dressed as a drowned rat, interviewing for a job. The same slouchy manager in a polo shirt is mopping behind him. I wonder if either of them recognizes me.

I barely recognize myself.

I hand him my debit card and print my family's mailing address on the envelope label. Then I tuck a copy of *Vogue* magazine and one of the *Dartmouth*, our student newspaper, into the envelope. A gust of cold air blows the back of my hair as the front door opens behind me.

"Sophie? Sophie Ha?"

I turn. "Oh, hi, Professor Horvath." He shakes snow from his plaid scarf. His navy coat is awesome—high collar and shiny gold buttons. Very dashing. My coat is unbuttoned, and I'm in a striped red cardigan over a flouncy satiny skirt and my kickass snakeskin boots—because this is how I'm feeling today.

"I saw your profile in the campus paper," Horvath says. "Congratulations on well-deserved recognition."

I smile. "Thank you. I'm actually here to mail a hard copy to my brothers and mom. She asked for it." I pull the *Dartmouth* from my envelope and show him.

"I'm sorry it didn't work out for you to join my class."

That's a euphemism. It ended up being pretty delicate. The head TA told Horvath that letting in Oliver instead of me could call his integrity into question, not to mention risk his billion-dollar lab if the story leaked. And of course, Victor knows the dean. So I got in. It was good not to be alone in this fight, because there will always be more Horvaths and Uncle Edwards.

But after a lot of thinking, I turned down Horvath's class and joined the entrepreneurship class instead. Professor Grieg was thrilled for me to work on Mirror, Mirror for my class project. The dear guy wears a *white undershirt* over his Hagrid-like belly. Most days, it's stained from breakfast or last night's dinner. Definitely not the most popular teacher at Dartmouth, but after sitting in for a class and speaking with him, I decided to go for it, and he ended up meeting with me once a week to advise me.

"You were right that the entrepreneurship class turned out to be a good fit," I say to Horvath now.

"I spoke with Professor Grieg," Horvath says. "He gave you rave reviews and shared a bit of your work. I wanted to tell you in person that I'm very impressed. Crowdsourcing tags for the clothing from your network—what was it? Your summer program?"

"Yes, that's right."

"Very resourceful. And your insights for how the tool can cross over to so many industries—it's that type of creative reframing that can make or break an invention."

"Thank you. I'm taking Applied AI in the spring and continuing to work on the app."

"Another excellent course. As for your summer, I've already told my friends in Silicon Valley that we have their intern dream hire here at Dartmouth. A few will be here next month." He smiles. "I'm hosting them at a private dinner with my top students, and I'd like to extend you an invitation." His smile deepens. "My students are my greatest assets—access to their talent is why these guys keep in touch with me."

"Thank you, and please count me in for dinner. I want to meet as many key players in this field as I can. But as for next summer, I've already committed to an internship."

"Already?" Horvath blinks.

"And I got internships for some students in your AI class, too. Owen, Trinity, and Natalie." His top three students, who I recruited to start an AI club with me when I returned from Taipei.

"Three students!" He frowns. His greatest assets . . . but I

420

didn't steal them. They came to me. "May I ask where you—all of you—will be interning?"

"Magic Silk." I pull out the *Vogue* I'm mailing to Mom, and show him a spread of Xavier's aunt and great-aunts, seated around the Mirror. The caption reads *Twenty-First-Century Magic*. "We'll be fine-tuning the algorithm and working on new capabilities. Shooting for the holy grail."

Professor Horvath folds his arms. "I'd hoped to refer all of you to my colleagues in Silicon Valley."

"Try Oliver," I suggest. "I know he's still looking for a job. Maybe you can hook him up."

With a smile, I hand my package to the clerk, and slip away.

42

XAVIER
DECEMBER 21

When I take the seat before Dean Ramchandran, I don't feel that same gulf between us that I felt the first day. His desk is smaller somehow. He's smaller. Kinder, with more color in his cheeks, set off by his checkered blue shirt. Or maybe it's my eyes that have changed, and now I can see the nuanced shades of gray and shadow that form him into a complex human being.

"How are things going?" he asks.

"Great," I say. "My film project earned an A across all three classes, so I'm in solid standing. Thanks for your support." Even Mr. Abadi, the only one I worried wouldn't approve, loved what he called making *her*story. He's trying to get my film shown in a local festival, and since I've already shown it at the Yeh's moon-cake pavilion, Jane has become resigned to letting me—at least for this project—loose on the world.

"I'm glad to hear. That was quite an ambitious project you took on." He clears his throat. "We, uh, have the results back from the additional diagnostic tests your specialist recommended. I think we were all surprised by your dysgraphia diagnosis . . . though it's much less well-known or understood. That you've had both dyslexia and dysgraphia helps explain the depth of your struggles these years."

Yes, that had been a big surprise, along with the zigzaggy curve of my abilities. Dysgraphia—I'd never heard of it, and I'm sure Ba hasn't either. It's why writing's been so hard for me. And learning Chinese—kids with dysgraphia may not see the extra dot or stroke that turns one complicated character into another. Musicians might miss notations on their sheet music.

But on the other hand, somehow, I see the world more magnified than other people. My head is where my paintings and drawings come from. It guides the images I catch on camera. So if I had the chance to trade my brain in for one that could read like everyone else . . . just like Sophie and her tornado . . . I wouldn't.

The dean pushes a bell-shaped chart at me. "As for the IQ tests, this is a bell curve of scores. This is yours." He marks an X at the far right, where the curve flattens. "You're at the extreme upper end. What's called 'twice exceptional.'"

"Twice exceptional?"

"Yes, 2e. Off-the-chart aptitude coupled with a learning difference. Kids like you are able to hide under the radar because you compensate so well. But you're laboring three times as hard as everyone else to get to the same place."

That's exactly what my life has felt like. And there was a term for it.

"So what will it take?"

"To do what?"

"Graduate. I mean, *really* graduate. Learn everything to legitimately earn my diploma. No hand-waving and pretending I'm even qualified to be a senior."

Dean Ramchandran folds his hands on his desk. "You're brilliant. You couldn't have come as far as you have unless you were. But you're behind in the curriculum. Not as important these days with information on the internet, I'll grant you, but high school gives you a critical baseline. At your current rate of progress, I'd say . . . in three years, you'll be able to hit the benchmarks to earn your diploma."

"And I'll be able to read by then?" I lean back in my seat. "Please be honest."

"There's a school of thought about the critical age for neuroplasticity. It's similar to foreign language acquisition—it's harder for an adult to pick up a language than a child. It may be similar for reading. There are studies, but nothing conclusive yet," he admits.

"So at the end of three years, I still might not be able to read?"

"I believe determination and tenacity conquer all."

It's what I expected, but it's still a letdown. A medley of might-have-beens plays through my mind. If I'd understood the problem sooner. If I'd gotten the right tutors from the start. If I hadn't been a part of my own cover-up, or even if I'd come to this school and these people sooner. Maybe then this magical skill that so many have would simply have been mine, too.

I rise and hold out my hand. Xavier-style diplomacy.

"Thanks, Dean Ramchandran. I appreciate your honesty."

On December 24, Aunty Three calls to let me know Ba is awake. Bernard comes for me, and I board the *Lynn* and fly back to Taipei.

When I enter the hospital room, Ba is alert and upright in bed, strangely thin in his blue hospital gown. His steel-gray hair is neatly parted as always, fighting the curls, and he keeps his eyes on me as I approach. If his doctor hadn't told me the truth, or if I hadn't spent my life hiding who *I* was, I wouldn't be able to tell.

Post-surgery, post-coma, my dad can barely see.

His world is now cloudy waters, colors, and blurs.

"Xiang-Ping, what is going on?" Ba demands. "I can't get a straight answer about anything. You hoodwinked my bankers and took your trust. My brother has left the continent in disgrace. What did you do? What have you done to our family's reputation?"

I drop into the chair beside his bed. Ma's photo is closer to him than it was last time I was here. In another time and place, I would not have wanted to be the one to tell Ba what his own

425

brother did to him. But though I may never feel ready for this role, I'm his son, and so I will be as I need to be.

"Uncle Edward was trying to oust you from Dragon Leaf."

Ba levels his eyes at his hands as I explain how Uncle Edward instigated the protests and conspired with the Crusaders. Ba's expression remains unchanged, but as I talk, he shrinks into his own body.

"As for my trust, I only took what Ma gave me. And our family reputation . . . I've been saving it."

He's quiet after I finish. A beeping sound comes from the hallway outside his closed door, where the bodyguards stand.

"I covered up for my brother for too long," he says finally. "Maybe that was my mistake."

It's my moment to pay him back. I could point out his own failings. How he hurt me. My body and my heart. He would take it. Because he knows he hasn't earned any right to me or my loyalty.

But that would make me just like him.

And so I reach for his hand, which is warmer than usual. His skin is rougher than I expected for a guy with servants to carry the bags of his servants.

"I'm glad you're awake," I say, and I mean it.

Ba's hand tightens tentatively around mine. His eyes shift to his blanket, but he doesn't withdraw his hand. "I'll be back at my desk next week. I have a lot to catch up on."

I put a new reader pen in his hand and my phone on his lap. "I'll show you how I do it."

"Do what?" Ba's voice sharpens. "I don't need anything."

"How I get around not being able to read."

For the next half hour, I show him how to use the reader pen. How to set up his phone to play his text messages and emails with a simple click. I tuck the pen into his pocket. I've donated a thousand reader pens like it to Harvard-Westlake to give to other schools—and pledged another thousand every year like the thousand mooncakes. I hope it will help more kids like it did me.

"If anyone had to be born into a century with dyslexia and dysgraphia, this is the one." I mean it as a joke, but I'm startled to see moisture in Ba's eyes.

"It was hard for you, wasn't it?" he asks.

An understatement from anyone else, but from Ba, a ground-shaking breakthrough. My throat aches. I nod, but he can't see me, so I say, "Yes."

His hand shakes as he reaches toward his nightstand, missing Ma's photo by several inches. I place her in his hands. He flinches, realizing I'd seen him grasping. But he still clings to her frame like a life preserver. "I hated whenever anyone criticized you, so I made sure I was the loudest of all. I thought I was doing you a favor."

Second chances. I didn't believe in them, but I do now. Because sometimes it's about having the tenacity to work through the shitstorm.

Besides, forgiveness isn't for him. It's for me.

"I get it, Ba."

"I heard Edward tried to buy Dragon Leaf. Even after the Crusaders failed."

"Aunty Three bought it."

"I heard that, too, but I didn't realize she had access to that much money."

"I loaned her my trust funds."

He trembles. "There is no greater way to tie you back to us."

There are greater ways, but yes, this was big. The trust was supposed to mean freedom from him and my family. Instead, I took on his shitstorm with everything I had.

"Ma trusted me to do what I thought was right with the funds. And so I did." Including, as I'd planned, hiring my own bodyguards, who are outside his door now. Ba and his body-guards will never touch me again.

Although I hope, over time, I won't need them against him.

Ba turns his face toward the window, the sunlight he can barely see.

I take a breath. "So no more games between us, okay? I'm not going to pretend I'm passing high school. And you're not going to pretend you don't see any redeeming worth in my art."

"Aunty Four shared your film with me. You have an ability the rest of us don't. Not Victor, not Edward, not me." Ba's eyes are on his clasped hands. "I should have been more open with your schools from the start. I should have trusted them to do right by you."

"I'm not ashamed of the way my brain works anymore, Ba. I'm proud of it."

He loses a tear that splashes onto his hands. "I was right about one thing. Your future is not tied to Dragon Leaf. Your future is boundless."

"Thanks, Ba." I squeeze those hands. "I hope so."

Two days later, I walk into our apartment foyer with Ba holding my arm. Almost the entire Taipei-based Yeh family is there to welcome him home—Aunty Three, Aunty Four, Ye-Ye and his sisters, and of course Haru, Kai-Fong and Jessica visiting from Kyoto University, Bernard and Alison. They don't crowd forward to hug him. They didn't bring balloons. But they're here.

In the hallway across from Ba's office, Haru and Kai-Fong help me remove the dragon mural from its frame. It was my idea, and Ba isn't resisting. I hand Ba his chop, which he stamps onto the mural in red as a symbol of his ownership.

Just above his, as the artist, I press my own chop: the dragon, inked in Yeh purple.

Epilogue

SOPHIE

APRIL 4

"New England looks like Taiwan," Xavier says. "Green everywhere."

"With little white steeples instead of pagodas," I say. Forested mountains surround us on all sides: New Hampshire to the east, Vermont to the west. We are lying on a blue blanket in a field of grass, pinkies hooked, gazing at the clouds. Only the chirp of birds and the buzz of insects break the cocoon around us. "We're going to have an amazing summer in Taipei."

"We're going to have an amazing rest of our lives," he says.

I turn my head to meet his eyes. "Turns out my summer on Loveboat wasn't a disaster after all. Because I met you."

"That makes it the best thing that's ever happened to me."

My phone chimes with a text on the group chat from Ever. I read the thread to Xavier as it comes in.

Ever: Guys, I got into Tisch—again!

Rick: WHOOHOO!!! She's coming east, gang!

Debra: Way to go, Ever!

Emma: Congrats!

Sophie: Congrats from me and Xavier!

Marc: You and Xavier?

Sophie: We're on the border of Vermont and New Hampshire.

"Tell them why I'm here." Xavier brushes a strand of hair from my face. His fingers linger on my arm.

Sophie: Xavier got into film school at Vermont College

Sophie: An hour from me!!!

Debra: Way to go, Xavier! Love from me and Spencer. #reunion #success!

Sophie: LOL that's amazing! Who'd have guessed?

Debra: 💔

Sophie: All right, gang. Go forth and run the world.

Ever: You guys, too!

"Loveboat forever," Xavier says.

Sophie: LOVEBOAT FOREVER

Ever: LOVEBOAT FOREVER!

Xavier takes the phone from my hand. He raises himself onto an elbow and looks down at me.

"I see you."

"I see you, too."

"Let's make a tornado together," he says.

Then he plants a very serious kiss on my mouth and I laugh and lock my arms around his neck and pull him down.

Assistive Tools for Dyslexia and Dysgraphia

Since technology changes quickly, the following examples are intended to help with identifying similar tools, but may no longer be on the market.

Writing: Voice-to-text or dictation software (e.g., Dragon Naturally Speaking, iPhone)

Penmanship: Applications to minimize demands on hand-writing (e.g., SnapType, Notability)

Reading: Dyslexic-friendly fonts; text-to-voice files (e.g., Voice Dream Reader, Audible)

Math: Typing apps to reduce handwriting load (e.g., Mod-Math, EquatIO, GeoGebra)

Note-taking: E-pens with recording (Livescribe ECHO); note-taking apps (e.g., GoodNotes, Notability)

Organization: Mind-mapping tools for visually oriented (e.g., Ayoa)

Acknowledgments

Thank you to all who helped bring this novel to life. Each of you has left a mark on me and I am grateful for your generosity, expertise, and passion. All mistakes are mine.

To my agent, Joanna Volpe, and her incredible team at New Leaf. To my editor, Kristen Pettit—this book would not be what it is without your brilliant insights. To my family at HarperCollins. To the talented Janice Sung and Jennet Liaw for another gorgeous cover.

To my writing community and beta readers: Sabaa Tahir, Stacey Lee, IW Gregorio, Kelly Loy Gilbert, Sonya Mukherjee, Stephanie Garber, Chienlan Hsu, Amanda Jenkins, Judy Hung Liang, Anne Ursu, Noa Wheeler, Lyn Miller-Lachmann, Lianna McSwain, Suma Subramanian, Sam Marsden. Charlie Oh for talking through characters you know as well as I do. Stephanie Sher, Lisha Li, Clare Chi, and Jen Rankine. My tour buds Adam Silvera and Farah Naz Rishi.

For help with and during my Taipei research trip during a global pandemic: Shannon Shiau at TECO, Elisa Chiu, JD Chang. Dave Tsai, Randy Tsai of Tsar and Tsai (Trusts and Estates, M&A), Joan/Hungry in Taipei, Anita Guo. Phoebe

Chen and Natalie Scheidel from Taipei American School. Gabriel Ellsworth, Rick Yu, and Jessica Chen at TG3D Studio Inc. for sharing your incredible tech with me—you are ahead of your time!

For speaking about this novel in its early stages: Carey Lai, Dave Lu, Hanlin Tang, Amir Khosrowshahi, Kelvin Au. Sam Liu for modeling Xavier's hair. Boba Guys.

For wisdom, support, and grounding: Kavitha Ramchandran, Jennifer Wu, Tony Wang. The Harmans, Itoi/Voths, Hessler/Sunwoos, Kims.

To my family: Ray and Barbara Hing, Byron and Liza Hing, my wonderful cousins, aunts, uncles, and those incognito.

To my children, who are part of everything I am and do.

To my best friend and partner in life, Andy.

And to Him who guides my path.